IN THE MOOD FUR LOVE

Also by
Eve Langlais, Milly Taiden, and Kate Baxter

Thanks Fur Last Night
The Big Alpha in Town

IN THE MOOD FUR LOVE

Eve Langlais Milly Taiden Kate Baxter

St. Martin's Griffin New York

These novellas are works of fiction. All of the characters, organizations, and events portrayed in these novellas are either products of the authors' imaginations or are used fictitiously.

For information, address St. Martin's Press,
175 Fifth Avenue, New York, N.Y. 10010.

www.stmartins.com

The Library of Congress Cataloging-in-Publication Data
is available upon request.

ISBN 978-1-250-16672-2 (trade paperback)
ISBN 978-1-250-16673-9 (ebook)

Our books may be purchased in bulk for promotional, educational, or business use. Please contact your local bookseller or the Macmillan Corporate and Premium Sales Department at 1-800-221-7945, extension 5442, or by email at MacmillanSpecialMarkets@macmillan.com.

First Edition: October 2018

10 9 8 7 6 5 4 3 2 1

CONTENTS

IN THE MOOD FUR LOVE

BEARING HIS TOUCH

Eve Langlais

CHAPTER 1

The slap rocked her, and not for the first time Becka tasted blood. The pain, however, no longer touched her. It would take more than a "well-deserved tap"—his words—for her to cry out.

Actually, crying was a proven waste of time. Tears never helped. Pleading never halted the abuse. And praying for hell demons to rip a hole between the dimensions and drag his ass into the flames of the pit never came to pass. Submission appeared to be the only way to survive.

But that was when I still had hope. When she believed someone might actually be looking for her, giving a damn about her disappearance. A hope dashed.

Her poppa was gone, dead in the fire that had taken her home, her things, her very existence. *He'd* had no choice but to tell her when she finally agreed to obey but only if she could see her beloved grandfather. A dead man, though, couldn't reassure Becka that everything would be all right. Nothing would be all right, never again, but at least her poppa never knew of the abuse she now suffered. A month now, and counting, with no end in sight.

No one cared about the bruises on her body or the fact that, when he dragged her out of one of his many hidey-holes, she piled on the makeup, dressed in long sleeves, and then faked that everything was okay. It was pretend or pay the price later. Becka got the impression he rather enjoyed the punishment part.

Bastard. I wish he would die. She would even love to help. Show her a cliff and she'd shove him off. Hand her a gun and she'd shoot him. At this point, she'd settle for a butter knife and a running start.

Becka hadn't been raised to be violent. Becka didn't understand violence. *He'd* taught her. Usually with his fist. But she preferred that to the other things he did.

Where was justice when you needed it? Apparently, saving other orphaned women.

A second slap landed atop the first, and she barely noticed.

"Have you learned your lesson, wild rose?" He used the nickname he had for her, a supposed term of endearment. She'd never believed it, not when his eyes always regarded her with such coldness. When she'd first met him, by chance when on a coffee and donut run, she'd turned down his request for a date. He didn't take no for an answer. He didn't accept the word "no" for anything.

"I hope you get hit by a bus." A swollen lip didn't change her sentiments.

"So fucking stubborn." Uttered with irritation. She braced for another slap. She'd earned the first one for refusing to eat her dinner, the second for not reacting. "I'll deal with you later. I've got business to attend to."

Ah yes, his mysterious business, which had brought them out of his last hidey-hole in Seattle to California. The land of sunshine and beaches. Not that she got to enjoy either. He kept her locked away even here. But she found it interesting to note they stayed in a hotel and not a reinforced bunker like before.

Why do we keep moving? Who does he hide from?

"Watch her." The order was tossed to his second-in-command, a big brute of a fellow named Brian. She hated Brian almost as much as *him.* Think Neanderthal mixed with dog and you got a hairy, hulking moron with absolutely no moral compass, and with rough hands.

She kept hoping he'd choke on a chicken wing. He ate them, suicide hot, by the pound.

"Rest. I'll be back later for our session."

No. No more sessions. She didn't know how many more she could stand. If it didn't kill her, then the madness might just win.

With her back turned, she stood and stared at the wall rather than acknowledge her kidnapper leaving the suite. She hoped he tripped and smashed his face in a wall. Or that the elevator would plunge him to his death. She'd even take him getting mauled by sewer rats. The door clicked shut, and she didn't hear any screams.

Pity.

Time ticked, and her guard shifted restlessly at his spot by the door, the leather of his jacket creaking. Boredom made her want to do something, but what?

Turning on the television didn't appeal. Seeing people laugh and smile was too hard to bear. She didn't recall the last time something had made her giggle. To her, laughter equaled freedom.

One month. One month a prisoner. How much longer would she last?

She licked her lip, tasting the copper still coating the swollen surface. That would be hard to cover with makeup. Of late, he had gotten more careless with his slaps. It used to be she had to pretend for his staff and he took care to only leave bruises that could be covered by clothes. Not anymore.

Something had changed. *Has he gotten what he needed? Is this a sign I'm about to be discarded?*

A girl could hope.

She stared out the window, the city vista awash with lights. For this trip, he insisted they stay in the heart of town at a high-end hotel—the kind that looked the other way when rich patrons skewed the rules.

It still blew her away how he moved among regular people without any of them realizing what kind of monster hid underneath the suits. Evil had a face, but no one seemed to recognize it.

Evil should be ugly and wear a dark cape. But no, *he* bore the face of a chubby accountant and the body of a pear. Add in a unibrow and she mocked him mercilessly, which peeved him to no end.

A knock at the door took her and her guard by surprise. Room service had come and gone, leaving behind a tray she refused to touch. At this late hour they expected no one else. The fewer people who saw her, the better.

Her guard, Brian the bastard, ignored the pounding.

"Shouldn't you answer that, Lurch?"

A glare and a grunt were the reply.

Whoever it was outside in the hall didn't leave. Someone knocked again, firmly. "Hotel security. We've had a report about suspicious activity in this room. If you're in there, please let us in."

Brian didn't budge, and she had to wonder what he'd do if she yelled *Save me!* Hit her for sure. But he also had strict orders to not cause any permanent or meaningful damage. Must protect the investment. However, whatever innocents stood beyond the door might not fare so well. Only once had she begged a stranger for help. He tried and got rewarded with a bullet.

She held her tongue.

The lock clicked as the hotel employee used a key, and she whirled in time to see Brian facing the door, hands empty. Guns were noisy and brought trouble. Besides, Brian claimed the personal touch was always more fun.

The door swung open, and Brian snapped, “Get ou—”

He never did finish the sentence, as a shotgun blast hit him in the chest and pushed him back. As if that would stop Brian. All the guards wore body armor and were tough as nails, tougher actually, and they filled the rooms on this floor. But how many of them were here, and how many had gone with their boss?

The attacker in the doorframe was dressed head to toe in black combat gear from his mirrored visored helmet to his black combat boots.

“Give us the girl.”

Brian got to his feet, his brow furrowed. “Like fuck, asshole.”

The guy with the shotgun tossed it to the side and pulled a knife from a sheath at his side. That didn’t daunt her guard.

With a snarl of rage, Brian went barreling at the attacker, taking the scuffle into the hall.

From her spot in the suite, Becka could hear them thumping and banging. The door slammed shut, muffling the sounds, and for a moment she stood there as if frozen. What should she do?

Move, you idiot.

She flew to the door, opening it and darting through, only to hit the wall hard as a pair of grappling bodies bumped into her. The force of it knocked her down, but she didn’t let that stop her from scrabbling on the carpet, moving in the direction of the elevator.

A hand grabbed at her ankle, and she peered over her

shoulder to see Brian gripped her tight. Her free foot kicked out and connected with his nose. He yelled but didn't release her. The visored assailant managed to loosen Brian's hold on her with an elbow to the back of his head.

As soon as the fingers gripping her ankle loosened she yanked, freeing herself. She got to her feet and ran toward the bank of elevators, only to halt abruptly as someone stepped into view from around the corner, taking up a position between her and the elevator. Given he also held a gun and wore a black helmet as well, she immediately distrusted him. The weapon rose and she squeaked and ducked, but he wasn't aiming at her. The shot went wild, hitting the ceiling and showering the hall with plaster because someone, another guard dressed in jeans and nothing else, hollered "Drop the weapon, asshole" before tackling the fellow.

The distraction got her moving again, only she didn't get far, as an arm curled around her waist and hoisted her off her feet. "Come with me." She recognized the voice as being that of Brian's usual partner in crime, Jim. She'd thought he'd gone with the boss, but apparently he just guarded from another room.

Like hell was she going anywhere with him. She struggled like a wildcat, squirming and twisting, hearing her blouse rip as seams gave way.

"Stop fucking fighting me," he snarled, turning to slam her into a wall. Old bruises screamed at the impact, and new ones surely formed.

"Let me go!" Becka yelled.

Instead, the grip tightened, but only for a moment. Jim grunted as someone hit him. More than one person, actually. More black-clad bodies wearing the concealing helmets filled the corridor, and one of them shouted, "Don't shoot. You might hit her!"

Good to know they didn't want to kill. Bad to know they wanted her. But the guards on this floor knew better than to lose the master's prize. Several doors were open now, and *his* minions filled the hall, wielding fists and, in one case, a metal rod.

She wanted to shout at them to go away. She didn't need more people standing between her and freedom, but at the same time, the distraction proved her salvation. Jim lost his hold on her, and she stumbled away from him, streaking past an attacker grappling with Brian. She could have cried in relief when the elevator doors opened and disgorged hotel security, adding to the general chaos. She darted into the cab and slapped the ground-floor button as the hotel guard yelled, "The police have been called!"

"You shouldn't have done that." One of the attackers, his face an expressionless mask of black plastic, twisted Jim's neck. *Crack.* Jim dropped like a rock. The hotel security guard fumbled for his weapon, and as the elevator doors closed, Brian yelled, "Get back here, you little bitch!," and the attackers shouted, "Don't let her get away!"

The doors sealed shut, and the elevator descended, rendering her safe for the moment, but that would prove fleeting. Brian and the others would surely take the stairs, and if the elevator stopped for even one floor she might not arrive before them.

She hyperventilated in the cab, her palms sweaty as the ride to the main level took forever. Her heart pounded so fast she feared dropping of fear.

When the doors slid open to reveal the lobby, she fully expected to see someone waiting for her and wasn't disappointed. She came face-to-face with a hotel manager, whose eyes widened upon seeing her. "Ma'am, are you all right?"

"No." The word bubbled from her, edged with hysteria.

She stepped out of the elevator, shying away from his hands when he would have touched her. "Don't. Just leave me alone. I have to go." Go before her brief stint of freedom ended.

She burst through the glass doors of the hotel, hitting the sidewalk, where the noise of cars passing, mufflers belching, engines roaring, and at times cars honking muddled her already-frantic mind. She didn't know where she was. She had no clue where to go. Where could she hide where *he* wouldn't find her?

Nowhere. *He'll find me wherever I go.* But she had to try. Had to make an attempt.

She ran, choosing a direction at random, ignoring the prying glances of those she passed, the evening hour still early enough for pedestrian traffic. That was good for her. It would make following her that much harder. However, blending in might prove hard, given her bare feet and ragged appearance. *I look like a woman running from something.* She should have trained for this day—done a few laps around the bunker room they kept her locked in—then maybe she wouldn't huff and puff so noisily.

The first street corner she stumbled on she turned, sprinting its length before making another sharp right. Sirens wailed in the distance, the cavalry to the rescue. Cops wouldn't stop Brian or *him,* and she had a feeling it wouldn't stop those that also came after her.

Everyone wants me, and I've yet to figure out why.

The next street she turned on had blaring neon signs, noise, and more foot traffic. Welcome to the club district. The thump of deep bass from more than one spot provided a cacophony that masked her own panting breaths, but it couldn't mask the distant yells of people.

Someone chased her, but she didn't want to be found. *I won't go back.*

She ducked into an alley and ran the length of it, only to cry out in frustration at the dead end. No escape. She headed back to the mouth of the alley but hesitated. Out there, anyone chasing could see her, but what if she were to hide? Hide where, though?

There were some doors lining the alley, none with handles, all locked from the inside, but the alley wasn't completely bereft of hiding spots. Between the trash bins, she spotted a wedge of space, big enough for her. She ducked in, the miasma of garbage almost gagging her as the hot, humid air rendered the scraps rancid.

Ass hitting the ground, she hugged her knees and huddled, wondering how she'd gotten here. What bad thing had she done to deserve this?

I did nothing. She'd been just a regular girl, with a regular job, living with her grandpa, when *he* entered her life. From that day on, her world changed, for the worse.

For a moment the music trying to hum through the building walls got louder as someone opened a door. She tucked tighter into her hole. No need to freak. Probably someone having a smoke.

The door shut, muting the music, and she heard nothing. Not even the scrape of a shoe or a hint of cigarette smoke. Had they left? Just in case, she ducked her face, hiding it in her tucked knees, hoping to make herself invisible.

It didn't work. Her skin prickled, and she couldn't help but peer outward. She saw a man staring down at her with the most curious brown eyes, and for some reason she blurted out, "Save me."

CHAPTER 2

The coppery undertone of blood hit him as soon as he entered the alley, the unmistakable scent waking his inner beast.

The heavy metal door clanged behind him as he tucked his cigarettes back into his pocket. Nasty habit that he kept trying to quit. He didn't smoke much anymore. Often, he'd light one only to stare at the smoldering tip before tossing it to the ground to stub it out. And yet he always kept a pack on him. They provided cover when he needed an excuse to lurk in places he shouldn't, like dark alleys at night.

Never know what you'll find.

His nose twitched at the bloody scent of violence, but his bear didn't rumble in warning, nor did he sense any danger. He let his refined sense of smell lead him, his shifter side stronger than most, even in his human shape. It was what made him such a good detective—before he got kicked off the force. Who knew they'd care about the baggie of weed he took to make brownies? The stuff was legal in just about every other state.

The loss of his legal career didn't bother him too much. There was plenty of work in the city as a private eye, so much work that he could pick and choose his jobs. He often chose the ones that took him to strip bars where wives suspected their husbands of cheating. The eye candy was fun, even if the beers were kind of pricey, but that was where creative invoicing came into play.

Given he stood in the alley of Bubble Butt Babes, he wondered if that was who hid out here: a stripper looking to make a few bucks, only to end up with a client who got rough.

The bass of the music emerged in a muted thump in the alley. While it was close to the witching hour, the street out front still had a decent amount of foot traffic. If someone wanted privacy, then there were few places to hide. The alley itself was a dead end, finishing in a roll-down garage door, which was currently bolted. A pair of trash bins, tall suckers on wheels, were lined like sentinels along the brick wall. They might have been emptied that morning, but the smell clung, a miasma that made his inner beast grunt in annoyance.

Smells bad.

Yes, it did, and above it all lingered the sharper scent of blood. Something wounded this way came, and he couldn't leave it alone.

With a silent tread, he paced the alley until he found her wedged between two trash bins, her head turned away from the alley, as if by not seeing she could prevent being seen.

He crouched down and noted she stopped breathing, her body going still.

An anticipatory hush fell, and he studied her, studied her hunched frame, the tattered clothes, the scratches on her arms, the fading and fresh bruises.

Trouble.

So much trouble. Despite her wounded status, a part of him urged him to walk away, knew if he didn't run that his life would change.

He didn't budge. How could he leave when she turned

bright green eyes his way and said in the softest whisper, "Save me"?

Save her? As if she had to ask. His cousins always claimed he had a hero complex. More like he couldn't stand to see women and children getting hurt. Which meant he couldn't turn his back on her.

He reached out and touched the exposed skin of her arm, just a poke that caused her to flinch as if he'd slapped her, while he fell on his ass. No grace at all.

Mine.

His voice, his bear's? Did it matter? The realization kicked him in the gut. She was his mate. His fated mate. His one and only. Forever and ever and . . .

"Fuck." He said it aloud, and she flinched again. *Not good.* "Who are you?"

For a moment he thought she wouldn't answer. "Becka."

"Who hurt you, Becka?"

A shudder went through her, and she didn't reply. Someone else did. "No one hurt her. She's fine and needs to come with me."

Getting to his feet, Stavros held in a sigh as he beheld the big brute at the end of the alley. Stavros had met his type before while on the force, too many times to count. A big bully and, worse, a bully who picked on women.

Can't stand those guys.

Let's maul him.

Sounded like a good plan. Now to get the guy to swing first—it helped in case the police and lawyers got involved later on. "I'm afraid I can't allow her to go with you."

The guy with the goatee sneered. "This is none of your business."

Actually, it totally was. She'd become his business the moment he set eyes on her. And even if she weren't his mate, he'd still get in this asshat's way just on principle. "I'm making this my business. See, I've got a problem with guys who think it's okay to hit girls. My mother always taught me"—usually with a wooden spoon—"that only pussies and cowards hit women."

"You meddle in things you don't understand." The crack of knuckles was probably meant to intimidate.

Ha. This goon had obviously never met his uncle Marcus. "I think you should leave before I teach you a lesson in how to treat a lady."

"I think your face needs rearranging." The brute began stalking toward him, and Stavros felt more than heard the woman rise behind him.

She stepped around his frame, careful to not touch any part of him, her arms hugging her body. "I'm coming, Brian. Don't hurt him. He was just trying to help me."

Did she seriously think he was going to allow her to hand herself over to this douche bag? "Get behind me," he ordered.

Eyes the color of spring grass looked at him with weary resignation. "I appreciate what you're trying to do, but I won't let you be hurt on my account."

She didn't get to decide that. "Who says I'm going to get hurt? I'm rather insulted you think this big goon can take me."

"You don't understand. He doesn't play fair. I won't have someone else killed on my account."

Killed? Ooh, things just got a lot more interesting. Just who is this fucker who likes to hit women and kill people? This inquiring mind wants to know. Because you're in bear country now, which means I am the predator, not you.

"Stand aside, sweetheart. I've got this. I'm a cop." He didn't tack on the used-to-be part.

The big dude heard him and snorted, "Here, piggy-piggy."

The idiot poked the bear, and Stavros replied by charging. The goon didn't sidestep his rush, and so Stavros hit him midsection and no further. Buddy was solid as a brick wall and held his ground.

Oooh, a little bit of competition. Usually that only happened with others in his sleuth—fancy word for his giant bear clan that ruled these parts.

Since pushing Brian over didn't work, he resorted to a bit of grappling and thrown fists. More like mallets, given they both had a granite-hard punch.

Grunt. Smack. Jab. *Oomph.* Poke. Pummel.

They traded blows for a bit until Stavros noted his lady trying to inch past. *She's not leaving without me.* He'd never find her again in a city this size. Never mind the smart thing to do involved letting her go.

I don't want a mate. Don't want. Don't want.

That was the man part of him. The bear part?

Lick her! Yeah. His beast side had simpler needs.

Time to wrap things up. He drew on his bear strength and got an edge on the dude, his blows hitting faster and harder until the guy staggered. A foot hooked around his ankle sent the goon tumbling to the ground, and in a moment Stavros had him handcuffed, arms behind his back. Not being a cop didn't mean Stavros had gotten rid of all his cool toys.

"Release me," Brian snarled. "You don't know who you're messing with. If I don't bring her back to him—"

"Who's him?"

"You'll see."

I should hope so. Stavros rather liked the ominous tone. A man could use a little spice in his life, and a woman—especially the one who'd scurried off. "Tell your boss that if he comes near her, I'll make him wish he was the load his mother swallowed."

"Suck my dick."

"Not my style, but don't worry. I'm sure you'll find someone to play with where you're going." He patted the goon on the cheek. "Say hi to my friends in blue. I hear the cells are nice this time of the year. Expect me to come by later for a little chat."

Sirens blared nearby, and he'd wager they were looking for the prick at his feet. As Stavros rose, he juggled his phone from his pocket and sent a quick text to a buddy at the precinct—*Left you a present in the alley*—with the name of the bar.

Then he went after his woman.

Not mine.

So mine.

He could see he and his bear would need to have a talk, because Stavros sure as hell wasn't ready to settle down, despite what his mother and sisters seemed to think. "*We need a son to carry on the name.*" "*You're not getting any younger.*" Never mind his uncle Horatio had just fathered his eighth child at fifty-five. If the women in his family caught wind of this woman, his single life as he knew it would vanish and the shackle of mating would bind him.

Choke. Gasp. He could feel the invisible collar of fate squeezing.

CHAPTER 3

Run while they're distracted. Becka left the stranger grappling with Brian behind. A part of her didn't want to. His Good Samaritan act would cause him a world of hurt—maybe even kill him—but sticking around would hurt her more in the end. Sometimes a girl has to be selfish. Besides, the guy had said he was a cop. He should be used to dealing with criminals.

Decided, she ran out of the alley, bare feet slapping the pavement. Despite the hour, she noted the number of people out and about had grown. Many of the pedestrians milled in groups, and as she passed she caught snatches of their conversations, most of them wondering about the wail of police sirens.

They're looking for me. Probably not to arrest her specifically, but they would want her as a person of interest. Getting nabbed by the cops, even for questioning, wasn't something she wanted to endure. As it was, she considered it bad luck that the fellow in the alley had mentioned he was a cop. A cop wouldn't have believed a false story of her falling down some stairs to excuse the bruises. A police officer would find it suspicious she didn't have any identification or a home address. *He'd* made sure of that.

I can't let them take me. That was her first impulse, and

yet getting arrested or taken into protective custody would put her in a cell, and that would make it harder for *him* to find her. And he would be looking. He wouldn't let Becka go that easily because, as he'd told her more than once, she tasted much too delicious.

Shudder.

Don't think about that.

Don't. Think.

She shuttered her mind and adopted a quick stride, just short of a run. People walking with rapid purpose drew less attention than those wildly fleeing. Or so she hoped. She turned at the first intersection, then turned again. She didn't slow her steps until she'd managed to make it around another corner, the stitch in her side a hitching pain she could no longer ignore.

"Do you know where you're going, sweetheart?" The casually asked question from behind managed to squeeze a little yelp of surprise from her. She halted and spun on a heel to find the stranger from the alley, the one with the kind brown eyes. With them both standing still, she noted that not only was he tall; he was pretty freaking wide too. Football-shoulder wide, and hairy, his head sporting a thick mop of dark hair, his brows thick and expressive, given one arched at her perusal. His square jaw held a bit of a beard, covering it from ear to ear and highlighting the sensuality of his lips. He had a strong nose, an arrogant one, and yet his eyes twinkled with mischief. He was also very much alive, unharmed, and waiting for an answer.

"Why did you follow me?"

"Perhaps I'm mistaken, but given I just had to put down a goon who claims he was fetching you for another, I was kind of under the impression you needed help."

"The police can't help me."

"I'm not a cop."

"But you said—"

"I used to be a cop, but the department and I had a slight misunderstanding. I work in the personal investigative realm now."

"You're a gumshoe?"

Laughter barked from him. "Now there's something you don't hear often. But yes, I'm a gumshoe who specializes in investigation and protection services. And maybe it's just me, but you look like you're in need of a protector." His eyes cataloged her from head to toe.

Before his gaze she felt stripped bare, every single bruise and scratch glaringly evident. She resisted an urge to duck her face. "I can't afford your services."

"Who says I'd charge you?"

At that, she took a step away from him and held out her hands. "I am not that kind of girl."

For a moment his mouth hung open, and then he laughed. "Sweetheart, I don't need to buy sex, or exchange favors for it. So you don't need to look like that. Can't a man offer aid to a damsel in distress just because it's the right thing to do?"

Her brow furrowed. "People don't do things for nothing." And when they did good deeds, sometimes it cost them their lives, like the poor man in the hotel.

The whoop of sirens drew closer. "Listen, I don't know about you, but given I don't know the whole story, and I don't get the impression you want the cops involved, what do you say we get off the street and talk about what I can do to help you."

"I don't want your help." She didn't need more deaths on her conscience.

Becka turned from him and would have walked away, but

he grabbed her upper arm. It wasn't rough by any means, but she still flinched, unable to stop the spurt of fear.

He released her and exclaimed, "Holy fuck, sweetheart! Just what did that bastard do to you?"

Enough to make her leery of being touched. She ducked her head. "You should go. It doesn't matter where I hide. He will eventually find me."

"Good. Because I'd like a word with him. My mother always did say I had expressive hands."

A peek at him showed one fist slamming into the palm of his other hand. "Do you have a death wish?"

"Nope, but I am a curious man. Just like a bear, I like to poke my nose in things and sometimes take a lick."

"You're strange."

"Thank you. Now shall we? I doubt we have long before my old workmates come across us. I'd rather not have them ask why I'm in the company of a woman who looks like she went a few rounds."

Go with him? She hesitated, especially since he held out a hand. A big hand. A hand marked with calluses from work. A hand that could hurt if it chose. A hand that asked for a measure of trust.

What do I have to lose?

CHAPTER 4

With only the slightest hesitation, she slid her smaller hand into his, and he was careful not to crush it. He had to be even more careful and not drag it to his lips and kiss it, or lick it like his bear thought they should do. The impression he got from her indicated she might not welcome slobber at this time. Maybe not ever. All of her trembled in fear.

Fear of him. It enraged him to know she was so frightened, and yet he couldn't express that anger. It would only scare her further, even if his rage was for whoever had done this to her.

He held her hand in a gentle grip, but at the same time he couldn't help a sense of urgency as he tugged her in the direction of his car. Lucky for them both, he'd parked a few blocks away from the club. The lights on his vehicle flashed as he approached, the doors unlocking as he pressed the fob button.

"This is what you drive?" She sounded rather surprised.

"What did you expect?"

"I don't know. Something more . . . I don't know. Didn't Magnum, P.I., drive a convertible?"

Not just any convertible, a Ferrari 308 GTS—also known as a boner car. "You watch *Magnum*?" His all-time favorite show as a cub. He'd devoured all the PI shows growing up. As an adult, he even tried emulating his favorite hero. He failed at the awesome mustache—mostly because all his female relatives laughed at it and told him it looked like he had a caterpillar crawling across his upper lip—but he did manage to grow a wicked beard, which his family told him made him look like a mountain man. He went clean-shaven most of the time now unless he wanted to irritate his sisters.

"*Magnum, Charlie's Angels,* even *M*A*S*H.* I like watching the older stuff. Things seemed so much more real then." How wistful she sounded.

If this were a regular date, he'd be plying her with the cheesiest line known to man—*Where have you been all my life?* But he doubted she'd appreciate it, so he stuck to simpler things.

"One thing I learned watching *Magnum* was to not be so noticeable." He patted the hood of his ten-year-old sedan, a navy blue that was both reliable and boring. "When I am working, I use this to blend in."

"What do you drive when you don't have to hide?"

"On my days off, I drive a Mustang convertible." He grinned. "Bright red." License plate MGNMBR—Magnum Bear, also the name of his agency. "What about you?"

"I don't drive. I don't even have a license." Her lips turned down.

It made him want to flip them upside down. It always made his nieces giggle, but somehow he didn't think it would work the same way with her.

Stavros opened the passenger door, but she deftly avoided touching him at all when sliding into the car. He, however, couldn't ignore her proximity or scent when he took the driver's seat.

Such an odd medley of scents: blood, fear, and something oily. But underneath it all, his other half noticed something yummy.

Only once he pulled away from the curb did he ask, "So where do you want to go? Is there a friend or family member that can take you in?" Because home obviously wasn't an option.

She shook her head. "I've got no family left. Just me. And I'm not from around here. If you could drop me at a bus station, I'll figure something out."

"Figure out what?" He cast her a quick glance. "You look like you went a few rounds with a brawler, you don't have a purse, and I'm going to guess those snug leggings of yours aren't holding a wad of cash or even I.D. You're gonna need both to travel."

Her shoulders slumped. "Thanks for pointing out my situation is hopeless."

"Not hopeless. Chin up, sweetheart; you're with me now. Things are already looking up."

"Says you. How do I know you're any better?"

He might have been more insulted if the abuse weren't so obvious. Of course she had trust issues. Someone had done a number on the girl and it made his inner bear rage, but he couldn't let that beast out quite yet. She was already scared enough. No need to frighten her more. But how to make her believe him when he said she was safe?

"You might not believe this yet, but trust me when I say I could not hurt you. Never. Not in a zillion years. And not just because my mother would beat me within an inch of my life."

"Your mother beats you?"

"Only when I deserve it." For some reason, she didn't look reassured. However, even he could admit he'd earned his whacks with a spoon. Jumping off the dining room buffet, which resulted in it falling over and smashing his mother's heirloom dish set, being the most notable example. "My mother is a wonderful woman. When she's not meddling in my love life. Apparently, a man my age should be married. I'm twenty-eight before you ask."

"That doesn't seem old."

"I'm the youngest of seven, the six others being sisters, all married by the time they were in their midtwenties."

"Sounds like you come from a big family."

"That's just the tip of the iceberg, sweetheart. I've got more nieces and nephews than I can count. Add in some brothers-in-law, and then there's my aunts, uncles, and cousins. . . . Family gatherings tend to be loud."

"Must be nice to have so many folk." She couldn't hide her wistful tone.

"Only when they keep their noses to themselves. Meddling isn't restricted just to my mother and sisters. Even my aunts and grandmother are bugging me too."

Her lips almost quirked into a smile. "My poppa never cared. He always told me to wait for love."

"Love isn't supposed to hurt." He regretted the words the moment they left his mouth.

A guarded look dropped over her face, and her hands clasped each other tightly in her lap. Her chin dropped. "I've never been in love."

"Then who's been hurting you?" he couldn't help but ask.

"A bad man. A very bad man." She whispered the words, and he could feel the fear radiating from her trembling frame.

His knuckles turned white as he gripped the steering wheel. He feared ripping it off in his rage. He took a deep breath and told himself to calm the fuck down. "In all the commotion, I just realized I never gave you my name. I'm Stavros. Stavros Georgopoulos. And you said your name was . . ."

"Becka."

He didn't push for a surname. Not yet. But he would find out. His curiosity wouldn't let him do anything less.

"Hello, Becka. Now, care to explain to me what's been happening with you? I get the impression you escaped a rather ugly situation."

"Very ugly. Which is why you shouldn't get involved."

"What did I tell you about trusting me?"

"I don't know you."

"Isn't that how all friendships start?" He shot her a smile, a meant-to-be-reassuring smile.

Instead, it made her frown. "I'm not looking for a friend."

"And yet you seem in dire need of one."

"If you want to be my friend, then how about telling me something about yourself, such as why you aren't a cop anymore? Were you a bad cop?"

"Actually, I was a very good detective. But I did a naughty thing. Actually, it was a yummy thing. I saved some marijuana slated for destruction and made some brownies with it. Someone ratted me out."

"You do drugs?"

He didn't consider pot much of a drug, at least the unmodified stuff. How to explain too that most drugs didn't affect him like they did humans? He said neither of those things but instead pushed for answers of his own. "That seems kind of the pot calling the kettle black, given the holes in your arms." They didn't quite look like needle marks, but no mistaking the punctures in her flesh and the bruising around them.

She crossed her arms. "It's not what you think."

"How do you know what I think?"

"I'm not a junkie."

"Then what are they from? Is someone sticking you with needles?"

"You wouldn't believe me if I told you."

"Try me."

Before she could reply, his phone rang, and the number was one he couldn't ignore. "Give me a second while I answer this." Since his car didn't have the bells and whistles of the modern ones, he had to answer it and hold the phone to his ear.

"Jenkins, did you find the present I left you?"

"If you mean the cuffs in the alley, then yeah, but whoever busted out of them was long gone."

"No fucking way." Too late he wondered if he should have curbed the expletive, but a quick glance at his passenger showed her looking out the window doing a shit job of pretending she wasn't listening in.

"I don't suppose he was about six and a half feet, built like a barrel, wearing a leather jacket and a goatee?" Jenkins asked.

"That's the guy I tangoed with. What's he wanted for?"

"Questioning for the moment. Seems he was involved in an altercation at a hotel. Some guys tried to bust him up. Him and some girl." *A girl?* Stavros tried not to react and tucked the phone onto his opposite ear.

"What are witnesses saying so far?"

"We're still taking statements, so I haven't had time to really sift through the reports, but indications are a few guys dressed in motocross gear and packing heat showed up at a hotel room. A brawl ensued. We've got at least one dead body and a few others injured. Plus the girl is missing. It's a fucking nightmare, especially since it turns out none of the cameras in that hotel recorded a damned thing and no one is saying shit."

"They were all broken?"

"Nope. Everything looked just peachy until the hotel went

to pull the video files. The drives are corrupt. Not a single one of them has anything usable thus far. But that could change. We're going to let the forensics geeks play with it and see if they can pull something out of the drives."

"You said there were some guys dressed in biker gear. Who were they? And who is the girl?" He knew Becka could hear him ask, but Stavros needed more info, and since his old partner seemed loquacious, best get as much info as he could now, before things got locked down.

"No idea. They disappeared along with your fellow in the alley and the woman. Speaking of woman, you didn't happen to see one, did you? Hotel clerk says he saw her running out of the place looking terrified. About five foot five, not scrawny but not chubby either. Shoulder-length blond hair. No idea about the eyes, but you'd notice her. She apparently looked a little beaten up and wasn't wearing any shoes."

"Nope, haven't seen her." He lied, and he knew she noticed because she stiffened.

"Well, if you do, let me know. She's a person of interest."

Damned straight she was. His interest. His business. He hung up with his old partner and for a moment silence stretched in the car.

He waited.

Waited some more.

"What are you going to do with me?" Asked so softly, so hesitantly.

His usual reply to a woman would be, *"I want to do dirty things with you."* Yet, quite honestly, this shell of a woman, hunched in on herself, bloodied, bruised, and so obviously frightened, didn't evoke any lust. How could she? She was a wounded creature, one that needed a safe place to lick her wounds. Lucky for her, he knew just the spot.

CHAPTER 5

"This is your apartment?" The fact that she'd even agreed to come here with him was a measure of her desperation, but for the first time in a long time Becka felt oddly safe. Surprising given what had happened at the hotel.

Who were those people attacking? Why were they after her? Did someone want to get back at *him*?

Whoever they were, they didn't mind getting their hands dirty and didn't fear the police. People were dead. Stavros had taken the news on the phone rather well, and yes, she'd eavesdropped. She couldn't ignore it when she knew it concerned her.

"What's wrong with my apartment?" he asked.

"I didn't say anything was wrong."

"Says the girl with the scrunched-up nose."

"It's just not what I expected." She'd expected to walk into a guy's place, the type with a big-screen television, game systems, chrome, and leather. It's what *he* and his cronies preferred. A décor meant for single guys.

This place bore a woman's touch, or so the flowered cushions on the sofa and the colorful vista paintings on the walls indicated. And what of the vase with real flowers in it?

It could mean one of two things. "Are you married?" she asked.

"Good God no. Very much single. For now." Said with a grumble.

"Oh, then you're gay."

"Excuse me?" he exclaimed.

"I'm sorry. That wasn't very politically correct of me. What is the proper term I should use?" Because she was pretty sure the vulgar word *he* used would be met with even more objection.

"I meant I'm not gay. The décor you see isn't my idea. Remember those meddling sisters I told you about?" He waved a hand. "Apparently, this is all part of making me look attractive to a possible mate. What do you think? Would you be more likely to date a guy who has needlepoint pillows?" He held one up with a cute bear wearing a bow tie lying on its back holding its toes.

"I think it's nice you're close to your sisters. I always wanted a family growing up." But for as long as she could remember, it was just her and Poppa.

"Remember that sentiment when my sisters kidnap you."

"Kidnap me for what?"

"Assimilation into their ranks. Before you can blink, they'll have you in an apron, popping out cookies and babies."

"Babies?" Her heart fluttered. How long since she'd last dared imagine a life that involved home and hearth with children? That happily ever after was never going to happen. Not so long as *he* was around.

"Forget I said that word. Anyhow, you can have the bedroom while we figure things out for you. I'll take the couch."

"I couldn't."

"You will. So don't bother arguing."

However, she wanted to argue. It didn't seem right that

she got the bedroom while he was forced to scrunch up on the couch. But how to argue with a man so determined?

In short order he had her in the bathroom with a T-shirt of his and instructions to cleanse herself. No point in protesting. She needed a shower. Just look at her feet. Filthy and sporting a few cuts, the pavement not very kind. He'd offered to carry her, but she'd refused, claiming they would look suspicious. He didn't like her reply but acquiesced. One of the few times he did, and it didn't stop him from glaring at her feet and asking every couple of paces if she was sure she didn't want to be carried. By the sixth time, she wanted to throttle him. Yet his very determination to do right by her eased her feelings about him.

A part of her hyperventilated at the thought of trusting someone, especially a man, but another part of her understood that most people were inherently decent. She just needed the strength to believe in it again.

Going to his apartment was another one of those faith things. She would have preferred a motel. However, he was right about one thing. She wouldn't get far without identification and money. Her escape would fail from stupidity if she refused the kindness he offered.

He used to be a cop. Surely he knows some people who can help me start a new life. As to how she'd make money to support herself? There weren't a lot of options for a girl down on her luck. Waitressing would take a while to build cash, as would most jobs. Which sucked. She was a girl who'd finished college and worked these past few years as a medical secretary. A great job, but not one she could claim without her papers, papers in her name. If she used her name, though, *he* would find her.

So what did that leave for a girl to make a few quick

bucks? A friend of hers in college had said she made great money stripping. However, Becka doubted she could stand a roomful of men staring at her, ogling her with their eyes, trying to touch. *Shudder.*

I can barely stand to look at myself.

She stripped out of her clothes, dropping the soiled garments to the floor. The shower proved delightful, loosening some of the tight muscles in her shoulders, making her gasp as the liquid burned at her cuts and reminded her of the bruising.

Once clean, she stepped from the shower and reached for a towel, only to have her gaze caught by her reflection. *That can't be me.* She gasped as she turned around and beheld her body. Her poor abused body.

She'd not seen it this way in a long time. There weren't any mirrors in the places *he* held her. *He* didn't like them. She took a step closer to the mirror, forgoing the towel.

The pattern of bruises was in different stages, painful to receive and painful to behold, but she refused to cry. Crying gave *him* power over her. Instead, she squinted her eyes and noticed the motley shadow over her ribs looked like a winged bunny rabbit. The one on her upper thigh, a vortex.

Some people found patterns in clouds; she found them on her body. The bruises would eventually fade. They always did until a new rage came on. Usually brought on by her defying *him.*

You'd think I'd have learned my lesson by now.

However, submission didn't come easily. A fear of pain didn't entirely quell her spirit. Although he did his best. *Gave it the old college try. Bastard.* A bastard who no longer had her because she'd gotten away from him, for the moment at least. The third time she'd managed to escape by her count but not yet a record attempt, given her longest breakout had lasted about thirty-six hours. Then he'd literally dragged her back.

It took her a while to rise from that beating. But at least he had hit her only with his fists and words. It could have been worse.

One day karma will get him. She hoped she could help that day when it came time to give that bastard the boot.

Stop thinking about him. She shouldn't give that asshole any more of her time. She should think nice thoughts.

What about her rescuer? If she were to judge him thus far, then she'd say he didn't seem like the kind of dick who would hurt a woman. Especially not given his obvious affection for female members of his family. It reminded her of the type of bond she'd shared with her poppa. *Rest his sweet soul. I will avenge you someday.* She'd tried once already, but the butter knife hadn't worked all too well and after that she mostly got to eat with a spoon.

Thank goodness for her memories of Poppa, a dear sweet old man who'd taken her in after her mother died. His oftentimes sarcastic love reminded Becka that all men weren't like *him*.

They say pain makes you stronger. Then she must be the strongest bitch around. She flexed for the mirror and almost laughed at herself. Almost. Hard to laugh at the broken woman in the reflection. Instead, a snort emerged, a loud ugly thing that was almost a sob, and the first tears rolled down her cheeks.

I'm not strong.

She was, however, very naked and thus screamed when the door bounced open and a wild-eyed Stavros leaped in, fists raised.

She cringed, dropping to the floor in a protective huddle, hugging herself.

"Sweetheart, what's wrong?"

"N-nothing." Stuttered through hitching sobs. So much for bravery.

She heard more than saw him dropping to his haunches before her.

"Don't say nothing. You're crying. Are you hurt? How can I help you? Please let me help you." He didn't touch her physically, and yet his words ghosted over her skin, pimpling it.

"N-no one can help me. I shouldn't be here."

"If you ask me, you're exactly where you need to be. You're safe, sweetheart." A towel dropped over her shoulders, huge and fluffy. "He can't get you here."

She clutched the ends of the fabric, unable to chase the chill inside. "You don't know what you're saying. You don't understand who you're dealing with."

"Then tell me. Help me understand. Who is this fucker that has you terrified? Give me his name, and I will teach him a lesson he'll never forget."

Stavros alone against *him* and his posse? "I won't tell you because you can't confront him. Ever. You don't understand what he's capable of."

"I have a pretty good idea." A wry reply. "And you seem to underestimate what I'm capable of. I'm a big bear when riled."

More like a teddy bear. He seemed much too nice to deal with the kind of evil in her life. "You'll get hurt."

"I think I just felt my balls shrivel up and die."

"This isn't funny." Even if she almost snorted. Her head lifted, and she noted he crouched before her, his brown eyes calm and steady. "Those guys I ran from won't hesitate to hurt you. You heard what happened back there. People were killed."

"Which is all the more reason why I should go after them. I can handle myself pretty good in a fight, sweetheart. And by the time I'm done with him, he'll wish his mother had a headache the night he was conceived."

Such brash confidence, but she knew better. "I'm so tired of being afraid."

He placed his hand over hers, a light touch, and yet she still trembled, not entirely in fear. There was something warm and reassuring about the skin-to-skin contact. *Something warm and nice about him in general.*

His eyes were locked on hers, his expression utterly serious, when he said, "I will be your shield. Let me protect you."

CHAPTER 6

Let me protect you. Did he seriously fucking say that? What next? Would he start singing "Lean on Me" off-key? He was a man. With balls. At least he still hoped he had some, or had finding his mate make them shrivel into oblivion? He jumped to his feet and pivoted before giving them a good grab to check on their status.

Balls? Check. One thing taken care of. Now for the other issue. The woman on the floor.

Mate.

I don't need to hear from you, he practically snarled at his bear.

M-a-a-a-a-a-te. Damned beast had a sense of humor.

So did Stavros. *Don't make me get the Yogi bow tie.* Because his furry half did so hate it when Stavros put on the metal band that proved impossible to rip off and sported a lovely welded green bow tie.

Meanie. His bear sulked, which meant Stavros could maybe now concentrate on Becka without his bear giving him inappropriate ideas. *Even if inappropriate ideas are usually so much fun.*

He paced the length of the bathroom.

"You seem agitated," she finally remarked, a hint of trepidation in her tone.

"Of course I'm agitated."

"Because of me." She sighed. "I'm sorry."

He whirled and fixed her with a wagging finger. "Oh no you don't. Don't you dare apologize. This is not your fault. Well, it is, but not for the reason you think. And you could never guess why because you're human. A cute human who is now looking at me like I'm nuts. You wouldn't be far from wrong." His little speech and wry attempt at a smile only served to widen her eyes to the point that he feared her orbs would fall out.

"Are you due for some medication?" She hugged the towel tighter around her frame.

"No. But I can see why you'd think it. This probably seems crazy to you. But I am not nuts, and I don't use medicine of any kind. Constitution of a bear." He thumped his chest.

"Isn't the expression 'horse'?" she asked, still watching him with wide eyes, but he noted they seemed mostly curious now.

"In my house, according to my mother, it's 'bear.' Just like, according to her, honey fixes everything."

"Let me guess. She read you *Winnie-the-Pooh* as a child."

He recoiled, utterly aghast. "Good God no. My mother read us *The Three Bears* and *Grizzly Adams,* although, in the version we got, the bears ate the humans. And in *The Three Little Pigs*—"

"Let me guess. The bear huffed and puffed at the houses?"

"No. It's *The Three Little Bears* and the bears ate the wolf."

"Why does it feel like I've fallen down a rabbit hole?"

"Because you're tired. It's been a long day for you. You need some rest." He offered her a hand to help her off the floor.

She hesitated and looked at her fingers, clinging to the corners of the towel.

He caught her dilemma, and were she not injured, he would have grabbed both her hands to lift her, and fuck the towel. However, Becka wasn't ready for that kind of intimacy yet. She might not be for a long time. A hurt animal needed time to lick its wounds.

"Take your time getting dressed. There's some pain meds in the cabinet over the sink. It can help with the soreness if you need it." Shifters healed quick, but even they didn't mind a bit of help when the hangover proved particularly fierce.

He exited the bathroom, closing the door behind him. He paced by his bed, a freshly made bed, meaning one of his well-meaning siblings had come by. It probably meant he'd find food in his fridge. His sisters weren't far from wrong when they claimed he'd starve without them. He definitely would, since he didn't remember the last time he did groceries. The only thing he usually stopped for on his way home from work was beer.

The shower came on, not for long. He knew the moment she finished and exited the bathroom, but he didn't react.

"If you'll give me a blanket, I'll sleep on the couch." The soft words came from behind him, and he turned slowly, not wanting to startle her. She stood looking utterly fragile, and by "fragile" he didn't mean in body. Her frame had just the right amount of flesh for him, but her frailty showed in how she held herself. Shoulders curled inward, a wary look in her eye that said she would bolt if given a chance. The shirt he'd loaned her hung around her loosely, the edges of the boxer shorts he'd also provided barely peeking past the hem. He'd never seen anything sexier.

Now if only she didn't look like he'd eat her all up.

Eating is good.

Not if the honeypot flinched.

He pulled back the covers on his bed and patted the mattress. "Get your butt over here. I'll be fine on the couch."

For a moment he really thought she'd run; he could see it in her tense posture. Then she took a step, then another mincing step until she reached him. She brushed him slightly in passing, and shivered.

She clambered into his bed. His really big bed. Alone.

It seemed so wrong. It also seemed wrong to pull the covers over her. But he did it and then snapped off the bedside lamp so she wouldn't have to fumble.

With darkness hiding expressions, she asked, "Why are you being so kind?"

"Because it's how I am." For her at least.

"So you'd do this for anybody?"

He rested his hand atop hers on the cover and noticed she didn't flinch. Progress. "Some of it yes. I would have stepped in for anyone against that thug. I would have offered to take them somewhere safe, but . . ." He leaned down close enough for his warm words to brush across her skin. "Only for you would I bring you home and give you my bed." He probably also would give her his heart, seeing as how she already had his balls.

"Thank you."

"Anything for you, sweetheart." Then he gathered what remained of his male pride—precious little at this point—and left her, to sleep on his short and uncomfortable couch. But at least he could console himself with the marinated chicken and rice he found in the fridge.

CHAPTER 7

Waking in a bed seemed so strange. When was the last time Becka had slept on a mattress? Usually she got the floor, and most times it didn't even have a carpet.

She stretched and enjoyed the tickle of sunlight creeping through the window. Another thing she rarely got to see. The other rarity was the smile pulling her lips wide.

Oh my God, I just smiled. Then she giggled. She didn't think she did it loudly, but a second later a head popped around the doorframe, a very shaggy head.

Stavros grinned at her. "Now that's what I like to see and hear, a happy woman in my bed. Did you have a good sleep, sweetheart?"

She nodded. "The best I've had in a long time."

"Let me guess, since you hooked up with Douche Bag?" Her smile began to fade, and he hastened to catch his words. "I'm sorry. I didn't meant to make you sad again."

"I'm not sad." At his pointed look, she shrugged. "But you are correct. I haven't slept well"—*unless drugged*—"since he took me."

"'Took' you as in . . . ," he gently prodded.

Tell the truth or lie? She had to tell someone. Someone should know what had happened to her. She took a deep breath. "I was abducted. I used to live with my poppa. And then, out of the blue, one day, this, this . . ." She didn't know what to call him. "Guy" seemed too trivial, but "monster" gave *him* too much credit. "This stranger took me and kept me prisoner."

"Didn't your grandfather call the police?"

Another roll of her shoulders. "Probably. But it didn't mean they found me."

"Why did he take you?" He clamped his lips tight. "No. Don't answer that. I can imagine why." Anger contorted his features, and for a moment he looked quite ferocious, almost animalistic.

"It's not what you think. He never touched me like that. Sexually, I mean." Her cheeks flushed.

"If not for your body, then why? Was he blackmailing your grandfather?"

"I'd rather not talk about it." She ducked her head and plucked at the fabric of the blanket.

"I shouldn't be grilling you this early. My bad. Feel free to spank me." He turned around and held his hands up, the movement pulling his shirt above his waistband and showcasing the way his jeans hugged his ass. *A nice ass,* she might add. "You can touch it if you'd like. I know I would." He tossed her a wink over his shoulder, having caught her ogling.

The shocking words might have made her recoil less than a day ago, but that was before she'd met Stavros. Her cheeks heated, and they weren't the only part of her body showing a rise in temperature. When was the last time that had happened? And it wasn't just since her capture. She'd been so involved with work she'd not bothered dating much. Mostly because the men she met didn't appeal. Stavros did, though. He made her body come to life, even if this wasn't the time.

His fault. The man was really cute and determined to put her at ease, which brought back her smile.

"That's better." He turned to face her and approached the bed. "You're much too young to appear as if you bear the weight of the world on your shoulders." He stopped at the edge of the bed, and he reached out a hand toward her cheek, hesitating before making contact. His eyes caught hers as if asking permission.

Did she want him to touch her?

An almost imperceptible nod answered his silent query and she held her breath as his fingers lightly stroked her cheek.

"How could anyone ever hurt you?" he murmured.

The gentleness of his words and touch roused something in her, and she leaned forward slightly, pushing into his casual embrace until her stomach growled. Loudly. Appalled, she recoiled, and her features tightened in embarrassment.

No surprise, he laughed. "I see someone has a rumbly tummy. And I've got just the thing to fix it. Can you handle being alone for a few minutes? There's a coffee shop with the most excellent pastries downstairs. How about I grab us some?"

"Sounds good."

"Any favorites?"

"Blueberry fritter."

"Mmm. Good choice. I'll also grab some honey crullers. They're a favorite of mine." He winked and disappeared from sight, a good thing because, for no reason at all, she began to smile like an escaped mental patient. Stavros was so nice. This whole morning was, so far, awesome.

Don't trust it. She shouldn't allow herself to relax and be this happy. The danger to her and Stavros was still so very real, and yet she couldn't help but relax. This was the safest she'd felt since being taken from her poppa. A pity she couldn't stay to enjoy it.

As soon as the apartment door closed she hopped out of bed and went sprinting to the bathroom, looking for her pants. Only they were gone. What to do? She couldn't exactly leave in a T-shirt and boxers. She scrounged through Stavros's drawers and had to admit defeat because his pants were just too enormous for her to wear. Perhaps no one would pay much mind to the girl walking about in men's clothes barefoot. Wait, not entirely barefoot—she found some flip-flops in his closet. Bigfoot sized, but at least they were something for her feet.

She exited the bedroom, conscious of the ticking time that would bring Stavros back. She had to make her escape before he returned. He'd made it clear he wanted to help her, but she liked him too much to see him get harmed.

Just as she approached the door to his place, it clicked as the lock was disengaged, and then the handle turned. She backed away, heart racing all of a sudden.

She didn't know who was more surprised. Her or the woman who walked in.

Eyebrows arched. Eyes widened. A woman sporting a dark ponytail and wearing an athletic suit stared at her.

Becka stared right back.

"Who are you?"

"Becka."

"Where's Stavros?"

"Getting coffee."

"Does he know you're here?"

"He brought me here last night."

"He did?" The watchful gaze took in her appearance, lingered on her bruised arms and then her similarly marked legs. "You slept here?"

"Yes."

For some reason, this tightened the woman's lips into a thin line, and Becka wondered if Stavros had lied about having a significant other, because when he walked through the door a moment later the woman whirled and began beating him with her purse.

"What is wrong with you? Hurting a woman like that?"

"I didn't do it."

"He didn't do it," Becka echoed, horrified at the beating he was taking.

He, however, didn't seem to mind, given he laughed, loudly. "Becka, meet my oldest, loving sister, Athena."

The blows slowed. "So you're not the reason she's bruised?"

"Do you really think I'd hurt a woman?"

His sister shrugged. "No. But it never hurts to be sure." Whirling around, Athena presented her with a bright smile. "Hi, I'm Athena Browning. Such a pleasure to meet Stavros's new girlfriend."

She waved her hands in front of her. "Oh no, we're not involved. He's just helping me out with a, um, problem I have."

"I rescued her," Stavros added.

"He saved you?" For some reason that seemed to delight the sister even further. "And brought you to his apartment?" Athena's face might crack if her smile stretched any more. "Are you wearing his clothes too?"

"Yes, but nothing happened. He was a perfect gentleman and slept on the couch."

"Oh my. This is getting better and better." Athena practically chortled with glee.

"Don't you dare start," Stavros growled.

"Start what, Brother dear?"

"I recognize that gleam of evil in your eye."

"What gleam?" A failed innocent blink by Athena just served to draw his brows closer together.

"The one that says you're about to plot against me."

"Would I do that?" Even Becka could read the falseness in her tone.

"Why are you here?" Stavros asked, stepping into the apartment and using his heel to shut the door. He'd managed to not lose his cardboard tray of coffees or bag of goodies. He put them on the counter and sighed when his sister grabbed one of the cups. "That was supposed to be mine."

"I'll share," Becka hastened to say before the siblings began another all-out brawl.

"At least someone here has manners," he said with a pointed look at his sister. To Becka, he displayed a gentle smile as he handed her the coffee. "Don't worry about me. I'll survive. I didn't know how you liked it, so I got it the same as mine."

"Don't you mean mine?" his sister taunted.

"Have a pastry too." He pulled out a blueberry fritter and handed it to Becka, along with a napkin. He then indicated she should take one of the two bar stools. No surprise, Athena took the other.

"So, Becka, who's the asshat in need of a beating? Or did Stavros already kill the fellow?"

The swallow of hot coffee choked her, and she coughed as Athena slapped her on the back. Stavros's sister certainly was direct and waited for an answer. "It was an accident."

"I'm not an idiot, dear girl. I work in the ER as a trauma nurse and know signs of abuse when I see them."

"I'd rather not talk about it." Because a part of her feared too much talk would draw *his* attention.

"Then let's talk about you. Age?"

"Twenty-six."

"Occupation?"

"Medical secretary." Becka answered the interrogation-like questions, more because she feared the sister would turn the purse on her if she didn't.

As if Stavros would let her. In truth, Becka didn't fear the formidable woman, and so far the questions were benign enough.

"Are you religious?"

"Not really. My poppa said religion was for fools who were too lazy to look for answers. He said we should have faith in ourselves."

A moue pulled at Athena's lips. "Hmmm. You might not want to tell our mother that. She's a big churchgoer."

"I doubt we'll meet. I'm only here temporarily."

"Where are you going?"

"Um—" She didn't know what to say, and Stavros jumped in.

"She's not going anywhere for the moment. I've already told her she can stay with me as long as she needs to get on her feet."

He did? When? Why wasn't he in a hurry to dump her? A normal man would want her to leave so she wouldn't cramp his style. Then again, nothing about Stavros was normal.

"Having a young, unattached woman living with you who's not your girlfriend? That's really not appropriate, Stavros."

"Your sister is right. I should leave."

"You aren't going anywhere." He glared at his sister. "And don't you dare tell the other apron minions about Becka. She needs protection."

"So why isn't she in protective custody?"

Did Becka imagine it, or did Athena seem intent on poking at Stavros?

"She's safer with me. 'Bodyguard' is one of my job descriptions."

"And will you be guarding her body from everyone?" Athena snickered. "This is going to be epic. Wait until I tell Momma."

Stavros groaned. "Athena!"

His sister grinned wider. "You know I can't keep this a secret. You should come to dinner tonight. Bring Becka."

"No way. I can't." He shook his head.

"You'd better." His sister exited, but her last words lingered in the air. "Or else . . ."

The door swung shut, and Becka asked, "Or else what?"

For some reason, he looked pained. Very pained. "The worst possible thing you can imagine."

She could imagine some pretty nasty stuff. "You'll have to give me a clue."

"Matchmaking."

CHAPTER 8

I still can't believe she laughed. He'd revealed his family was about to go on a matchmaking rampage and she thought it was funny.

Awesome. Seriously, hearing her laugh proved the most amazing thing, especially since it sounded kind of startled, then evolved into full-blown belly giggles.

It was the most adorable thing he'd ever seen. He resisted an urge to scratch at his shriveling balls. *Nothing wrong with finding her attractive.* Surely he got some man points back for his dirty thoughts that involved bending her over the arm of the couch, dropping those shorts, and getting to his knees to pleasure her.

Give me a taste of that honey.

Did something of his hunger show in his gaze? Eyes wide, she watched him.

"Finish your breakfast. Because then we have to go clothes shopping."

She peered down at herself, which meant he looked down at her too. So much to enjoy. Especially how the short boxers revealed her legs. More like taunted him. Those bare legs should be wrapped around his waist, not wasting time holding her up.

I am being completely irrational. The crazy attraction

made no sense. Yet every time he looked at her, every time she opened her mouth or smiled, he was turned on.

I am in so much trouble, because if looking at her pleased him so much, imagine when she gave him his first blow job. He just hoped he managed to not drool on her head.

"I don't think I can shop in this." She pointed at her ensemble.

"I'll have to buy you some stuff then. Will you be okay if I leave you here for an hour or so?"

"Of course." Her eyes shifted left, and her head dropped.

A fingertip under her chin lifted it. "Don't think you can fool me, sweetheart. I know what you're thinking. You're thinking, 'As soon as he walks out that door I am out of here.' Here's the thing. That door uses a key. A key to get in. A key to get out." He pointed, and she noticed for the first time the lack of a thumb-bolt. "Second, it's dangerous out there, especially dangerous when you're not dressed to blend." Becka would draw attention; she was too beautiful to evade notice. He wouldn't wax eloquent on the smattering of freckles on her skin or the snub tip of her nose. He would, however, say the T-shirt clung to her breasts in a way that would draw eyes, not all of them friendly.

"Would it do any good to repeat I don't want you to come to harm? Would you believe me if I promised to stay?"

"Depends on how you seal that promise."

The innuendo was clear, and he couldn't have said why he did it. It was probably too soon for her to think of being with another man. She'd just escaped a traumatic situation, and here he put the moves on her. It was beyond creepy. Yet she'd claimed the abuse never got sexual. Did that change all the rules? Did it mean he could show her affection? Would it make her feel more protected and safe?

Her head ducked. "I don't understand what you want from me."

"Would you scream and try to stab me with a knife if I said 'you'?"

The revelation caused her breath to hitch, and yet her heart raced, adrenalized by their interaction.

"You barely know me."

"Is that supposed to change my intense attraction to you?" Nothing would change it. Ever. *Becka is mine.*

Mine. His inner beast grumbled in agreement.

"It's flattering. Really it is, but it's too soon for me to think of getting involved with anyone."

"Because you're worried the guy who held you prisoner is going to come back. Let him. I'll take care of him."

"You don't understand what he is."

And she didn't yet know what hid under Stavros's skin. Showing her too soon would send her running for sure, though. Humans needed a certain amount of time to adjust to the idea of a man changing into a bear. The revelation usually proved less traumatic if the pair mated first. "Promise me you'll stay until I come back."

Her lips clamped tight.

He cupped the back of her neck and drew her to him, lowering his mouth to hover a hairsbreadth away. "Promise me, sweetheart. Have faith in me."

His turn for his breath to hitch as she touched her mouth to his, a soft embrace, so gentle he didn't dare move.

It lasted mere seconds, and yet the touch proved much too electrifying for him not to act. His hands gripped her more firmly, and he let his lips join the kiss, slanting them over hers, nibbling and tugging at her mouth. The sugar and fruit of the donut powdered her lips. Delicious.

Hot panting breaths emerged amid increasingly heated

kisses. More like one long embrace of sighs, and moans, and a bit of tongue. The skin-to-skin contact proved electric. His hunger for her roared inside.

Want her. Want her now.

A good reason to step back, his lips bereft and his eyes busy taking in every detail of Becka from her swollen lips to her glazed gaze. He couldn't resist rubbing that lower lip with his thumb. *So fucking sexy.*

"You are a temptation, sweetheart."

"Is that why you stopped?" Her query emerged a tad high-pitched.

"I stopped because if I didn't I wouldn't have gone shopping. And you need clothes." Actually, he needed a few answers too. But he doubted bringing her along was a good idea. Just like leaving her here alone wasn't the best option, which was why, when she went to brush her teeth, he contacted his sidekick, also known as Cousin Damian, to come keep an eye on his place, out of sight, of course. He liked Damian well enough, but not enough to leave him alone with Becka. Killing a friend would suck.

She emerged from the bathroom with her hair combed and tied back. She noted the shoes on his feet. "So you're really going. Can you at least promise to be careful?"

"Clothes shopping is not that dangerous." He winked.

She didn't buy it. "Please come back."

"Tell you what, if I am not here by suppertime, feel free to bust out." Because the only way that would happen was if he was dead.

"Be good."

"Always," said with a wicked smile, and just because he was a man he snared her and drew her close. He gave her one more kiss, a kiss that she didn't hesitate to return.

He stopped it—way too soon—and left before he took her

right then and there. It was too early, despite the promise in her kiss. He had to take things slow with her so he didn't frighten her.

Let her have some time alone, a time for her to regroup and rest. Time for her to miss him maybe too?

All the way down he couldn't help but think leaving her felt wrong. Yet truly what was the danger to her? No one knew he had her. His apartment was probably one of the safest places in the city. His apartment door was burglar-proof. His windows were stories aboveground, and the one with the outdoor fire escape had bars. Add in Damian outside keeping an eagle eye and nothing could get to her.

I should stay and protect her in person. The thought persisted.

However, sitting around his place wouldn't get him any answers, and he dearly needed some. Despite all his gentle prods, Becka just wouldn't reveal her abuser. She tried to protect Stavros, which truly was laughable. But cute.

Everything about her was cute. He considered it a huge victory she'd stopped flinching when he touched her. Hell, they'd progressed enough that she had touched him, initiating their kiss. He considered it a huge victory.

She's beginning to trust me.

The burgeoning trust needed help, though. In order to have her truly relax and feel free, he needed to prove to her that the guy who'd hurt her wouldn't ever do so again. Which meant finding the guy. And when he did . . .

Eat his face. A bloodthirsty sentiment he wholeheartedly agreed with.

After exchanging a few words with Damian—"Call me if you suspect anything." "Don't be such a pussy-whipped nerd" was the reply—Stavros grabbed his car and went back to the scene of the crime, the hotel where it all started.

As he drew close to it, he noted it still had more than a few police cars strung out front, including a forensics van. The fact that people had died and were assaulted would mean lots of yellow tape. If he didn't feel such a sense of urgency, Stavros might have waited for the reports.

Parking a few blocks over, he traveled the rest of the distance on foot, taking note of those gawking—because in some cases the guilty parties did enjoy returning to the scene of a crime.

Who didn't want to relive an epic fight? In his family sleuth, they were starting to use GoPros. Those body cams caught all the action—and misdemeanors. Uncle Leo grumbled a few times about the old trick of dropping it in the toilet, not working with new technology and its waterproof, shockproof casings.

Despite the police presence, Stavros managed to enter the hotel unmolested. A hotel couldn't shut down for a police investigation. However, that didn't mean he managed to pass with impunity. A few steps into the lobby—decorated in a lovely shade of blue, with hints of gold and white marble, and he only knew this because his sister had helped design the space, meaning he'd heard about it over and over and over—he saw his old nemesis, Landry.

Don't let him see me.

Luck wasn't on his side. Landry spotted him and, with his side comb leading the way, headed over.

"What are you doing here?" Landry asked, his thin attempt at a mustache a distracting strip of fuzz over his lip.

"I was in the neighborhood and saw the commotion. Being curious, I thought I'd wander in for a peek."

"Bullshit. I already know you're involved. I heard you collared the prime suspect last night but then let him get away."

"Just doing my part as a good citizen. Not my fault you took too long to arrive." Never accept blame. Another thing Uncle Leo had taught them.

"We were still securing the crime scene when you notified Jenkins. You do know the proper chain of procedure involves you contacting Dispatch."

"I'm not a cop anymore. Procedure doesn't apply."

A sneer pulled that upper-lip caterpillar in ways no furry thing should stretch. "That's right, you're not on the force anymore, which means you shouldn't be here. This is a closed investigation. So turn around and leave before I have you booked on impeding an investigation."

"Do that and I might not want to share information that I have about the case. Vital information, I should add."

"Such as?"

Stavros gave him a crumb, something that wasn't really a secret. "There is a woman involved. Seems there's some guys looking for her."

"We're already aware of that."

"Did you know she was being kept prisoner? That she was abducted and being held hostage in the hotel room?"

Landry's gaze narrowed with suspicion. "How do you know this? Have you talked to her? Do you know where she is?"

"Me? Nope. Just repeating some conversation I had with the thug in the alley. You know, the one you guys lost." Utter bullshit, of course, the thug hadn't said much before Stavros took him down, but Landry didn't know that.

"Who was the assailant? Did you get a name?"

"Well, hold on a second, I just gave you a tidbit you didn't know. Fair play says you should give me something in return."

The battle played itself out on Landry's face before he bit

out a reply. "The hotel confirmed there was a female staying in the room where the altercation began. That female escaped during the brawl on that level and apparently fled the hotel on foot. But that's all we know. We didn't find any identification in the room, just a few pieces of clothing."

"You managed to lose a terrified woman who escaped in her bare feet?" He couldn't help taunt the prick. After all, he was pretty sure Landry was the one who had ratted him out about the weed. *Uptight prick.*

"How did you know her feet were bare?" Landry's eyes narrowed.

"Because people noticed and I hear what they say." Stavros covered his gaffe.

"Sir, the boys might have found something."

The claim drew Landry's attention, and he shot a glance over his shoulder. "Coming." He turned back. "Do you have anything else?"

"Not yet."

"Sure you don't," Landry muttered. "If you happen to find the girl, let me know immediately. As a witness to last night's events, she could be in danger."

"Never fear; I will do the right thing." For Becka and himself.

As Landry joined his posse, Stavros wandered toward the front desk. He flashed his PI badge as he introduced himself. "Hi, I'm Stavros Georgopoulos with Magnum Bear Investigative Services. I'm here on behalf of the gentleman who died last night. Mr. Smythe." A name he'd gleaned from the news. "Actually, I'm here on behalf of his company. Apparently, they sent him on this trip with a company laptop. Given his demise, the company is concerned about its property, given there is some sensitive information on the drive and they're worried about it getting into the wrong hands. Do you know where his belongings are?" More utter bullshit. When dealing with folks, always make it sound like you knew exactly what you were doing. Most tended to just reply with the answer.

"The police have all his things, plus those from the other room where it all started. I still can't believe it. It's just awful what happened last night." So awful the clerk appeared as if he'd burst with excitement. While trauma sucked for those dealing with it, many times those on the outside found a perverse pleasure in feeding off the adrenaline of it.

"So fucking awful," he agreed. "So they've got all my client's things. That's a fucking bummer. The company won't like that. I'm surprised, though. I thought he was a victim."

"More like a hero from what I hear. He took on one of the ninja dudes," said the young man behind the desk, his Adam's apple bobbing in excitement.

"Ninja dudes?"

"Ken, one of the security fellows involved in the altercation, said it was like some crazy action movie. There were these dudes, all dressed in black, head to toe, and wearing helmets too, so Ken couldn't see any faces."

"How many of them?"

"Not sure. Ken thinks he saw about three, but in the chaos there could have been more."

"Any idea who they were? Or what they wanted?"

"Nope." A shrug of skinny shoulders. "Most of the staff think it's a drug deal gone bad."

"And what do you think?" Because it never hurt to ask what people had seen. Sometimes the oddest clue could crack a case.

"I think it was a war over the girl. One guy had her; another one wanted her. So they fought. Except she got away, and holy crap was her boyfriend pissed."

"Oh. He returned to the hotel?"

"He did and lost his shit when he got back. I was just coming into work, and I saw him, screaming in the lobby. Demanding to know where she'd gone."

"Did the cops take him in for questioning?"

The clerk shook his head. "Nope. They wanted to, though. He shoved through them like they weren't even there and left. Now the cops are looking for him too."

"Can I ask what he looks like?" Put a face to the asshole who would suffer for what he did to Becka.

"He's a tall dude, but chubby."

"Skin color?"

"Superpale. And his hair is dark, kind of greasy-looking and totally receding." The clerk shoved his hair back on his forehead.

"Anything about his features that stands out?"

"He's got one of those big hooked-nose deals going on and a full-on unibrow. Not an attractive fellow, that's for sure."

"Does this fellow have a name?"

At that request, the clerk wavered. A subtle slide of green paper across the counter bolstered his resolve.

"Don't tell anyone I told you, but dude's name has got to be totally fake. I mean who the hell calls themselves Vladimir Dracuul?"

"Seriously?"

The clerk bobbed his head. "He even had I.D. to back it up."

"And where is Mr. Dracuul from? Transylvania?"

The clerk snickered. "Seattle of all places. Can you imagine?"

Not really, but a strange thought was beginning to form in Stavros's mind. A thought that surely was wrong.

He thanked the clerk and thought he'd try to make it to

the floor of the attack, except when the elevator doors opened on the eighth floor the blue uniforms on duty wouldn't let him past. "Sorry, man, but Landry will have my badge if I let you in."

Since Stavros had no desire to see his former mates get in trouble, he left but didn't go to his apartment. Not yet. Even if he wanted to.

Really wanted to. Like now. This very minute.

Run.

Go.

He had to see her.

And that desperate need was why he wouldn't. The fact that Stavros had met his mate didn't mean he wanted to run headlong into commitment. Commitment meant being responsible for someone else. No longer hanging out with his buddies at strip bars. And splitting the last donut.

It meant spending time with one lady. Putting her needs above his own. Protecting her from life's adversities. Making love to her all night long. Waking up beside her. Sharing smiles with her.

Hold on; exactly what was wrong with this picture again?

Exiting, he paid no mind to the people around him until he reached his car and whirled suddenly.

The moderately tall man in the suit didn't even flinch.

"Why are you following me?"

"You were showing an interest in a certain hotel patron."

"Don't know what you're talking about."

"Don't act stupid, Mr. Georgopoulos. We know who you are."

"How do you know me?" His brow furrowed in suspicion.

"People say the most interesting things when they think themselves alone on their phones. In this case, someone in the hotel lobby recognized you. There was mention you were here last night."

"Their information is wrong."

"Is it? Then why were you questioning the desk clerk?"

"How about instead we start with who are you and what the fuck business is it of yours who I talk to?"

"I am Antoine Beauchamp." A cultured name for a suave fellow. "I am here on behalf of my client."

"And who is your client?"

"None of your concern. Suffice it to say he has an interest in the girl who went missing last night."

"Don't know nothing about no girl." And he wouldn't tell this slick prick if he did. Something about the guy set off a warning growl.

Doesn't smell right.

The whole thing stunk.

"You don't say. Well, if that changes"—a card appeared, a simple white card with a number on it and simply the name Antoine—"call me. There is a reward for information leading to her return."

Out of curiosity, he asked, "What kind of reward?"

The number dropped his jaw.

Exactly who is my sweetheart?

He planned to find out, and he'd start by asking her. No more evading his questions. He'd get some answers goddammit, except when he arrived home thoughts of questioning her disappeared. The doorknob and lock were a melted mess. Someone had used acid to chew through the metal and gain entry. Inside, the damage continued, the place appearing as if a tornado had gone through it. Cushions tossed. Couches overturned. Cupboards torn open and contents strewn everywhere.

And not a sign of Becka anywhere.

What happened?

He slammed the door shut and wedged a chair in front of it to prevent it accidentally opening. Then as he stripped out of his clothes, he called his partner. The phone went straight to voice mail. *"Hey, this is Damian. Leave a message, unless you're my ex-girlfriend; then you can get back on that broomstick and fly out of here. I'm keeping the dog." Beep.*

"You better be fucking dead because if you're not—" *Argh.* The phone went flying and hit the wall. The heavy-duty case protected it.

He finished stripping, just in time too, as his bear shoved through with a growl.

That's better. Now I can see. By "see" he meant what had happened. In his human form, he truly was restricted. When it came to deciphering events, he had only his eyes, but that didn't tell anywhere close to the whole story.

Scent, though, that was an entirely different beast. He sat his bear ass on the floor, closed his eyes, and took a few whiffs. He sifted the different flavors, sorting them for study. The usual ones—his cologne coming from the direction of the bathroom, most likely smashed given its potency. Sweaty socks coming from his gym bag equipment, usually kept in the closet, now strewn on the floor. Leftover pizza smell from the box still sitting beside the cupboard because it didn't fit in the recycling bin.

All familiar home smells. Now for those that were out of the ordinary. Some kind of cheap deodorant, two different scents, neither of them his and most definitely not Damian. Oregano, that was a leftover from his sister Athena. She loved to cook Italian—which drove his very Greek mother insane. Then there was honey, with a hint of delicious, that belonged to Becka.

He followed the smells around, nose sometimes pressed to the floor, other times held high in the air. He snuffled at cushions on the floor and stuck his nose in crevices. The picture that emerged proved interesting, and it wasn't long before he knew where Becka could be found.

Hold on, sweetheart. I'm coming for you. He just hoped he wasn't too late.

CHAPTER 9

"Where is she?" The bellow came a moment before the door swung open.

Amid much snickering—not by Becka, who was still in a stunned state—Stavros stormed into his mother's house, his brows pulled taut, his usual genial smile missing. The open floor plan of the main level meant Becka saw him quite clearly. There weren't many places to hide, but given he seemed quite angry, she kind of wanted to duck out of sight, especially when his gaze lighted on her. The anger partially faded as gentle concern filled his eyes. "Thank God, you're here. You're not hurt, are you?"

"No. Your sisters were very gentle when they came to dress me and then take me back to your mother's house."

"Dress you . . ." His gaze took in her appearance, lingering at her waist. In a blink, the last of his anger melted into incredulity, then mirth. "Are you wearing an apron?"

Wiping her flour-dusted hands on it, Becka couldn't help a sheepish shrug. "They kind of insisted." She thought it best not to argue. His family was kind of bold and bossy. Besides, the way they'd kind of taken her under their wing made her feel warm and mushy inside. She'd never had much female or motherly influence growing up, her mother having died at a young age, so young she didn't remember her.

"It's cute." He looked as surprised as she felt at the compliment.

She managed to hide her pleasure as his mother bustled around the island and headed toward Stavros, brandishing her rolling pin. "Is this how I raised you? To come barging into the house like an ill-bred country bear?"

I'm pretty sure the expression is "bumpkin." But Becka thought it endearing the way Stavros's Greek mother mixed things up. Callings kids cubs, likening her husband to a big old grizzly.

But she liked the woman, who insisted Becka call her Momma Lulu. Momma Lulu was apparently delighted to meet Stavros's lady friend—and no amount of protesting by Becka would sway her from calling her that. As a matter of fact, the more Becka defended his actions and played down what he'd done, the more his mother beamed. It also resulted in Becka being treated to album after album of Stavros growing up.

Such a happy family with so many memories. It made her wistful because, while she'd had some special moments with her poppa, all those pictures were gone. Burned to the ground in the fire *he* set to hide her disappearance. For all intents and purposes, Becka was dead to the world.

The conversation between Stavros and his mother heated as she waved around her kitchen weapon of choice. "What do you mean the girls left your place a mess?"

"My apartment looks like someone had a temper tantrum."

"Wasn't me," said Cyrena, another of Stavros's sisters. "Place was immaculate when we left. Alayla even made your bed and emptied your garbage cans."

"I don't suppose any of you wear cheap athletic deodorant?"

"Did someone wreck your place?" Becka caught on to what he was asking and felt all the animation and pleasure washing out of her.

He had found her. Or at least found Stavros's place. Which meant they might not be far behind. *They are probably on their way here. Right now. Oh God.*

Instant panic suffused her. Her fingers fumbled at the knot behind her back as she tried to remove the apron. "I should leave. Now. I never should have come. I'm so sorry." She heard herself blabbing as agitation made her clumsy and the knot refused to release. On the contrary, the stubborn thing drew tighter, and she could have sobbed in frustration.

Big, brawny arms came around her, trapping her. *Trapping me!* For a moment she panicked, drawn back into her nightmare. Becka pushed at Stavros and hyperventilated. "Let me go. Let me go. Let me go."

But he wouldn't move away, just hugged her tighter, murmuring against her ear.

"Shhh. Calm down, sweetheart; no one's leaving, and only a moron would show up here."

"Should I call James?" Persephone lifted her head from her phone long enough to ask. "He's home right now working on the back patio, but I'm sure he'd rather be here slapping around some thugs."

"Ooh, maybe I should call Pietro too. He's been harping about how he needs more boy time since the twins were born," Cyrena added.

"Will it make you feel better if a couple of the boys come over?" he asked.

"No." Because that was more people who might get hurt on her account.

She went limp in Stavros's grasp, and his hold relaxed, enough that she dropped low and scooted out of his embrace.

Her bolt to the door proved short-lived, as he plucked her midstride. "Excuse us. I'm going to take Becka out to the swing for a chat," he announced over his shoulder as he carted her out the door.

Becka remained behaved and silent until they hit the outside porch and the front door closed. "Put me down. Right now. And don't you dare stop me from leaving."

"Or?"

"What do you mean 'or'? You can't keep me prisoner. I have a right to leave. And if you don't let me, I'll—I'll call the cops on you."

"Okay." He handed her his phone and stood back, leaning his bulky frame against the house. "Go ahead. It's on speed dial."

She growled. "Stop treating this situation like a joke. This isn't funny."

"No, it's not. Which is why I'm not laughing."

"Not laughing and yet you're keeping me here. You're putting your whole family in danger. He knows I'm with you."

"We don't know that for sure."

"You said it yourself. Someone trashed your place."

"Could have been anyone."

She glared at him as she crossed her arms. "Now who's lying?"

A big shoulder lifted and dropped. "Fine. It was probably someone looking for you. But upside, he didn't find you. And all that shit can be replaced. You can't. Which means I'm going to have to thank my sisters for grabbing you or else you would have been there alone when they came. They'll never let me live it down." He looked so pained at the thought.

"Don't you see now why I have to go? Look at what he did to your place. *He* will stop at nothing to find me."

"By 'he,' I am assuming you mean Count Dracula?"

Her mouth rounded. “You know of Vladimir?”

“You mean that’s really his name?” Stavros grimaced. “And let me guess, he’s a vampire, hence the wounds on your arms.” At her continued shocked expression, his own changed. “Holy fuck, sweetheart. I was joking. Vampires don’t exist.”

“If you say so. Real vampires might not exist, but sometimes all it takes is belief.”

At that admission, his eyes widened. “Holy fuck. Are you telling me he truly thinks he’s a vampire? And let me guess, he’s been using you for a buffet dinner.” His face twisted. “That sick fucktard. I’m going to rip off his dick and force-feed it to him.”

A lovely sentiment. “There will be no ripping because you’re not going to meet him.”

“Oh yes I am.” Said with such menacing promise. It flustered and aroused, by nature, with its pure machismo. But it was also a very dangerous sentiment.

“You can’t go after him. You don’t understand the resources he has access to. The men he’s got working for him are rough. Real rough and not afraid to hurt people.”

“I can hurt people too.” His grin was back to being too open and wide.

“What will it take to make you go away? I don’t want to see you hurt.”

“I’m not leaving, sweetheart, and on the off chance I get a boo-boo you could always kiss it better.”

“You are the most frustrating man.”

He pushed away from the wall and loomed over her, but forget fear. Having him that close only served to fan the flames within her. All of her tingled, the anticipation of his touch almost too much to bear.

"I'm frustrating?" He chuckled softly and leaned down to brush his mouth ever so lightly against hers. "You're not the one whose balls hurt with wanting."

Did he imply . . . surely not? "I'm not doing it on purpose."

"I know. But that doesn't stop me from wanting you."

Wanting me? She gaped at him, flustered and hot at the same time. The situation was utterly impossible. The only thing she knew was she should get away from him as far and as fast as she could. Instead, she did something impulsive. She grabbed him by the cheeks and pulled him to her, meshing her mouth to his.

If she surprised him, he didn't show it, quickly pulling her to him and keeping his mouth pressed to hers, their breaths comingling. She fitted against him perfectly and, in his arms, felt such a measure of peace, but that peace didn't mean she didn't also feel extreme arousal.

Stavros only had to touch her to ignite her. A single kiss had her ready to do things, things that involved more touching. More kissing. More . . . everything.

I can't. Not right now. Not with everything still happening. She pulled away and tried to catch her breath.

"We shouldn't be doing this."

"Actually, we should be doing more of this, but if we get too frisky on the porch my mother is liable to come at us with the hose."

"Your family is very interesting."

"You don't know the half of it. And you're one to talk, escaping a guy who tried to make you think he was a vampire."

"Not just think, he is," she replied.

For some reason, that caused Stavros to recoil. "Wait, what? Hold on a second. Don't tell me you think he's a vampire too."

"Not think, know. You seem to forget I lived it." She held out her arm and showed the fading punctures, the skin no longer so mottled, but the scars would take longer to heal.

"Sweetheart." Said softly as his hands cupped her cheeks. His gaze caught and held hers. "Despite what he wants you to think, vampires aren't real. He's a sick cumwad who needs his ass kicked a few times before I end his miserable life."

"I don't think 'cumwad' is a word." Probably the stupidest thing she'd ever said yet the only thing she could say at his vehement exclamation. He was truly angry about her treatment and determined to avenge her. It was oddly sexy.

"Says the girl who believes in vampires."

"There are things out there that exist that you wouldn't believe." More than a few rumors abounded, and she'd been privy to them in Vlad's care. *Shit.* She'd thought his name. She peered around and hugged herself. The brightness of the afternoon didn't chase the chill.

"Actually, sweetheart, I do believe because I'm one of those secrets."

The odd reply drew her attention to him. "What do you mean?"

"I mean I'm not really human. I guess, since you believe in vampires, this is going to be easier than expected. I am a bear," he said, and then fixed her with an expectant stare.

"Bear what?"

"A bear shifter."

She shook her head.

"As in I change into a bear. Rawr." He lifted his arms for emphasis.

A snicker came from her. "Oh please. If you were going to screw with me, you could have at least used 'wolf.' Werewolves at least are on par with vampires."

"No, really, I am a bear shifter. A werebear if you will."

"And I'm a genie princess."

"Can I see you in the belly outfit?"

A frown pulled at her brows. "No, you cannot, because I'm screwing with you like you're screwing with me."

"Except I'm not fucking with you and I can prove it."

Sure he could. And to think she'd thought him normal. She should have known there was something wrong with him. He was just too perfect otherwise. "Then prove it." She leaned back against the railing and crossed her arms. "Let's see this badass bear of yours."

"Who told you it was badass?" He winked. "Just kidding. He totally is."

"Then stop yapping and show me. I'm waiting," she sang as she tapped her foot.

"Not out here. People aren't supposed to know."

"Of course they're not. Because people don't change into bears."

"Boy, are you going to feel silly when I show you. Come on." He dragged her inside but didn't stop at the main floor, just said "Gonna show her my bear" to the curious gazes tossed their way.

He took her by the hand to a set of stairs leading down to a finished basement, the main family room area large and open.

"You can stop screwing with me. This isn't funny. And we're wasting time. I should be putting distance between me and your family."

"You're not going anywhere. And in about two minutes, you're going to be utterly amazed. Or grossed out. But I'm hoping for amazed. Do you want me to do this in front of you, or change in another room?"

"Is that where you keep the costume?"

A smile curved Stavros's lips. "No costume. Just so you

know, we like to be rubbed behind the ears. Don't be afraid to give the fur a good hard scrub. Ready, sweetheart?"

"Go." She clapped her hands, and as if that were a signal, his shirt came off. *Oh my.* The top half of him was ogle worthy, his body thick through the chest, with muscle, not fat. But also furry too. But that didn't make him a bear.

His hands went to the waistband of his pants, and he unbuttoned.

"What are you doing?"

"Unlike cartoon bears, I don't wear clothes. And shifting in them is really hard on the wardrobe. When possible, I strip first." His hands began to shove the pants down, and she closed her eyes.

He really was taking the fantasy all the way. Really, though, a bear? He couldn't have chosen something believable?

There were a series of odd noises, kind of cracking and popping yet at the same time fluid. It made no sense, but she didn't look. Looking meant seeing a naked Stavros. A lovely sight surely, but a distracting one.

Speaking of which, dammit, he'd talked her out of leaving. For the moment. Once he was done messing with her, she planned to march back outside and—

What the fuck just licked my hand?

Her eyes shot open and opened even wider when she screamed, "You're a fucking bear!"

CHAPTER 10

Okay, so maybe she wasn't quite ready.

Still, the girl admitted to believing in vampires. Why was his shifter side such a shock? The logic didn't matter; his chagrin at making her faint did. At least he caught her before she hit the floor. And another bonus, she didn't die of a heart attack. But just in case, he switched back.

The fugue state didn't last long. She regained consciousness slowly, her eyes blinking, each opening of her eyelids a chance for her to gaze at him quizzically. Better than the blood-curdling scream of before.

He'd heard plenty of laughter after that upstairs. No way would his mother and sisters keep it to themselves. Soon, everyone in the family would know he'd made Becka scream.

Everyone will know I am the bear. The biggest and baddest.

Her lips parted, and she wet them with the tip of her pink tongue. "You're . . . I mean you were a bear."

"Still am inside."

"And you can change like that anytime?"

He shifted her in his lap, pleased she didn't try to escape, even though he was quite naked. Then again, she was still addled by his revelation. "I can shift within reason. Too many times in quick succession will drain me."

"Don't you need a full moon?"

He shook his head. "Nope. Although the urge to go swap into my furry skin is stronger during that time."

"I fainted."

A smile tilted his lips. "You did."

"I didn't get a chance to rub your ears."

"You can give me twice the scratch next time."

"Next time?" Her brow furrowed. "How is it that you can change into a bear, but you don't believe in vampires?"

"Because they don't exist. Don't you think I'd have noticed if there were vampires running around?"

"They don't run around. There actually aren't very many. Something about it being very hard to find the right type of person who can handle the vampire sequence. Or so *he* said." She shivered.

His turn to frown. How dare she fear that woman-beating coward? "From now on, when referencing your ex-vampire, use the term 'fucktard.'"

"That seems rather vulgar."

"Yes, it does."

Her lips split into a grin. "Fucktard." The foul word came out hesitantly the first time. "Fucktard. Fu-ck-tard." She drew the word out and smiled. He would have killed anything for her in that moment.

"Yes, he's a fucktard, and a coward. And, most of all, a fraud."

"A fraud with money." Her gaze dropped, and she stared at something under his chin. "It's amazing what throwing around some dollars lets some people get away with."

"You mean like the fact he thought his money gave him the right to take you? No one, not even the richest prick in the world, has the right to hold another person hostage. But why? Why you? What did he need you for? What makes you so special?" Other than the most obvious thing. She was fucking amazing.

"Apparently, I have a rare blood type."

"How rare?"

"As in rare enough to kill for. *He*"—at her inflection, Stavros poked at her ribs. She corrected it to—"Fucktard apparently got wind of my rarity after I gave blood during a drive for it at my work. He's got some mole working the blood banks just to keep an eye out for my plasma type."

"So he targeted you?"

"Yes. He found out where I lived and worked. He tried pretending an interest in me at first, but I wouldn't go out with him. So he kidnapped me."

"How long ago?"

"A month. For the first week or so, I kept expecting someone to find me. He told me to behave or he'd take my grandfather too."

At the mention of family, he could have slapped himself. "Where is your grandfather? We should contact him and let him know you're alive."

Tears filled her eyes. "Poppa is dead. Fucktard killed him. He killed my poppa so he wouldn't raise any alarms about my disappearance."

"I'm sorry." The sadness emanating from her couldn't remain unacknowledged. He drew her close for a hug, only to feel another set of arms wrap around as his sister Persephone cried, "That is so fucking sad. Don't worry, baby girl. The boys will make that bastard pay."

A nice sentiment, but Stavros wasn't willing to share Becka quite yet, not with her so fragile and finally opening up to him. "Do you mind giving us a moment?"

"Actually, I do mind." Persephone let them go and stepped away before tossing her hair. "No way am I leaving you down here alone with your new mate and the couch we conceived Jarrod on."

"I didn't need to know that."

"If it prevents you from soiling that precious memory, then I've done my job." His sister patted him on the arm and winked at Becka.

"Your family is demented." Said in an almost wondering tone. "So wonderfully demented."

And Stavros could tell she absolutely adored it. On the other hand, he wasn't sure he liked his sister much at the moment.

Persephone pinched a bare cheek. "Oho, someone lost his knickers. Don't let Ma see you misbehaving with our guest. She'll give you a few swats for sure."

"You're naked?" Becka sounded so surprised.

"When did you expect me to dress? Who do you think caught you before you face-planted?"

"It wasn't my fault I fainted. There was a bear."

"Still is, sweetheart. Right here in front of you."

"Is that why you're so hairy?" He gaped at her, and her lips turned down. "I'm sorry. I didn't mean to insult you." She scrambled off his lap and backed away, a hint of fear in her expression, and even though he hadn't done a thing, he felt absolutely horrified.

He dropped to his knees in front of her, trying to make himself seem as least daunting as possible. "Sweetheart, don't be scared. Never. I would never ever hurt you for teasing me. Or insulting me. You could hit me with a two-by-four or nail me in the sack and I would never do a thing to retaliate. Try it. Hit me."

Her head shook violently.

"Really. I don't mind." He thumped his chest a few times, but it was his sister, with a "He's tough, look," gut-punching him that did the trick. Suddenly Becka went from looking terrified to smiling and even chuckling.

Persephone grinned, quite pleased with herself. "See, no harm. No foul. And no retaliation."

"Wait until Christmas," he growled. "I see your boys getting a drum set under the tree."

His sister's eyes widened in horror. "You wouldn't dare!"

"I won't, but only if you give me some privacy."

"Fine. I'm leaving, but if you're going to get frisky stay off the couch."

"With cymbals."

His sister fled, and he sighed. "I told you my family liked to meddle."

"I'm sorry."

"For what? The fact my sisters have no boundaries?"

"No, for being so much trouble."

"What did I say about apologizing?"

"Am I allowed to say thank you?"

"For what?"

"For being you."

For some reason, the soft words brought heat to his cheeks. "I should probably get dressed before we have more company."

At the reminder, her gaze dropped from his face to under his chin. Red stained her cheeks, and she whipped around.

The shyness didn't hide her interest, not from him. He could smell her arousal. Totally wanted to taste it but knew he wouldn't have time to truly savor it. He located his clothes and pulled on his pants. When he finished zipping, he then approached her, lightly touching her shoulder to let her know it was safe to turn.

She whirled, careful to keep her gaze on his chin. "Despite the whole bear thing, I meant what I said before. We shouldn't stay here. If you feel a need to stay with me, then fine. But I don't want anyone else in your family involved. Please, Stavros."

The "please" did it. Took the last bit of his balls and shredded it.

That's it. I'm a goner. A man about to do anything this woman asked.

"I've got oven-fresh cookies!" his mother yelled.

Yeah, he'd do anything after his snack.

CHAPTER 11

Ditched for cookies. It was the most adorable thing, especially since Stavros grabbed Becka by the hand and tugged her up the stairs, insisting on sharing this extravagant delight. Hot cookies made from scratch.

A surreal set of hours passed as Becka experienced her very first large family gathering—a much noisier event than her past dinners with her poppa. Her fervent desire to leave proved hard to enforce, Stavros's cocky confidence keeping her in that kitchen, nibbling on all kinds of things, including those blessed cookies. Supper came and went with a potluck of dishes, so much food that her belly felt round and full for the first time since her capture. Nightfall came, then bedtime, and she was still in the house. Her escape foiled by good food and well-meaning folks.

As the evening hour waned, most of the sisters had departed, leaving only Becka and Stavros, Persephone, plus, of course, his mother and father—a gruff man, or so it seemed at first. He quickly made Becka feel welcome and comforted with his booming laughter, teasing, and he even gave her a big hug before he and Momma Lulu went to bed.

Eventually, Persephone wandered off to read a book, which left only Becka and Stavros awake for the most dangerous time of day. No point in warning Stavros once again. He just wouldn't listen. He didn't understand. He truly thought he could handle the situation.

Maybe he can. But she feared more finding out he couldn't. The door he showed her on the second level opened into a girl's pink paradise. Becka walked in to find dark pink shag, complemented by white furniture and light pink walls.

"I won't be able to stay in here with you," he mentioned. "My mother"—a glare shot down the hall—"has certain ideas about boys and girls. One involves being married before sharing a room."

"Oh. Um. But we're not, um—"

"Having sex? Not yet." He winked as he leaned against the doorframe.

How many more times could she blush before she looked permanently sunburned?

"I guess this is good night." More like good-bye. But she couldn't tell him that; he'd probably tie her to the bed if he suspected what she planned.

"That's not a good night." He wound an arm around her waist and drew her close. "This is a good night." He proceeded to give her insomnia by shooting sexual caffeine into every atom she owned until a thump on the far wall led to him pulling away.

They drew apart slowly, her cataloging every inch of him to remember. She wished she could stop time and live in this moment forever. *I don't want to leave.*

"I'll see you in the morning, sweetheart." He dropped one last soft kiss on her lips, and then he was gone, the door shutting softly after him.

A sigh escaped her. *I'm going to miss him.* A shame she'd never see him again. She rather liked him. He made her believe in good guys. Almost made her believe in a happily ever after.

The only way that would happen was if she did the right—and yet so very hard—thing. Still fully dressed, she sat on the bed, reading a book she found—involving the pairing of a bunny and a bear that had her smiling—waiting until the house went silent.

Midnight came with a dark cloak of silence. Time to leave. She stood and moved in her bare feet to the door—her shoes were, she hoped, still by the front entrance. She pressed her ear against the wood-grain panel and listened.

Nothing but the frantic thump of her own heart. She exhaled, then breathed deep again before gripping the knob and turning it ever so slowly. The door pulled inward on well-oiled hinges. She took a step and hit something.

"Eep." She flailed as she fell and landed on something unyielding and welcoming at the same time.

"Sleepwalking, sweetheart?" Stavros asked, his arms coming around her in a cage.

Caught! So she lied. "I needed a drink of water."

"There's an unopened water bottle on the nightstand."

"Fine, I was trying to leave," she hissed. A part of her couldn't believe his lack of trust in her, sleeping on the floor outside her room. Really?! Then again, apparently he knew her better than she'd suspected.

"I knew you would, hence my comfy spot. Why don't we continue this conversation in your room before we wake the whole house?"

Moving to her room would mean getting off him. A shame, because she was quite comfortable where she was.

"You're bossy," she grumbled as she rolled off him. She made it back into her room and paced by the bed as he entered, softly shutting the door behind him.

"I'm only bossy because you're trying to do something stupid."

"Taking responsibility is not stupid."

"It is if you're just planning to offer yourself up like a sacrificial picnic basket."

"Isn't the expression 'lamb'?"

"Gross." He made a face. "We don't eat anything cute. Most of our meat is bacon and fish. Maybe the occasional crustacean." He shrugged. "But we're killers when it comes to berry season."

A lightbulb went off, and she blinked. "Oh my God, I just realized all those comments you keep making about bears . . . it's because you're a bear."

"Well, yeah. It would be odd to compare ourselves to other animals."

"I never asked before"—mostly on account she was in shock—"but is your whole family bears?"

"Only the men."

"And you're born that way?"

"Nope. We're one hundred percent human at birth, but once we hit our teens we go through a ritual whereby our father turns us."

"But only the boys? I'm surprised your mother and sisters are okay with that."

"They don't have a choice. The virus that is transmitted via the saliva of a bite only works on men, and even then, not all men will change. Direct family has the best chance of conversion, but even that's not foolproof. Poor Julio has been bitten a dozen times now to no avail. For a while, my uncle thought my aunt cheated on him, until the DNA test came back proving Julio was his. However, it turns out he's immune."

"This is all very strange to me."

"Yet you believe in vampires."

"Because I lived with one."

"And now you live with me. A bear." He grinned, white teeth flashing.

"For now. But I can't stay with you forever."

"Why not?"

"What do you mean, why not? Because it's not your responsibility to take care of me."

"What if I wanted it to be? What if I said I wanted to date you and do deliciously decadent things to your body?"

"I'd say"—*Do me. Yes. Now. I'm yours.*—"that you're insane."

"I get that from my father's side. We've got a bit of grizzly in our line."

"And what about your whacked-out sense of humor? Is that from your father too?"

"Probably, although I'd say that's more the panda in me. Apparently, we've got a great-ancestor who visited China."

She sat down on the edge of the bed and flopped on it, closing her eyes and covering them with her arm. Perhaps by blocking him out she could think clearly, because he seemed determined to muddle her mind.

The bed dipped alongside her. "No hiding, sweetheart."

"Why not?"

"Because I want you to see me when I do this."

"Do what?" She opened her eyes and removed her arm as she turned her head to see him. He took that moment to draw her close and kiss her. A soft and sensual kiss. A kiss meant to melt.

It worked. Her mouth parted, and she welcomed the foray of his tongue.

The embrace didn't last long enough. He pulled away and stared at her. "I want you, sweetheart."

She wanted him too. "But—"

He silenced her protest with another kiss. A longer one

with dancing tongues that brought her blood to a boil and left her slightly breathless.

Again, he pulled back. "I understand you're worried, which is why you can't think of a future with me yet. But don't worry. I'm going to fix that."

"Fix it how?"

"Don't you worry ab—"

He cut off what he was about to say. His brow knitted, and an instant later he was off the bed and moving to the door. Much like her, he put an ear to it.

"What's wrong?"

"I thought I heard something. Stay here."

Before she could protest, he'd ghosted out of the room, quickly and silently, latching the door behind him.

"Stay here," he'd said. But he wasn't the one waiting, straining to hear what had roused his attention. She rose from the bed and paced, pausing a moment before the window, only a moment before cursing her stupidity. With the lamp on behind her, she cast a perfect silhouette if anyone watched outside. She whirled and clicked it off. She moved to the bedroom door again and pressed her ear against it.

Nothing.

For a moment her fingers lingered over the knob. No, he'd asked her to stay. She owed that to him. She whirled around in time to see a shadow against the window a moment before it crashed through the glass. Her mouth opened on a scream, and she turned to fumble at the door.

Only in her clumsy haste and panic she couldn't get it open. An arm clad in black fabric wrapped around her upper body, cinching her tight. Something pressed against the side of her neck and . . .

CHAPTER 12

The alarm system showed green, and yet Stavros's bear radar insisted something was wrong.

Very wrong.

He stripped before letting himself out the side door, a quick glance outside showing nothing, the motion sensors not activated at all. *Are they working?*

It wasn't hard to test. As he padded past them, nose lifted, scenting the air, they came to life, bathing the yard in a soft glow. Nothing appeared amiss. Yet still a sense of unease lingered.

Always trust your gut. Something taught by his father at a young age. He put his nose to the ground and moved toward the edge of the yard, meaning to patrol, but a scuff of sound on the far side of the house attracted his attention.

Becka!

With his fur bristled, he turned around and bolted on four legs to the side where Becka's bedroom resided. Bursting around the corner, he looked up in time to see a body, clad head to toe in black, rappelling down from the roof and kicking the glass window leading into the bedroom.

He roared, which didn't do much considering his enemy was two stories above. The intruder emerged from the window, sitting on its edge, a limp Becka over his shoulder. The fucker gave him a wave before jumping and swinging to the side, his harness pulling him back to the roof. But where did he plan to go from there?

How did he get here? Stavros raced around the building, looking for the intruder's ride. Unless he could fly, he needed some wheels. Sure enough, on the far side, behind his own car, he found a vehicle that didn't belong. He charged at it, wondering where his backup was. He'd called in some family favors to cover the outside, and yet he seemed to be the only one acting.

If they hurt anyone . . .

Grawr!

His bear charged at the SUV, whose driver threw it into reverse and burned rubber as he tried to escape. Much like in an action movie, it suddenly spun, tires screaming, ass end fishtailing before it gripped asphalt and shot forward, only to crunch as something big and furry barreled into its side. The SUV tilted on two wheels, and Stavros's grizzly cousin stood on two legs to finish its tilt.

Despite the vehicle lying on its top, the wheels spun, and Stavros left the driver to Damian. He turned back to the house and noted the guy standing on the roof, Becka still draped over his shoulder.

Got you trapped, you bastard.

He roared a challenge.

The guy lifted a gloved hand and gave him the finger. That took some fucking balls. Then again, the guy thought himself safe on the roof. He apparently didn't know Stavros's daddy climbed that roof every December to put up Christmas lights.

Stavros's father stood on the far side and bellowed, "Put the girl down and I might not kill you."

The intruder didn't even turn to face Stavros's father. Bad

move, since Stavros's daddy, with no regard for his pj's, burst into his bear. However, his roar was overshadowed.

A strange *whup-whup* sound filled the air, and Stavros could only look on in disbelief as a helicopter swooped into view over his house, flying low. Too low, as it dropped a ladder. The intruder shifted Becka on his shoulder and grabbed hold of the rungs and began to climb.

Oh hell no. Who the fuck are these guys? Stavros's father charged, but he would never make it in time.

Bang. Bang. Stavros swung his shaggy head and noted his sister Persephone—an excellent markswoman, much like the goddess—taking aim at the helicopter. The helicopter dipped, and the guy clinging to the ladder swung, his legs losing purchase, one arm tearing free. Of more concern, he lost his grip on Becka, who fell several feet and hit the rooftop, then rolled.

Rolled like a snowball gathering speed right off the fucking edge!

Shit.

Stavros's claws left furrows in the ground as he raced toward the house, running faster than he'd ever run in his life. He stood at the last possible moment to catch her in his arms.

She roused enough to crack one eye and say a slurred, "Saved by a teddy bear." Then passed out again, safe in his arms.

As for the helicopter and the dude hanging from the ladder, they disappeared from sight.

But good news. The bears still had the car and its driver.

Except they didn't have the driver.

A few minutes later—one of those minutes spent getting pants for the men who'd shifted—Stavros bellowed, "What the fuck do you mean he escaped?"

Damian, back in his human shape, shrugged. "What would you like me to say? When I wrenched the door open, the damned thing was empty inside."

"He must have left a trail, though." Even if the man wasn't bleeding, Damian should have tracked him.

"The inside of that car smelled like new. If I'd not seen the damned guy behind the wheel, I'd have said it was driven by a ghost." Because what else wouldn't leave a scent?

Stavros sighed and ran a hand through his hair. "We'll run the plates. See who it belongs to."

"Wouldn't that be her ex?"

Except from all signs, Vladimir was a moron, whereas this had been a pretty slick operation, foiled only by chance.

And me. His bear thumped his furry chest.

More like my sister.

His bear slumped in shame.

"What are you going to do now?" his cousin asked. "If they tried once, they might try again."

And next time, they might bring more firepower.

There was only one thing to do.

"Are you thinking what I'm thinking?" Stavros's papa bear grumbled.

"Family Jamboree!"

CHAPTER 13

Becka woke in bed, which she found kind of surprising given the last thing she remembered was someone breaking through a window.

I was attacked!

She sat bolt upright in the bed, in the pink room she recalled, and she wasn't alone. Stavros lay beside her, looking entirely too much at ease as he leaned his head on a crooked arm.

"Morning, sweetheart."

"Don't you 'morning' me. I was attacked. And drugged. I think. There might have been a bear." She recalled a sensation of falling and then a big furry muzzle. But she might have dreamed that part, maybe dreamed it all, given she was still in her room, except for the fact that the window now sported a lovely expanse of cardboard with crawling babies extolling the virtues of diapers.

"Don't get your panties in a twist unless you're going to let me untangle them with my teeth."

She slugged him, too shocked to even feel horrified by her actions. "Don't joke. Your house was attacked. I told you this would happen."

"And I told you not to worry. We sent them packing, and look, you're here in one piece."

She patted herself and didn't notice any missing body parts or feel any new bruises. "So I didn't fall off a roof?"

"You did. But I caught you."

She flopped back onto the bed and closed her eyes. "How can you be so blasé about this? Someone could have been hurt."

"Someone can get hurt walking across the room. My cousin Josephine is so clumsy she managed to break her own leg making her bed."

"That's an accident, though. What happened last night was a targeted attack against you and your family."

"Actually, against you. Whoever came visiting last night wasn't out to hurt anyone. We found two of my cousins sleeping off tranquilizers in the woods."

"Vlad—"

"Fucktard."

"—tranqed them? That doesn't sound like him."

"Because it's not. We have a new player. The same one that came after you in the hotel, I'd wager."

"Why do you sound so giddy?"

"It's a guy thing you wouldn't understand."

Understatement. There was a lot she didn't understand. The one thing she did know? Stavros was too damned cute in the morning, and way too dangerous in her bed. The man wore only track pants, nothing else, which meant that big, muscled chest of his was in plain sight. The hair on it only served to define his bulk and narrowed into an interesting V that disappeared below the waist.

"Keep looking at me like that and we won't make it to breakfast."

Funny how his threats didn't frighten her, just like his proximity didn't. She felt so safe with him, safe and sexy, which might be why she reached out to run a finger down the middle of his chest.

"Fuck breakfast," he growled, drawing her close. "The bacon can wait," he whispered against her lips.

"Bacon?" She wrenched herself free. "Really? I haven't had bacon in . . . Damn, a long time. Fucktard was all about keeping my blood clean, so I wasn't allowed fatty foods."

She hopped out of bed, and she noted him staring at her, rather incredulously.

"Are you ditching a morning make-out session for food?"

"You did it for cookies. And I mean, we're talking bacon." When he didn't show signs of understanding, she repeated it more slowly. "Baaaa-c-onnn." Her tummy rumbled.

He sighed. "Do you have any idea how incredibly sexy you are when you get excited about food?"

"Tell me later, after my bacon."

Except later didn't come right away, as hordes of people descended on his home, family, he claimed. So much family that it was decided to pack them up and move things to the bigger family homestead owned by his grandparents, where Becka was absorbed by the army of aprons and barely allowed a glimpse of Stavros as they baked.

Well, the women baked; Becka mostly tasted and listened as they argued, good-naturedly. Something about dresses and which one would work best. She couldn't follow it and, when she asked, was met with giggles and vague statements of, "You'll see."

What she saw was a bunch of lunatics with no regard for the danger. They treated the whole attack as an adventure. They were eagerly planning for more.

More! Maybe she'd fallen off the roof last night and cracked her head. Even now, she probably was in a hospital bed, heavily sedated, which meant this wasn't real. None of it was real.

Which would be a shame, because she really liked Stavros. Like really, really liked. Speaking of whom, where had he gotten to?

Hearing some loud male cheering, she ventured outside to find the men shirtless and wrestling. A lot of skin showed, and she wasn't the only woman to stop and stare.

"Cole is going to win," remarked a strapping blonde.

"Please. Ark is totally going to twist him into a pretzel," said a darker-skinned woman. "What about you? Who are you rooting for?"

"Me?" At their expectant stare, she ventured his name. "Stavros."

Their eyes rounded, and one of them uttered, "Oooh. So you're that *girl*."

"About time the love bug caught him," snickered the other.

"Excuse me? We're not in love."

"Yet. It will hit you soon enough, and you'll realize there is no escape. But it's not so bad. I'm Anja." The big blond girl held out her hand. "And that's Jade.

"And you must be Becka. Welcome to the family."

Her hands waved, as did her head, as she replied, "I'm not family. Stavros is just a friend."

Anja snickered. "Not for long."

"She's right," Jade agreed. "There's no fighting the mating instinct."

"The what?"

"You know what he is?" At Becka's blank look, Anja rolled her eyes. "The bear. You know he is a bear? So is my Cole."

"And Ark. He's the one who explained the mating instinct to me, once I stopped freaking out about the bear thing."

"It was a bit of a shock," Becka admitted.

"So he showed you the bear but didn't explain why he refuses to leave your side." Anja rolled her eyes. "Typical male."

"He's only been sticking close because there are some bad people after me."

"That might be part of it, but I'll bet the real reason is because he can't help himself. The mating instinct makes it impossible for him to walk away from you."

"I don't understand."

Jade's turn to jump in to explain. "The mating instinct is what happens when a shape-shifter encounters his fated mate. Think of it as love at first sight."

"More like lust," snickered Anja. "But accurate. Once they catch your scent"—she snapped her fingers—"it's all over for them."

"That seems awful. To not have a choice." Becka shook her head. "What if the woman doesn't want him?"

Anja uttered a derisive sound. "Seriously? Have you seen them?" The glistening male bodies still wrestled.

"Good looks and hot bodies aren't the only thing that's important."

"How about the fact he'd chew off his own arm before he'd hurt you?" The pointed look at Becka's fading bruises made her tuck her hands behind her back.

"Those had nothing to do with love." But everything to do with why they were here, all of them gathered. A protective barrier between her and whoever wanted her. So many people who could now get hurt to protect one.

"Why the sad face?"

"I shouldn't be here."

"If you weren't, then we wouldn't have a cause for celebration."

"Aren't you worried? Hasn't anyone explained to you that the guys after me are dangerous?"

"And?" Anja cocked her head.

Even Jade seemed unperturbed. "If they decide they're going to help, it's best to just go with the flow. Trust me when I say they don't accept the word 'no' as an answer."

"I'd prefer to have a choice."

"That I can understand." Anja's gaze turned thoughtful. "So let me ask you, how do you feel about using yourself as bait?"

If it meant saving these people a world of trouble? "Tell me what I should do."

CHAPTER 14

"No. Fuck no. Hell no." It didn't matter how many times he said it. It still happened. They were going to set a trap using Becka as bait.

Stavros hated the plan, even as he had to admit it was a good one. The bad part? It involved putting Becka in harm's way, long enough to draw her enemies out of hiding so the sleuth could strike, because the fuckers were proving elusive.

He'd been so excited to have the SUV as a clue until a DMV search on the trashed vehicle showed it as stolen. No prints inside or out of it either. The first dead end.

As for the aerial rescue? Stavros still had people working on locating the helicopter, but without any kind of markings to identify it that was proving worse than looking for a needle in a haystack, dropped in a puddle of mud in the dark.

Whoever was behind the dudes in the black suits was good at hiding. So Stavros also turned his attention to his other problem, Fucktard, except he'd also disappeared. They'd yet to find any trace of him or his goons at any hotels.

While Stavros's buddies on the force were more than happy to do some minor searches for him, they didn't know enough about Fucktard to be able to put a trace on his credit cards. If he even had a credit card. He'd paid cash to the hotel.

Which left only two options to resolve the situation. Wait for the fuckers to show again, which would mean fun for everyone, but only if they did it soon. Keeping this many bears close by meant lots of food and chaos. They could do it for a few days, but if Becka's enemies showed patience and waited weeks . . . things could get hairy. Not to mention, Becka would keep using it as an excuse to not let him get close.

Not acceptable.

She was his mate, and the sooner he could get her on board with that idea, the better for him, his bear, and a certain blue-balled pain centered in his groin.

Option two to fix the situation was to flush their prey. For that they needed the right kind of bait, aka Becka. Using her as bait, however, meant danger, and he didn't like the idea of her being put in harm's way. She'd suffered enough.

Of course she didn't see it that way. She jumped all over that plan with no regard for herself or safety.

"I'll do it."

Wish she'd do me.

But in order for that to happen, he needed to kill Fucktard. So be it. Time for this bear to go from defensive to offensive, which meant planning, and for that he trusted only a few guys.

Stavros eyed his cousins—Cole, Ark, and Matthias—in the den, a real den with a desk and not a hole in a hill. Although the family did own a nice cavern in the Rockies. They spent a few family vacations there, swimming in the lake, eating the berries, scaring off tourists, and stealing their coolers. The ones with beer, not food.

Apart from his three cousins, he had a shitload more family on standby, all raring for a piece of the action. They could get some, given the brazenness thus far of the attacks.

"Okay, boys, given the fact someone showed up at my parents' house, I'm going to assume the police investigation is compromised." Because who else would have leaked his involvement? And even if his brothers in blue weren't involved, he'd bet a certain lawyer he met outside the hotel was keeping close dibs. "Here's the plan. I'll drop Becka at the police station to give a deposition. She'll ask for police protection, which means they're going to put her in a motel with a few cop guards. I expect Fucktard or the other asshole will attack at night, only we'll be ready for them." *Ready to fuck them up.*

"About the guy we're expecting. Are you sure you're not shitting us about the whole vampire thing? 'Cause, if you are, I'm going to be massively disappointed." Ark had loved the *Blade* movies as a cub and always wanted to fight the undead forces of darkness.

"Only you would be." Stavros shook his head at Ark. Mating to Jade hadn't tempered him one bit. Still a giant meathead. It was why Stavros loved the fucker so much.

"Let's say buddy is a vampire. Did she mention which of the rumors are true? How do we take one out?" Cole, the family assassin, ever practical when it came to looking for ways to take down the enemy.

"She claims he avoids sunlight. His safe houses had metal shutters, and at the hotel he insisted they have the curtains closed even at night. But she doesn't know for sure if sunlight will hurt him. Crosses and holy water don't do shit. He can also eat garlic and pass as a human by eating and drinking like they do."

"But he adds in a few pints of blood to wash it down." Cole shook his head. "Fucking vampires. Who would have thought it."

"I say we bring a few wooden and silver stakes," which

proved easier to acquire than expected. The internet was a wonderful thing, and a certain giant online store had same-day delivery for so many odd items, including a vampire-slaying kit.

"I'll stick to using my hands. Ain't too many things that will survive if you twist off their heads." Ark cracked his knuckles. Given their size, not too many things would survive being crushed between them, period.

"Ready to do this?" There was no fear, no hesitation, in their enthusiastic "yes." Bears feared nothing and no one.

The plan started off well, with Stavros driving Becka to the police station and his old partner Jenkins expecting her.

She seemed so cool and composed. "Seemed" being key. He could sense the trepidation trembling just beneath. "Are you sure you want to do this? I can turn around; we can try something else."

"I have to do this."

"You don't have to do anything." *Except me. She should totally do me.* Not the most appropriate thought given the situation but better than letting out a very beastly roar.

"If I don't do something, then he'll just keep coming after me."

"No he won't, because I'll kill him." Said perhaps a little more growly than he'd intended, yet oddly enough, it eased the sharp scent of fear emanating from her.

She placed her hand over his on the gearshift. It didn't entirely soothe the beast. *She should move it over a bit, say to the V of my thighs.*

Bad bear.

"Can I ask you something?"

"Of course. Anything."

"Some of the women mentioned something interesting to

me. Something about a mating fever. They seem to think you might be afflicted."

He shot her a quick glance and noted her chewing her lower lip. "If you mean that from the moment I met you I was ready to lay down my life and give you my balls, then yes. I am a goner. You are destined to be my one and only."

"And you're okay with that?"

Not at first, but now . . . now he couldn't imagine anything better. "How could I not be okay? Have you seen the awesome chick destiny paired me with?" He shot her a grin and loved that she didn't duck her head at his frank words.

"But you barely know me."

"I know enough. I know that, despite adversity, you showed enough strength to not only escape but bounce back. Or haven't you noticed you're no longer cringing every time someone touches you or looks at you?"

"It wasn't strength but fear that had me escape. And I'm still scared of people, just not you."

"Which is how it should be, and with time, you'll learn to trust people around you again. That kind of experience doesn't just evaporate. But you can get over it. You will get over it, because I'll be there to help you."

"I'm scared," she admitted.

"So am I. Scared for you. But I've got a goal that I'm aiming for."

"What is it?"

"You and me, naked in my bed fucking like bears."

"Isn't the expression 'bunnies'?"

"They come too quick. Me, on the other hand . . ." He shot her a slow smile. "I can go for hours."

"Oh."

Yes, oh, and he couldn't help but smile as her cheeks

turned pink. The moment didn't last. The police station drew into view, and he parked in the visitor lot. He gave her one last glance.

"Ready, sweetheart?"

She nodded her head.

"Showtime."

CHAPTER 15

Showtime indeed. Becka couldn't help but tremble inside at the realization of what she was about to do.

The police station loomed in front of her, a modern building with mirrored windows, concrete walls, and lots of men in uniforms with guns walking around. It should have made her feel safe, but from the moment she exited Stavros's car nervousness assailed her.

A hint of her trepidation must have shown, because Stavros grabbed her hand and laced his fingers with hers. "No worries, sweetheart. This is the easy part."

Funny how it didn't feel easy, not when she walked in and felt as if everyone stared at her. Perhaps they did.

A guy came to greet them, sporting a comb-over that really could have used a razor. "I should have you arrested for hindering an investigation," snapped the fellow.

"And you should be arrested for wearing those pants. Where's Jenkins? He was supposed to be the one meeting us."

"He got called out on a tip. Don't worry. I can handle questioning the woman."

Except she didn't want to go anywhere with the man. She didn't like the look of him at all. She clung closer to Stavros.

He bent low enough to whisper, "No worries, sweetheart.

Nothing bad will happen to you here either." He raised his head to ask, "What interview room do you want us in?"

"Us?" Landry shook his head. "There is no us. You know the rules. Unless you're her lawyer, I have to question her myself."

The muscles in Stavros's face tightened. "That wasn't the deal I had with Jenkins."

"I don't know anything about a deal, but I do know protocol. Do you want to argue about this all day, or shall we get this over with?"

"Give me a second."

Stavros pulled her aside and tilted her chin so he could meet her gaze. "A little change in plans, but don't worry. Landry might seem like a prick, might even be a prick, but he's straight as they come. Remember, we're in a police station. Tons of cops around. Nothing to worry about. And I won't be far. Just tell him the truth like we discussed."

She nodded. His thumb rubbed the skin on her jaw. "It's almost over, sweetheart. Just a few more hours."

He dipped low enough to brush a kiss on her lips, meant as a light embrace, but she couldn't stop herself from flinging her arms around his neck and hugging him close, desperate for some of his courage.

The wolf whistles and catcalls forced them apart.

"Save it for later. This is a cop station, not a bordello," Landry snapped.

Becka pulled away from Stavros, following the ill-fitting blue jacket of the brusque officer. A peek over her shoulder showed Stavros staring after her, and then she lost sight of him as they buzzed her and Landry through a door that swung shut and clicked behind them.

A short while later she was in a room, a plain room with

light gray walls, a metal table bolted to the floor, and sitting in the world's most uncomfortable chair.

Landry dropped a folder in front of her, causing her to flinch.

"Someone is jumpy."

"I'm sorry. I still haven't recovered from my time in captivity."

"I want to hear all about it. First, though, I need a coffee. Can I get you a drink? Water? Coffee? I think we have some tea too?"

The kind request took her by surprise. "Water, please."

The detective left, leaving her alone with her thoughts and fears. She chose to focus instead on the future. What would she do if Vlad was arrested?

If she didn't have to fear capture, she could return to her old life. A life that no longer existed with her poppa and the house she'd grown up in gone. She could probably still go back to her old job, especially once they found out she was a victim, or, with her education and experience, she could start over. Here. With Stavros.

He seemed pretty determined to keep her in his life, a concept she didn't mind at all. She quite enjoyed his presence. His droll wit, outrageous innuendos, and the way he made her feel like the most attractive woman alive helped.

What of his bear side? Could she handle it, though? She'd fainted the first time she saw it, but more out of shock than fear if she were being honest. She didn't think he'd ever hurt her as man or beast. And really, how bad could being mated with a shifter be? Look at how happy all the women in his family were. They too once upon a time found out their husbands were something "more." If they could accept, why couldn't she?

Minutes ticked as she waited for the detective to return. Inside the little room, she couldn't hear a damned thing. Not even passing traffic in the hall.

But she sure as hell noticed when the lights went out.

CHAPTER 16

Out in the lobby, Stavros paced. Something didn't feel right, and he didn't mean the fact that Landry instead of Jenkins had taken the lead on the case.

His bear paced inside his head, and the hair on his body stood on end. The unease wouldn't leave him, so he stepped outside the precinct house and placed a call to Cole.

"Why are you not inside with the girl?" His cousin wasted no time on such trivialities as "hello."

"Landry pulled procedure on me. He's got her in an interview room."

"By herself?"

"It's a police station. How much safer can she fucking get?" He no sooner said it than the doors to the station swung open and stayed open as bodies streamed out, cops, civilians, perps in cuffs. He could hear an alarm ringing.

He grabbed a rookie he knew and barked, "What the fuck is going on? Why are they evacuating the building?"

"Bomb threat."

The words sent a chill through him and not because he believed for one minute there was a bomb. *This is a distraction.*

Stavros pushed past the emerging bodies into the building

itself, Cole still on the line but forgotten in his hand as he looked for a sign of Becka or Landry.

The lobby emptied quickly as he moved against the flow toward the locked door to the inner sanctum.

Billy still manned the desk, his florid face even more flushed than usual as he hollered, "Move out in an orderly fashion and set up a perimeter. Please find your duty officer and report in once you've reached a safe zone."

"Billy, I need to get in there." He pointed to the door.

"No, you need to get out. In case you didn't hear, we've had a bomb threat."

"It's bullshit, and you know it. How many of those do we get a month? Two, three? And we've never had a real bomb yet."

Apparently, a god of mischief was waiting for that moment, because Stavros had no sooner said it than a slight rumble rocked the floor underneath and the lights went out.

"Everybody out now!" Billy screamed, and then his corpulent frame was vaulting over the desk and following the mad dash of those still trying to get outside.

Stavros didn't join them. Becka was in here somewhere, and he had to find her. The good thing about a power failure was it meant the locks disengaged, a weird safety feature installed just in case the electricity failed and folks needed to exit the building. It meant he could yank on the handle for the inner sanctum and the door opened. A good thing too, because its solid bulk saved him from the spray of bullets that suddenly hit it with a *rat-tat-tat.*

Someone is shooting! He ducked behind the door and slammed it shut, then cursed as the lack of power meant it wouldn't lock. More bullets peppered its surface, leaving dimples on it that showed whoever attacked meant business.

Holding it one-handed, his foot braced on the wall for leverage, he slapped his phone to his ear.

"Cole? You still fucking there?"

"Yeah, but I'm moving to the rear entrance. Is it me, or did something just blow?"

"The power is out, and someone is inside shooting."

"I'm on my way." No surprise his cousin sounded excited.

The cavalry was coming, but Stavros was unarmed, the joys of coming to a police station. No guns allowed, not even for ex-cops and PIs.

He thought of shifting into his bear; with the power out, the cameras were down. But before he could fully commit to that idea, the backup generators kicked in, random lights illuminated, and the door clicked as the lock engaged.

One less worry for him, a pisser for the shooter who'd gone on a rampage trying to Swiss-cheese the portal.

With no time to waste, because the generators were only a stopgap measure, he sprinted to the interview rooms.

Boom. The second explosion sputtered the lights, plunging him into darkness again, which might have been a good thing, because it made him a harder target to spot. It didn't take a genius to realize the shooter had taken advantage of the once-again-unlocked door and come through it. Judging by the sound of gunfire behind him, the shooter was taking no chances and spraying the hall as he went.

Time to swap to fur. Not only would he heal better; he'd see and smell better too.

Good enough to hunt.

Time to catch me some varmints.

CHAPTER 17

She tried to not panic when the lights went out, but the room had no window, which meant she was in complete darkness.

I don't like the dark. The dark was for monsters.

It also meant something wrong had happened. *Oh God, he found me.*

So much for being safe here. She knew, without a doubt, this was no coincidence. *I have to get out.* But the door was locked electronically. The question was, would it remain that way with no power?

Only one way to find out. She felt her way along the wall, fingers running over the drywall, feeling the occasional ridge indicating a plaster repair. She found the corner and turned, her fingers soon bumping over the frame for the door. Her fingers clutched the handle, and she took a deep breath, tossing up a quick prayer that it would open. Before she could turn it, a single light bloomed into existence, and as she blinked her eyes against the sudden illumination she heard a click at the door. She tugged the handle and could have cried when it wouldn't budge.

She'd taken a moment too long. Frustrated, she whirled from it and paced, wondering if, behind the one-way mirror, someone watched.

A noise alerted her to the fact that someone had opened

the door to the interview room. She spun, her elation at not being forgotten turning into icy fear. It wasn't Landry or any police officer standing there.

Terror instantly flooded her veins, and she scrambled to the far end of the table, looking to put some distance between them. She'd thought herself cured of the fear; a few days spent with Stavros and she'd remembered a decent world, a world without pain. Seeing Vlad again brought it all back, and the cruel twist of his lips let her know it was about to get ten times worse.

"If it isn't my wild rose. Did you really think you could escape me?"

"You won't get away with this."

"Stupid bitch. I already have. Your human laws are no match for me. I am practically immortal. Soon, I will have enough of your blood running through my veins to truly transform."

"No. I won't let you."

"Won't?" He raised a mocking brow, which, considering he had only one giant one, gave him an odd appearance. "You don't have a choice. I chose you for a reason. With your blood, I shall ascend to greatness. All will bow before my reign of darkness."

"There won't be much bowing when you're behind bars, asshole." Landry shoved Vlad into the room, sending him reeling. He turned with a snarl on the cop.

"You dare to touch me, human."

"Yeah, I dare. This is my witness, and she's gonna put your ass behind bars." In that moment, she took back all the unkind thoughts she'd had about Landry. Until he said, "And then I'm going to collect the bounty on her head."

A cruel smirk twisted Vlad's lips. "Good luck collecting it when you're dead." *Bang.* The gunshot to Landry's back, a cowardly shot, caused red to blossom on the front of his button-down white shirt. Landry opened and shut his mouth while his eyes widened in surprise. He fell to the floor. Another victim to the madness.

"Where were we?" Vlad turned to her and approached on the left of the table while Brian, gun still in hand, stepped over the body and tried to block her on the other side.

She retreated until her back hit the wall, her breath coming in short, terrified pants. No escape. What to do? She couldn't go back. She couldn't. Just couldn't. And that was when the lights went out for a second time.

Dropping to her knees, she didn't think of smashing her face in table legs, just scurried forward under the table while listening to Vlad and his minion cursing.

But so long as they cursed behind her they weren't ahead of her, and she made it out of the room into a dark hall. She hit a wall with her hands and stood. Where should she go? Did it matter? She couldn't stay here. With her fingers on the plaster, she half-walked, half-ran, stray windows in offices with their doors open providing a faint illumination, but if she could see, then so could—

"There she is. Get her!" The rabid scream brought forth a frightened hitch of noise.

Bang. Bang. From ahead, she could hear gunfire. No escape that way. She saw an exit sign and shoved through the door. She found herself in a stairwell. Up or down?

Bang. Bang. Up it was.

At least in here there was some light, the windows providing fading daylight. Would it be enough to stop Vlad? She now regretted the choice to arrive so late in the day. The bears had hoped to make this quick for her, a few hours at the police station, enough to have night fall, then a motel to lay the trap. They'd never expected Vlad to act so brazenly.

Not Vlad. Fucktard. She could hear Stavros's voice so clearly and wished he were with her. She needed him right now.

However, she was currently on her own, and it would be dark soon. Soon, not yet, so when she saw the stairs ended in a door marked "Rooftop Exit" she gladly ran onto the flat top of the building, sobbing in relief.

Vlad with his affliction to sunlight wouldn't follow. She couldn't say the same for Brian.

Up here, there was nothing to use as a weapon. In the movies, the heroes always found a metal bar for swinging or a forgotten tool like a nail gun. All she saw was bird poop and cigarette butts. Reality sucked.

She ran to the edge and looked down, seeing people milling on the street, too far away to help her, and before she could shout to ask she heard the disdainful chuckle. She turned around to find Vlad on the roof with her. Alone. In daylight. He didn't burst into flame. He didn't even get a sunburn.

Pity.

He sneered at her. "Nowhere to run, bitch. Come with me now without a fight and maybe I won't hurt you too much."

"Or maybe," said a figure dressed in black from head to toe, including a helmet, "you should take a leap off this building and save me the trouble of tossing you." The new player stepped out from behind a thick air vent, hands empty and yet oozing menace.

The voice seemed somehow familiar and, yet, not. Whoever it was, she wouldn't argue, not if he wanted to kill her tormentor.

And what about after? One problem at a time.

Vlad didn't look pleased at being interrupted. "This is none of your business."

"Oh, but it is. You made it my business when you took the girl. She's a very special girl, not for the likes of you."

"You know about her blood?" Vlad sneered. "Too late. It's mine. And once I've completely replaced mine with hers, I'll be able to ascend and become a true vampire."

"Stupid human." Spoken with clear disdain. "That's not how it works. And even if it did, we'd never accept your kind. We do have standards."

The conversation had taken an odd turn, and she still couldn't shake the feeling of familiarity. But who did she know that stood so tall and spoke with such confidence? It wasn't Stavros; he would never hide.

"I don't know who you are, but you're too late. She belongs to me." Vlad dove toward her, and she screamed as she dashed away, toward the man in black.

"Get behind me, little Bee."

Little Bee? Only one person ever called her that. Before she could speak, a gunshot rang out and the guy with the helmet moved, moved so fast she didn't see where he went.

She also didn't see the uneven spot on the roof, and she hit it hard with her toes. Instant pain that sent her falling to her knees. "Ooww." She couldn't help but cry out, which, in turn, was answered by a grumbly roar. Rolling onto her back, she pushed herself to a sitting position and noted the giant bear on the roof. A giant bear that grappled with Brian. The gun went flying, a victim to the savage pummeling. And then there was a wolf on the roof too. A wolf where Brian used to be.

Dear God. Could no one be what they seemed? As the two animals tore at each other, Vlad approached her, hands outstretched, his eyes wide with manic glee.

"Don't touch my little Bee." The vehement words emerged with a deep chill, and yet she still smiled.

Smiled as her poppa, somehow, was still alive, and stronger than expected, given he held Vlad over the parapet. Poppa looked back at her, his eyes masked by the helmet, but she could still see him asking for permission.

She nodded. "Do it." A cold, cruel justice, and yet after what Fucktard did to her? Totally deserved.

He screamed on his way down. A short scream. And then she was running at the man in black.

He caught her in a hug, and she heard him murmur, "My little Bee. I'm so glad you're safe."

"How are you here?" she asked. "I thought you were dead."

"I am in a sense. But I don't have time to explain right now. We have to leave. Come." The familiar *whup whup* of a chopper got louder, and for a moment she looked at the offered escape.

Rawr!

She turned her head to see Brian taking the same route as his master and a very angry bear charging at them.

When her poppa would have put her behind him, she stopped him. "No, it's okay. He's with me."

And despite the fear trembling in her, she walked toward him, trusting in Stavros, even if he was kind of furry and scary.

He stopped in front of her and cocked his head. *Growr.*

She could almost hear the question in his voice. "It's okay. I don't know how, but that's my grandfather in the suit."

"A grandfather who's come to take you home. Hurry now, little Bee. We have to leave."

"Not without Stavros" was her stubborn reply.

"She's mine," he growled, suddenly not a bear anymore.

But that didn't stop someone in the chopper from shooting at him at her grandfather's signal.

"No!" she screamed, and then she was shot too.

CHAPTER 18

Stavros stretched and almost knocked her out of bed. Luckily, he grabbed the body before it went far and snuggled it against him. He nuzzled his face in Becka's hair, breathing in her scent, soothed by it.

And then remembered what the fuck had happened.

In a single bound, he was out of bed, pacing.

"What the hell? How did we get here?" He raked a hand through his hair and looked around the very pink bedroom, the window already fixed—more than likely by his cousin Ivan—and a very happy-looking Becka still lying in bed—wearing entirely too many clothes in his opinion.

She stretched and kept smiling. "About time you woke up. Do you know you snore?"

"I'm less interested in discussing my sleeping habits and more about how the hell I got here."

"I had a little help."

He arched a brow.

She giggled. "Okay, lots of help. Or so I was told. We both kind of slept through it. Apparently, the chaos of the bomb and the shooting provided cover while your family smuggled us out of the police station."

"How exactly does one smuggle people"—one of whom

would have been naked—"out of a police station under attack?"

"Well, first of all, the attack was over by then. And second, the fire marshal"—ah yes, his second cousin Travis—"said there was a gas leak and had the area evacuated. That gave the gas company guys, which included even more of your family, time to get your ass out of there."

"What of you?"

She shrugged. "I woke up before they were done. I only got shot with one tranquilizer, unlike you. It was suggested I stick around for a while since too many people saw me going in. But that Jenkins guy sped things along so I'd be here when you woke up."

He owed Jenkins a pitcher of beer.

First, though, "Where are my pants?"

"Why do you need pants?" She eyed him, and there was no hiding his happiness at seeing her.

"You're not safe. Those dudes in black are still out there."

"Yeah, about those guys. Turns out they're the good guys. Of a sort. They're bad, but bad on my side if that makes any sense."

"No, that makes no sense. They shot me. And you apparently."

"With a sleeping agent. My grandfather—"

"Your grandfather? I thought he was dead."

"He is. Kind of." She laughed and then took a moment to bring him up to speed, and he blinked several times during it. Said "fuck" a few times too.

"So you mean to tell me," he said slowly, "that you're the great-times-a-couple-granddaughter of some big pooh-bah in the vampire world, and he raised you after your parents died, but someone found out who you are on account your blood is stupidly rare and thought they could use you to become a vampire too."

"Yes." She smiled. It was cute, and a good thing, since she was delusional.

"Vampires don't exist. Fucktard wasn't a vampire."

"No, he wasn't, but he wanted to be one. Which would have never happened. According to my granddad, you have to be born with the right kind of blood. I'm the last of our line, but we're not the only family apparently with the right kind of genes."

"So you're a vampire?"

"Not quite. Apparently, having the blood is only part of the deal. To fully turn requires some kind of ritual that requires an actual vampire and me dying."

"But you could totally be a hot undead chick if you chose?"

"I'd rather be a chew toy for a bear."

The remark pulled a barking laugh from him. "I think that can be arranged. After a shower." Because that smell coming from him was not sexy.

"How big is your shower?" Becka asked with a slow, sexy grin. Which now and forever would be known as a boner grin.

Then again, was there anything about her that didn't make him hard?

He couldn't help but grab her off the bed in a hug that squished her. "I'm so glad you're safe, although I do wish I'd had a chance to take a bite out of Fucktard."

"The important thing is he's gone and isn't coming back."

"Good, because the only thing I want to see coming tonight is you."

"Then what are you waiting for?"

He tossed her over a shoulder and ran them to the bathroom. In moments Stavros had the water streaming, but she still wore too many clothes. Offensive things. He wanted to tear them from her body but restrained himself. She'd shown herself resilient thus far, but he had to remember she was recently out of a traumatic situation. He had to take things slow.

She must have noticed his hesitation, because she cupped his cheeks. "What's wrong?"

"I'm sorry. I shouldn't have manhandled you like that."

"Don't be sorry. I'm not afraid with you. And I like it when you touch me. I'd like it even better if we were both naked."

Her clothes then hit the floor in a simple strip show that almost had him panting like a dog.

With a swish of her hips, she entered the shower, and he could only stand and stare for a moment, stunned at how sexy she appeared, even more so with water glistening over her flesh. The soap she grabbed and lathered over her body was surely meant as a tease. Especially when she slid that slippery bar between her legs, back and forth in a manner that seemed more about pleasure than cleaning.

Mmm. Wanna taste. His mouth almost watered he hungered so badly for her. He followed her into the shower, crowding her on purpose, and she didn't flinch or move away. On the contrary, her hands flattened on his chest, stroking suds over his flesh.

"Need a hand getting clean?" she teased.

"Seems a waste since I'm planning to get us dirty." He leered, and she giggled, a giggle that turned to a gasp as he slid his hands down her back, tracing her skin to the tops of her buttocks. Her nipples, pressing against his chest, puckered and begged him to nibble. Instead, he kissed her, claimed that mouth of hers, and groaned as she responded, fiery hot and passionate.

But he'd waited forever, it seemed, for more than just a taste of her lips. Angling her so her back pressed against the shower wall, he ducked that he might suck one of the buds that tempted him. She inhaled sharply, and he rumbled around the breast in his mouth before sucking it hard. His tongue slid around her nipple, toying with it, teasing it into a sharp point before switching to the other side. Back and forth, he licked and sucked, pausing to occasionally rub his scruffy jaw against her skin. Mostly because she shivered so wildly each time.

He could have played with her lovely breasts all day. But something else beckoned.

He dropped to his knees before her, a supplicant to her altar of honey. Her thighs parted at his gentle touch, exposing her but, best of all, showing him her trust.

A trust he would never abuse. Although he might make her scream.

In pleasure.

His tongue lapped at the core of her, tasting her slick honey, the sweetness of her making him throb. Her swollen flesh quivered against his tongue as he licked. Her body tensed and shuddered as pleasure mounted within her.

A peek upward showed her staring down at him, her lips curved in a wanton smile. He almost came just with that one look. He'd never seen anything more perfect.

All mine.

While a part of him wanted her to come on his lips, he was a selfish bear. He wanted her first orgasm to be on his cock. He wanted to feel her coming apart as he penetrated her. Claimed her.

Took her and made her his.

He stood and gasped as she gripped his rigid cock and slid her hand back and forth.

"My turn," she whispered before dropping down before him.

As if he'd say no. Hell, he wasn't sure he knew how to speak after the first flick of her tongue against the head of his cock. He couldn't help but tangle his fingers in her hair as she lapped the swollen head of his shaft. A groan escaped him when she stopped teasing with her tongue and took him into her mouth.

The fingers in her hair tightened and he had to remind himself to stay gentle, but apparently she didn't feel the same qualm, because she sucked him hard. So hard, and she dug her nails into his thighs as she suctioned, deeper and deeper into the warm recess of her mouth. He groaned again when she fondled his heavy sack.

He wanted to come so badly, but he held back. Held on. He was still determined to have his first orgasm buried to the hilt within her. Pure torture and bliss.

Time to finish this.

He drew her to her feet and took her mouth, took her lips with passionate urgency, as his hands spanned her waist. Then he spun her until she faced the shower wall. A gentle pressure in the middle of her back bent her so that she presented her delectable backside. Apparently, she understood where he was going with this, because her hands flattened on the wall and she shot him a sultry look over her shoulder.

"Is this the part where we get dirty?"

"So dirty," he murmured as the swollen head of his cock nudged against her nether lips. Her sex parted for him, and he pushed into her, slowly, so slowly, wanting to take it easy. To control himself. To—

"Ahhh." He couldn't help the noise, not when she shoved back hard against him, impaling herself on him, forcing him to sink so deep.

He almost came. As it was, it took him a moment and a breath or two to control himself.

No coming until she does.

That was the plan. And he was sticking to it. Despite the shower water making things tight, he managed to thrust into her, his cock, throbbing and hard, driving deep, each stroke wringing a moan from her. Hell, each stroke drew a groan from him.

Their tempo increased, faster and faster, the steam of the shower almost as hot as their panting breaths. When her orgasm finally hit, he felt it, not just with his cock or his body, but with all of his being. In that moment, as her flesh shuddered around him, a bond was forged between them, something unbreakable and perfect.

Almost as perfect as his own orgasm. He claimed her with his seed, the hot spurts of it welcomed by her pulsing channel, leaving them spent and breathless.

But happy. So fucking happy.

As a guy, he didn't do fucking poetry or flowery words and shit, but on this occasion, the first time he truly claimed his mate, he felt it needed something special. Something she would never forget.

"That was awesome." Okay, not the most incredible of speeches, but good news; he doubted she'd ever forget the hollered, "Now that you're done making the kitchen light shake, are you coming down for dinner?"

Eat them. Maybe later. First he needed to dine on some honey—*my mate's honey*—for dessert.

Grawr.

EPILOGUE

Imagine that, Stavros snored like a bear. Deep, and rumbling, but Becka didn't mind it. *Probably because I love him.*

The realization didn't shock her, even if a part of her still thought it was too soon to feel it. Then again, exactly what constituted love? Did love come only over a predetermined stretch of time? Or did it really come down to something as simple as divine fate? Why couldn't love be two people meeting and instantly recognizing they were meant to be together?

Like me and Stavros.

What a strange series of events had brought them together. So much had changed, and for the better.

Vlad was gone. His body splattered on the sidewalk, and the autopsy revealed there was nothing vampire about him. The teeth? Implants. His aversion to sun, fake. He was just a rich boy who thought he'd found the secret to immortality in her rare blood type.

The blame for the attack on the station was fully placed on him. Most of the thugs he'd brought were dead or languishing in cells, bitching he had them mesmerized with his vampire powers. The district attorney wasn't having any of it.

As for the bear some people claimed they saw at the station during the fight? Chalked up to a hallucination brought on by major stress.

The incident did have one interesting side effect. Being short a few officers meant Stavros got his job back with a stern warning to stay away from any marijuana cases. An easy promise to make because, as Stavros confided, his cousin Niko had a stash almost ready to crop.

A few days had passed, a few days of whirlwind depositions, and meeting more family, and eating massive amounts of food with said family, followed by intense lovemaking to work off the food.

As of last night, they slept at his place, the army of aprons having swept through, repairing and cleaning the damage done by Fucktard—*snicker*—and his thugs. The wonderful women who'd taken her in as one of their own had even strewn the bed with rose petals—which set her off sneezing. But once Stavros cleared the room of flowers, changed the sheets, and got her an antihistamine, they had a wonderful time.

So why was she awake at three in the morning? She didn't know, but she wouldn't deny a certain restlessness, which was why she rolled out of bed. He grumbled in his sleep, his arm waving around for her. He loved to snuggle.

A smile stretched her lips as she leaned down to place a light kiss on his cheek. "I'm just going to get a drink of water."

Yet it wasn't thirst that drew her to the living room, more like . . . anticipation. She walked in and stopped, not out of fear or even surprise. Somehow she had known he was there.

"Poppa." His name spilled out softly.

He looked the same as he always did, the streetlight outside providing enough illumination through the living room window for her to notice his thinning gray hair, stooped shoulders, and weathered features so different from the man hidden within the helmet on the rooftop.

"My sweet little Bee. I came to see if you were all right."

"Of course I am. Even better now that I know you're not dead." She approached him, not fearful at all of the man who raised her, despite what he was.

"I'm hard to kill." For some reason that struck her as funny, and she laughed, a mirth he shared with her.

They soon got serious again.

"Are you going back to Seattle?" The place they'd lived before Vlad barreled into her world and stole her.

He shook his head. "There's nothing for me there. I'm thinking of starting anew in this city. I thought I might stay close in case my little Bee needs me."

"I'll always need you, Poppa." She couldn't help the tightening of her throat as she said it. Here was the man who'd raised her, always been there, who loved her. When she'd thought he was dead, she was devastated. Now he was still kind of dead, but that didn't change who he was at heart. *My poppa.*

"About the whole poppa thing, we might have to perhaps change that to 'uncle.' I only ever adopted the persona of an elderly relative to forestall questions, but now that my secret is out . . ." He smiled, and as he smiled—without the giant fangs legend gave vampires—he straightened, his hair thickened, and the creases on his face smoothed. The transformation took only seconds, and at the end of it a man in his prime stared back at her. The face might be younger, the posture much better, but the eyes? She'd know those eyes anywhere.

"Are you sure I shouldn't call you Daddy?" She smirked as he cringed.

"You're a naughty girl, little Bee. Good thing you have a strong man to watch over you."

Speaking of which . . . "Is it truly over?" And by "over" she meant not just Vlad and his insane quest for immortality but also someone else who might get the crazy idea to use her rare blood.

"The blood test results that led him to you have been modified. You needn't fear, but just in case, I recommend you don't give blood in the future."

"I'll make sure she doesn't." The rumbled words came from behind her a moment before Stavros's arms wrapped around her. She relaxed into his embrace, her days of flinching over.

"Ah yes, the teddy bear she insists on keeping. Take care of her. Or else you'll find a place in front of the fireplace as a rug at my cabin."

"You needn't worry, sir. I'll take good care of Becka."

"I do believe you will." Her poppa's expression softened. "I'm going to miss seeing you every day."

"Me too," she whispered.

"I'll text you my new address in a few days. I'm thinking something penthouse-ish with a balcony. The ladies love that, and it's been a while since I entertained." A rakish wink made her laugh. His piece said, her grandfather/uncle/vampire whirled and dove through the open window, probably the same one he'd used to get in. Except . . . it didn't have a fire escape.

"Poppa!" She couldn't help but gasp and run to peek, but he was gone. Gone but always watching. Watching over her, the last of his ancestors.

"Is this the wrong time to say how much I love you?"

Startled, she turned in Stavros's arms. "Why do you say that?"

"Because you're mine, and I'm so happy that, as it turns out, you can bear my touch."

And if they kept making love at the rate they currently enjoyed, she'd be bearing his cub in no time too.

FAKE MATED TO THE WOLF

Milly Taiden

For everyone that loves a happily-ever-after

ACKNOWLEDGMENTS

Sheri Spell—Thanks for your help all the time when I get stuck. You're such a wonderful friend.

Tina Winograd—Thanks for always having my back, girlfriend.

CHAPTER 1

Shawna Goode slammed the phone down and cursed silently under her breath. The rat bastard boss of hers was going to drive her into a room with padded walls, and not the kind you stuck to in those Velcro suits either. She was destined for the insane asylum or maybe even the courtroom on murder charges. Shawna smiled evilly when she realized that she'd have a good chance of being acquitted of all charges when she explained to the jury, who would be at least partially women, the things the man said and did that caused her to explode.

"'Your system is broke; fix it now. And no more long breaks. You're abusing the time clock,'" Shawna mocked as she scowled in the direction of her manager on the other side of the wall. Up until two weeks ago, she'd never had one complaint about her system. Now all of a sudden, every day it was something new. The matches weren't good.

The ringing of her cell phone made Shawna jump in surprise as she glared at the offending little object. Damn caller ID was blank again. She knew better than to answer, but she was in a foul mood and who better to take it out on than the lunatic stalker who kept calling?

"What?" she snapped as she opened the phone and waited for his response or, more to the point, his lack of one. Heavy breathing didn't count, she figured. "This is getting ridiculous; either stop calling or talk to me, you coward."

She jabbed the end button as the breathing continued; how she missed the days when she could slam the receiver down and let out some of her frustration and anger. By the time quitting time rolled around, Shawna was ready to tell her boss where to shove the computer software sideways.

A few more steps and she'd be free. As soon as her car door shut, she would be dialing her two best friends and begging for some girl time, ice cream, alcohol, and cookie dough included. That's all she could think about as she waited for the elevator to open.

"Shawna, I need to speak to you before you leave for the day!" Clark Benoit called nasally from his stance in his office door.

"I'm already clocked out for the day, and have someplace to be," Shawna replied as nicely as she could as she clenched her hands into fists, trying to hold back the urge to let her tongue loose on the imbecile.

"I'll adjust your time clock to reflect this meeting, but you might be unaware you still have three minutes until it's time to clock out officially."

Shawna gritted her teeth and turned around to face him. "Since I wasn't able to take a lunch due to a last-minute emergency that you handed to me, I figured leaving three minutes early wouldn't hurt anything."

Clark sniffed in annoyance and headed back into his office without waiting to make sure she would follow. The bastard knew she didn't have a choice. Thanks to him she was one strike away from being on probation. Two strikes away from the unemployment line.

This was not how she wanted to end this day, she thought as she stalked forward with barely controlled anger. If this job didn't pay so well, she'd have quit a long time ago. But sadly, she needed the money too much to let her Latin temper have free rein. Clark's secretary smiled apologetically as Shawna passed by her and stepped into the cretin's office.

"Please have a seat," Clark offered with a barely disguised smirk on his thin, lipless face.

It was all Shawna could do to not shudder in revulsion as the man's eyes scanned over her body and finally stopped at her eyes. Clark was not a good-looking man; to put it nicely, he looked like he'd fallen out of the ugly tree and hit every limb on the way down. His personality was even worse; he spent his days sucking up to the management and making snide, degrading comments to all the staff that worked for him. He was the worst to the women, though, and if you had curves then you could forget getting anything other than insults and innuendos out of the man.

"Ms. Goode, I hate to have to say this, especially since it's not the first time we've had this discussion. Today alone you left your desk and went to the ladies' room four times. Your behavior is causing this company wasted time and money. This has to stop. I'm sorry to say I had to write you up and this means you are on probation. One more incident within six months and you will be let go."

Shawna gaped at the buffoon masquerading as a man across from her. Had he been stalking her to see where she went and how long she was gone?

Clark pushed a piece of paper across the desk to Shawna. "Do you have anything to say in response?"

She grabbed the sheet and scanned the list of reasons he'd used to explain writing her up and gaped in astonishment. How in the hell did he think he could get away with this sexist bullshit?

"If you'll sign it, I'll have it entered into your personnel record," Clark continued without waiting for a response to his earlier question.

"No" Shawna slammed the paper down on his desk and glared at her boss. "I refuse to sign it and I want a meeting with HR to discuss these allegations."

Clark leaned back in his chair and smiled in satisfaction. "Ms. Goode, you're fired."

Shawna opened her mouth to respond, but no words would come out. Could he fire her after claiming she had one more chance?

"Yes, I see your confusion. I spoke to HR earlier today as a matter of fact. Explained the situation and that you would probably refuse to sign the document. After I outlined all of your transgressions, I was informed I didn't have to place you on probation. I could fire you and be covered since you were already given multiple warnings."

She wasn't sure what to say; she knew what she wanted to say, but she wasn't sure if it was worth it. *Fuck it,* she thought as she stood up and leaned over the desk. "You should be ashamed of yourself. You aren't a man; you're a pig in a suit. One of these days one of your employees will file a sexual discrimination suit against you. When that happens, I hope they call on me for information. I'll be happy to tell them about your disgusting treatment, your leers and your obsessive stalking and counting trips to the restroom and how long we're in there. You are a sad piece of shit."

Clark's face was purple with anger as he pointed to the door and screamed for her to collect her belongings and get off the premises before he called Security to escort her out.

Shawna laughed at his threat and headed back to her office with her head held high. No way would she let the foul little troll know how she trembled and wanted to cry at what had just happened. Her world had just collapsed around her and she didn't know how she was going to fix it.

"Shawna?" a hesitant voice called from her doorway a few minutes later. She looked up in surprise to see Clark's secretary, Penny, standing there.

"Yes, Penny?"

The woman stepped in and closed the door softly behind her. "I just wanted to tell you I'm sorry and that I wish I could stand up to him like you just did. We heard every word of what you said to him. We wanted to cheer, but we were afraid he'd write us up or fire us too."

"He'll get what's coming to him one day. No way can a man who created a company based on women with curves allow a chauvinistic pig like Clark to work here for long."

"I hope you're right," Penny whispered sadly as she slipped back out of the office.

"We'll meet you at your apartment in half an hour with supplies," Josie said, and hung up before Shawna could reply. She really did have the best friends in the world. She'd barely made it to her car before she was in tears and speed-dialing them. Honestly, she wasn't sure how they'd understood a word she'd said between her tears and curses.

Shawna knew she looked a fright, and if she'd had any doubt of that all she had to do was see the shocked face of the homeless man who lived in the building's garage to prove it.

"Miz Shawna. You okay?"

"I will be, Robbie. Thanks," she said as she climbed out of her car and wiped at her tears.

"It's that idiot boss of yours, ain't it. I knew he was worth nothing. This just proves my point. Makin' a beautiful lady like you cry and all."

Shawna smiled sadly. "My friends are on their way."

Robbie saluted. "Robbie's on the job. I'll watch out for them and hang around until they leave. What else can Robbie do for you, miz?"

"Come by when you see the pizza man. Dinner's on me. And no, don't protest. You always look out for me and my friends. It's the least I can do to repay you for your kindness."

"Ain't no big deal. You're a sweet lady, who don't belong in this area of town. Makes me feel like the man I once was, knowing I can help you out."

Shawna smiled softly, placed a kiss on his cheek, and headed to the stairs and the four flights she had to climb. Some days, like today, she longed for her old apartment with its elevators and security gates. Neighbors who didn't get their doors busted down by the cops once a month, and an area that was safe to walk outside at night.

Thoughts of her two young stepbrothers and mother locked in their hell quickly vanished all those thoughts, though. They were worth this and so much more. Another six months and she would have had enough money to get them to safety. Who knows how long it would be now? What were the chances she'd find a new job in time to pay off their debts for this month? Thanks to Clark, they were in servitude for extra time. How she hated that bastard.

She'd barely had time to take her shoes off after walking in her front door before there was a knock. Damn, her friends really were the best, she thought as she opened the door and waved them in. "Did you guys hit all green lights or what?"

Ally winked as she hip-checked Shawna and placed her bag of goodies on the kitchen table. "You clearly needed us and chocolate. Not sure which is rated higher, though."

Josie laughed. "You're just lucky we were together and able to slip away from our mates so quickly. I expect we have an hour before one of them is calling to check in on the situation. They weren't happy we wouldn't let them come get firsthand information. They want to kill whoever made you so upset."

"Not yet. Where's the wine?" Shawna grumbled as she stalked to the table. "Pizza's on the way. I need alcohol and then I'll explain everything."

"It's that rat bastard dickless wonder of a boss, isn't it?"

"Yeah," Josie agreed. "We both know how hard he's been on you. We figure it has to be him again. I really think we need to let the guys have a go at him."

"Or better yet," Ally piped in, "let us tell Hawke what type of guy he really is. I still insist there is no way he'd have hired Clark Benoit if he'd known his true personality."

Shawna rolled her eyes, grabbed a couple wineglasses, and filled them. She hesitated for a second, then shrugged, grabbed the bottle, her glass, and headed to her couch in the combo living, dining, and kitchen area.

"He fired me tonight," Shawna said without preamble to the two shocked faces staring at her in stupefaction.

"On what grounds?" Josie demanded indignantly.

"He wrote me up again and I refused to sign it. I said I wanted to speak to an HR representative. Apparently, he had already cleared it with someone and they told him he could fire me, so he did."

Ally growled low in her throat, startling Shawna for a moment, until she calmed down enough to reply, "What was his reasoning for writing you up this time?"

Shawna smiled sarcastically. "Oh, you're gonna love this one. Too many trips to the restroom in a workday and taking too long in the ladies' room. Leaving early, even though I worked through lunch and overtime is forbidden and I was doing something for him that he said couldn't wait."

"Did you say using the bathroom too much?" Ally demanded.

"Yup, you heard me right. It's that time of the month: what was I supposed to do: sit at my desk and bleed all over myself? I even asked him that on one of my trips back from the ladies' room to my desk. His reply, and I wish I was making this up, was to hold it until I got home."

The two women exchanged glances before collapsing into laughter. Shawna wished she were joking about that, but the guy was clueless apparently to women's anatomy. Some of the other employees had whispered that he'd said similar things to them.

Shawna and her friends' laughter only died when the doorbell rang and she got up to pay for their dinner. "Food!" they called excitedly.

Shawna paid, set the boxes down on the table, and waited for the delivery guy to disappear down the stairs. Once he was gone, she called out for Robbie, knowing he wouldn't be far away. "Robbie, I know you're here somewhere; don't make me come looking for you!"

Robbie shuffled into view with a blush covering his face. "I told you not to worry about me, Miz Shawna."

"Take the pizza; I won't accept no for an answer."

Robbie gave in and smiled. "You're too good for this place. You have a good time with your friends. I'll be here when they're ready to leave."

"So are you, Robbie. It's not often I meet a gentleman of your caliber. Thank you and be safe out here, okay?"

"Always, Miz Shawna," he replied as he melted back into the shadows with the box she'd given him.

Once the ladies were settled back in the living room, wine and pizza in hand, Josie asked the one question that had been weighing on Shawna's mind.

"What are you going to do now?"

"Honestly, I don't know. Try to find a job, any job for now. I can't afford to be out of work. Every penny I make goes toward my mom and brothers. I'm so close to getting them free. I talked to her yesterday. She sounded so defeated and tired. I'm worried about her; I think she's getting sick from the lack of care."

Ally jumped to her feet and moved to sit beside Shawna. "How much more do you need? Let us help and then you can pay us back if you insist as slowly as you want."

"Yes, let us," Josie chimed in as she leaned forward and placed her hand on Shawna's knee with a gentle squeeze. "I don't like you living here, but I understood your reasoning for moving. Now your hands are tied and we are in a position to help. Let us do that for you."

"You don't understand," Shawna started to say but had to stop to take a sip of wine and wipe the tears that were falling freely. "It's a lot of money. Even after I pay them off, I have to find a way to get them someplace safe. Be that here or someplace else. Just out of there and the hell they are trapped in."

"Ally, I think our friend here forgot who we mated. Keir and Xander have the money, but if they don't have the power then you can bet your ass Julia and Bess will."

Shawna couldn't help but laugh at the looks of determination and anger on her friends' faces. She'd always known they'd do anything to help, if she'd only ask. But this was her problem and she didn't want to impose on the friendship. It was her family's problem; she should be able to solve it.

"I know that look, Shawna Elisa Goode. We've been friends way too long." Josie turned to Ally and indicated Shawna. "That look means she is going to refuse and try to do this on her own. She's going to ignore the fact that she's been there for us whenever we needed something in the past and that she will be in the future. She's going to ignore the fact that she is our sister and that what hurts one of us hurts all of us."

"Stop!" Shawna called in exasperation. "All right, I get it, point taken. You don't have to beat the dead horse into the ground, revive it, and beat it dead again. Just give me a few days to figure some things out and I'll let you know what I need." She paused and sighed in weary consternation. "Deal?"

"Agreed; now is it time for the cookie dough or what?" Ally sang as she danced happily in her seat. "'Cause, come on, ladies, we all know cookie dough makes everything better."

CHAPTER 2

Hawke Hawke dropped down on his desk the files he'd spent the better part of the morning staring blankly at and leaned back in his office chair with a groan of frustration. He let his thoughts drift to the dinner party where he'd first seen his mate. She'd been breathtaking, and when she'd snubbed him it had shocked the hell out of him. She was his mate, his other half. He'd spent every waking moment thinking about her, if he was honest his sleeping moments too. The things he dreamed of doing to her body might be illegal in some states.

Two excruciating months had passed since that day and he wasn't any closer to Shawna. Not for lack of trying, though. He'd quickly found out where she worked, manufactured an excuse to go down to the department only to be told she didn't work there. He'd done some digging and discovered her whereabouts and raced down there only to discover she was on vacation for the week. Next trip down he'd been ambushed by Clark Benoit, the guy he'd put in charge of running mateforhire.com, and he hadn't been able to escape quickly enough.

Why in the hell he'd ever hired Clark was anyone's guess. The man always left him feeling like he needed to take a shower to wash off all the brownnosing. On it went for two months; either she was out or he was, she was in a meeting or Clark bombarded him.

Sheer desperation had made him ask two of his closest confidants for ideas on what to do. Something he knew he'd never live down.

"Hawke, what's up?" Keir answered with a laugh. "Looking for more advice?"

"Yeah, because your last bit has helped so much," he retorted in annoyance.

Keir's laughter filled the phone, "If it helps, Xander's here. Maybe he has something helpful to add. Let me put you on speaker."

"Hey, brother!" Xander called out. "Fill me in on what you've done and let's see what we can come up with. Though I'm surprised Keir with all his women couldn't come up with something worthwhile."

Hawke grinned evilly. "He's gone soft, I think. He's mated now, must have lost his hunting instinct." He waited for the laughter and curses to die down before he spoke again. "I've done nothing, and I know that sounds stupid, but it's true. It's like she knows when I'm coming and hides. Two months now, and not one sight of her. I'm practically stalking her department. Her manager says she is out, or busy, or something. If I didn't know better I'd think he was hiding her from me."

Silence filled the air for a minute. Hawke wasn't sure if he should keep going or wait for the idiots on the other end to speak up and help out like the good friends they were supposed to be.

"This may be a stupid question, but what reason would he have to keep her from you?" Keir questioned hesitantly. "I mean, you're the head of the company; it makes no sense."

"Hell if I know. It's not like he can get away with lying to me or anything. For that matter, I'm not even sure what she does in his department. He runs mateforhire.com, but I never authorized anyone else to have access. I might have to check her files and see if she's his administrative assistant or something along those lines. That wouldn't explain why she's always busy, though, with him running interference or why she was supposedly at some conference. Wouldn't it be the other way around? She'd be the one taking all his calls." Hawke rambled on. "Things aren't adding up. I think it's time I cornered Clark and got some answers."

"Well then," Keir said with humor lacing his words. "Glad you called us and we could be of such help."

"Bite my hairy ass, you overgrown house cat."

Xander cleared his throat and spoke quickly before the insults escalated. "If you need help, just let us know. I'll talk to Josie and see what she can find out. Those three are thick as thieves. If something's up, Josie and Ally will know or will find out what it is."

"Thanks, guys. I appreciate that. Now if you'll excuse me, I have some things to get settled here."

Hawke hung up after they exchanged their good-byes and smiled the first smile he'd had in weeks. His wolf grinned in anticipation and excitement. It was time to plan and hunt. His mate was done running from him, and her days as a single woman were coming to an end.

He glanced at his desk clock, saw it was still early afternoon, and called his assistant into the office.

"You wanted to see me?"

Hawke nodded and waved her to a seat in front of his desk. Rebecca was a rare gem he was lucky to have working for him. "You up for a mystery?"

She cocked one eyebrow, leaned forward, and smiled devilishly. "Are we finally going to track your mate down?"

"Bloody hell, woman. What do you know of it?"

Rebecca smirked, sat back in her chair, and started to tick off points on her upraised fingers. "One, you've been grumpy as hell, but I've also caught you staring off into space lost in thought. Didn't mean much until rumors started flying."

"What rumors?"

"Two"—she pointed to another finger as she moved through the count—"you've been visiting your pet project's department a lot. Speculation is you're being matched and checking in."

"Not exactly."

"Let me finish, please." She glared before shaking her head softly and continuing on. "Three, I've heard you've been up in HR asking about an employee, and no, I don't have a name. That part isn't being spread about. It is common knowledge it's a woman and she also works in the aforementioned department."

"What if it's innocent and I was checking her record for violations to fire her?"

Rebecca rolled her eyes, "Sure. The man who has demanded every manager let him know of any significant events in his employees' lives. The man who goes out of his way to help employees in every aspect of their lives and has not once ever gone to HR to do any of this. They come to you, remember!"

Hawke blushed but didn't comment. She was right; there wasn't much he could say on that point at all.

"Four, word might have spread from . . . another office that you'd met your mate but were having problems with sealing the deal."

"For fuck's sake," he bellowed as he jumped to his feet

and glared down at Rebecca. "That's being spread around the office?"

"If it helps, the women are eating it up. They think it's romantic to see you working so hard to win her over."

Hawke slumped back into his chair, dropped his head onto his desk, and groaned in embarrassment. He knew whose fault this was. His so-called friends loved to stir the pot; they told their assistants knowing damn well they'd love to see him squirm.

"Don't cry, boss man. I'll stop teasing you. What's the mystery anyway?"

He sat up and glared at his former favorite employee. "You're an evil woman, Rebecca. I pity the man you settle down with." He straightened his tie, grabbed a pen, and fumbled for the words to explain without sounding like a lovesick lunatic stalker.

"You're fidgeting. This is awesome. If I didn't love my job so much I'd be the most popular person at lunch tomorrow with that tidbit. And you can stop growling now. I won't tell . . . for now, at least."

"What did I do to deserve this torment? I've tried to be a good person; I've never purposefully hurt anyone that didn't deserve it. Yet the fates have saddled me with this misery and grief."

Rebecca couldn't contain her laughter any longer. Hawke grunted, closed his eyes, and waited. Five very long minutes later she wiped the tears that were running down her face and settled down.

"You done now? Ready to hear what I called you in here for?" He waited for her to nod in agreement. "Good. Her name is Shawna Goode. I met her a few months ago at a party Xander and Josie threw for Ally, who has since been mated to Keir. Anyway, I asked them who she was and they all found it hilarious that she worked for me and I had no clue."

"How's that possible?" Rebecca exclaimed in confusion as she sat up straighter in her chair and studied him.

"Exactly. That's one of the things I want checked out. Make sure no one is hiring without informing me so I can meet the candidate. I don't know when or how that got changed, but I want it stopped. No employee joins my company without a proper introduction and welcome."

"Hold on." Rebecca stood, raced out of the room only to return a moment later with a pen and pad. "I want to take notes."

"Since when do you need to take notes?"

"Since you started acting love-sick crazy. I want to jot down all the things I've seen and what you want me to do. I don't want to forget a thing."

"Why haven't I fired you yet?"

Rebecca laughed. "I'm too valuable and you wouldn't know what to do without me here. Don't worry. I won't tell everyone yet. . . . I'll wait until you've pissed me off, and then it's payback."

"Also, we need to check into HR," Hawke said loudly, trying to drown out her words. "There's something odd going on there. The employee list on my computer has Shawna listed as working in one department, but in actuality she works for Clark Benoit."

"How is that possible?" Rebecca paused, stuck her pen in her mouth, and started chewing on the end as she thought about what he'd said. "Have you checked their records?"

"No, I'm afraid it will tip someone off that I'm looking into it. I've never gone there before; I've only ever had to look on the computer for the information I need."

"Good point. I can do it without suspicion. I have my ways."

"Okay, ninja Rebecca. Next thing, I need to find out everything I can about Clark Benoit and his department. If I'm honest, I don't recall setting him up with a department. He was hired to run the computer. I can see him having an assistant, but from what I saw he has two or three people there, besides him and Shawna."

"Have you seen the latest stats on the matches, by the way?" Rebecca asked hesitantly.

"No, why? What's wrong?"

"In the last few weeks the matches haven't been working out. We went from an almost perfect match rate down to about half that. I've sent memos to Mr. Benoit asking what the status is and for an explanation. The only response I received was, well, to put it mildly, sexist, degrading, and rude."

"And why have you not let me know this before now? I'd like a copy of that response ASAP. Please schedule a meeting with him first thing tomorrow as well."

"It was verbal. He's too smart to put it on paper. I can give you the gist of the conversation, though. Basically, told me to go eat another cake and leave the computer stuff to people who knew what they were doing and that he didn't have time to answer my questions."

"Hold off on the meeting for a day or two. First, I'd like to look at his file and talk to some of his coworkers and get their take on the man. I want to know everything about him and his time here before I call him in and hand him his ass."

CHAPTER 3

"It's been two weeks, Shawna; open up the door and talk to me," Josie demanded.

Shawna groaned, climbed to her feet, and opened the door for her pain-in-the-ass friend. "I talked to you yesterday, and Ally a few days before that. It's not been two weeks."

"Since anyone has seen you yes, it has. And no offense, but you look like shit. What's wrong? Are you sick?"

"No." Shawna yawned and moved back to the couch to flop down in exhaustion. "I'm just tired. It's my first night off in a week and a half. I have to be back at the gas station at four A.M., though. I'm just trying to catch up a bit."

"When did you start working at a gas station?" Josie asked in confusion.

"Couple days ago. I needed more money."

Josie huffed out in annoyance, "Stop killing yourself and let us help. You're working what, three jobs? This is insane."

"What do you want? I don't have the energy to fight with you right now. I want to sleep, not argue."

"Fine. I'm here because Hawke fired your old boss this morning. Apparently, the day you got sacked was also the day he found out some disturbing things about Clark. He's spent the last two weeks doing some research and gathering evidence and justification so the man couldn't file a grievance."

That was the best news Shawna had heard in days. If she weren't so dead tired she might just celebrate. It couldn't have happened to a nicer man; now if it had only happened before the ass licker had let her go.

"Are you listening to me?"

Shawna cracked open one eye and peered at her friend. "Sorry, what was that? I was throwing a party in my head. It's all the energy I have right now."

"*Carajo!* I said Hawke has been trying to reach you. They've discovered that you were running the Mate for Hire site and they want you back. Apparently, once you left, things got bad quick. Your old boss didn't know how to do it. He screwed things up so bad that they had to temporarily shut the site down."

"You're kidding me, right?" Shawna jumped up with more energy than she'd felt in weeks. He'd gotten what was coming to him after all. Karma did come back around sometimes. "I'm sorry the computer got screwed up, but so damn happy they discovered what a useless person he was."

Josie rummaged through her purse and pulled out a business card. "Here. Take this. It's got Hawke's direct office and cell number. He's desperate to get you to come back and work for him. He's got incentives for you to come back too. Things were pretty screwed up; he wants to fix them."

"Why are you bringing that to me? Why hasn't he called or something?" she asked skeptically.

"Your file with Naughty Goddess still has your old address and phone. No cell or email address on file. He wanted to come in person, but we persuaded him to let me try. If he doesn't hear from you soon, though, he will show up here. Mark my words, he's determined."

They spent another half hour catching up on their lives and then Shawna fell back onto her couch and closed her eyes before the door was latched. She quickly fell into a deep sleep.

Days passed in a blur as Shawna ran from one job to the next, never staying home longer than it took to change clothes or take a catnap before she was off again. She knew her friends were worried about her, they continued to offer money and support, but Shawna wouldn't accept it. The amount of money she needed to pay off wasn't something she could borrow from them. No matter how much they insisted. She'd been able to make this month's payment, but it had been late and a fee had been added on. She was drowning and didn't know how she was going to survive this.

"Shawna." A weak voice spoke softly on the other end of the phone.

Shawna strained to hear the woman's voice. "Mama, is that you?"

"*Hija.* I miss you."

It took all Shawna had to not break down in tears at the frail sound of her mother's voice. It'd been almost six months since they'd last been able to speak. Letters were not enough; she needed her. "What's wrong? Are you okay?"

"Calm yourself, *hija.* I'm just tired. They got your payment, they—"

"What? They what?" Shawna pleaded, worry and terror fighting for dominance now.

"It's your brother; he's very sick. I don't have long to talk, so just listen. I've got a plan; I'm going to get him to someone who can help. Just remember we love you very much. I'll call again when I can."

Before she could respond the line was dead. Ice flooded her veins as she recounted the cryptic words her mother had spoken. What help was she getting? How was she getting him help? Nothing Shawna could come up with settled her mind. Her family was in danger and there was nothing she could do.

Her knees buckled and she collapsed onto the hard walkway to her apartment; giant sobs of terror wracked her body as she clutched at the phone, willing it to ring back.

"Miz Shawna?" Robbie rushed to her side, pulled her to a standing position, and half-carried, half-dragged her the rest of the way to her apartment. "Where's your key?"

Shawna could hear him, but words failed her as she dug in her pocket for the key to her house. She blindly handed it to him, lost in her world of pain and worry. She'd already lost too much; she couldn't lose her mother and brothers too.

"Come on, Miz Shawna. Almost there," Robbie's soft voice cajoled. She collapsed onto her well-used couch and let the sobs free once again.

She wasn't sure how much time passed before the sound of soft voices roused her from her semiconscious state.

"*Carajo,* Hawke, I said put him down," a low voice demanded. Shawna struggled to open her swollen eyes as she heard Hawke's voice reply in a menacing tone.

"He's in her apartment alone with her like that. He's going to tell me what's going on or I'm going to rip out his intestines through his nose."

"As graphic and disturbing as that sounds, you need to chill the fuck out. If you'd listen to me and stop your masculine posturing, you might hear better."

Shawna finally managed to open her eyes in time to see

Josie and Ally standing next to Hawke, trying to pull his hands off poor Robbie's tattered shirt.

Robbie nodded his head vigorously. "I've been trying to explain. I found Miz Shawna like that and helped her in here. I'd never hurt her. I called Miz Shawna's friends to come help."

She watched as Hawke released his grip and took a small step back. "Fine, but he will explain and it better be the truth."

Shawna had had enough of this; she pushed herself to a sitting position, wiped the tears from her cheek, took a deep breath, and gave a demand of her own. "Leave him alone; he's done nothing wrong."

Everyone froze in stunned shock before they all began talking at once. She was exhausted physically and emotionally; hearing all of them try to talk over one another was more than she could handle.

"Quiet!" she screamed as she jumped to her feet like a deranged lunatic and glared at everyone. "I'm having a very bad day and I don't have the patience to sit here and listen to you scream at each other. If you want to talk to me, you can all sit down like the adults we are or you can get the hell out."

Shawna didn't wait to see if they listened or not; at this point she didn't care. She dropped back down onto her couch and closed her eyes. As the seconds ticked by and she didn't hear the front door open and close she knew it was time to figure out why they were all here.

"I can feel you all staring at me," she grumbled as she opened her eyes and took in the faces around her. "Why are all of you here? And don't even think about all talking at once. I am so close to going postal today."

Robbie sat up a bit straighter and quickly explained, "Miz

Shawna, that's my fault. After I helped you in and you collapsed I was worried, you see. So, I found Miz Josie's number in your phone and called her for help. A lady needs women around when she's hurting like you." He lowered his eyes and wouldn't meet hers before continuing on. "I didn't mean to cause you more stress, and I'm sorry I went through your phone like that."

"I'm not mad at you, Robbie. You've done so much for me, for all of us. How could I ever get mad? If you hadn't been there when I got home, things would be so different right now. You probably saved my life." Shawna pulled Robbie down so she could give him a hug and whisper in his ear, "I can never repay you for all your kindness. Thank you for being my friend."

"It wasn't nothing, Miz Shawna." Robbie smiled bashfully and stepped back with a nervous glance to Hawke. "Is he okay? I mean, are you ladies safe with him?"

"He's an old friend. He'd never hurt any of us. Don't worry. I promise," Shawna replied, which was quickly seconded by Josie and Ally.

"All right then, I'm gonna go, but I'll be close by if you need me."

Shawna watched him walk quietly out of her apartment before turning her attention back to Josie and Ally. She couldn't deal with Hawke right now. His presence was like that of a living, breathing entity standing over her, breathing down her neck. She was too on edge and aware of his every movement. She hated that he was seeing her life falling apart. He was too put together and in control and it just made her feel worse. She wanted to hate him, she knew she put on a good act, but deep down inside she wanted to tie him to her bed and never let him up.

"Talk to us. What's happened? Why did Robbie sound

so scared when he called us for help? What's going on?" Ally pleaded desperately.

Shawna was wrong, she could deal with him after all, and it would be easier than explaining to him. Besides, if she was honest with herself, she was curious as to how he came to be in her run-down shitty-ass apartment in the first place. She turned her attention to him and was shocked at the expression of fear and worry evident on his face.

"What are you doing here?" she whispered, still in shock over what she'd just seen.

"He . . . I told you . . . Well . . . ," Josie tried to explain before giving up and shrugging.

"What she is trying to say is that we warned you he was looking for you. That he might show up here if you didn't call him soon. This morning he . . . um . . . Well . . . he asked for your address. They"—Ally indicated Josie and Hawke—"were arguing when I showed up. A few minutes later Robbie called freaking out, and here we are."

"You're stalling," Hawke pointed out. "What happened and why are you living in this shithole anyway?"

That pissed her off; as concerned as he was, he didn't have the right to demand answers or disparage her living space. She huffed and turned her back to the overgrown oaf and faced her friends. "I don't have time to deal with him right now. Were you guys being honest when you said you could help me or that maybe Bess and Julia can? I don't know what to do and I'm so scared."

"Of course, anything. Just tell us what we can do." Josie replied without hesitation as Ally nodded in agreement.

"I got a call this morning; my brother is sick. I think my mother is going to try to sneak away and get him help. She said they loved me and she'd call back when she could. I've been dealing with these people for long enough to know they won't let her or my brothers get away. I don't know where she is or how to help her. I just know they will hurt them and if they survive they'll probably make them pay for the time and energy they spent tracking them down."

"This is a job for the big guns. I'll talk to Xander and between us, Bess, and Julia we'll find them and get them to safety."

Ally nodded in agreement with Josie. "What about the money? Are they going to demand you keep paying?"

"Excuse me, ladies, but—" Hawke started to speak but was quickly silenced by Josie.

"This isn't your concern," Shawna said with a glare before taking a deep breath to reply to Ally's question. "I don't know, to be honest. I think to be safe I need to keep making payments until I know they are safe someplace else. But if those bastards do get them again, at least they won't take that out on them. I can't afford to take that chance."

"Fine, that makes sense, but you should hear Hawke out then. He could help with that part. You're killing yourself working three jobs and barely making enough to cover your bills here. Add in what you send to them and you're drowning in quicksand." Ally smiled weakly before glancing to Hawke. "Just hear him out for me. And don't worry either way, because you'll have the money you need to pay them off with or without taking him up on his offer."

She hated that he was listening to her problems, but she couldn't hold it in much longer. Her friends were her rocks in the tidal wave of grief and worry that was sweeping her away. She knew with every fiber of her being that they along with Keir and Xander would do anything and everything to help her fix this. Hawke, on the other hand, was an unknown quantity. She knew of him by reputation only. Most of the employees she'd worked with at his company adored him;

they raved about his compassion, care, and personal attention. Though none of the people in her department had ever seen it, too many people had said it for it not to be true.

Shawna gathered her courage and faced Hawke Hawke, hoping that he really was here to offer her something she desperately needed. Hope, short and simple.

CHAPTER 4

He'd never been so furious in his entire life as when he'd walked into Shawna's hovel and seen her so broken on the couch. His only thought had been to destroy whatever and whoever had hurt his mate. Robbie was the only unknown entity and closest target. Before he'd known what he was doing he'd grabbed the smaller man and thrown him against the wall. He had to give the man credit; he didn't cower from Hawke's superior strength or anger.

Robbie had stood tall and proud and looked right into Hawke's eyes as he attempted to explain. Again, Hawke had to give the man credit; few people had the courage to do what he'd done. Sadly, Hawke's rage at seeing his mate so hurt had closed his ears to anything the poor man had said. If it hadn't been for Shawna's demand for him to be released, Hawke didn't know what would have happened.

Then the strangest thing had happened: Robbie became a kicked puppy begging for Shawna's forgiveness. At first Hawke had thought it an act, but as he watched the man he realized he treated all three women that way. As if they were queens and he their lowly servant. Nothing but respect and courteous behavior until his eyes met Hawke's again and then finally he realized what he saw there. The man was protecting his charges from Hawke. Robbie thought Hawke was a threat to the girls. It was the damndest thing he'd ever seen.

He was sure his jaw had dropped when Robbie asked if they were safe here with him. What did Robbie think he was gonna do if they weren't? Hawke could have snapped the man's neck with hardly an ounce of effort.

He was lost in his thoughts when he heard the girls use his name. He quickly focused in on the conversation in time to catch the drift of it and see his mate trying to distract them. That was going to end now. He had too many questions for her to get away with that. When he'd agreed to follow the ladies here, he'd never in a million years thought it would be to such a run-down tenement. What had happened to her old apartment? He'd never been there, but he'd looked up the address that was on file and it had been in a good area.

"You're stalling," Hawke pointed out. "What happened and why are you living in this shithole anyway?"

So, he needed to work on his tact, he thought as he quickly watched Shawna shut him out. He hadn't meant it like it'd come out, but his patience was running thin. He just wanted to help her, keep her safe, and worship her delicious body. Was that too much to ask?

Especially now, his mate needed him even if she didn't want to admit it. Nobody was going to make his mate cry and get away with it.

"Excuse me, ladies, but—" He tried to interrupt so he could get them to give a clear answer. It was obvious the ladies were all in on whatever was happening, but he couldn't help if they wouldn't spell it out a little more clearly for him.

"Hawke?" Ally called with a frown. "Are you going to explain or not?"

"Yes, sorry, I was trying to decipher your cryptic words. I seem to be only hearing the CliffsNotes versions and it's left me with more questions than answers."

Shawna stiffened. "That's because it's none of your concern. What is it you wanted to talk to me about?"

"A job," he replied without formality, "to be exact, your old job with added benefits and pay. Plus, all the things you should have had all along. As I'm sure you've been told, I fired Clark. While there were many reasons, one of the biggest was that he hired you and the other ladies without my consent or knowledge. That's not how my company is run. He was brought on to build and run Mate for Hire. Once he'd fired you, things quickly made it apparent that he was not doing that job."

"What happened? How did it become apparent?" She cursed and glared at him. "Did he break my program? I'll kill him!"

"I asked him to make some changes to my profile and match me up as an experiment, because it had come to my attention that matches in the last few weeks hadn't been working out. To put it mildly, my dates were total disasters. My hired mates were so off the mark it was frightening; I couldn't even bring them with me to the functions."

Shawna groaned, "How bad did he screw up my work?"

"Let me put it like this: My last 'mate' was allergic to dogs." Hawke rolled his eyes in annoyance before continuing on. "She freaked out and ran out the door as soon as she discovered what type of shifter I was. Mind you, this was clearly marked on the form I filled out and should have been part of the information she was provided."

He glared at Josie and Ally as they snickered at his words. It hadn't been funny to him or his wolf in the least bit. "Anyways, like I said, he's been fired. I want, no, need you to come back and fix everything. I'm willing to double your salary, and before you protest, consider the amount of work it'll take to fix his screw-ups."

Shawna nodded slowly. "Can I think about it?"

"*Carajo,* Shawna, what's there to think about? Take the damn job; he's practically on his knees groveling at your feet. Take advantage, girl," Ally said with a wink to Hawke.

"Ladies, I assure you if I was on my knees in front of her, groveling would be the last thing on my mind."

He grinned wickedly as he watched the blush creep up Shawna's beautiful tawny face. She was gorgeous and now that his mind had gone back in the gutter he was struggling not to pull her to her feet and stake his claim like his wolf urged him.

"Besides," Josie chimed in, pulling him from his thoughts. "Think of the resources he has at his disposal. You've said it yourself how fantastic the company is to most of its employees. Between all of us"—she gestured between the four of them—"our mates, and their superscary and highly effective assistants, there isn't anything we can't accomplish."

Hawke nodded in agreement. "I don't know for sure what's going on, but I gather your mother and brothers are in trouble. Whatever it is, whatever you need, I will do or find a way to get it done. You have my word on that."

He wasn't sure what he could say to convince her to come back to work for him. He'd offer her the CEO position if it would help; he just needed her to be there in the building. It would be so much easier to manufacture reasons to see her and seduce her if she was close. For the life of him he couldn't figure out what she had to think about. It was a no-brainer: come work for him and earn three times as much as she made now for a third of the work.

"Fine. I'll come back," Shawna said with a sigh. "But only if I get free rein to make some changes and upgrades to the software."

Hawke bit his lip and eyed her dubiously for a moment in consideration. "Can we at least agree to discuss them before you do anything? I'm not saying I won't let you do what you want, but I'd like to be kept in the loop."

Shawna nodded slowly before offering her hand. "It's a deal. When do I start?"

He let out the breath he hadn't been aware he'd been holding and smiled. He couldn't remember the last time he'd had to work so hard to get a woman to do anything. His mate was going to be a constant thorn in his side and he didn't want it any other way.

"Tomorrow too soon for you? I wasn't kidding when I said the program is screwed up. I have a pile of complaints on my desk and I have a date lined up for a function tomorrow, and no 'mate' to go with me."

Shawna gaped at him in shocked disbelief. "You want me to come back to work tomorrow and get you a mate in the same day?"

"I'm a customer too; I already RSVPed and the per-plate cost was probably what you pay in rent here for a month. I'm not letting that money go to waste."

He watched in amusement as she opened and closed her mouth attempting to find the words she was looking for. In all honesty, he could easily go alone or not go at all. The money had gone to a wonderful cause and that's all that mattered to him really. But he couldn't pass on the opportunity to get Shawna one step closer to him. Now to just wait for her to catch on to his way of thinking.

Ally cleared her throat to gain their attention and winced.

"Why don't you be his date, Shawna? It will solve his problem and you get paid for being his 'mate.' It's a win-win situation."

Hawke could kiss her for inadvertently offering what he was working on suggesting himself. He made a mental note to send her flowers at the next opportunity.

"You can't be serious?" Shawna gritted out between clenched teeth. "No one would believe I was his mate, and besides, I have nothing fancy enough to wear to something that cost that much!"

Hawke ignored her protests and stood up to leave. "I'll see you at eight tomorrow morning and I'll pick you up here at six thirty to head to the benefit."

CHAPTER 5

She wasn't going to survive the day, or rather she would, but there were no promises in Hawke's case. It wasn't even eight yet and the rat bastard was waiting for her outside her former office looking like a freaking *GQ* model, holding two steaming cups of coffee. If one of those wasn't for her he was a dead man. By the gods, why did he have to look so damn good this early?

"Morning, my beautiful!" he called out as he handed her one of the cups. "A welcome back gift."

Shawna glared at him: How could he be so damn chipper this early in the morning? Hell, she'd only had two cups of coffee. She'd need at least a dozen more to make her ready to face the day ahead. After his abrupt announcement and departure yesterday she'd spent the rest of the day arguing with her besties, crying in worry about her family and finally giving in to their pleading to borrow an outfit for the damn benefit. Once they'd left she'd lain awake most of the night clutching her phone, pleading with whatever deity was listening to make her phone ring with the sound of her mother's voice.

She grumbled a thank-you and moved past him to drop her bags off at her desk. His smothered laughter followed her and raised her hackles even higher. She huffed and turned to face him and waited to see what he wanted. Yes, he'd begged her to come back and said he'd see her at eight, but she hadn't really thought he'd be waiting. Didn't he as CEO have much better things to do than come stare at her? She knew she was being a bitch, but she was tired and frustrated, emotionally and sexually.

"Not a morning person, are you?" He glanced around the small office and frowned. "This is your office, really?"

She bristled at his acerbic tone. "What does that mean? What's wrong with it? This is what I was assigned to when I was hired, after all."

Hawke sighed. "I didn't mean it's bad. Just that as the person in charge of Mate for Hire you shouldn't be in this small, windowless room. Don't get me wrong, it's a nice office, but you're the top of the food chain for my dating business. You need an office that represents that."

"Why? It's not like I entertain clients or applicants here."

"What if I said I wanted to change that? Make a separate entrance right into the offices? Have your secretary greet people as they come in and sit in a small waiting room? Maybe have a couple of the employees Clark hired sit down and do interviews with them so we can have a much more rounded application process? Have a physical presence and not just an online one?"

Shawna stopped rummaging through the desk drawers and stared up at him in shock. She'd asked Clark for a meeting to discuss that very thing multiple times. Half of their clients were from surrounding areas; to bring them in for that personal touch would make the program and the matches that much stronger.

"Why are you gaping at me like that? It's slightly creepy, you know." He paused, nodded slowly. "Okay then, was that too much for this early in the morning? Should I come back later and finish . . . ," he trailed off as she raced around the desk to stand in front of him.

"Are you kidding me? Do you know how long I've wanted this very thing? I have a new questionnaire I've created that was a thousand times more comprehensive, but Clark wouldn't even look at it."

Shawna suddenly realized how close she was standing to Hawke and backed away slowly as she felt her face burn in an embarrassed blush. What was it about this man that made her forget herself? Sure, he was a top-of-the-line prime Grade A piece of hunk, and he smelled so good she had to fight to keep her mind from wandering to the places she'd like to lick him, but she wasn't a schoolgirl who couldn't control herself.

Hawke winked at her and nodded toward the door they'd entered a few minutes ago. "Come with me; I've got something to show you. I think you'll like it, and as to your new questionnaire, I'd love to see it. If it helps us be more accurate, I'm all for it. I'll even volunteer as your guinea pig and get matched for my next couple of functions to see."

Shawna followed behind him lost in thought of him on dates and wondering why that left her feeling so livid at the thought. She'd known he'd signed up and been matched. It's how she got stuck being his date tonight, after all. She hadn't really cared until now. What had changed so drastically to alter this?

"You might remember that I mentioned we'd fired Clark a few weeks ago. We've been busy since then, as you'll see. I'd already lined up contractors and began work the next day to get this completed as quickly as possible."

His words brought her back to herself as she listened in

astonishment at what he was saying or what she assumed he was saying. Could he have really already built the new area and she hadn't noticed driving in?

She stopped suddenly and stared at the beautiful double frosted-glass doors in front of her as she read the writing on them.

Mate for Hire

a subsidiary of the Naughty Goddess company

Hawke Hawke

CEO

Shawna Goode

General Manager

"You . . . I'm . . . Holy shit on a shingle." She breathed softly.

"I hope you being speechless means you accept the new title. Now, if you can manage to walk with me through the doors, I'll show you the rest of your new offices and you can meet your staff." He winked as he grabbed her hand and pulled her through the doors.

"I think you're insane, in case you were wondering. Amazing and gorgeous but insane all the same."

She watched as Hawke smiled so devilishly that it made her want to run to the nearest bathroom and ease the ache that had begun when she'd run up to him in her office. That look was 100 percent wicked delight.

"You think I'm gorgeous?" he whispered as he stepped closer and crowded her back against the door. "It's okay; you don't have to lie. I heard it from your very own plump lips. Furthermore, I can smell your arousal and need and it's mutual, baby. But first we have some work to do. But just maybe I can find us an unused room or area so I can finally taste you. It's all I've thought about since the minute I laid eyes on you at Keir's party."

Shawna gulped and pushed at the rock-hard chest inches from her face. As much as she wanted what he was offering, there was no way in hell she was letting anyone see anything inappropriate between them. Last thing she needed was someone to start gossiping about how she was given her position within the company.

Hawke smirked and stepped back from her as she straightened her clothes and took a deep breath in an attempt to calm her rapid breathing and heart rate. Damn the man, all he had to do was get close and she was a puddle of need at his feet.

The first person she saw after she tore her eyes off Hawke was Penny, Clark's old secretary, with a big grin standing behind a desk a few feet away.

"I'm so glad you finally agreed to come back to work here. You wouldn't believe the changes and everything that's been going on. We all made sure to tell Mr. Hawke what you did here and we all agreed unanimously that you deserve the title on the door. You ran this place, even if you never got credit for it." Penny paused and took a deep breath before blushing. "Sorry, I tend to ramble when I'm nervous. I'm just so happy you're here."

"Penny, it's so great to see you too, and thank you. I think I'm excited to be back, a little overwhelmed at the moment, to be honest."

"Oh, you'll get over that real quick. Mr. Hawke has fixed everything; all those things we heard about working for him, well, they're true. I've never been as happy as I was the day he called us in for a meeting and told us Clark had been fired. Listen to me going on and on. You go get your tour and get settled in."

Before she could respond, Hawke took her hand again and pulled her around the desk and through the arched doorway into the inner sanctum of her new work space. Shawna was awed by what she saw around her. The office was so homey feeling, with pictures of families and couples on the wall. Every person she passed was smiling and waved happily and welcomed her back. She was overwhelmed and speechless. Hawke took advantage and continued the tour, explaining each area and greeting everyone by name.

"This is the last stop on your tour. It's your office, as you can tell by the nameplate. You have the option of hiring a personal secretary if you need one. The applicant has to meet with me for final approval once you've selected them, but that's more a formality so I can welcome them to the company."

Shawna nodded dumbly as she stared at her name stenciled on the door. How had her life changed so drastically in a matter of hours? With the salary that came with this job, she could afford to get a better place to live and bring her family to live with her and pay off their debts without a problem.

Her good mood vanished as she thought of her mom and brothers. For a few minutes she'd been able to ignore her problems, but like a tidal wave they were back and as strong as ever. She opened the door and rushed inside to hide the tears that threatened to fall. Last thing she wanted was the whole office to see her fall apart on her first day as boss.

"Shawna, what's wrong, babe? Talk to me. Is it the office? What? I can't fix it if you don't talk to me."

"It's nothing. Just lack of sleep and I'm struggling to hold in my fear for my family. For a minute I'd forgotten about their situation, and it came crashing back." Shawna took a deep breath and steadied her nerves. "I'm fine. I need this; it will help me focus on something I can do instead of sitting at home waiting for them to call. Bring me up to speed, please."

He nodded in understanding and dove into what had been done since she was gone. He explained the mountains of papers on her desk and the complaints of bad matches as he pointed to a three-inch pile of papers.

"Those are all complaints?" She exhaled loudly and shook her head. "Tell me again why I can't track that bastard down and skin him for ruining all my hard work."

Hawke laughed. "Will it help to know he's been blacklisted from working anywhere I have a friend? Which in case you were wondering is huge. And trust me when I say that goes for Keir's and Xander's friends too. He'll be lucky to get a job at the local gas station when we're done with him."

Shawna laughed. "It does a bit for now, at least. After I get in there and see just exactly what he's done I'll reevaluate and let you know."

"It's a date. In the meantime your schedule is clear for the week. I had a temporary shutdown implemented on the site, with a letter explaining it's down for maintenance and an overhaul to fix some of the issues that had come to light. You might still get some walk-ins, as I did include the address and invited people to come in in person and talk to a staff member with any comments, concerns, or to begin the process. Your staff will handle that, of course."

"That leaves me free to work on the program and fix what he broke and make the changes I've been begging for?" Shawna asked eagerly.

"It does indeed. If you don't mind, though, when you've

got the new questionnaire filled out can I look over it and fill it out again. Might as well have the staff be the first people to use it and look for anything we might have missed. In fact, I can have Keir, Ally, Xander, and Josie take it again. Once the software is up and running to your satisfaction, let's test it and see if they get matched again."

Shawna narrowed her eyes at him, bit her lip in thought, and finally gave in and laughed. "Challenge accepted."

The next few hours flew by as Shawna sat hunched at her desk going through all the paperwork and getting organized. She was just about to give up and throw it all in the trash when a knock sounded at her closed office door. Startled and annoyed at the interruption, she shoved back from her desk and pulled the door open with a scowl.

"Not happy to see me, I take it by that look," Hawke drawled as he pushed by her and dropped onto the leather couch set against the wall on the other side of the room from her desk. "Come on, I brought you lunch and you look like you could use a break."

"Sorry." Shawna shrugged and moved to sit beside him on the small couch. She tried to put as much distance between them as she could, but the huge man beside her took up more than his share of the small space.

"I won't bite, you know, unless you ask me to, that is."

Shawna rolled her eyes and leaned back into the comfort the couch provided and moaned in happiness. "I've only been here a few hours and you've already made inappropriate advances half a dozen times. How have you not been charged with sexual harassment by now?"

Hawke gave her a lopsided grin. "There's nothing inappropriate about this. I want you; you want me. I'm just making sure you don't forget that fact. But for your information, I've never and would never harass a woman. My mother and grandmother would skin my hide. They created this company because they believe women with curves are goddesses. They taught me well. Your curves, for example, have kept me awake for hours every night dreaming of the things I want to do to you, to hear the things you'll scream as I pleasure you."

"Well, my son has one thing right; that's for sure. I would skin him alive if he were to act in such a disgusting way to a woman." The woman gave Hawke a sardonic look that said she'd heard every word he'd said. "I hope I'm not interrupting anything, but I came to visit my son and was told he was here checking out the new office. I guess they had it partly right," she said with a wink as she stepped fully into Shawna's office.

Hawke jumped to his feet. "Mother, what a pleasant surprise." He glanced at Shawna and smiled. "Shawna, I'd like you to meet my mother, Patricia Hawke. Mom, meet Shawna Goode."

"Call me Patti; 'Patricia' is too formal," she said as she moved closer and sat in the chair across from their positions on the couch. "I've heard so much about you, it's nice to finally put a face with a name."

Shawna wanted to die of embarrassment. His mother had heard the things he'd said and yet here she sat as calm as can be. Was she a shifter too? Could she tell how hot her son's words had made her? She couldn't think of that; she'd never be able to look the woman in the face if she did.

"It's a pleasure to meet you too. You've created one amazing company and I'm so fortunate to be able to work for it."

Patti laughed. "I notice you didn't mention working for my son or how delightful he was to work for. Not that I blame you, of course."

"Mom," Hawke groaned, "don't embarrass her. I just got her to agree to come back to work for us. Today is her first day back."

"Calm down, Son." Patti winked at Shawna. "You'd think I was going to tell you secrets about his childhood or how he used to practice his growl and roar in his bedroom. It was so cute, seeing my little wolf trying to act so tough and powerful."

"That's it, Mom. Let's go. Shawna, babe. I'll see you later," he said as he leaned down and placed a soft kiss on her cheek before escorting his mother out of the room.

Shawna sat there stunned as her cheek burned with the feel of his lips long after he'd walked away. What in the hell had just happened? She was exhausted from the multitude of emotions over the last few minutes. From lust to embarrassment to laughter and shock. The ring of her cell pulled her back to the present and she fumbled it out of her pocket.

"Hello?" she answered, and quickly scowled as she pulled the phone away to see the unknown number message. The damn stalker again. What was this asshole's problem? "Look, you douche canoe, stop calling me, leave me alone, and go take a long walk off a short pier."

She'd no sooner hung up than the phone rang again; she growled and answered with a barked "What?" but again got no response. It was time to call the phone company and see what they could do. This was starting to get on her nerves!

"Shawna!" Hawke called as he entered the office again with a scowl. "Why aren't you answering me?"

Shawna frowned in confusion. "What are you talking about? I didn't hear you call me. Sorry. It wasn't on purpose."

"No, I mean on the phone. I keep calling you. Have been for weeks, actually." Hawke shrugged sheepishly. "I talked Xander into giving your number to me."

"The only calls I got today were from an unknown number. The person either breathes into the phone or there is silence. . . ." She trailed off and stared at him, waiting.

"That wasn't me. The phone just rings and rings until it hangs up when I call. But I did literally just call you twice." Hawke waved his phone at her as if that were proof. "I'll do it again right now."

She watched as he hit a button and then put the phone to his ear. Within seconds her phone was ringing too. Shawna opened her mouth to say something, but confusion left her speechless. The caller ID showed "Unknown," the same as the other calls. With a sneaking suspicion, she pressed accept and said hello into the receiver.

"What the hell?" Hawke grumbled as he put his phone on speaker. "It's still ringing on my end."

"What number are you dialing? Are you sure it's mine?"

"It's the number your bestie's mate gave me." He recited the number and she nodded slowly. "Here, let's try this. Let's hang up and you dial my number."

She typed his number in and made a mental note to save it to Contacts later. She heard his phone ring and looked up in time to see him frown. "What?"

"It says unknown number too. You're programmed into my phone, so that makes no sense at all." She watched as he accepted the call and now it was her turn to frown.

"My phone is still ringing. This makes no sense."

"I have no suggestions at all. I've never heard of anything like this happening before. By the way, what phone is that? I don't think I've seen a flip phone like that since the early nineties. Can you even text on that thing or do apps or search online?"

"Leave my phone alone. It makes and receives calls . . . most of the time. It works for me," she growled as she cradled the phone to her chest to hide it from his mocking view. "It was the best I could do, I had to downgrade so I could afford one. I had this one laying around from years ago and was able to talk them into switching my service to it at a much-reduced cost. Thank you very much."

Hawke raised his hands in an "I surrender" way and nodded. "Sorry, didn't mean to offend you or anything. Just took me by surprise."

"What did you want anyway? You just left five minutes ago and called twice."

"Oh yeah." Hawke pointed to the bag he'd set on the floor beside the couch when he'd walked in earlier. "I brought you lunch and I wanted to tell you because I kinda forgot this morning that you look beautiful today."

Shawna melted. How could she stay mad at a man who brought her lunch and complimented her like that, not to mention he'd talked to his mother about her?

"Also, you're on salary and I trust you. So feel free to leave a bit early today if you want to go home so you don't feel rushed for the benefit tonight. I've gotta go; my mother is waiting and I shudder at what mischief she could be up to unsupervised."

The next few hours flew by in a haze of questions from Shawna's staff, sorting through the never-ending paperwork, and staring off into space lost in thought. Between her family and Hawke, she had a lot on her mind. She wasn't sure what to make of Hawke; he was gorgeous to a level that left her whimpering in need. When he'd walked up to her to be introduced at Ally's party, it had taken all she had to not throw herself at him and beg for the release she knew only he'd be able to supply.

Her mama had taught her better than that, though; she'd ignored the man and walked away with her dignity intact.

Even if she did go home and dip into her toy drawer a couple of times. She couldn't seem to satisfy the cravings he evoked in her. But she knew all she would ever have was her fantasies. People like her old boss, Clark, had taught her well enough through the years to know a man like Hawke Hawke wouldn't want someone like her.

As her best friend from college used to say, Shawna had more curves than a highway through the mountains. The college guys didn't appreciate them, but it was okay. She knew one day she'd find the right man to worship her body. Until then she'd do it for them.

"Shawna!" Penny called hesitantly from the door. "I hate to bother you, but this just came for you. Said it was urgent." Penny held out the small box in her hand and shrugged. "It came by personal messenger."

"Did they say anything? Are you sure it's for me?" Shawna stood up and moved to meet Penny halfway. Her curiosity was killing her.

Penny shrugged. "Nope. He said he was told to take this box to you and say it was urgent. That's all he knew."

She took the box and began peeling the tape away. She couldn't imagine who'd be sending her something on her first day in such a small box and so cryptically either. She gasped as she peered inside and saw the last thing she had been expecting.

"Is that a phone?" Penny asked hesitantly.

"Yes, the bastard. I'm going to kill him," she grumbled as she pushed past her assistant and stormed out of the office. She had no idea where she was going, but she'd find him and give him a piece of her mind. Who did he think he was: her fairy godfather? Last time she looked he hadn't been wearing tights or carrying a wand.

The mental image that brought to mind almost made her

laugh out loud. Too bad she was mad at the overbearing brute.

"Is this place a freaking maze?" she yelled in frustration after wandering down the same hall for the third time.

"Excuse me, are you lost?"

Shawna spun in surprise and blinked as one of the most beautiful women she'd ever seen stopped beside her.

"You're Shawna, aren't you?" the perfectly proportioned blond bombshell cooed before enveloping her in a bear hug. "I've been dying to meet you; I am so glad you came back to work. Life has been so much better today. I know it's 'cause you're here."

Shawna awkwardly patted the stranger in an odd sort of hug and quickly pulled back. "Do I know you?"

"Oh, excuse me. What was I thinking?" The blonde laughed. "I'm Rebecca. Hawke's assistant slash gofer slash detective slash 'stop talking and do what I said' girl."

"You're his . . . assistant?" Shawna's thoughts whirled a mile a minute. Why would he want someone like her when he could have this woman instead?

"Yes, I helped him track down and document everything we needed to get rid of Mr. Benoit. I don't know how you could stand working for such an arrogant, woman-hating Neanderthal." The blonde smiled and offered her hand. "We haven't been formally introduced. I'm Rebecca or as he calls me when he doesn't think I can hear him 'royal pain in my ass.'"

She didn't want to like this woman, but there was just something about her that put you at ease and made you feel welcome. "It's nice to meet you too."

"Oh, you got the phone. I'm so glad it arrived in time. We were worried it wouldn't. Come on, I'll show you how to get to His Majesty's den. But don't tell him I called it that. I am so not in the mood for one of his tirades on what it means to be a good assistant. The first thing is always don't talk back."

Shawna had to bite her lip to keep from giggling at this woman's infectious attitude. "It's not like he didn't know what I was like before he hired me. We've only been friends since we were in diapers. Anywho, the phone. So, do you like it?"

Before she could reply, Rebecca froze. "Wait, is there something wrong with it? Is that why you were headed to his office? 'Cause if it is, I gotta go. I don't wanna be there when you tell him. It'll all be my fault, even though I had nothing to do with it other than giving him the phone number."

"No, calm down." Shawna sighed. "I just . . . can you explain why I was sent the phone? I don't understand."

Rebecca grinned happily. "Simple, yours was wonky and unreliable. Besides, this is a company phone. All the managers of each department get one. It's yours, though, so feel free to download apps and stuff. Oh, and we pulled some strings and this phone has your old number already transferred to it."

"I'm so confused," Shawna mumbled as she trailed behind Rebecca's retreating form. Had she fallen down a rabbit hole to a place where nothing made sense and everything was ass backward?

Before she could ask any more questions, Rebecca opened a door and breezed in, calling out in a loud singsong voice, "Guess who's here?"

CHAPTER 6

He couldn't remember a time when he was as nervous as he was now, watching the hours tick by until he could pick his mate up and take her on their first real date. Even if she didn't know it was real. His assistant's voice pulled him from his thoughts as she used that irritating high-pitched singing thing she did to yell at him.

"Guess who's here?"

He didn't have to reply; if he knew Rebecca at all she'd just march into the office and bring their guest with her. She was a damn efficient assistant, he reminded himself as he eyed the stapler he was tempted to throw at her.

"I know what you're thinking and you really don't need me to call your mother back in here, do you? She was fishing for gossip, but I didn't give in . . . yet."

Hawke narrowed his eyes. "You wouldn't dare."

Rebecca smiled evilly. "You want to bet on that?"

He rolled his eyes and turned his attention to the woman standing half-hidden behind his annoying friend. "Shawna, is that you?"

"Yes, it is. I found her wandering the halls; you didn't give her a proper tour, did you?"

"Sorry, we got distracted. I'll rectify that first thing tomorrow. Now, don't you have someplace to be . . . that's not here?"

"Spoilsport. Fine. I'm going. Actually, I think I have some errands to run, and since you said, be someplace not here to there sounds perfect to me."

"Why do I keep you here again?"

"Simple, I'm fantastic at my job and I'm not scared of your temper tantrums. Though why you didn't outgrow them is beyond me. I mean really, most boys have given them up by the time they're hitting puberty."

"Get out, before I change my mind about this stapler," Hawke growled.

"That's my cue. Shawna, it was wonderful meeting you. Let's do lunch sometime so I can tell you all his dark secrets. In the meantime"—Rebecca pulled her into a hug and squeezed—"I'm so glad you're here. I've finally got a sister."

Hawke bit his lip to keep from bursting into laughter at Shawna's wide-eyed stare as she watched Rebecca run out of the room. If you weren't used to the woman, it could be quite overwhelming. "You okay?" he asked as he moved from behind his desk and stepped closer to his mate.

"I'm not sure, to be honest. Did I get sucked up into a tornado and get spit out in Oz or something?"

"No, that's just Rebecca when she's excited. She's not always quite like that. Usually it's a bit more subdued, but she was happy to meet you. Gave me the cold shoulder for hours for not introducing you to her first thing this morning as a matter of fact."

Shawna nodded slowly. "Okay then. Well, I came to . . . well . . . Thank you for the phone."

"More like scream at me for it," Hawke said with a wink, "but since you ran into the whirlwind I'm assuming she explained it's a perk of working here?"

"Yeah, she told me. I didn't expect that. Thank you and thanks for getting them to keep my number like that."

"I didn't want you to miss a call in case your mother was able to get through. By the way, I was going to tell you tonight, but we've already got people on finding your family and safely getting them here."

"Already?"

Hawke grabbed her by the hand and pulled her to sit on the couch he kept in his office for late nights. "Of course, babe. We put the ball in motion last night. We weren't going to let you handle this alone; we have the resources to help."

Shawna sniffled as she wiped her eyes and gazed up into his. All he could think was how beautiful she was. Without a second thought, he pulled her across his lap and wrapped his arms around her. Offering what comfort he could.

"I know, hon, you've been so strong all alone, but you don't have to anymore. We're here to help. We'll stand beside you, babe."

He wasn't sure how long they sat like that; all he could concentrate on was the warmth of her in his arms and the intoxicating smell that was uniquely hers. He leaned his head back on the couch and closed his eyes as he attempted to memorize this moment. He never wanted to forget it.

"Loosen your hold," Shawna whispered. As soon as he did, she flipped around and straddled his hips.

"What are you doing?"

"Something I've been dying to do since the moment I first met you." With that, she leaned down and stole his breath. Never in a million years had he expected her to initiate their first kiss. With a growl of uncontrollable hunger at the feel of her lips, he stood up and shifted them so they were lying on the couch.

Just when he thought he'd died and gone to heaven, she

pushed at his chest until he backed off. "What's wrong?" he panted.

"Nothing. I . . . It's just . . . I'm not sleeping with you today. Not here, not like this." He watched as she slid out from beneath him and stood up. "I've got to go . . . get ready . . . for the benefit tonight."

"Wait!" he called, but it was futile; she was gone out the door before he'd barely finished the one word.

What in the hell had just happened? He climbed to his feet and sighed. Every time he got close to her something happened to end it. What had he done to deserve this? He'd finally gotten his first time at the lips he'd been craving for months and she took off on him. He wasn't sure how long he stood there staring out the door as if he thought she'd actually waltz back in like it had all been a huge joke.

"Boss man, you all right?"

Hawke jumped at the older man's voice and spun to see Henry, the night-cleaning man, standing beside him.

"What? How?" Hawke shook his head and stared in confusion. How in the hell did Henry get into the office and beside him without him being aware of it?

"That's what I'm talking about. You been standing there staring off into space for the five minutes I've been in here. You didn't even acknowledge me when I was talking to you. Should I be calling for an ambulance or your momma?"

"What? No, I'm fine." Hawke took a deep breath and tried to center himself. "Sorry, I was lost in my head. What can I do for you, Henry? It's a bit early for you, isn't it?"

Henry nodded. "That's what I figured. Not much in this world that would make a smart man stupid. You got female problems, don't you, Son?"

"No," Hawke denied vehemently.

"Yup. I've seen it a thousand times before. And the grapevine says you've found your mate."

Hawke gaped at him in astonishment. "You too? What, is there some underground gossip train or something? I've never seen anything like it."

"People talk, boss man. I've been around since you were in diapers. Ain't much I don't know about the goin'-ons around here. I know where all the skeletons are, I guess you'd say. I can even tell you a few things that would surely shock your delicate sensibilities to the core. Though a lot of that got fixed when you fired that no-good scoundrel Benoit."

"Why didn't you tell me how bad he was? I can't be everywhere and run this place. I don't understand why no one ever talked about him before. It was pure coincidence I discovered it this time." Hawke grinned at Henry. "I've got a proposition for you, old friend."

"Never you mind. I came here to tell you something important. Not to get roped into something. Don't think I don't remember some of your schemes from when you were a kid. You spent many evenings in my company helping me take care of this old place because of them."

"That's true; those are some of my fondest memories. You always treated me like a son, made me feel welcome and special. I couldn't have asked for a better role model. I'd be honored if when the time came I could count on you to do the same with him."

"Well, that's kind of what I came to talk to you about. I'm gettin' old and these bones aren't what they used to be. It's time for me to think about retiring."

Hawke frowned and dropped back onto the couch, staring at Henry in shock. How could he retire? The man was an institution around here; everyone knew and loved him.

Last year when Henry had come down with the flu and was admitted to the hospital for dehydration, half the office had left at some point to go see him. The other half sent him flowers, candy, and stuffed toys. Hawke hadn't seen anything like it.

"Don't get like that. I'm thinking of going part-time for a while. I don't know what I'd do with myself if I didn't have something to keep me occupied, but I wanted you to know that it was time."

"I can handle that, but I've got an even better idea. How about you train your replacement, and then you come work for me during the days? Trust me, this job is perfect for you."

Henry scratched his cheek and eyed Hawke before slowly nodding. "What do you have in mind?"

"You know we just opened the new area for Mate for Hire, right?"

"Of course I do. That's your mate running it. Today was her first day back. Always liked her; she's got backbone. If you ask me, she's perfect for you. Won't take none of your crap and she'll keep you on your toes. She's as stubborn as you are. Never thought I'd say that was a good thing, but in your case it's just what you need."

"Thank you for that glowing recommendation." Hawke rolled his eyes good-naturedly. "Anyway, I was thinking you might be of use to Shawna. What do you think about working with her to get things up and running? I've never met a person as astute about people. You read them and are uncannily accurate. She's going to be seeing people in the office that want to sign up. I'd like you to be there to help get the read on them, give feedback, and help make sure we get everything we need to match them perfectly."

Henry cocked one eyebrow. "You want me to help play matchmaker?"

"Yes, in a way. I'm sure you know we took a hit with Clark in charge. Shawna is working to fix that, but she could use the help to perfect the program. When you're not needed, you can make the rounds of the building, talking to all the employees and give me the inside scoop. Things I should know. Clark should never have been allowed to get away with what he did. If you'll help me, we can make sure it never happens again."

"Don't you think you should ask your mate about assigning me to work with her like this? My missus never took kindly to me interfering in her areas like that."

Hawke winked. "Don't worry. I've got that covered. Can you give me a few days to hire someone and then we'll move you to your new position?"

Henry shrugged. "Why not? It's your funeral. And by the way, if you don't get outta here you're gonna be late picking up your girl. That is not the way to start any relationship, Son."

"Shit," Hawke swore as he glanced at the clock. "I'm going to be late. I have to run home and change. I'll talk to you later, and thanks, Henry."

Just as he was about to break into a run, his phone rang, startling him. He pulled the phone out of his pocket and groaned at the caller ID. *Xander.* This was going to be painful; he just knew it.

"Hey, brother. What's up?" Hawke said in greeting as he answered the phone.

"Be thankful it's me calling and not Keir. I'm saving you that pain. Though not completely, as he's here listening in. And for the sake of full disclosure, the women are on speakerphone with Shawna as we speak, getting her side of things."

"They're rubbing off on you, aren't they?" Hawke groaned. "What do you want to know?"

"Answer one simple question and we'll let you go," Xander replied with laughter tingeing each word.

"Can't I save us all the trouble and just tell you both to go fuck yourselves?"

Laughter filled his ears as his former best friends delighted in his response. Why did he answer the phone again? He'd known this was coming; hell, he'd done the same thing to them, practically. It was only fair they get their revenge after all.

"How bad did you fuck up?" Keir called from somewhere in the distance.

"Fuck off," Hawke growled, knowing he'd hear him with his shifter hearing. "I didn't, if you must know. Everything's been great up . . . until a few minutes ago at least." He mumbled the last part to himself but knew they'd hear him anyway.

"What did you do?" Xander asked, feigning sympathy.

"Nothing; she kissed me and then took off. I don't know what the hell happened, to be honest. I will never understand women. Look, I'm getting in my car. I've gotta race home to get changed before picking her up for the benefit tonight."

They exchanged good-byes and he hung up feeling a bit better. Even if his friends hadn't said anything of importance, just them caring enough to call was pretty special. Now it was time to focus on the woman of his dreams and convince her she belonged with him.

CHAPTER 7

Shawna pulled into the parking garage and blinked in surprise. She'd driven home on automatic pilot and hadn't even realized it. The last thing she remembered was hanging up with the girls and promising to call them later with all the details right before she'd left her office after fleeing from the passion she'd found in Hawke's office.

Thoughts of that one amazing kiss and the things he made her feel had scared the living shit out of her. She couldn't allow herself to lust after a man she had no hope of ever having for herself. It had been bad enough she'd kissed him like that. Sure, he'd reciprocated, but he was a man, any stimulation was enough to turn them on, and she'd been sitting on his lap in a dress. He must think she was a wanton hussy after that display.

A soft tap on her window made Shawna jump in surprise. She opened her door and smiled up at Robbie. "Hey, sorry, didn't see you there." Shawna's smile slowly fell as she took in his worried expression. "What's wrong?"

"There's been some nasty-looking guys asking around about you, Miz Shawna. I ain't told them anything, but I don't like the looks of them."

"I'll be fine. Come on, let's go up to my apartment. My boss brought me lunch and it was enough to feed a small army. Since I have plans tonight, you have dinner," she said with a wink as they crossed the dingy garage. "And don't worry so much. I'm sure everything is fine."

Robbie sniffed in disdain. "Don't know about that. You didn't see these guys."

He was right, she hadn't, but she could just imagine who they were. She'd been expecting people might come stake out her apartment looking for her family. They were in for a surprise if they actually thought any of them would be stupid enough to be sitting here where they knew to look. With any luck she'd be gone on her date with Hawke before they showed up. She didn't want to drag him into any more of her drama.

"Robbie, I want you to do me a favor and hide whenever these guys come around. You're right; they aren't good people and they don't have a problem with hurting people or making them disappear. Trust me on this."

"Miz Shawna, are you in trouble?"

Robbie looked so sad at the possibility that it nearly broke her heart. Underneath the worn-out dirty clothes was a man with a heart of gold who'd fallen on tough times. She knew she was lucky to have him as a friend and vowed to help him get back on his feet as soon as she could.

"Not me, but my family. I'm pretty sure these guys are looking for them. I don't know anything to help, though. Something tells me they aren't going to believe me or care. So, please just be careful and stay away from them. I'll be okay; I promise."

He didn't look convinced but, thankfully, didn't argue with her about it. They walked quietly to her door and she handed him his dinner. "Please be safe. My friend Hawke is coming to pick me up. He won't let anyone get near me; I promise."

Robbie nodded but didn't look happy. "Fine, I'll stay away from them. But you'd best be promising me that I won't ever find you like you was yesterday. I can't take scares like that. Have fun tonight and thank you for the dinner, Miz Shawna."

Shawna smiled and stepped into her apartment. It felt like years since she'd left this morning. So much had happened in a short time. Add in that smoldering kiss with Hawke and she was on fire all over again. A quick peek at the clock told her she had just enough time to use the new toy she'd picked up. It'd cost her a pretty penny, but damn if it wasn't worth it. She stripped as she raced to the bedroom and pulled open her bedside drawer.

The Womanizer was a godsend; when she'd first heard about it, she'd been disgusted by the name. Now that she owned one, she didn't care what it was called. As the ad she'd read said, it was as close to oral sex as you could get with a machine. It not only vibrated but sucked your clit too. It was a handheld mother of all orgasms. She was vibrating in anticipation already; thoughts of Hawke filled her head as she quickly lay on the bed.

It wouldn't take her long, she knew; ever since she'd locked lips and felt the heat radiating off his large body she'd been a goner. She wasn't even sure how she'd gotten off the couch and out the door her legs had been shaking so hard. As her thoughts conjured the kiss again she let her hand trail over her erect nipples as she gasped at the pleasure. What she wouldn't give to have Hawke's large, muscular hand kneading her breast instead of her own.

"Hawke," she moaned as she slipped the toy between her folds and turned it on low.

She couldn't contain the moan as she felt the vibrations.

She could feel his eyes on her as she writhed on the bed in desperate need of his touch. "I need you so hard." She panted as she used her left hand to pinch her swollen nipple.

"Don't stop, baby," she heard Hawke whisper as her need pushed her higher than she'd ever been before.

Shawna bit her lip and moved the toy slightly so it aligned and began to suckle at her clit. This time the ragged moan was ripped from somewhere deep inside at the overwhelming pleasure that filled her body.

"You're fucking gorgeous. I can't wait to be the one making you scream in pleasure like that," Hawke growled.

"Yes, god, yes," Shawna begged. She was losing her mind. The pleasure was causing her to hallucinate, but she didn't care. That voice was driving her pleasure to unbearable new depths.

"If you taste half as good as you smell, it will be like nirvana. I want to bury my head between your thighs and make you shake and beg for mercy."

"Fuck me, Hawke." She didn't know what she was saying anymore; it was mindless pleasure as her body danced to his tune alone now. If he actually touched her, she was afraid she'd spontaneously combust. "Oh, fuck me, fuck me," she cried as his voice filled her once again.

"That's it, baby. Ride that toy; show me what you'd do to my face, my cock."

"Hawke!" Shawna screamed as her whole body splintered into a million pieces and fell back to earth.

"That's it, baby; ride those waves. You're so beautiful when you come apart like that. I can't wait to feel you wrapped around me when it happens. I want to take you to the stars and hold you tight as we float back to reality."

She'd never felt so relaxed and exhausted as she did at

that moment. That was an orgasm to end all orgasms. Never in her life had she experienced anything even close to that. She'd hallucinated! That was a first.

As she lay there trying to catch her breath she became aware of a feeling of being watched; she slowly eased up her heavy eyelids and gasped as she saw the man standing a few feet away.

"Hawke!" she exclaimed as she jumped up and attempted to cover herself with the bedspread she was lying on. "What in the hell are you doing here in my room?" she screamed as she tugged unsuccessfully at the blanket trapped under her wriggling body.

"Don't cover up on my account. I could stare at your luscious curves for eternity and never get tired of them. You are the epitome of a goddess, love."

She bit her lip as she saw the lust that shone from his eyes. His wolf was close to the surface. The knowledge both excited and scared her.

"I came to check on you after you ran out," he said as he took a few more steps, easing his way closer to where she lay panting in shock. "I knocked, but you didn't answer. Then the most intoxicating smell reached me and I heard your moan of need."

"What are you doing?" Shawna whispered as she watched him kneel beside her on the bed.

"I just watched you, listened to you call my name and beg me to fuck you. Babe, I want to claim what's mine more than I want my next breath."

"We have to go. . . ." She trailed off as he lowered his head to her chest and took her swollen nipple into his mouth. Her back involuntarily arched off the bed as she felt his teeth scrape against the sensitive bud. Shawna felt his hand trail its way down her thigh and sweep closer and closer to where she secretly wanted it the most. She knew she should stop this, but it felt too good to be touched by him. To have what she desired come to life.

"Hawke," she gasped out as he rubbed one finger through her slick, moist heat.

He leaned back and smiled. "We don't have time right now for me to do what I'm craving. For now, this taste will have to satisfy us."

She watched as he pulled his hand back to show her his glistening fingers covered in her juices before he licked them clean with a moan of delight.

"Just as sweet as I'd imagined you'd be. Now, get up and get dressed. No shower; just get some clothes on."

She started to protest, but one look at his steely-eyed stare and she knew it would be futile. There was barely controlled need staring back at her. She nodded and climbed to her feet on wobbly legs that didn't want to support her.

"I need to clean up," she said as she felt her face burn in embarrassment.

"No," he growled before stopping himself and taking a deep breath. "No, baby. Please don't. Just put on some clothes and let's go before it's too late."

She paused and glanced back at him over her shoulder in confusion. "Too late?"

"My control is going to snap if we don't get out of here soon. The smell of your arousal and orgasm is going to push me past my limits. If you want to make it to the benefit, we have to go now. Otherwise I'm going to throw you on that bed and worship at the altar of your body for the rest of the night."

Shawna knew he was telling the truth; she could see how he was straining to hold himself in check. But a part of her wanted what he said. She knew she'd probably never have this opportunity again. To have a man like him lusting after her, to see the evidence of his need so strongly, was a heady thing.

"I'll get dressed, but I hope that when you drop me off you'll consider joining me back in this bed. I want one night of the promise I see lurking in your eyes. I want to feel the power of your wolf as you claim my body."

Never had she felt so wanton as she did now getting dressed. Part of her felt dirty and ashamed for not getting cleaned up, but one look at the man standing a few feet away almost drooling and that was quickly quelled. She was tempted to get dressed as slowly as she could to watch him mesmerized by her body, to feel his gaze devouring her, but the quicker they got to the benefit, the sooner they'd be back here, she hoped making her scream.

"I'll be outside. I can't," Hawke grunted out as he took deep breaths. "You're killing me."

With those few words he spun on his heel and exited her small apartment. The sexual tension left behind was still strong, though. She shook her head and quickly grabbed her most sensual matching panties and bra set. If she was honest, it was also one of the only ones she had that actually matched. Next she pulled out the dress Josie had let her use. It was not her usual type of dress, but she couldn't deny it was gorgeous.

With a grin of pure evil, Shawna had an idea. She could zip up the small zipper on her lower back, but it would be so much more fun to have Hawke do it. She called out to him knowing he'd hear her with his superior shifter senses.

"Hawke, I need your help, please."

Within moments the front door opened again. She tracked his footsteps as he moved closer to her. Without a word, she spun and gave him her back. "Can you zip me, please?"

"Beautiful, you know my goal is to get you undressed. Not put clothes on you."

She laughed, but her breath caught as she felt his warm breath against her ear. "You are the most mesmerizing creature I've ever seen in my life. You have enchanted me," he whispered as he pulled the zipper up slowly while trailing one finger against her skin, leaving goose bumps in its wake.

"I'm almost ready," she said breathlessly as she stepped away and shivered. "Five minutes."

"That's fine. We've got a bit of leeway." He grinned ruefully. "It's a bit easier now that you're dressed and I'm not seeing temptation quite as much."

Five minutes later she was ready as promised. She took a moment to stand in front of her full-length mirror and take in her appearance. It wasn't often she had the time or inclination to dress up anymore after all.

She was glowing, not that she expected any different after that mind-blowing orgasm a short time ago, but it was more than that too. It was the way she felt in the dress, the way Hawke's eyes tracked her every move with hunger.

"I see I'm going to have a long night ahead of me fighting off everyone who sees you in that bit of witchery," Hawke drawled with a wink.

Shawna shrugged impishly as she took in her dress, seeing what he did. The long-sleeved black dress fit her to perfection with its teasing glimpses of skin under the lace and beaded sleeves and bust. It had an empire waist with a keyhole back that left a good portion of her smooth, tawny skin exposed. But by far her favorite feature of the dress was the slit that went from her toes up to midthigh.

"I'm ready; just let me grab my purse and we can go." Shawna bent over to retrieve her black clutch from the floor of her open closet and heard Hawke's indrawn breath.

"I swear, woman. You will be the death of me. Do not bend over tonight or I will end up killing someone."

Without waiting for a reply, Hawke led the way back out of her apartment. When he reached the door, he faced Shawna and grimaced. "I really don't want to share you with the world after I've seen what you're hiding under there. Just please stay close to me tonight, so I don't have to call Keir or Xander for bail money. It's a benefit for charity, after all. It's bad enough you'll probably end up giving one of the old geezers a heart attack as it is."

They made small talk as they headed to the garage and his waiting car. Nothing important, just "get to know you better" things. Shawna was amazed at how much they had in common. They came from entirely different worlds, yet they were so similar in so many ways.

"Have fun, Miz Shawna!" Robbie called from his corner of the garage with a wave and a nod of greeting to Hawke.

"Night, Robbie, be safe for me," she replied as she climbed into the car.

"What's his story?" Hawke asked as he joined her and started the car. "He's very protective of you."

"I don't really know. He was here when I moved in. I'd say hello or wave when I saw him and we just sort of became friends. Robbie's one of the good guys. He always watches out for the people he calls too good for this place. When Josie and Ally come by he escorts them to and from my place. Does the same for me too, actually. He's a vet; I know that from something he let slip one day."

They lapsed into silence as she watched the scenery pass by the car window until she suddenly realized she had no idea what tonight was about. "What's the benefit for? I mean, what's the cause they are raising money for?"

"It's for a group called Tomorrow's Hope. They run shelters for homeless kids, give them a place to live, feed them, and get them in school."

"I've never heard of them. How did you get involved?"

"I used to volunteer with at-risk kids. Through them I heard about this group and all the good they've done. I began helping them too. Actually, twice a year all the employees of my companies get a paid day to go volunteer for a few hours at a charity of their choice. I believe in giving back and doing what I can."

This man was a mystery to her; every time she thought she knew him he surprised her with some other detail. Had she been misjudging him the whole time? "Why did you create Mate for Hire?"

Hawke grunted out a small laugh. "That was out of the blue."

Shawna shrugged. "I was just thinking it was an odd thing for you to do. Then again, most men don't run lingerie companies either, I'd imagine."

"True, but you know my story. My family created it and I just took over. As to the matchmaking side of things, that was all me. My grandparents have one of those relationships most people only read about. You know, the ones where they met, fell in love and married, and stayed together for seventy years until death separated them hours apart."

"Of course, everyone's heard of those. Some part of me always wondered if they were true, though, you know. I'd love to believe they were. I mean, to live your whole lives together and when one dies the other follows quickly because they can't live without the other. To be so in love that you've been inseparable for five times as long as you were apart. It's surreal and kind of awe-inspiring."

"That's my parents. They met when they were in middle school. They were twelve years old, but they knew right then they'd be together forever. They dated all through high school and got married the day after graduation. Even now, they don't go more than twenty-four hours without seeing each other." Hawke grinned. "Do you know that last week I surprised them and found them slow dancing in the living room? They've been married over fifty years and the love I saw on their faces for each other blew me away."

"That's beautiful, but that doesn't explain why you started it."

"Because I think everyone should have a chance to find their soul mate, their other half, the person that brings meaning to their lives. Yeah, shifters know when they meet their mate, but they still have to find them. I created Mate for Hire to help them achieve that goal. Some of the matches don't end up being their mates, but they usually at least end up being friends. That we do have such a high success rate, or at least we did, is in part thanks to you."

"What about you then? You put your information in, but you haven't found your mate yet. I know the system was flawed and the matches weren't working, but what about before that? How did your dates go?"

"To be honest, I didn't sign up until recently and that was only for a couple reasons. One, I wanted to see for myself how bad the matches being created were, and two, I needed a date until I could convince my mate that she belonged to me."

Shawna gasped in surprise and alarm. "Wait, you've met your mate?"

"A few months back. She's been rather a pain in the ass up until recently, though. Wouldn't give me the time of day. Things might be coming around now, though, finally."

She didn't know what to say. All her thoughts were focused on that one word: mate. He'd found his mate; he belonged to someone. She wanted to weep at the news; all she'd wanted was one night of unbridled passion, but how could she do that with him now? Her eyes burned and her heart hurt from the sudden sense of loss. Never in a million years had she expected that, and she wasn't sure how to react now that she had heard it.

"Is she a shifter too?" Shawna asked hesitantly. The last thing she needed was a female shifter chasing her down for daring to encroach on her territory.

"No, she's human. She knows about shifters. A couple of her friends are mated to shifters, in fact. But for some reason, she's got it in her head that because she has curves no one would want her. I'm trying to prove to her how wrong she is. Stubborn wench."

Shawna grunted, "What do you expect when you spend your whole life being judged and deemed less than because you aren't that model size zero? Women with curves are looked down on, called names, and ridiculed. Hell, I went to see my doctor and he harps on losing weight even though he admits I'm healthier than ninety percent of his patients."

"I guess I never thought of that. I don't see any of that when I see her. Just the woman I want to spend my life with. The woman that makes me want to worship her body in ways she can't even begin to imagine."

The silence filled the car once again as they both thought over the things that had been said. For Shawna's part, she wanted to scream and cry and run home to drown her sorrows in a bowl of ice cream. "Does your mate know you're out with me tonight?"

"We're here. I hope you're ready for this," Hawke said as he ignored her question. "I'm sure as hell not," he grumbled softly.

CHAPTER 8

He wasn't sure how he was going to survive this night. He was already rock hard and aching and now he had to watch these old perverts fawn and drool over his clueless mate. He was just lucky she hadn't maimed him when she realized she wasn't alone earlier. When he'd walked up to her door and heard those sounds, smelled her arousal, there was no way he could have stayed away. Lucky for him he knew how to pick a lock and within seconds he was in the door and watching the most erotic moment of his life.

His wolf had pushed him to claim his mate right then and there, but he knew she wouldn't accept that yet. Instead, he watched, fantasized, and waited. When she'd called his name, he'd almost lost his mind. It'd taken all he had not to climb between her luscious thighs and take over for that toy.

Hawke groaned silently as he remembered the taste of her on his fingers, the way her eyes darkened as she watched him. Only his iron control kept him from coming right then and there.

"Are you okay?" Shawna asked as he stopped beside her outside the entrance to the benefit. "You look like you're in pain."

If she only knew the half of it, he thought. "I'm fine, babe.

Just remembering the taste of you." He grinned wickedly as he heard her intake of breath. "Come on, let's get this over with."

Hawke placed his hand on the small of her back and led them into the overflowing abundance of people littering the entryway. He hated these types of people. They were only here to be seen and to see. Always ready to spread a rumor or gossip no matter who they hurt. He'd have hoped, considering this was a charity event for kids, that they'd be better behaved. It was clear that wasn't going to be the case. And if that one Botoxed, leather-wrapped harlot didn't stop sneering at his mate, she was going to find herself in a world of hurt.

"Hawke, stop," Shawna whispered as she pulled on his arm. "Ignore them. They aren't bothering me. I swear I'm used to it, nothing they say can hurt me; I promise. Let's have fun and ignore the old biddy."

Hawke laughed as she said that last bit, loud enough for the shrew to hear. Her gasp of outrage could be heard all around the room. His mate was perfect and apparently a bit more tactful than he was at the moment.

"Excuse me," a cultured older voice said softly beside them. "I couldn't help overhearing and observing what just transpired and I wanted to say that was, to put it mildly, fantastic. It's about time someone, and pardon my French for saying this, had the balls to put that bitch in her place."

"Reginald, it's wonderful to see you again. May I introduce you to my date and very good friend, Shawna Goode. Shawna, this is an old friend of my family, Reginald FitzWilliams."

"It's a pleasure to meet you," Shawna said with a blush. "I'm sorry if I offended you."

Reginald's smile broadened. "Never, my dear. You merely

did what I wish I could have so many time before you would have. I'd be delighted if you'd both join me for dinner at my table tonight. I fear if I have to sit with the usual people I will go quite mad."

"We'd be delighted to; wouldn't we, Hawke?"

Hawke found himself nodding without thought. He'd do anything she wanted to keep that smile on her face. She was radiant and so full of happiness it almost took his breath away. He quietly followed behind them as the two made small talk while latched onto each other's arms. If he had to be replaced he was just happy it was to a man old enough to be his grandfather.

The next few hours dragged by as man after man manufactured reasons to come up and be introduced to Shawna. It was beyond Hawke's comprehension why she thought people wouldn't want her; did she not have eyes to see how many men braved his icy glare to talk to her?

"Excuse me; I need to take this call," Shawna murmured politely as she got up and hurried out of the ballroom.

Hawke watched her go, debating whether he should follow her or wait. After five minutes and she still hadn't returned, he gave up and went after his missing mate. He found her in a small alcove, clutching the phone and sobbing.

"Babe, what happened? Are you okay?"

Shawna shook her head no, before throwing herself into his arms. "My mom. It was my mom. They are safe for now. They're in hiding and won't tell me where, but they're still safe. She got my brother to a doctor."

"That's great news, right? Why are you crying then?"

"You don't understand. Just because they're safe now doesn't mean they'll stay that way. Those people won't quit until they find them and make them examples. I'm not stupid and neither is my mom. They will have to hide and stay hidden; I probably won't ever see them again, and that's if they don't get caught."

"Come on, let's get out of here." Hawke tucked her under his arm and led the way out. His mate was one hell of a woman, so strong and independent, but now it was time to let the big guns handle things.

"Shawna, here's the car," he whispered as he opened the door and helped her buckle in. Within a few minutes they were driving down the road and he was making a call.

"Xander," Hawke barked into the phone. "Any luck with tracking down Shawna's missing family?"

"Still working on it. Why? What's happened?"

"Her mom called; they found a doctor to treat one of the boys. We need to find them before they are caught again."

Xander sighed audibly. "I know. Trust me we have more people on this than you can imagine. Between all of us we should have found them already."

"What are we going to do when we locate them? I want them here so Shawna can be with them. I'm not letting them be separated under any circumstances."

A bitter laugh filled Hawke's ears. "Yeah, well, that's not goin' to be so easy. Has she told you who has been holding them? Or why they were there in the first place?"

"No," Hawke growled. "Something tells me I need to demand answers. But mark my words, I will find a way to make this happen."

"I know, Brother. I'll call Keir and see if he has heard anything. We'll get your mate's family back; don't worry. Just stay with her. I've heard of some reports of suspicious people asking questions."

They said their good-byes and Hawke jabbed the off button. His anger was mounting by the second. How was he supposed to help when he didn't have the whole story?

"Shawna, beautiful, I need you to talk to me. Tell me everything. No more holding back. I can't protect you if I don't know what is really going on."

Shawna sniffed and glared at him. "It's not really any of your business. You're my boss, but that doesn't give you the right to demand personal things."

He wanted to laugh, but he knew she was just lashing out in pain and he was an easy target. "Demand?" he bit out angrily. "I asked you to talk to me. I didn't demand yet, but don't get me wrong. You will tell me everything starting with why there are people here asking questions about you. And if you want to see me demanding wait till I get you in bed."

"You don't get to go to bed with me. You have a mate; I don't poach on other people's territory, you asshole."

Hawke stared at her in amazement. How could she be so brilliant and so bloody stupid at the same time? Her two best friends were mated to shifters; did she really not know anything about how they lived or mated? Did she really think he could sleep with her, do the things he'd done to her earlier if he was mated to someone else?

Before he could form a reply, she started talking again.

"You're right, though. I'm sorry; I shouldn't have snapped at you. I know you're trying to help and can't do it without all the information. Two years ago my father was seized for debts he owed to a gang in our hometown. My brother has a chronic illness that costs a lot of money to keep under control. I sent what money I could to help each month. My father borrowed money from the wrong people in desperation for emergency surgery. My brother made it through and has been doing fairly well since then. Two years ago, like I said, they came and took my father to make an example of him. He was making payments, but they were often late or only half of what was due."

"Where is your father now?"

"We assume dead; we haven't heard from him since that day. A year ago they came back for my mother and brothers. They contacted me and said they'd keep my family until the debt was paid off, but that we'd owe more every day it took until it was paid off. They charge them for the place they sleep, for the food they eat, and anything else they can come up with. So on any given day my family ends up owing more than they earned for the day. I've been sending the payments each month. What's owed for the original payment plus a bit extra to help offset my family's incurred debts."

Hawke wanted to destroy all of those bastards. It was unthinkable that they were getting away with what basically amounted to extortion. There was no way that Shawna's family would ever be free of debt at the rate they were going, even with Shawna sending money.

"When Clark fired me I was late on the payment and they beat my mother bad. She ended up needing to be taken to the hospital. They added that to the bill, plus her lost wages for the time she was too hurt to work. Two days ago my mother called me frantic; my brother is sick again and the gang won't or can't get him the help he needs. She was going to escape with the boys and get him help. She called to say good-bye in case she didn't make it."

"Shit," Hawke cursed. That explained her breakdown; he was only surprised she's held up as well as she has under these circumstances. If it had been his mother and siblings, he'd have torn open hell itself to get them back safe. "What about the people asking questions?"

She shrugged. "I figured they'd send people to see what I know, and if they'd come here I guess I was right."

Was she insane, acting so nonchalant about all this? If the men were part of this gang, then they were dangerous.

How did she expect to take on two men determined to get information from her? In the area she lived in, no one would bat an eye if she screamed or called for help. Sure, Robbie was around, but Hawke wasn't about to put the life and safety of his mate in someone else's hands. "I don't think you should be alone with them around asking questions," he blurted out, knowing her reaction was going to be borderline nuclear.

"I'm not endangering any of my friends, and what if somehow for some insane reason my family is able to get here? They have my address; I'm not running away and hiding when they need me."

"You said it yourself: The chances they'd show up at your place are minuscule. Your mom isn't stupid; she would know they'd look there for her. It's why she hasn't told you where they are. She's trying to protect you."

Shawna grunted, shook her head in the negative, and glared at him. "I don't care what you say; nothing will get me to leave there."

Hawke silently fumed the rest of the way back to her dump of an apartment as he tried to come up with something that would convince her to leave. But he knew one thing for sure: His mate was stubborn as the day was long. Nothing he could say would sway her. If she wouldn't leave, then he was coming to stay there, and god help anyone who showed up that didn't belong. He protected what was his, and this woman was his life.

"Fine, stay there. But before we head back I need to stop by my place and grab a few things."

"Drop me off and then go get whatever it is you need."

Before she'd finished, Hawke was already shaking his head no. "Unacceptable. I'm not leaving you alone now that I know they're here."

Countdown three, two, one, ignition, he thought just as she caught on to what he was saying. "You are not staying with me. Go find your mate and shack up with her. I don't need to be under constant supervision. I'm a big girl, if you hadn't noticed. I can take care of myself, and I don't need you thinking otherwise."

Well, that went well, he mused. "How about a compromise. I'll walk you to your apartment and leave you there while I run home, but I want Robbie to stay with you. He may be smaller than me, but something tells me he'll defend you with his life."

"I don't need a babysitter, *carajo.* What do you take me for?"

Hawke sighed. *Time for a new plan of attack.* This one obviously wasn't working at all. He pulled to a stop in the garage and put the car in park as she glared at him.

"Robbie's right there. He can walk me to my apartment. No need to come back." She seethed as she climbed out of the car and slammed the door shut.

Hawke rolled his window down and gave Robbie a pointed look and nodded toward Shawna. He smiled in relief when Robbie agreed and took off after Shawna with a grin. "I'll be back in a few minutes!" Hawke called to them.

Life with his mate was never going to be boring; that was for sure.

CHAPTER 9

"Miz Shawna, wait for me!" Robbie called as he raced behind her. "You shouldn't be walking around here by yourself. Especially not with those guys around. They were here earlier and they didn't look happy."

Shawna groaned at the news. Why couldn't those guys just go away and leave them all alone? She'd made this month's payment even after her family had left. That should have given her some leeway, but nope. Why was life such a bitch? The last few days had been a whirlwind of highs and lows. Every time she thought things were turning around there was life kicking her in the heart again.

"Are you all right? Your friend seemed pretty upset when you stormed out of his car like that."

"He can go roast in the fiery pits of hell for all I care. He's got a mate, a freaking mate, and here he was making me think things, impossible things."

Robbie scratched his cheek. "I don't know much, Miz Shawna, but I do know a thing or two about shifters. I had some old friends that were and they taught me a lot. If I recollect correctly, there is no way your man there would be taking you out or looking at you the way he does if he had a mate. You see, when shifters find their person that's it for them. They never look at anyone else."

"But he admitted he'd found his mate a few months back. He flat-out told me he had a mate, Robbie."

Robbie bit his lip and tried to hide his smile, which just made Shawna even more confused. "What?" she asked as she put the key in her lock and opened the door. "Come in and tell me what you're smirking about."

She took two steps into the apartment before she realized they weren't alone. She froze in terrified shock as she took in the two men standing in front of them with guns pointed directly at their heads.

"Come in and shut the door. Both of you," the uglier of the men snarled. "Don't think you will get far if you try to run. We've been watching; around here no one will care if we shoot."

Shawna nodded slowly and stepped farther into the room. She glanced over to see Robbie standing next to her glaring at the two men. "Don't do anything stupid," she whispered quietly.

"Shut the door. We've got things to discuss," the smaller man said with a sneer on his smarmy face.

"What do you want?" Robbie asked as he stepped in front of Shawna as if he was her human shield.

As much as she appreciated that, she couldn't let him get hurt trying to protect her. This was not his fight. "It's okay, Robbie. Let me handle this." She placed a gentle hand on his shoulder as she stepped around him and faced the two men.

"If this is about my mother, you're wasting your time. I don't know where she is. She isn't stupid enough to tell me that. She had to know you'd come here looking for her. As to your money, you got this month's payment, and I'll keep paying until the debt is gone."

The two men glanced at each other and rolled their eyes as if to say this woman was loco. "It's too late for that, my sweet. Your family has to be taught a lesson. No one makes us look like fools and lives to tell the tale. When she ran off with those bastard kids, she signed her own death warrant. Pay or don't, but their future has already been decided. Yours, on the other hand, is still up for discussion."

"Don't touch her," Robbie growled as he took a step forward.

"Brave man, but you know what they say about bravery, don't you? The line between bravery and stupidity is so thin that you don't know you've crossed it until you're dead."

The ugly one laughed at his friend's words. "Maybe we'll take him to help pay off their debt. What do you think?"

"What do you say, Miz Shawna? You and your friend willing to come work off your family's debts with us or will you keep paying so we don't have to come back and pay you a visit?"

"I'll pay. Just get out of here and leave me alone," Shawna demanded.

"I'm afraid it's not that easy. There's still the matter of your missing family." The ugly man walked into the kitchenette and pulled two chairs behind him as he headed into the bedroom. "Bring them and come on. We're wasting time."

Shawna trembled as the man approached with an evil gleam in his eyes that said he was enjoying this way too much. "What are you doing?" she choked out.

"Getting our answers. Let's hope for your sake you have a low tolerance for pain and this ends quickly," the smaller man said.

"No!" the ugly one called back with a laugh. "I like to watch them cry out in pain and beg for mercy. It gets me so hot to see that."

Robbie cursed as he tried to push the man away from Shawna. "I told you not to touch her."

Shawna screamed a warning, but it was too late. The pistol whipped across Robbie's face, knocking him to the floor in a blur of movement.

"Help me carry him; the stupid gringo got himself hurt." The man pointed the gun back at Shawna and gestured for her to go first. "Don't try anything or you're next."

Her thoughts were going a mile a minute. Was Robbie okay? What were the men going to do to them? Why hadn't she listened to Hawke and let him stay? He'd said he was coming back; with any luck she could hold on till he got here. He'd hear what was going on and get help. She had to believe that.

"Sit down and put your hands behind your back," the ugly man demanded as he helped drag Robbie in. "Don't move; I promise you won't like the consequences."

Shawna dropped into the chair and surveyed the room as unobtrusively as possible, looking for anything that would help her out of this nightmare. If she survived this, she'd never be vulnerable like this again. She'd take self-defense classes or carry mace or . . . Who was she kidding? None of those things would have helped against a loaded gun.

"You got him? I'll grab the rope and we can tie him up first."

Shawna turned her attention back in time to watch Ugly lean to the side and pull a coil of rope from her bed. With quick, deft movements Robbie's hands were tied behind his back and the duo were advancing on her. She tried to remember everything she'd ever heard about what to do if you got tied up, but her brain couldn't comprehend what was happening to give her a good answer. Was she supposed to flex her wrists? Like that made sense; how do you flex your wrists?

Ugly smiled as he leaned over. "You ready for some fun?"

She closed her eyes and tried not to breathe in his foul smell as he leaned back with a laugh. *Go to your happy place,* she thought frantically as she listened to the two men discussing their plan of torture and which questions to ask first in case she passed out too quickly.

CHAPTER 10

No one had ever dared to stand up to him like Shawna did. She was all fire, grit, and beautiful passion. She didn't care who he was, how much money he had, or what type of shifter he was. She wasn't giving in without a fight if she believed she was in the right. Hawke had never seen a more beautiful sight than his mate storming off, anger radiating off of her in waves. Now if she'd only listen when he was right, their life would be perfect. The danger was still here, but his stubborn, sexy-ass mate was determined to do things alone.

The ringing of his phone pulled him from his thoughts as he pushed the hands-free talk button and answered.

"Hawke, where are you?"

He tensed at the tone of Keir's voice on the phone. "A couple miles from Shawna's place. Why?"

"We filled Bess in, and she had her nephew put some people on the place. She just called because she got a report that those men were in the building. There was some communication breakdown and she was just informed fifteen minutes ago. They've been in there for a couple hours, though. We're on our way, only about five minutes away."

Hawke cursed, did an illegal U-turn, and raced back the way he'd come. Thankful that it was quiet on the streets at this hour in this neighborhood. If the men laid one finger on his mate, they were going to wish they were dead by the time he got done with them. The coroner would need a sieve to sort things out.

"Hawke, dammit, answer me, man!" Keir yelled through the car speakers. "Don't go half-cocked on us. You can't kill them. We need them alive, to shut the gang down and get her family free. Are you listening to me?"

He growled audibly. "They might already have my mate and you want me to let them live?"

"Only so you can make her happy by giving her family their freedom. I promise you can hurt them, scare them, and make them wish they were never born. But they have to be alive for questioning."

Hawke scoffed. "I can question them and relay any information they provide."

Keir groaned in response. "Listen, we are two minutes away, tops. I'm not going to ask you to wait for us, but we are asking that you try to use some caution and not get killed or kill them. Bess can have her nephew only do so much, and if there isn't anybody to take into custody . . ."

"Only because I want my mate happy will I spare their lives. And that's only if she's unharmed."

Keir sighed. "Agreed. If they've hurt her, you know we'll clean up any mess and make sure there are no bodies to be found, ever. Just make sure you get the answers we need first."

He jabbed the end button as he pulled into the garage and opened his door before he'd even put the car in park. His mate was in danger; his wolf wanted to destroy anyone who touched her. Their breaths were numbered if she even had a hangnail while in their custody. He wanted to let out a primal howl of fury at the audacity of these men. Within seconds he'd climbed the stairs to her floor and stalked down the hallway like the predator he was.

Only caution made him slow as he approached her door and listened quietly for any clue of what was happening inside. A soft thud was the only sound and it didn't tell him nearly enough. The man in him wanted to kick the door down and say to hell with it; the wolf in him was more cunning than that. He didn't have a pack at his back yet, but his friends would be here soon and that was good enough for him. It was time to take down the prey.

Hawke slowly rotated the doorknob so it would make as little noise as possible and pushed the door open an inch and waited for a cry of alarm. As the seconds ticked by without anyone coming to investigate he pushed the door open a bit farther and peeked around it. The living room and kitchen were clearly empty. That only left one logical place, Shawna's bedroom.

He made sure to leave the door cracked so that his friends could get in without detection and began his trek across the small space. His focus sharpened with each step he took and every word he heard them say.

"Let's try this again. Where is your mother?"

Shawna's defiant voice was music to his ears: "I already told you I didn't know. No matter how many times you ask, the answer isn't going to change, you half-witted buffoon."

Hawke wanted to laugh out loud at his mate's interesting insult. Yup, life was not going to be boring with her around.

"I'm going to ask you one more time. If you don't answer me, I'm going to start breaking your fingers knuckle by knuckle."

"Don't you touch her, you filthy piece of shit. You won't live to regret it if you do. Her mate will destroy you. He'll keep you alive as long as he can while causing the most pain you can imagine. You think you're badass gang members, but have you ever dealt with a shifter whose mate you're holding tied up and threatening physical harm to?"

A loud thump filled the air and then Shawna's shriek: "Robbie, are you okay? Stop; don't hit him anymore," she pleaded.

Hawke's wolf was done waiting, pack or not. His mate was in danger and they couldn't stand by any longer. He stepped purposefully into the room and leaned against the doorjamb.

"Boys, I think you have something that belongs to me."

The two men jumped and spun to face him, surprise and fear evident on their faces. That's right, fuckers; it was time to pay the piper. The taller man with the face that clearly only a mother could love raised his gun and pointed it at Hawke.

"Don't move," he snarled. "You're outnumbered and we've got your girl."

Hawke rolled his eyes and turned to look at Shawna. "They hurt you, babe? Your answer determines if they walk or get carried out of here."

The ugly man blustered, but Shawna ignored him. "No, they haven't hurt me. Just threatened to. Robbie, though, they've worked over pretty well. He kept drawing their anger to him so they wouldn't touch me."

"They get to live then. Wouldn't you agree, boys?"

"I think you're the one who's going to get hurt," the shorter of the two men growled out.

Hawke laughed sarcastically. "I wasn't talking to you two cumsickles. I was talking to them." He nodded behind the two men as he said the last words.

Ugly rolled his eyes and smirked. "Like we're stupid enough to fall for that trick. We're not amateurs."

"You might not be, but you're dealing with shifters now. We protect our own at any cost, and you forgot about the fire escape," Xander whispered from behind Ugly.

This time the two men did spin around and look behind them to see Xander and Keir standing there with giant smirks.

"You have two choices: You put your guns down and go with the nice officers waiting outside and answer all their questions or you take your chances with us. Like my brother here said, we protect our own. You took my mate; that is a death penalty in our book."

Much to his disgust, the shorter man dropped his weapon and raised his arms in the air. "My momma didn't raise no fool. I've heard about the lengths your type is willing to go for revenge."

Hawke grunted, "Well, that was anticlimactic. How about you, Ugly? What's your choice?"

Ugly glared at him with an evil smirk as he turned the gun on Shawna. "I think I'll see you in hell!" he screamed before pulling the trigger.

CHAPTER 11

Shawna squeezed her eyes shut as she heard the ugly man's words. If she was going to die, she didn't want to see it coming. The loud retort of the gun droned out all other sound. The seconds ticked by, second by agonizing second, as she waited for the pain or oblivion to overtake her. With trepidation she slowly opened her eyes and screamed as she saw Hawke and Ugly lying on the floor. There was blood everywhere.

"Hawke!" she screamed in desperation as she tried to go to him, forgetting for a minute she was still tied to the chair. "Help me," she begged as she rocked the chair from side to side in her attempts to get her arms free.

"Shawna, listen to me."

Slowly she calmed down enough to hear Xander. She focused on his face a few inches from her own.

"That's it. Come back to us. Keir is trying to untie you, but you have to stay still. He doesn't want to cut you instead of the rope," he explained over and over until finally it sank in and she stilled.

"What are you doing? Help him; *carajo,* what kind of friend are you anyway? Call an ambulance; do something," she pleaded as tears poured down her face.

"Hawke, are you done yet? He has to be alive, remember;

your woman needs you. Stop playing with your food and get over here before she gives herself a heart attack."

Shawna turned to stare in amazement as Hawke pushed himself to his feet and rushed to her side. He was covered in blood, but he didn't appear to be hurt himself. She wanted to throw herself into his arms and never let him go. Then she was going to kill him for scaring her like that.

"Babe, I'm okay. Stop crying. He didn't hurt me. It's *his* blood; he'll think twice about attempting anything like this ever again. Especially with two broken hands. It's over, babe; calm down."

As soon as her arms were free, she wrapped them around him and held on as tightly as she could. She never wanted to experience that kind of fear again. "So much blood."

Hawke grunted in agreement. "Yeah, well, he's going to be hurting for a while. I broke his nose, knocked a few teeth out, probably cracked some ribs, and I know I broke his hands. All in all, he's getting off easy for touching you."

"I heard a shot?"

Keir answered for Hawke this time. "As Ugly there turned the gun on you Hawke leaped forward and punched the guy, just as Xander knocked his hand up so the shot went into the back brick wall. The two of them went down swinging, or should I say Hawke did. The other man went where he was put. He didn't even lay a single finger on your man; I promise."

"Guys, the paramedics are here to take him away. Bess's nephew is here with his guys. They're gonna take custody of the wayward kidnappers," Xander said quietly as he nodded to the door and the people waiting there.

"Robbie?" Shawna cried out as she suddenly remembered her friend. "Is he okay?"

"I'm here, Miz Shawna. Don't worry. I'm fine. Takes more than what these two can dish out to keep me down for long."

Shawna released Hawke and rushed to Robbie's side and pulled him into a tight hug. "I can never repay you for what you did tonight. You are my hero."

"Miz Shawna, I'm just glad I was here, but if you don't mind please let me go. Your shifter is eyeing me, and after seeing what he just did to that man I don't wanna take any chances."

All three men laughed at his words. Shawna grunted but relented and pulled back from him. "Do you need a doctor?"

"No, I'll be fine," he replied with a soft smile. "Trust me, I've had worse."

"I'm sorry, but that's not going to be acceptable." They all turned to see a young man standing in the door with an apologetic frown on his handsome face. "I'm Nathaniel, Bess's nephew. Well, great-grandnephew or something like that if you want to be technical. Anywho, my point is we need you to get checked out. Pictures will need to be taken of your injuries as well."

Robbie sighed but nodded dejectedly. He turned to face Shawna. "I'm glad you're okay. Don't be getting in any more trouble while I'm gone." He looked to Hawke and nodded. "Take care of her; you don't find many like her anymore."

"Don't I know it." Hawke stared at him for a brief moment and nodded back. "Always," he whispered quietly.

Shawna glanced between the two men and frowned. "Are you guys communicating without talking? What do you mean, 'always'? Always what?"

The other four men chuckled as they filed out of the room, leaving Hawke and Shawna alone. Her frown deepened as she gazed up at him. "What am I missing?"

"He told me to take care of you or he'd come kick my ass. I replied that I would and I'd let him if I hurt you," Hawke explained as he stepped closer to Shawna to wrap her in his arms once again.

"You guys said all that with just a look? And you claim women are difficult to understand?"

She willingly let him pull her into his arms, finding comfort in the beat of his heart under her ear. She never wanted him to let go, until reality set in a few minutes later. She stiffened in his arms and pulled away. "You should let your mate know you're okay. She won't like that you're here with me like this."

Hawke groaned and pulled her to sit beside him on the bed. "It's time we had a talk, babe."

Shawna glared at him and jumped up to stand in front of him. "No, don't you dare. Let me say something first. Yes, I'm deliriously happy you're okay, and yes, I am probably in love with you. But I don't get involved with other women's men. And yes, I'm so excited that you gave me my job back and the promotion, but that doesn't change the fact that you have a mate. Don't even try to deny it. You admitted it yourself earlier."

"I'm not—" he started to say, but Shawna wasn't having any of his excuses.

"I have too much respect for myself to become the other woman. I may have more curves than a lot of men like, but I know that one day I will find one that doesn't care and in fact loves me for them."

"That's just—"

"I know I acted like a fool earlier all over you, but I can control myself. I promise not to do that again. I just hope your mate doesn't kill me for it."

"You're my—"

"So," she interrupted once again. "I'm going to say this

once and only once. I love you, Hawke Hawke, but you have to go and you can't come back."

"Excuse me, I hate to interrupt, but," Keir said with a shit-eating grin as he leaned in from the other room. "But since you aren't giving him a chance to speak, I thought I'd do my friend a solid and tell you the obvious."

Shawna scowled at him and cocked one eyebrow, waiting for him to finish and leave.

"You're his mate."

"What?" she said, not comprehending what he was saying at first. She was sure she was hearing things.

Keir smiled. "I'll speak slowly and enunciate for you. You . . . are . . . his . . . mate." With those words the former playboy winked and retreated from the room.

Shawna slowly spun back around until she was facing Hawke straight on and gaped at him in astonishment.

"It's true. I've been trying to tell you, but you listed all your reasons I had to leave; hell, I tried to tell you on the way to the benefit tonight too. As soon as I met you at that party a few months ago, I knew you were the one I'd been searching for. You were my other half, the one my heart beat for. When you snubbed me, I was shocked. No one had ever done that before. It took me months to track you down, and when I finally did it was to discover you'd been fired."

"But you went on those dates with your hired mates? You told me you'd found your mate and let me believe it was someone else?"

"I signed up for the service and was going to enter the database and make sure it matched us together. I wanted you to be my fake mate until I could convince you that you really did belong with me. But then he fired you and I used that opportunity to see if the reports were true, that he was making bad matches. It had an added benefit that it gave me more reason to get you to fill in as my fake mate when they didn't work."

"I'm your fake mate and your real mate?" she asked with a laugh. "Is this a bad time to tell you I never filled out a form and entered it in there? Your plan wouldn't have worked."

Hawke stared at her in shock. "Why in the hell not? I was sure being the creator you yourself would have been one of the first."

Shawna knew she was blushing now as she felt her face flame in embarrassment at what she was going to have to admit. "You may have only met me at that party, but I had seen you from a distance for a while. I heard about what you did for the employees and I had a crush on you. I knew no one in that system could compare to you in my mind. Once I met you, and Josie and Ally told me stories, I fell more and more in love with you. That's part of the reason I was so mad when you showed up here. I didn't want you to see what my life had come to."

"I could never be ashamed of you. You've done nothing but sacrifice to keep your family safe. You awe me, babe." Hawke grabbed Shawna and pulled her close. "You know what?"

"No, what?"

"I believe you mentioned something about the two of us and this bed earlier. . . ."

"No, our friends are still out there. I've learned my lesson about shifter hearing. I am so not doing that with them anywhere in this building."

Hawke burst into laughter at her words. "Beautiful, they left five minutes ago. They gave us our privacy, and to be honest I don't think I can wait much longer to make you mine.

My wolf and I didn't like seeing you in danger. He's pushing me hard to claim you and put our mark on you forever."

"Kiss me, Hawke." The words were barely out of her mouth when he dragged her onto his lap and their lips met in desperation. Her arms twined around his neck. Pulling him closer, she brought her chest flush to his. Heat took over every cell of her body. His kiss devoured her.

Lord, the man was a kissing god. With soft strokes of his tongue, he caressed the inside of her mouth. Whimpering in the back of her throat, she moved restlessly on his lap. The long, steel length of his cock was poking at her ass. He glided his hands under her top, making her belly flesh quiver. When his warm hands touched her skin, desire increased inside her tenfold. Breaths turned to pants. Her body thrummed with arousal. She tuned everything but the sight of him out of her mind.

She smiled. "I want you, Hawke."

Her bra was now the only barrier between her breasts and his hands. Swollen into tight points, the peaks of her nipples called for his touch under the satiny material. A combination of lust, hunger, and desperation flared in his eyes.

"Fuck, Shawna. I want you too." In a smooth move worthy of any professional stripper, her hand reached behind her back, unsnapped her bra, and pulled it off.

"Fuck me, Hawke. I want you inside me, right now. It's all I've dreamed about for weeks." His hands curled around her head and held her immobile. Raw hunger made her body shudder. Their kiss turned into a greedy need to consume each other. Moisture gathered in her pussy, and an incessant throbbing took hold between her thighs. In a frantic mating, their tongues danced, rubbed, and curled over each other until passion overrode all else. Blind lust shot through her when she rocked her hips over his hard cock.

He kissed wet trails from her jaw to her breasts until he was sucking on one of her erect nipples. Her pussy clenched when he enveloped her breast with his firm lips. Soaked in her cream, her thong became a new point of friction on her swollen pussy lips. She tore at his shirt. A wanton urgency took hold of her and guided her actions. To feel his skin on hers became her only mission.

When he helped her take the shirt off, she splayed her hands over his bulging shoulders and sighed. When his warm muscles contracted, she groaned. He was a work of art. His chest was corded with muscles and bronzed to perfection. Just looking at him made her pant. Whimpers rushed past her lips when his teeth grazed her turgid nipple.

"Oh yes. Do that again." Again he sucked and then nipped at the tight bud. She moaned and pushed her chest farther into his face. He released her nipple from his lips and rolled the wet tip between his finger and thumb, tweaking the sensitive flesh while his mouth latched onto the other one for a taste.

She dug her nails into his shoulders, holding him in her grip while rocking her hips over his cock. A smile curled her lips when she gazed into his golden eyes. He licked his lips and pulled the dress slowly up over her hips, belly, breasts, and finally off altogether.

"You take my breath away. My wolf demanded I claim you the moment I saw you. It's been hell fighting that instinct. Tonight you become mine forever." He motioned for her to stand and once she'd complied he pulled her lacy black thong down her legs, placing kisses along her thighs as he went. Afterward he kissed his way back up to her stomach. She groaned and stood in place. He licked circles on her stomach and around her belly button. He caressed her breasts, down the sides of her breasts to her waist, and squeezed the flare of her hips.

She took a choppy breath. He fluttered his fingertips down from her hips toward her core, and she bit her lip to keep from moaning. When he massaged her thighs, she was ready to beg him to touch her. Before she had a chance to, he moved a hand between her legs and dipped his fingers between her waxed pussy lips.

He groaned. "Fuck, Shawna. You're so hot and wet. Is that for me, baby?"

"God, yes. Just for you." She moaned. Each dip of his fingers into her wet sex made her whimper louder. He stood, and she had to tilt her head back to look him in the eye. His eyes were sexy, stormy. He put his arms around her waist and held her tightly to him. Their hearts beat in a furious, identical gallop. He switched their positions and pushed her to lie on the bed. Her legs ended up spread-eagled, showing off her dripping cunt. Possession filled his eyes when he glanced over her naked form.

"Fucking gorgeous. Seeing you earlier like that in bed, so wet and wanting, made me believe that good things do come to those who wait. But now this. This is heaven. This sight will be one I burn into my memory forever."

Her whimpers and moans made it hard for her to catch her breath. "Hawke, please."

Kneeling at the edge of the bed, he leaned his body between her legs. His gaze locked on her swollen folds. "I have to taste you."

She was going to explode and he probably wouldn't have to touch her. He pushed her legs wide open with his massive shoulders, and her ass came off the bed. He curled his arms around her legs and gripped her hips with his hands. Arousal flashed through her when he licked a lazy trail around her wet pussy lips. He raised his eyes to look at her and licked his lips.

"Mmm. Delicious." Harsh pants coming from her own lungs were all she heard while she watched the erotic vision of him licking at her cunt. He stroked his tongue around her entrance until she was ready to tear at her skin. After multiple quick flicks, he used his tongue to pierce her sex and fuck her.

She groaned and rocked her hips under his face. "Oh yes, yes, yes."

Moans tore from her dry throat while he circled her swollen clit with his warm, wet tongue. With her arousal worked up to an uncontrollable inferno, she clawed at the bed. He wrapped his lips on her needy clit and then brushed his tongue mercilessly over it. Her muscles tensed and shook. She screamed when she came. Her head lifted, slammed back down on the cushion, and thrashed from side to side. Pleasure thundered and washed through her. His hot, muscled flesh grazed her body when he moved up on the bed.

Their gazes met, and she smiled. Satisfaction still hummed in her veins. She curled her hands into his dark hair and pulled him up. He kissed her with hunger and passion, ramping up her desire once again. She was still shaking from coming so hard. She held her legs wide open and peered down to watch while he slid his hard cock across her dripping pussy, coating it with her juices. She grabbed his thick length and guided him to her entrance.

"Fuck, Shawna, I don't want to hurt you." The sound of his gravelly voice sent pricks of lust down to her clit. She was slick enough for him to slide his big dick in without causing pain. Her legs curled around his waist. When he glided his cock down into her pussy, she lifted her hips off the bed and helped him impale her until he was balls deep in her cunt.

"Fuck, baby," he groaned into her shoulder.

At the same time, she moaned at the amazing fullness inside her. "Oh my God."

"Goddamn. You feel fucking incredible." He pulled back and plunged in a fast thrust that fanned the flames inside her body.

"Yes, yes, yes. More!" The words left her throat in a garbled mess of pleas. She rocked her hips trying to get him to move faster. One minute he was taking his sweet time driving her crazy, and the next he turned into her very own sex machine. He fucked her with faster, harsher drives. Pummeling her pussy with his stiff cock, he had her so far gone she was ready to beg for more. The scent of sex and passion filled the humid air.

He circled his tongue over the shell of her ear and bit down on the lobe. Then he whispered in that deep voice that made her nipples tighten and her pussy flutter, "You're going to come for me. I won't stop fucking you until you do. Want me to fuck you until you come?"

"Yes, yes. I want to come. Please make me come." Digging her nails into his shoulders, she clung to him. He drilled her in harder slaps of skin on skin, and she moaned louder at the delicious friction inside her pussy. She wanted to feel his chest on hers and pulled him into her, raking his arms and back with her nails in the heat of the moment. Tension gathered inside her, heightening her need for more. She tilted her hips, and he hit her G-spot with so much force she trembled. Everything cracked inside her. Her back bowed, and she screamed his name. Air rushed out of her lungs, and bliss rushed through her. He continued to drive his cock into her body, her pussy contracting around his cock until he'd wrung every shudder out of her body.

"We're not done, babe." Shawna bit her lip in confusion as he pulled out and flipped her over. "Up on your knees, baby. I need to claim you." She shivered at the thick layer of lust that infused his words. She glanced over her shoulder to meet his eyes and saw the raw hunger he was fighting to keep in check for her sake. His wolf was close to the surface.

"I'm yours always." She'd barely finished speaking before she was impaled on his cock. Her slick channel squeezed at his shaft repeatedly. Shawna was on fire, her whole body was on fire, she wasn't sure how it was possible, but Hawke felt bigger this time. Like he'd expanded inside her somehow.

"Hold on, baby. I won't be able to last long," he panted as he began thrusting. She could feel his fingers as they dug into her hips as he pulled her back to meet him. Shawna had never felt so full in her life. Shudders began to wrack her body, stronger than before. She gasped as she felt him lean over her back, changing the angle of each thrust.

"I love you, baby," he whispered right before he sank his teeth into her shoulder and began to shake. He slowed his thrusts until he held himself immobile above her and groaned into her shoulder. His cock jerked inside her and warm semen filled her womb. With their bodies still twined tightly together, he lifted his head and kissed her, a slow, languorous stroking of his lips over hers.

EPILOGUE

"It's only your mother and brothers. You don't have to be nervous, babe!" Hawke called as he stepped into the bathroom and gave her a droll stare. "What is taking you so long?"

"Hush, now. I'm just nervous. It's been so long. I never thought I'd see them again and now they're here."

Hawke smiled and pulled her gently into his arms. "Didn't I tell you we'd find them and bring them home? It took some time, I'll admit, but it was for their safety."

Shawna nodded. "I know. And I was able to talk to them, so that helped, but it's been six months since they were rescued. So much has happened since then."

"Yes, it has. But just think: It's finally over. The trial is done, they're all going away for a long time, and your family is safe. They don't even have to hide anymore. Nathaniel pulled a lot of strings to make that happen."

Shawna smiled and pulled out of his arms. "I know, and I will be forever grateful. You and our friends have done the impossible. They have a new life thanks to all of you. I wouldn't have been able to pull any of this off."

Hawke winked. "Come on, we're late."

She rolled her eyes but let her mate pull her out of the bathroom and down the hall. She'd moved into Hawke's house the day after he'd confessed they were mates. Six months and she was still overwhelmed at the amount of space and rooms this place had. One of her greatest joys was teasing him by calling it the Hawke Manor. "House" just seemed so inadequate.

"You're fixating again, aren't you? I told you it's just a house, and in a few more weeks it won't be that quiet here anymore."

"Shhh," Shawna scolded as they turned the corner in the living room where all the guests were waiting for what she was told was a welcome home party for her family.

"Surprise!" a chorus of voices screamed at once.

"What?" she exclaimed as she took in the faces of her friends, coworkers, and acquaintances. "What's going on?"

"We're shifters, remember? We knew probably before you did!" Keir called with a wink. "Congrats, lil mama."

Shawna couldn't contain the tears as she saw her mother standing a few feet away wiping at her own cheeks. She looked tired and a bit older but healthy. "You're really here?" Shawna asked as she took a step closer, almost as if she was afraid her mom would disappear as soon as Shawna got too close.

"I'm here, baby girl. I've missed you so much," her mother replied before she rushed forward and pulled her into a tight hug. "I love you, sweetie."

Xander walked over to where Hawke was watching from his place in the doorway. "She hadn't a clue?"

Hawke smiled. "Nope, she's been too focused on the reunion to notice anything else. Everything all set?"

"You doubt me?" Xander scoffed. "Yes, it's all good. Keir gave them an apartment in the building he owns. Ally's mom, Arlene, is their neighbor, actually. It's rent-free for as long as they want to live there."

"It's true!" Keir called as he stopped beside them. "Besides, it helps me out too. Arlene could use someone close by to help out sometimes. Ally is getting exhausted; I'm about ready to tie her to the bed."

"Do you really need to tell us about your kinky sex life at my baby shower?"

Xander laughed at Hawke's dry tone. "Still think it's pretty amazing all our mates are pregnant so close to each other."

"I'd like to think you'd know how that happened, but you are shifters, so who knows if things work different with you all."

Hawke smirked as he turned to face the newcomer and offered his hand. "Robbie, it's wonderful to see you. How are you?"

"Gettin' better every day. Thanks to you all. I don't know how I'll ever repay you for all you've done for me."

"Don't thank me. You saved my mate. The least I could do was help you. Besides, you did me a favor by taking that job. Henry has been a lifesaver for Shawna. Business has skyrocketed and my employees' morale has improved by almost double everywhere."

"I kept meaning to ask, but what exactly is old Henry doing anyway to help Shawna?" Xander questioned. "I mean, when I think of Henry I really don't think matchmaking, you know."

Hawke laughed. "No, but he's got an uncanny ability to read people and get them to open up to him. Shawna has him set up to meet the new clients and welcome them. He talks to them and learns things that end up helping her tweak the clients' profiles so that they are matched right the first time. When he's not working with her, he's playing spy and reporting back to Rebecca and me anything that's going on anywhere in the organization that needs attention."

"Like last week, right?" Robbie interjected, grinning.

"Yes, exactly," Hawke replied. "Henry overheard one of the data analysts talking about how she was struggling to find a babysitter for her sick child. Henry brought it to our attention and we decided to implement a new policy. The analyst checked out a laptop and is working from home until the child can go back to school. She didn't lose her paid time off and doesn't have to put money out she may not be able to afford."

Keir looked stunned. "Can I hire Henry away? I could use someone like him."

They made small talk until Shawna made her way over with her mother in tow. Hawke wrapped his arms around his mate and winked at her. "You okay, love?"

"I am now. I've got my whole world here in this room together finally."

THE WITCH, THE WEREWOLF, AND THE WAITRESS

Kate Baxter

ACKNOWLEDGMENTS

Thanks to Kevin Courtney, for helping me in my research of all things Lowman, Idaho. Also, a huge thanks to my amazing agent, Natanya Wheeler, and everyone at NYLA, my kick-ass editor, Monique Patterson, as well as Alexandra Sehulster, and the amazing cover artists, copyeditors, and marketing team at St. Martin's Press. You guys rock!

CHAPTER 1

"I hereby call this meeting of the Lowman Liars Club to order."

The six old men at the table chortled at their weekly Sunday-morning greeting as Ellie Curtis filled their mugs with coffee. The Lowman Liars Club, as they called themselves, never missed a Sunday morning at the Sourdough, and they were hunkered down and fully prepared to whittle the morning away, laughing, arguing, and telling tall tales, until the conversation inevitably wandered to politics, which usually started a fight or two and sent everyone home.

Ellie wasn't about to complain. Sundays were usually slow and her shift at the little restaurant and general store had a tendency to crawl by on broken legs. At least the ornery old farts hanging around this morning would offer her a little entertainment. God knew she needed a distraction. Immortality could be *so* boring.

"Hey there, sweetie, can I get my cinnamon roll?"

Ellie shook herself from her reverie to find Frank Burns looking up at her expectantly. His grin was part charming octogenarian, part dirty old man. He never missed an opportunity to try to flirt with her. Though in Frank's case, he thought flirting equated to giving her antiquated nicknames like "sweetie," "toots," "honey," "girlie," "sweet cheeks" . . .

The list went on and on. Ellie had heard them all in the forties and fifties when they'd actually been popular. The patriarchy still thrived among the members of the Lowman Liars Club. She doubted they even knew what feminism was.

"I dunno, Frank." Ellie gave him a sweet smile. "I talked to Marge yesterday and she said you're not supposed to be eating too much sugar."

Frank harrumphed. "What Marge doesn't know won't hurt her," he grumbled. "Now get on to the kitchen and grab me a cinnamon roll. Extra icing."

Ellie pursed her lips and cut him a look. "You're lucky I like you, Frank." She ducked behind the counter and poked her head through the kitchen service window. "Hey, John, Frank wants his cinnamon roll. Extra icing."

John, the owner of the Sourdough and one of the fifty or so full-time residents of Lowman, Idaho, grabbed a spatula and scooped a platter-sized cinnamon roll from a large cookie sheet and slapped it on a plate. He baked them fresh every Sunday and they were Ellie's only weakness. Warm, soft, gooey, and oh, so cinnamony. And the homemade cream cheese icing was the stuff of legends. Before the day was over, she'd serve up at least a dozen of these babies. Every Sunday, Frank made sure to order the first one fresh out of the pan. If he didn't get the first one, there was always hell to pay.

"Here you go." Ellie set the plate in front of Frank. She pulled a notepad from her apron and addressed the table at large. "Okay, gentlemen, what are we having?"

One by one, the five remaining men placed their orders. Ellie didn't know why she even bothered to ask anymore. They ordered the same thing every Sunday, never deviating from their routines. If she'd been thinking, she would've had John start everyone's food beforehand so she could have it waiting on the table for them when they got there.

"You got a crush on Frank or something, Ellie?" Tom McKenzie asked. He never wasted an opportunity to give her a hard time. "Why does he get his food before the rest of us?"

"You know why, Tom," Ellie said with a grin. "If I don't give Frank that very first cinnamon roll, he'll ruin all of our day."

Her reply earned her a round of laughter from everyone at the table, including Frank.

"You've got her trained good, Frank," Tom teased.

Ellie rolled her eyes. She wasn't about to get these guys into a discussion on why it might behoove them to join the twenty-first century in regards to their attitude toward women. Instead, Ellie humored them, knowing their time on this earth was short. Human lives passed in the blink of an eye. She'd seen too many of them come and go. Their fragility earned them a pass every now and then.

Ellie busied herself around the restaurant, filling salt and pepper shakers and ketchup bottles and folding napkins around silverware while she listened to the table of elderly men ramble on about nothing and everything. The sounds of their voices became white noise in the back of her mind as her thoughts wandered. In two centuries, not much had changed. Then again, in a place as small and isolated, how could it? Very few people were interested in carving out a life in this little corner of the world. Even by Idaho standards, Lowman was nothing more than a blip. The sort of place you drove through on your way to somewhere else.

The area hadn't even been called Lowman when Ellie's family had settled here. The town got its name a little over a hundred years ago when Nathaniel Winfield Lowman breezed into the area and homesteaded here. He'd claimed discovery over an area that had been populated by both

Native American tribes and trappers and explorers for ages. But until Mr. Lowman had seen fit to set up a post office, no one had cared.

Ellie's family had settled in this area long before any of that. When the wilderness was still truly wild and those who inhabited it lived in tandem with one another and nature. It hadn't been the easiest life back then, but it had been a good life. Until a vindictive witch decided Ellie needed to be punished for something she'd had no control over, changing her life forever.

Forever. The word never used to scare her. It had always been such an intangible notion before she'd known better. Now the prospect of forever chilled her blood. It filled her with such despair that some days she didn't know how she managed to drag herself out of bed. Forever wasn't a blessing. It was a curse. One she was desperate to free herself from.

Of course, the chances of that happening were about as good as the chances she'd sprout a tail by the end of the day. Nonexistent.

"Honey, can I interrupt your daydreaming over there to get another cup of coffee?"

Ellie snapped to attention and jerked upright. The men at the table chuckled, each of them taking a turn to tease her for being a total space cadet. They meant well and all of them were harmless. Ellie forced a customer-service smile to her face and grabbed the carafe from the coffeemaker. It wasn't their fault she lived in purgatory.

"Sorry, guys." Ellie topped off each one of their cups with fresh coffee. "Your breakfasts should be up in a second."

"Good thing," Tom groused. "Frank's almost got that cinnamon roll put away."

The group shifted their sarcastic comments back to Frank, and Ellie used the opportunity to duck into the kitchen. John was busy plating everyone's breakfasts and she slipped into the pantry to take a few deep, cleansing breaths. Anxiety always got the better of her when she let her mind dwell on her situation and the adrenaline that pooled in her limbs created a fight-or-flight reaction that needed to be burned out of her system. There was no one to fight and certainly nowhere to run. Ellie was stuck here.

Literally.

For eternity.

"Yes!"

Colin Courtney pushed out his desk chair and pumped his fist. Since relocating to Stanley, Idaho, with his pack several months ago, he'd been trying to become a sentry—the supernatural world's equivalent of special forces law enforcement—with the governing body of the Sawtooth Mountains Territory, and finally he'd been accepted to join their ranks.

The supernatural world didn't subscribe to human laws. They were apart, separate, and as such, they had their own systems of government and law enforcement. Throughout the world, territories were marked off and policed by sentries assigned to each region. The Sawtooth Mountains Territory wasn't the largest in the Northwest, but it was quickly growing. Colin's pack relocating here had seemed to set off some sort of supernatural population explosion. The SMT wanted to boost the number of sentries stationed here in preparation for potential threats and issues that might crop up as a result. Since moving to Stanley, Colin had found himself with *way* too much spare time on his hands. Becoming a sentry was exactly what he needed to occupy his time.

His only obstacle in accepting the position was his alpha,

Liam. Their leader had been a high-ranking sentry once. Before they'd come to Idaho. And his experience with the supernatural organization hadn't exactly been a positive one. His tenure had left a bad taste in Liam's mouth and he'd forbidden any other members of the pack from taking up with them.

Liam might have been alpha, but Colin wasn't about to let him dictate his life. Especially since he'd sacrificed his own happiness to pack up and come to this gods-forsaken territory in the middle of fucking nowhere. Pack came first. Always. The only thing that trumped the pack was a mate bond. And in this isolated corner of the world, his chances of finding his true mate were less than slim.

"What are you celebrating?" asked Colin's brother, Owen, as he strode through the door with a wide grin on his face. "I could hear you shout all the way from the main house."

Colin closed the lid on his laptop and crossed the ten feet from his desk to his living room. The pack's living situation always made privacy a bit of an issue. But even without the pack dynamic, Owen would have walked in like he owned the place.

The pack lived on a few hundred acres of land nestled against the Sawtooth National Forest and Bench Lakes Trailhead. Liam lived in the main house a quarter mile away, while the rest of the pack lived in tiny cabins. It wasn't a bad deal, really. Colin's cabin was perfect for him and sat at the periphery of the row of other cabins. Stanley was a nice little town and the country surrounding it was breathtakingly gorgeous. Being so far from the city—any city—didn't bother him too much. That's what Amazon was for. What stuck in his craw were the endless days of boredom that stretched out before him. Colin was itching for an adventure, and so far he'd yet to find one.

"I beat Dark Souls." Colin wasn't about to tell anyone—including his brother—about the sentry position. At least not yet. "That end boss was a tough motherfucker."

Owen glanced over at the dark TV screen and the PlayStation beside it. He didn't need physical evidence to know Colin fed him a load of crap. Werewolves could smell a lie from a mile away. Owen's brows shot up and his jaw squared, but he didn't press Colin on the matter. *Thank the gods.*

"Deer season opens next week." They were predators, after all. Hunting, whether in their human or wolf forms, sort of came with the territory. "I'm making a trip into Boise tomorrow to grab some ammo and supplies. Want to come?"

Any other day, Colin would have jumped at the chance to get out of Stanley for a couple of days. But the director of the Sawtooth Mountains Territory wanted to meet with him tomorrow in Garden Valley. No way was he missing that appointment.

"Nah. Go ahead. I think I'll scout instead. Find a few good game trails before next week so we know where to start looking."

He was headed to Garden Valley, but Colin could totally do some scouting on the way home. Which made the excuse he'd given Owen truthful enough to cover his tracks. Supernatural creatures could find ways to circumvent deception being sniffed out when they needed to.

"Okay. . . ." Colin might have covered his tracks, but Owen was obviously still a little skeptical. "I've never known you to pass up a trip to the city in favor of a hike, though."

Colin shrugged a shoulder. "Maybe I'm just getting used to living out here."

"Suit yourself." Owen headed for the door. "Want me to pick you up anything while I'm in town?"

It was Owen who'd settled comfortably into his role as a

local. Referring to the city more than two hours away as "town" was about as local as you could get. "I'm good. I'll text you if I think of anything."

"All right. If you change your mind, let me know."

Colin nodded. "Will do."

The door closed behind Owen, and Colin let out a slow breath. He headed back to his desk and opened his laptop to look over the email. It would feel good to have a sense of purpose again. Not that his place in the pack wasn't important, or even . . . enough. That wasn't the point. Pack life could get complicated. Communal living had its drawbacks and complications. Tight-knit families like his had a tendency to squabble and get on one another's nerves from the constant togetherness. Especially when the togetherness spanned centuries. Colin loved the members of his pack. Would die for each and every one of them. But he wanted something that was *his.* Something separate from the pack. Something he could take pride in and excel at. He could be an amazing sentry. He just needed the chance to prove himself.

Colin hit reply and fired off a quick email, thanking Wade Robinson, the SMT director, for the opportunity and confirming he'd be in Garden Valley tomorrow morning to meet him. He'd been worried about finding an excuse to be gone all day, but Owen had inadvertently given him the perfect alibi. It wasn't like he needed a hall pass to leave the pack's property or anything, but he didn't want to have to answer any questions about where he was going and why no one else could come along. He'd of course come clean to Liam once he knew his position with the SMT was confirmed and solidified. But until then, he was keeping it a secret from his alpha.

CHAPTER 2

The week had gone by tediously slowly. Ellie couldn't believe it, but she was actually glad Sunday had managed to roll back around, bringing Frank, Tom, and the rest of the Liars Club back into the Sourdough to argue, drink coffee, and stir up trouble all morning. Of course, by lunchtime she'd be ready to get them out of her hair and send them back to their respective homes. It was pretty much their Sunday routine.

She checked the clock above the counter as she started the coffeemaker. Her Sunday regulars were nothing if not punctual, and if she didn't have their table set and ready to go by eight on the dot she'd hear about it. T-minus ten minutes and counting . . .

Frank was the first one through the door, as usual. Ellie flashed a welcoming smile as he headed straight for their usual table.

"Morning, Frank!" she called. "Coffee's ready and John says the cinnamon rolls have a few more minutes."

Frank shucked his jacket and settled into his usual seat. Ellie poured him a cup of coffee and the other members of the group began to filter into the restaurant as she set the cup in front of him. The quiet of the empty restaurant was filled with the booming voices of the complaining old men as they shucked their jackets and followed Frank's lead by settling themselves into the same chairs at the same table they'd occupied every Sunday for as long as Ellie had been working at the Sourdough, which was going on two years.

"Morning, gents!" Ellie called out.

She headed back to the counter, grabbed five more mugs, looping her thumb and fingers through the handles, and grabbed the coffeepot with her other hand. Since taking the waitressing job here, she'd become pretty adept at balancing plates and carrying more mugs/glasses/silverware at a time than her hands should logically have been able to handle. She headed back to the table, set the mugs down one by one, and filled each with coffee. Mike Pedersen cleared his throat and Ellie knew what he was going to ask before he even got the opportunity.

"Sweet'N Low and cream is on the way, Mike."

He grinned as he turned his cup so the handle pointed to the left. "I probably oughtta be worried you know me so well, Ellie."

She laughed. As regimented as these guys were, they weren't too tough to get a bead on. "A good server always knows her customers. How else am I going to get you to give me a decent tip?"

The bell above the door chimed. A short partition separated the tiny general store section of the building from the restaurant, preventing her from seeing the customer who'd just walked in. Ellie topped off the last cup of coffee at the table and returned the carafe to the coffeemaker before heading toward the front of the building to help the customer who currently wandered around in the store.

"Good morning." Ellie smiled at the woman standing near the cash register.

"Hi. My husband is trying to fill our tire with air and your compressor doesn't seem to want to turn on."

Crap. The problem with working at a place that was essentially your last stop for groceries, food, and fuel for the next fifty-plus miles was that Ellie sometimes forgot to check everything off her list of morning tasks.

"Sorry about that." She grabbed a key from next to the cash register. "I just need to turn the compressor on. We turn it off at night." She rounded the counter and headed for the door. "John!" she called toward the kitchen. "I need to run outside for a sec! I'll be right back!"

A pickup pulled into the parking lot as Ellie followed the woman out toward the gas pumps where the air compressor was located. She glanced at the truck and the man inside before turning her attention back to the woman in front of her. This Sunday was turning out to be busier than most. Ellie hoped the pace would build momentum and the day would fly by.

Ellie quickly unlocked the power box for the air compressor and turned it on. She said a quick good-bye to the woman and offered a wave to her husband, who bent to fill their tire with air as Ellie headed back into the building. No doubt Frank would be champing at the bit for his cinnamon roll. The others would be more than ready to order their breakfasts as well. Disruption of the Sunday routine was never well received.

As she headed back into the restaurant, Ellie noticed the man who'd pulled up in the pickup seated at the counter, his back turned to her and bent over a plate. She glanced at Frank, who looked absolutely appalled. *Oh boy.* She rounded the counter just in time to see the guy hunkered over the platter-sized cinnamon roll, fork in hand, prepared to dig into the soft, warm cream cheese–coated goodness.

"Stop!" Without thinking, Ellie reached out and snatched the plate away. The guy's fork bit into the Formica countertop with enough force to chip it. She spun toward the kitchen and showed the plate to John as though he hadn't just served the cinnamon roll to the guy at the counter. "This is Frank's cinnamon roll!" Ellie didn't know why it bothered her so much. "You know he gets the first one out of the pan!"

"Relax, Ellie." John looked at her like she'd lost her mind. "I've got twelve more cinnamon rolls. Number two is going to be just as good as number one." He slid a plate with another roll covered in extra icing her way. "Now give that poor guy back his breakfast."

John was the boss. The Sourdough was his and he could serve whoever he wanted, whatever he wanted. That didn't mean she had to be happy about it. With a huff of breath, she turned and slapped the plate back down in front of the cinnamon roll usurper before retrieving the second plate and stomping toward the Liars Club's table.

"I'm so sorry, Frank." As apologetic as Ellie felt, John might as well have just given away Frank's firstborn. "I had to run outside to turn on the compressor."

Frank's gentle smile and confused expression made Ellie feel even more like she was making a mountain out of a molehill. "Don't you worry about it," he said. "John's right. I shouldn't get bent out of shape about it and neither should you. I mostly just like to tease you about it. This one's going to taste just as good as the first one out of the pan."

Ellie set the plate down in front of him with a sheepish smile. She brushed off the tension that pulled her muscles taut as she retrieved a pen and her notepad from her apron pocket. "Okay, guys, what'll it be?"

The sensation of eyes on her sent a shiver of not-unpleasant anticipation down her spine as she took down everyone's orders by memory. What in the heck was wrong with her today? Either she was more hormonal than she'd thought or immortality had finally begun to take its toll. Somehow she didn't think that PMS was to blame.

Colin stared at the woman who'd just tried to steal his breakfast before angrily slapping it back down in front of him. She huffed and puffed as she stomped across the restaurant to the table of old men who'd been arguing about the sad state of the local water district when he'd come in. His wolf surged to the forefront of his psyche—unusual since the full moon was still a couple of weeks off—excited and keyed up.

Mine.

The single word echoed not only in Colin's mind but also throughout his skin, muscles, bones, and marrow. The very cells that constructed him. It was an instinctual urge he couldn't ignore or deny. The animal part of him was in charge right now. He recognized his mate on sight and wasted no time in letting Colin know the truth of it.

Well, fuck.

Wasn't it just his luck that his wolf would find them mated to a freaking psychopath? Colin's wolf gave an excited yip in the back of his mind and he willed the animal to settle the hell down. Whereas the wolf's first impression of the woman fervently apologizing for not serving the old guy at the table what was apparently a very *specific* cinnamon roll was a positive one, Colin could safely say his own first impression of her was less than glowing.

"Well, I hope you're happy with yourself."

The unreasonably angry woman in question rounded the counter and snatched the carafe of coffee from the warmer. She topped off Colin's cup as she kept her narrowed gaze on his. A quiet moment passed, and if he hadn't been so monumentally annoyed he would have acknowledged how striking she was. Dark mahogany hair, navy blue eyes with dark lashes, a pert, almost upturned nose with a splattering of charming tiny freckles. Her lips weren't full, but they were expressive. Perpetually downturned. She wasn't waif thin but curvy. Lush, with a womanly fullness that practically had Colin's wolf howling his approval. But Colin ignored all those things, instead opting to hold on to his annoyance with her abrasive attitude.

"I am." Colin shouldn't have antagonized her, but he couldn't help himself. He stabbed his fork into the gooey cinnamon roll and tore off a chunk, popping it in his mouth. He didn't bother to swallow before he spoke. "This might be the most delicious cinnamon roll I've ever eaten." He followed it up with a hearty swallow from his coffee and dug into the warm roll once again.

Every bite seemed to crank her temper up another notch. And subsequently made every bite more delectable. His wolf let out a warning growl in the recesses of his psyche, unhappy with the way Colin treated her. Well, too damned bad. Mate or not, he wasn't about to let some woman he'd just met berate him for eating a damned cinnamon roll.

"It wasn't yours," she snapped. "That was Frank's cinnamon roll."

"Ellie!" The cook's warning tone drew Colin's attention. "It's just a cinnamon roll. Frank's okay with it, so get over it."

Ellie.

The name had moxie, just like her. Colin had no idea why this cinnamon roll had her so riled up, but he could only imagine the storm she'd bring over something truly important.

"I didn't see Frank's name on it," Colin replied, totally ignoring the cook's attempt to calm Ellie down.

She opened her mouth to lay into Colin once again when the cook rang a bell at the service window and set several plates on the stainless-steel counter. "Orders up, Ellie." His warning tone indicated he wanted the subject of the cinnamon roll closed for discussion.

Ellie threw a hateful glare Colin's way before turning her back on him to retrieve the plates. He watched as she artfully balanced five plates laden with food on her arms and hands before hauling them over to the table of rowdy complainers. Her demeanor changed in an instant. Cordial, lighthearted, almost . . . flirty. Colin's wolf let out a jealous growl. Why did those crotchety old bastards get something he didn't? His preternatural hearing didn't miss a syllable of the banter exchanged, and by the time Ellie made her way back to the counter Colin's wolf was as cranky as he was.

Good. At least they were both on the same page now.

"That your fan club over there?" Colin jerked his head toward the table. The words came out a little gruffer than he'd intended.

Ellie's eyes widened a fraction of an inch before narrowing once again. "Maybe."

Colin's wolf didn't appreciate her vague answer. No one at that table could've been younger than seventy. And all but one of them wore a wedding band. Colin was almost embarrassed that he'd checked each one of their left hands when the opportunity arose.

"Is that why they get cinnamon roll preference?" He wouldn't let it go. Couldn't. His own stubborn pride refused to. It was a damned pastry for shit's sake! What was the big freaking deal? And why did that stupid chunk of baked dough on his plate prod her to treat him like a second-class citizen?

"Something like that."

Another vague answer. Colin couldn't back down from the challenge in her deep blue eyes. If she was going to push, he was going to push right back. He met her look for look and slowly dug his fork into the cinnamon roll, pulling off another healthy chunk. He swirled it around the plate to coat it in the sweet icing and popped it in his mouth, letting his eyes drift blissfully shut, as he chewed.

"Mmmm. I have to say, Frank's cinnamon roll does seem like it must taste better than all of the others."

Ellie's expression went from plain angry to enraged in a beat. She snatched the plate out from under Colin's hovering fork. "That's it. Get out!"

The cook poked his head out of the service window, his expression no longer playful but stern. "Give that man back his breakfast, Ellie. What in the hell is wrong with you? Last time I checked this was *my* place, and you don't have the right to kick anyone out of here."

Her face turned a shade of dark pink. Either from anger or embarrassment. Guilt stabbed at Colin's chest. He'd baited her. Practically dared her to take their little tiff a step further. Mostly because her anger amused him. That, and Colin had an insufferable habit of refusing to back down from a fight.

Ellie's eyes glistened as though she might cry and Colin's wolf let out a forlorn howl in the back of his mind. To hurt one's mate was a serious offense. One that required atonement. It didn't matter whether they'd only just met each other or not.

"Look, I'm sorry." Colin acknowledged the guy in the service window first and then Ellie. "This is my fault. I was giving you a hard time and I shouldn't have."

"You didn't do anything wrong," the owner replied. "Your breakfast is on the house."

"I'm sorry too, John." Colin tried not to be annoyed that Ellie apologized to her boss and not to him. "I shouldn't have let my temper get the better of me."

"Don't apologize to me," he said to Ellie. He bucked his chin in Colin's direction. "Apologize to him."

Ellie's gaze dropped and her jaw took a stubborn set. "Sorry."

Colin wrinkled his nose. She totally wasn't sorry. He could smell the lie on her. He cocked his head to one side as he continued to study her. How had he missed the spark of magic that clung to her? He'd been so preoccupied with the suddenness of the mate bond, and then her show of temper, that he hadn't even noticed. He thought her merely a woman, but could she be more? A witch, perhaps? It seemed that Colin's mate was full of surprises.

"Can we start over?" He offered her his hand. "I'm Colin Courtney. And don't apologize. Everyone has bad days."

She looked down at his hand but made no move to shake it. "Enjoy your cinnamon roll, Colin," Ellie said as she rounded the counter and headed toward the little store area. "Have a good rest of your day."

Well. So far, his relationship with his mate was off to a *stellar* start.

CHAPTER 3

The bell above the door chimed at Ellie as though it was as angry with her as everyone else. She stepped out into the cool early-morning autumn air and took several deep, cleansing breaths to slow her racing heart. Her cheeks flooded with heat and she waited for the breeze to do its job and banish the color she was certain had settled there. The sound of her pulse rushing in her ears mingled with the breeze, but it wasn't enough white noise to drown out her thoughts.

She'd absolutely lost her freaking grip in there. What was wrong with her?

Just last weekend, she'd contemplated for the millionth time the fragility of humans. Their short lives, delicate bodies, susceptibility to illness. Any day could be their last and Frank and the other members of the Liars Club were just another reminder that death was an inevitability that would soon catch up with them.

You used to be human too. Stop thinking of them like they're aliens.

Ellie banished the thought from her mind. Humans got sick. Humans died. Humans possessed free will that allowed them to do simple things like leave the boundaries of their own towns. She hadn't been able to do any of those things in a long damned time. She wasn't human. She wasn't a ghost. Truth be told, she had no idea what she was.

A freak. That's what you are, Ellie.

The bell above the door rang and she hustled around to the side of the building, unwilling to face whoever had just walked outside. She was angry and embarrassed and it would be bad enough to have to go back in and face John, Frank, and the others after her little temper tantrum. A truck door opened and slammed seconds before the loud engine growled to life. She let out a slow breath as the crunch of gravel beneath tires trailed off into the distance. If she ever saw Colin Courtney again, it would be too soon.

Ellie leaned against the log exterior of the building and took a few more minutes to calm herself down. The more she thought about it, the more she realized the worst part of the entire situation hadn't been the cinnamon roll, or the affront to Frank, or even the way Colin had managed to push her buttons. It was the way he'd strode in there and had the audacity to be so goddamned confident and good-looking.

She didn't think she'd ever seen as striking a man as Colin. Tall, every inch of him corded with thick muscle. Expressive blue eyes and hair the color of early-autumn wheat. His face could have been chiseled from stone, square jaw, sharp cheekbones, and a straight nose that made his face seem almost too symmetrical. Ellie thought men like that only existed on television and in magazines, airbrushed to perfection. For a second, she'd thought his ribbing was meant to be playful. Or flirtatious. That, of course, had set her already-heated temper on fire. She couldn't flirt back. Couldn't even entertain the idea of it. All it would get her was a heap of disappointment.

One of the many problems of being a freak of nature was

that there weren't any other freaks of nature to keep company with. Encounters with eligible men were few and far between. Most of them one-night stands that promised no possibility of anything more. Really, how could she ever have an actual relationship with anyone? There's no good time to start up a conversation with the words, *So . . . It's probably time I tell you that I'm practically indestructible and can never die. Oh, and by the way, I hope you like this tiny town, because I can't* ever *leave.*

Anyone with even a shred of sense would tuck tail and run for the hills.

Ellie pushed herself away from the building and straightened her spine. A personal pity party wouldn't make her feel better, nor would it change what had happened to her. She'd learned a long time ago that living in either the past or the future would only bring her heartache and so she stayed in the moment, attached herself to the present. It was the only way to keep her sanity intact.

She dusted her hands down the front of her shirt and apron and smoothed her palm over her hair as she rounded the building and went back inside. Frank and the others were engaged in a heated debate over whether or not the ponds near the dump would freeze over before the snow flew, and she was grateful they were too wrapped up in their own speculations to pay any attention to her. She slipped past the counter and through the swinging doors into the kitchen, where she found John doing prep work for the potential lunch crowd. Weekenders on their way back to the city from Stanley and those who owned vacation cabins in Lowman often made the Sourdough their last stop on the way home.

"John, I really am sorry." A lump formed in Ellie's throat as she swallowed her considerable pride. "I don't know what got into me. I mean, I've never lost my temper with a customer—with *anyone*—like that before."

John set his knife down on the cutting board and turned to face her. His pitiful expression only managed to make the golf ball–sized knot in her throat feel more like a goose egg. "I know. Sometimes, being out here . . . it weighs on people. You get used to a routine and having things a certain way and any disruption seems like a big deal. I get it. Maybe you should take a couple days off and go to town. Mingle with civilization."

If only. Tears stung at Ellie's eyes, but she threw her shoulders back and stuffed her stupid emotions to the soles of her feet. "Sure." There was no point in arguing or telling John that she didn't need time off. She had a feeling it wasn't a suggestion. But she wouldn't be going into the city. She wouldn't be going *anywhere.* "Thanks."

"No problem." He laid a comforting hand on her shoulder. "You okay?"

"I'm fine." She was so far from fine it wasn't even funny. "I really am sorry about the outburst."

John responded with a wink. "It's all good."

It really wasn't, though. Nothing had been good for a long damned time.

Ellie left the kitchen and went back to her station behind the counter. She busied herself with clearing Colin's empty plate, silverware, and coffee cup from the counter and wiping it down. As far as John, the guys at the table, and anyone else in Lowman was concerned, Ellie had only lived here for a little over three years. What none of them realized was that in reality she was older than the town itself. Had lived here since before it had been settled and had never left.

Over the years, she'd developed a system to keep her

existence more or less a secret in order to not raise any suspicion. She'd come out of the hills for ten or fifteen years, rejoin their little society, and get a dose of human interaction before telling everyone she was "moving." Then she'd go back into hiding, hole up in her little cabin in the woods until anyone who might have known her was no longer around—or alive—to recognize her. She'd reemerge with a new name and a new story and start the process all over again. That way, no one wondered why she never went anywhere, never aged, never got sick, never got hurt, et cetera, et cetera, et cetera. It was easier this way. And after two centuries of the same routine, she was starting to get used to it.

Until Colin Courtney walked through the door and reminded her of all the things she wanted and would never have.

Damn him.

Colin hadn't wanted to leave the Sourdough, but he had an appointment to keep and he wasn't about to miss it. The drive to Garden Valley passed in a blur as his tires ate up the miles of winding highway through the steep canyon of Highway 21. His brain was too full of Ellie to think about anything else. Not his appointment, his excitement at becoming a sentry, or his own worries over how his alpha would react when he found out. No, the only thing on Colin's mind was Ellie's haunting beauty and the way she'd claimed his wolf with nothing more than an angry frown and a few shouted words. She was definitely one of a kind, and she'd made it pretty damned clear exactly how she felt about Colin.

Problematic considering what she was to him.

Colin's wolf let out a forlorn howl in the back of his mind.

The animal was loath to leave his mate behind. The animal didn't give a shit that she'd obviously rather sit through a double root canal than spend time with them. The animal didn't care that Colin had obligations and appointments that needed to be kept. The animal had only one fuck to give and that was for his mate.

The mate bond trumped everything. Including familial obligations. Including pack obligations. It was the most sacred of bonds. Once a wolf chose its mate the only thing that could break the connection was death. There was a reason why werewolf mates died in pairs. One couldn't live without the other. If anything were to happen to Ellie—a virtual stranger—Colin's wolf would never recover from the loss. It would slowly drive him mad until the other members of his pack had no choice but to put him down. Even now, the animal urged Colin to turn his truck around and race back to her.

Sorry, buddy, that's not going to happen.

Colin rolled into Garden Valley, a town not much bigger than Stanley and about thirty miles from Lowman. The area was a major hotspot for second homeowners thanks to its generally mild winters, early springs, and gorgeous scenery. Colin always marveled at the difference a few thousand feet in elevation could make. He'd come to love Stanley in the months since they'd settled there. Loved the Sawtooths, Redfish Lake, and the surrounding territory that the pack hunted every full moon. But there were times, the previous winter specifically, when he wished that Liam had chosen to relocate the pack to Garden Valley instead.

He'd likely be making regular trips to Garden Valley now that he'd been accepted into the sentry's ranks.

Colin pulled into a parking spot at the Boise National Forest substation and killed the engine. Wade Robinson, the territory's director, worked a day job with the Forest Service, which gave him an in with the human goings-on in the wilderness areas so many supernatural creatures called home. Colin wondered how he managed to juggle both jobs. Did he never sleep?

The offices were closed for regular business on Sunday, which was why Wade had chosen today to meet. Apparently, regular office hours for the SMT were whenever his human job was done for the day/weekend/whatever.

"Hi, Colin." Wade greeted him at the door with a friendly smile. "Thanks for driving down today. Come on in."

Colin followed Wade into the building. Tall and sleek, Wade's human form was very reminiscent of his animal form. He was one of a handful of mountain lion shifters in the territory and had a reputation for being pretty damned formidable when he had to be. Colin had to admit he was a little envious of the male. Werewolves were different from shifters in that the way to become a werewolf was to be bitten by one. Not so for shifters. They were born dual natured. Some weird mystical process didn't invasively insert another consciousness into their brains and bodies. And unlike werewolves, a shifter could transition from one form to another with ease no matter the time of the month. Completely painless. The transition for a werewolf was incredibly painful and avoided at times other than the full moon. *Lucky bastard.*

"Have a seat."

Colin settled into the chair opposite Wade's desk. His stomach muscles tightened with anxious anticipation. He was about to be assigned to his dream job and his wolf had claimed a mate. So far, today was turning out to be pretty damned epic.

Wade fixed Colin with a serious stare. "I have to say, I was pretty surprised to get your application considering how your alpha feels about the sentry."

Colin figured Liam's opinion of the sentry would come up, though he hadn't expected it quite so early in the conversation. He guessed it was best to get it out of the way sooner rather than later, though.

"Honestly?" There was no way to sugarcoat this. "Liam doesn't know I applied. I haven't told him yet."

Wade leaned back in his chair. His lips pursed as he considered Colin. "I'd like to move forward having a solid relationship with the pack. I can't say this is the way that's going to happen."

Colin had hoped his keeping his application from Liam wasn't going to be as big a deal as it apparently was. It wasn't as though he'd planned to keep it a secret forever. There were no secrets in the pack. But he'd wanted his position to be solidified before he went to Liam with the news.

"I understand that and I totally agree." Colin would be damned if he wasn't 100 percent the professional. "Of course Liam will be made aware of the situation. As soon as I get back to Stanley. I wanted to wait until after our meeting so I had all my ducks in a row when I talked to him."

Wade nodded. "I get that. You're more than qualified for the position I need you for and I'd hate to lose you before you even get settled in because of Liam's bias."

Colin smiled. Gods, it felt good to know he was going to make a difference. That he was valuable. "It sounds like the Sawtooth Mountains Territory is light on sentry enforcement."

Wade let out a chuff of laughter. "The entirety of the Boise National Forest is light on sentry enforcement. It's such a sparsely populated area for both humans and supernaturals alike. No one wants to be stationed out here. Especially those who have established packs somewhere else. But this area is attractive to rogues and troublemakers. It's the perfect place to hide out and stir up trouble. This area isn't nicknamed The Badlands for no reason. It's got a growing reputation as being someplace where anyone can get away with anything. I want to squash that rumor—and the reality it's creating—for good."

Which was exactly why Colin wanted to work as a sentry in the first place. It was also a position that could be potentially dangerous under certain situations. Which would be the main bump in the road as far as Liam was concerned. He'd been a high-ranking member of the sentry once, and one of his missions had gone south, causing the death of an innocent shifter whose brother later nearly killed Liam and his mate in the name of vengeance. His worries were totally founded, but that didn't mean Colin wasn't going to be a stubborn son of a bitch until his alpha saw things his way. Colin wanted this job. Period.

"I'm up for the challenge and I'm ready for this assignment," Colin said. "Liam isn't going to be a problem. He'll be concerned, but I know he'll see things my way once I talk to him. I'm anxious to get to work."

"Good." Wade rested his arms on the desk. "We need a dozen more like you, Colin. We're glad to have you come aboard."

In the span of a couple of days, Colin had everything he'd ever wanted. A family. A pack. And now a purpose, and a mate. Life couldn't get any better. So why couldn't he quell the sense of foreboding that intruded on his happiness?

CHAPTER 4

Colin left his meeting with Wade riding a high of optimism. His moment of nervous anxiety was long forgotten as he parked his truck along the Kirkham trail, ready to do a little scouting and track some game. He hadn't intended to scout so far from Stanley, but Wade had let him know that the deer had been hanging out close to the ridges at the top of the trail and Colin was anxious to see for himself. A sure thing was better than chasing his tail closer to home any day of the week.

Besides, when he was done Colin planned on stopping by the Sourdough. He needed to make peace with his mate and start them off on the right foot before his wolf intervened. Unfortunately, the animal part of him wasn't half as diplomatic.

Bright autumn colors painted the brush and trees that dotted the hillside. Fiery reds, bright oranges and yellows. Muted browns and golds. The previous winter had been hard, which saturated the mountains with plenty of groundwater to sustain the land throughout the summer heat. The grass didn't crunch beneath Colin's feet as it had last year. A good sign. Game would be easier to track when the grass and underbrush didn't give away his presence.

Thanks to his preternatural senses, Colin had one up on

the animals he tracked. The sound of the wind, of every blade of grass that stirred, was intensified so he recognized even the tiniest shift of motion or bending branch. He continued to hike upward, searching for a vantage point to scan the lower hillsides and valley below. He didn't need binoculars thanks to his keen eyesight. Aside from a light daypack with water and a couple of snacks, Colin didn't need anything else in the way of gear.

The Kirkham trail was popular with hikers. From the top of the ridge, the trail wound downward for five or six miles and ended up near the hot springs, which was one of Lowman's main tourist draws. Colin had stopped at the hot springs once last winter with his brother, Owen, and Owen's mate, Mia. But being the third wheel was never fun and Colin hadn't found the soak in the geothermal waters all that relaxing.

Maybe now that he was mated and no longer a tagalong, he'd find a reason to go back there.

Colin's mind wandered to Ellie as he continued to hike. The wonders of the mate bond were as sudden as they were unfathomable. He didn't know anything about her other than her first name and that she coveted Frank's Sunday-morning cinnamon roll with a ferocity that rivaled that of the wildest of wolves. Magic clung to her, although Colin had been certain she was human. A curiosity he planned to get to the bottom of ASAP. Her heritage could be considered problematic but not insurmountable. His alpha, Liam's, mate had been human and she'd become a werewolf soon after their mate bond was established. If Ellie was, in fact, human, a simple bite would ensure that she would be stronger, infallible to human sickness and injuries. She'd be practically immortal like Colin.

He could ease her into the idea. Give her all of the facts

and let her come to the conclusion on her own that becoming a werewolf was the best course of action. That is, if he could get that hot temper of hers to cool long enough for her to hear him out. Even then, the chances of her believing him were slim to none. Hell, Colin hadn't believed in things like werewolves either until he'd been bitten by one. To say there was a bit of an adjustment period after learning creatures you only thought existed in myth actually walked the earth was an understatement.

His mind turned even deeper inward as he continued to hike. He found himself greedy for information about Ellie. How did she end up in Lowman of all places? How long had she worked at the Sourdough? What did she do for fun around here? What sort of music did she like and what were her favorite books and TV shows? Did she have a favorite flavor of ice cream? What was her go-to comfort food? Were her lips as soft and inviting as they looked? And how would she react if Colin leaned in and put his mouth to hers to find out for himself?

His wolf grew anxious in his mind, no longer interested in stalking prey and more than ready to get back to their mate. It further divided Colin's already half-assed focus. Not good. Especially when the pack was counting on him to scout good hunting grounds. He could think about Ellie later. When this part of his responsibilities had been fulfilled. Right now, he needed to get his overactive mind—and his wolf's overactive mind—off of her and back onto the game trail.

The path began to narrow the higher uphill Colin walked. His balance was better than a human's, and he was infinitely more surefooted. It was easy for him to track game in places a human couldn't get to. The narrow trail didn't bother him. Neither did the steep drop to his right. It wouldn't bother the deer either. They'd be hanging out in terrain like this, without a doubt.

Colin took a step and the trail gave way without warning. The ground fell out from under his feet and there was nothing he could do to stop himself from falling backward. Not even superior werewolf instinct and reflexes could save him when there was nothing but air beneath him and to either side of him. Gravity affected even supernatural creatures and Colin could do nothing but bow to its will and fall.

The sheer cliff face offered him nothing to gain footing on and the lack of foliage on this side of the mountain gave him nothing to grab on to. He tumbled ass over teakettle down the steep embankment, arms and legs flailing like a rag doll. Over rocks, tree stumps, and the hard dirt. His body felt as though it had been run through a meat tenderizer as bones broke, muscles bruised, and his body contorted in ways that no human would have rebounded from.

Colin grunted as a rib snapped and he reached for a clump of grass with a hand that refused to work after the bones in his forearm shattered. Pain exploded through every nerve ending in his body as his wolf let out a howl in the back of his mind. The fall wouldn't likely kill them, but it would sure as hell fuck them up.

He continued to roll, tumble, flip, and fall for what felt like forever. There wasn't an inch of his body that wasn't broken or battered to shit. The hillside began to taper and then level off, which meant his wild ride was about to come to an end. He would have let out a sigh of relief if he weren't worried about his broken rib puncturing his lung in the process.

One last flip toppled Colin's body over itself and he landed hard on his spine. The back of his head hit a large rock and the sickening *pop* of the impact nearly made his stomach heave. Stars swam in his vision as darkness encroached at the periphery. He was going to pass the fuck out and there wasn't a damn thing he could do to stop it.

Colin only hoped his supernatural healing would kick into high gear and get him back on his feet before some hungry cougar or bear came along to finish what the mountain hadn't managed to do.

Damn it. His day had been going so well. . . .

So far, the first of her two days off alone with her thoughts definitely hadn't done Ellie any good. Rather than clear her mind, she'd spent too much time overthinking every little detail of her existence to death.

Existence, because she absolutely didn't have a life.

When she'd left the house this morning, Ellie had thought a hike might do her some good. It had been a while since she'd gone out and worked her muscles, and she'd yet to get out and really enjoy the autumn colors. For as much as this stretch of land felt like a prison, its beauty had always captivated her. Left her breathless at times and made her feel small and insignificant at others. It wasn't the wild beauty of this place that hadn't changed much over the course of a few hundred years that saddened her. It was her own inability to break from the land and her own body that, like the land, hadn't changed with the passing of so much time.

Ellie had always considered the land surrounding Lowman as such a lonely, isolated place. It was a mirror image of her own loneliness and isolation. Unchanging. Inescapable. Bleak. Hopeless . . . *Snap out of it!* She gave a shake of her head as though to dislodge the depressing thoughts. Today was supposed to be about banishing those dark emotions, not wallowing in them.

A low groan drew Ellie's attention and her heart leaped

up into her throat. It wasn't uncommon to come across animals on the trail. Deer, elk, the occasional raccoon or chukar. Predators were a little rarer, though she'd seen a cougar once and heard the wolves howl. This wasn't a predator's growl, however. Or the grunt of a buck or bull elk. The sound was all too human for Ellie's peace of mind and it wasn't a pleasant sound by any stretch of the imagination.

She turned toward the rustle of brush to her left and caught sight of an arm jutting out from the crisp yellow leaves. A gasp lodged in her throat as she ran toward the still body sprawled out on the ground. Ellie paid no mind to her own safety. Didn't even wonder why anyone would be out in the middle of nowhere, passed out on the ground. Whoever he was, he needed help. And Ellie would do whatever she could to make sure he got it.

Her chin dropped as she stepped over a fallen tree, wound her way through the sage, dried weeds, and grass, to set eyes on the nearly unconscious man tangled in the brush.

"C-Colin?"

His name caught on her lips, awkward and yet so familiar. Ellie dropped to her knees beside him. Her breath raced in her chest and her heart slammed against her rib cage to pump the blood through her veins. Adrenaline dumped into her system, causing her limbs to quake.

"Hey." Her voice sounded small, fearful, in her ears. "Can you hear me?"

He appeared relatively unscathed. *Weird.* Dried blood and dirt crusted his skin and his clothes were torn as though he'd taken quite a fall. His chest rose and fell with slow breaths and Ellie's gaze ventured upward, to the sheer cliff face of the mountain. Had he fallen from there? If so, he should've been dead, or at the very least battered and broken to a pulp.

"Colin?" She gave his shoulder a gentle squeeze and she

marveled as the muscle flexed beneath her grip. The guy was absolutely cut from stone.

His eyes flew open and Ellie stifled a gasp. An otherworldly gold light blazed behind his irises, lending him a wild, feral quality that made him seem more animal than man. She jerked backward, blinked, and leaned in only to find the gold light gone and his eyes once again blue. Tamer. Though much less lucid. Had she imagined what she'd seen? If so, he wasn't the only one in trouble.

"It's Ellie." She brushed the hair away from his brow, wondering at her own tenderness. "Do you remember me? We met yesterday at the Sourdough."

Had it really only been yesterday? It felt more like a year ago. Colin studied her for a quiet moment and his gaze cleared of the confusion that had glazed over his beautiful blue eyes. He brought his arm up and cupped the back of Ellie's neck with his palm. His lips moved and his voice rasped in his throat as he uttered a single word. "Mine."

Mine? His what? Ellie's brow furrowed. Had he been up here with someone? A wife or girlfriend, maybe? A friend or even a child? What—or who—was he looking for? "Are you missing something, Colin? Someone? Can you tell me what happened?"

Without warning, he pulled her down and put his mouth to hers. Ellie was too shocked, too off balance, to do anything but fall headlong into the kiss. Colin's mouth was soft yet insistent as it moved over hers. Warm, wet, conveying a passion Ellie couldn't fathom or understand. His hand on her neck went limp and fell away as his mouth went slack. She pulled away, confused, only to find him unconscious. Out like a freaking light.

She didn't know if she should take it as a compliment or an insult.

Ellie had no car, no phone, no way to move what she assumed was a mass of muscle that couldn't weigh less than two hundred pounds. She might have been immortal, but that's where her freakiness ended. She'd kill for a little superhuman strength right about now. Without help—a truck, four-wheeler, extra bodies, a *crane*—she had no idea how she was going to get Colin out of here.

"Colin!" Ellie shook him by the shoulder. "You've got to wake up."

He didn't budge. Ellie cringed as her hand flew out and delivered a slap to his cheek. Apparently, today was for doing all sorts of unexpected shit. He let out a groan and he stirred. A good sign. Maybe a couple more slaps to the face and she could get him up and walking.

"Colin!" She slapped him again. Harder. "I can't carry you, so you need to get the hell up!" She had no idea if she was helping or hurting. At this point, she didn't know if it even mattered. His eyes came slowly open, once again alight with something she could neither identify nor understand. She had a feeling whatever it was, she'd managed to piss it off. Were they sitting over some sort of natural gas vent that caused her to hallucinate or what?

He pushed up from the ground, much too quickly for someone who'd managed to survive a life-threatening fall. Ellie scrambled to her feet, reaching out to steady him as he swayed and stumbled to his right. He was upright, at least. Progress.

"Hang on. I've got you." Okay, so maybe that was a bit of an overstatement. Ellie's knees nearly buckled under the bulk of his weight. Two hundred pounds? More like two-fifty. She propped her shoulder under his right arm and gripped his wrist. He hadn't managed to speak a single word since passing out, which made her worry that maybe he had a concussion. The nearest hospital was a couple hours away. She could call the ambulance and have a Life Flight helicopter airlift him to the city faster, but none of that would happen until she got back to her cabin and a phone.

"I know you're not doing all that hot, but do you think you can walk? My cabin is about a mile and a half downhill from here. I definitely can't carry you, because honestly, I think you weigh as much as a bull elk, but I can help you if you promise to stay on your feet."

Colin leaned against her and buried his face against her hair. "Mmmine."

Oh shit. She'd almost forgotten. "Colin? Is there anyone else up here with you? A person? Pet? I don't want to leave anyone or anything up here."

"No." She was thankful he was upright and talking. Even if it was only monosyllabic words. "Just. Me."

"Good to know. Okay." She hitched her hip against his leg for extra support. "This is going to be slow going, so let's get a move on."

Mine. Ellie wasn't sure why the simple word gave her pause. Maybe it was the emphatic way Colin had said it. She sure as heck hoped she wasn't getting herself into trouble by being in the wrong place at the wrong time.

Because for once, she really wanted to be in the right place at the right time.

CHAPTER 5

It was far enough from the full moon that Colin's body didn't want to heal as quickly as it usually did. It hadn't helped that he'd rolled for nearly a mile without stopping, breaking every bone in his body, sustaining multiple cuts and contusions, before smashing the back of his skull on a chunk of granite. No one—not even a werewolf—healed from that shit in an instant.

He'd been tangled in the brush for twenty-four hours, exhausted, hurting, and forced to lie there while the preternatural force that lived within him healed every tiny square inch of him from his toes upward. Thank the gods he'd been unconscious for most of it. The first few hours had been excruciating. Colin might have lain tangled up in that fucking brush for another twelve hours if Ellie hadn't come along. His mate had awoken the wolf first.

In times of distress it was common for the wolf to occupy the forefront of their shared consciousness in order to protect the human part of their dual nature. All it had taken was Ellie's scent, her voice, her gentle presence, to wake the wolf. But no matter how much the overanxious bastard wanted to get up and tackle their mate to the ground so he could run his nose along her fragrant skin, it wasn't going to happen when their shared body wasn't ready to cooperate.

It would have been lights-out for a few more hours if Ellie hadn't gotten frustrated and decided to go slap happy. Whereas it had amused Colin, the wolf hadn't found her hard-core slaps half as entertaining. Her tactic had gotten the job done, though. It had roused the wolf enough to get Colin up on his feet. His head still pounded like a motherfucker and his footing was as sure as if he were standing on a boat deck in a storm. He just needed a few more hours. A little more rest to get him back to 100 percent. Easier said than done with his mate within such close proximity. She was a beautiful distraction who could tempt a male from the grave.

She sort of already had, hadn't she?

His body might not have wanted to cooperate, but with every step Colin's mind sharpened. What bothered him more than his sorry physical state was that his second impression on Ellie couldn't have been much better than the first. He was a werewolf for fuck's sake. Vicious. Powerful. Strong. Practically immortal and more than capable of protecting what belonged to him. The male Ellie had come upon on the hillside was none of that. The blow to his pride was far worse than any other injury he'd sustained in the past day.

Colin was going to have to do some serious damage control. Once he could actually stand on his own two feet.

"You're doing great, Colin. My cabin is just over this next ridge."

He swallowed down a groan. Yep, he was the epitome of male power and strength. The last one hundred yards of the mile-and-a-half walk were by far the hardest. Not because Colin was weak. On the contrary, he healed more and more with every step. Rather, it was the knowledge that once he was at full strength he'd be alone with Ellie. In her house. All he could think of was kissing her again.

"We can call an ambulance once we get inside."

"No." Finally, Colin found his voice. "No ambulance. Just need to rest."

"Are you kidding?" Ellie paused to look up at him. The concern in her expression caused Colin's chest to swell. "Did you see the cliff face you fell down? It's a wonder you're alive. You've got to have a broken bone or two."

Try two hundred and six. Most of the broken bones had healed. Colin's ribs were still a little tender and his right wrist tilted at an odd angle. A few more hours and he'd be right as rain. The last thing he needed was for Ellie to call an ambulance and get a bunch of know-nothing human doctors involved.

"Not as bad as you think." Taking a deep enough breath to talk hurt like a bitch thanks to the broken rib that had yet to heal. Colin hated that it made him sound like a gods-damned caveman. "Really. I'll be fine."

Ellie let out a disbelieving snort. "You sure seem fine."

Colin didn't have the energy to argue with her. But he'd be damned if he let her call an ambulance or anyone else. "Believe me, I've been worse."

Ellie turned to stare at him once again and took a stumbling step that jostled her shoulder into Colin's ribs. He let out a grunt of pain and she cringed. "Sorry. I'm sorry. I didn't mean to hurt you. I just . . . You've been *worse*? What sort of life are you living?"

Colin wanted to laugh, but he knew it would hurt like a son of a bitch. Ellie would find out soon enough exactly what sort of life he was living. "Wild and free, honey."

Ellie laughed. The sound was music to Colin's ears. It warmed him from the inside out and his wolf practically purred with contentment in the recess of his psyche. "Wild and free, huh? Sounds like a recipe for danger."

Could it be that maybe they were finally getting off on the right foot? Colin sure as hell hoped so. "Obviously. Since you're practically packing me down the mountain right now."

"No offense," Ellie said with a laugh. "But you are *heavy.* I couldn't carry you if I tried. Call me a crutch, because that's literally all I am."

Thanks to their sheer muscle mass, werewolves were denser and thereby heavier than humans and even some supernatural creatures. Ellie was stronger and sturdier than she gave herself credit for. Without her help, he'd still be lying in that damned bush with its prickly branches poking him in the back.

"What do you do for a living?" Ellie seemed almost embarrassed to ask the question. "Are you like a personal trainer or something?"

"Law enforcement." It was close enough to the truth, though probably not what Ellie's idea of law enforcement would be. He was thrilled she'd kept the conversation going. That she was curious about him. Wanted to know more about him.

"For Boise County?" Ellie glanced up at him from the corner of her eye.

It was impossible for a werewolf to lie to its mate. "No. I'm more of a freelance, special forces type of law enforcement." Yeah, that might've been the most transparently bullshit answer Colin had ever given anyone. But telling her the whole truth wasn't an option, yet.

"Hmmm." Ellie kept her pace slow as they walked. Her cabin came into view, a rustic log structure that fit perfectly with its surroundings. "No offense, but that answer was a little vague."

Colin smiled down at her. "It was meant to be."

Ellie's brow furrowed and her lips quirked in a half grin.

She obviously didn't know what to make of his honesty and he wasn't about to give her any more information than he already had. At least not until he could set her down and explain their situation to her.

"You're sort of a mysterious guy, you know that?"

"No one's ever called me mysterious before," Colin said with a laugh. "But I'm gonna take it as a compliment."

From the corner of his eye, he noticed Ellie's grin widen. "You go ahead and take it however you like."

Well, shit. It definitely *hadn't* been a compliment.

Ellie didn't know what to think of Colin. Her first impression had been that he was nothing more than a cinnamon roll–stealing, mouthy jerk. Intentionally antagonistic. Inherently annoying. Of course he was at a disadvantage right now, probably concussed, and definitely dehydrated, but he seemed almost . . . tolerable. Friendly. Charming and even a little funny. Right now, he was the sort of guy Ellie might find herself interested in. There was no denying Colin was an attractive man, but she'd always needed more than good looks. She wanted to be attracted to someone's personality. His heart. His soul.

Stop it, Ellie. This is a dead-end road.

It didn't matter what she thought about Colin, because he would never be anything more than the guy who'd pissed her off and the guy she later had to help down the mountain. He was someone she'd met in passing and would likely never see again. And that was probably for the best. Because even if she wanted it, there could never be anything between them.

Ellie was destined to be alone.

A pang of regret tugged at her chest the closer they got to

the house. She'd call an ambulance for Colin and it would likely be the last time she ever saw him. She found herself wanting a few more minutes with him. Wanting to know any small detail about him. She hadn't been kidding when she'd called him mysterious. He had an odd way of guarding personal details about himself, keeping everything nice and vague. Ellie knew that game. She played it well. Had been playing it for the past two centuries. She'd never met anyone as good at it as her, though. Which made him even more interesting. Her curiosity burned.

They walked on a gravel path that skirted the modest garden at the back of the house. Everything had already been picked and preserved for the winter, leaving nothing but the empty raised beds and the churned-up earth. They stopped at the back door and Ellie reached out to ease it open. Colin was so tall he practically had to duck to get inside. His sheer size astounded her and he seemed so much bigger once inside the cabin.

"Let's get you to the couch. I'm sure you're thirsty too."

Colin didn't argue as they negotiated their way through Ellie's modest kitchen into the living room. She eased him down on the couch and let out a breath as she straightened and stretched her spine. She might've merely been steadying him for the mile-and-a-half walk downhill, but man, that much muscle was *heavy*.

"Don't move." Colin's brow furrowed at the order and he gave her a lopsided grin. Ellie swallowed down a groan. Where was he going to go? He could barely walk. "Um, yeah, I mean just relax. I'm going to get you some water."

She had no idea what had her so off her game. It could've been the intensity of his eyes, the strange golden glow she could've sworn she'd seen in their depths, his charming smile, the deep rumble of his voice, his imposing size and presence, or any of a few dozen other things. Once again, Ellie considered that he might have a girlfriend or be married. He wasn't wearing a ring, but that didn't mean anything. And if he was, in fact, single, there had to be something wrong with him. Only a fatal flaw would keep women away from that kind of perfection.

Ellie grabbed a glass from the cupboard and filled it with water from the tap. She grabbed the cordless phone from the cradle and headed back into the living room, handing the glass to Colin before she settled into the chair beside him. He chugged the glass of water in less than five seconds, making Ellie think he'd been on the hillside a lot longer than she'd initially thought. She stood and took the glass from his hand. "Be right back."

She went back into the living room and handed him the refilled glass. He drank this one a little slower, which was a good sign. Ellie studied his deep blue eyes, searching for any trace of the strange gold she'd seen there. It could've been a play of sunlight, but somehow she doubted it. Which meant she was probably just losing her damned mind.

"Okay." She reached for the phone she'd set on the end table. "Let's talk about that ambulance."

Colin leaned forward and plucked the phone from her grasp. "I told you, I don't need an ambulance. Just rest."

One thing was certain: The man was stubborn. Ellie's jaw clamped down and she let out a huff of breath. "You absolutely need an ambulance. And the nearest hospital is two hours away. If I call an ambulance, the EMTs can ask for Life Flight. You need a doctor to check you out, Colin."

He flashed a sardonic smile that sent a thrill through Ellie's core. *Do* not *fall for it. You are* not *allowed to lust after him.*

"If I didn't know any better I'd think you were concerned."

Ellie cleared her throat. "No. Well, yes. I mean, I'm not a monster. Of course I don't want you to be hurt." What was it about this man that flustered her so? Why did his very presence set her on edge with the promise of something she couldn't quite identify and yet knew she would never have? Ellie rubbed at her chest, as though she could somehow banish the pain that had settled there. The past few days, she'd been unable to stop feeling sorry for herself. The endless days, months, years, decades, and so on had finally begun to wear on her. The appearance of this new, beautiful, interesting person in her life only added to her distress.

"Ellie? Are you okay? What's the matter?"

She looked up to find Colin studying her, his expression intense. She hated that this perfect stranger could read her so easily, and she straightened in her chair as she forced a pleasant expression to her face. "I'm fine. You're the one who's not okay. You need to see a doctor. I'm sure you need X-rays and who knows what else."

Colin brought the glass to his lips and finished off the rest of his water. His eyes bored into hers, and behind those blue depths Ellie saw something much too intimate for having only met him. It should have frightened her, but all that gaze managed to do was draw her in.

"I don't need X-rays." His voice was as smooth and decadent as rich dark chocolate. "I don't need a doctor. I don't need stitches, braces, casts, or anything else. I don't need an MRI. I don't even need a physical. So I definitely don't need an ambulance, and I absolutely don't need Life Flight."

He wasn't trying to start an argument or even antagonize her. In his tone, Ellie sensed he was trying to convey something to her. Something he desperately needed her to understand. "You just need rest." She finished his train of thought, her own words barely a whisper.

"That's right." His voice went low to match hers. "And maybe another glass of water."

Ellie hustled to the kitchen, grateful for a reason to put a little distance between them, and refilled his glass. Her stomach tied in knots and her limbs quaked. She'd never met anyone who had such an instant and visceral effect on her. She didn't know how to act, how to react. She was in uncharted territory and as nervous as a fawn waiting in the brush for its mama. She went back to the living room and held out the glass. Colin reached out and took it from her, brushing his fingertips along hers in the process. Their eyes met and once again she caught a glint of gold.

She had no idea what was going on, but she had a feeling this man would be her undoing.

CHAPTER 6

Colin's wolf scratched at the back of his psyche like the bastard was trying to break out. The animal was anxious, excited, and impatient. The animal wanted Ellie to know what she was to them, how vital and important she was to their very existence. The damn animal didn't care that she was human. Or, at the very least, close to human. That she'd think Colin's words were the ravings of someone with a concussion who needed to go to the hospital. He needed the animal to calm down. He needed his wolf to focus on healing and not on Ellie. Colin could hardly blame his wolf for being focused on her, though. He even found it difficult to pay attention to anything else.

The moment his fingers brushed against hers, electricity arced between them. Colin's stomach twisted and turned, tying itself into an unyielding knot. The sudden lust that surged through him nearly shocked his system. His cock jumped to attention, almost as annoying as his damned wolf, ready and willing to take their superficial relationship to a more intimate level.

His body turned traitor to ally with the wolf. *Great.*

"Thanks." Colin cleared his throat as he brought the glass to his lips. The walls seemed to close in around them as he broke out into a sweat. He needed to calm the hell down. But most important, Ellie needed to quit looking at him with such intense interest. Because right now, both his wolf and his body were making a good case for why he should throw caution to the wind.

"Is there anything I can do to convince you to go to the hospital?"

Colin smiled. "No. But I appreciate your concern."

A light blush painted Ellie's cheeks and she looked away. He found her sudden modesty a little charming. Especially because he'd already seen her fire and knew she was anything but quiet and demure.

"Okay." Ellie didn't sound happy, but at least she wasn't going to argue further with him about it. "Is there anyone I can call for you, then? Or maybe someone you want to call yourself? To come pick you up?"

Was she already trying to get rid of him? Colin wasn't close to being ready to leave. "No. I don't need to call anyone. And my truck is parked at the trailhead. If you want, you can give me a ride up there, or I can always hike back up."

"Of course I can give you a ride," Ellie said. "But you probably shouldn't be driving. How far to your house?"

Colin took a drink of water. "Stanley."

Ellie's expression turned sad and he wondered at the change. "Oh. Stanley. Probably why I've never seen you around."

Stanley was only fifty or so miles from Lowman, but it was true that Colin rarely ventured past their home base. Now that he'd been hired as a sentry, that was about to change. A lot of things were about to change.

Colin had no idea how to move forward. How to breach the subject of his mate bond with Ellie. Had she been a supernatural creature, this would've been so much easier. Had she been a werewolf, there'd be no problem whatsoever.

It was true that magic clung to her skin, but it was so faint that he had to assume she was a descendant of a witch many generations ago. She might have seemed "other," but she was as mundane as any human. She wasn't any of the things he'd hoped, and wishing it were different wasn't going to help him.

"Ellie—"

"You kept saying 'mine' up on the hill," Ellie interrupted. "What were you talking about?"

Huh. His wolf had obviously made his stake while Colin had been on the verge of unconsciousness. Maybe this wouldn't be as hard as he'd thought.

He met her gaze and held it. "I was talking about you, Ellie."

Her lips parted on a breath. Colin was struck by her soft beauty.

"Me? Why?" Her disbelieving tone wrenched his heart. Was it so unfathomable that he—or anyone—would want her? "What do you mean?"

"You are mine, Ellie." Colin hiked a shoulder. There was no way around it. It was best to be straightforward and honest. "My mate."

She shot up from her seat, eyes wide. "Okay, you definitely have a concussion. Either that or you're a freaking psychopath who needs to get the hell out of my house right now."

Well, that could have gone better. Colin pinched the bridge of his nose between his thumb and forefinger and let out a slow breath. It's not like he'd expected her to be immediately receptive. But he'd really hoped she wouldn't reach straight for the mentally unstable card.

"Try to keep an open mind." No one ever reacted well when a sentence started that way, and Colin instantly regretted the words. Ellie opened her mouth to speak and he held up a staying hand. "Ellie. The world isn't as simple as you might think it is. There are things, forces, creatures that exist . . ." Gods, he was fucking this up big-time.

Ellie's scent soured with fear and anxiety. She pulled her bottom lip between her teeth and studied Colin from beneath lowered lashes. "Like witches?"

She spoke so quietly that, even with his preternatural hearing, Colin had to strain to hear her. Her words drove a spike of fear through his chest. He'd been right about the magic that clung to her, but he was beginning to think it wasn't because of her heritage like he'd assumed. Perhaps the supernatural world wasn't as foreign to her as he thought. "Yes," he replied. "Like witches. But there's also so much more." His wolf gave a low whimper in the back of his mind. "What do you know about witches, Ellie?"

"I know they're real," she whispered. "And that they're evil."

His wolf's whimper turned into a menacing growl. Colin took a deep breath and held it in his lungs. Her scent didn't bear a hint of deception. Very few humans were privy to the supernatural world. And her experience with it had obviously been unpleasant.

"Some of them are, yes." Witches, like any creature, weren't inherently good or evil. The intent of their magic and the spells they cast determined that. "But not all of them. Ellie, do you know what I am?" Colin figured it was best to test the waters and see what she knew about his world before moving forward.

Her brow furrowed. Once again her scent soured. What she knew about his world was superficial at best. "A man?" Her words lacked conviction.

"No. I haven't been a man for a very long time. I'm a werewolf."

Ellie backed away and her fear sliced through Colin's chest. "You hit your head harder than you thought," she said with a nervous laugh. She reached for the phone. "I think we'd better call that ambulance."

With preternatural speed, he reached out and snatched the phone from the end table before she could get to it. "I don't have a concussion, Ellie, and you know it."

"H-how did you do that?"

"I told you, I'm a werewolf."

Ellie's eyes went wide. "No one can move that fast."

"I can. Supernatural reflexes." He realized her brain would have trouble reconciling what her eyes saw. He had to be patient because he needed her to understand the magnitude of their bond. "I *am* a werewolf, Ellie. And you are my mate."

Ellie's heart beat a mad rhythm in her chest. Colin moved in a blur, so fast it was like the phone had been on the end table one second and was in his hand the very next. Witches were real. She knew that firsthand. Magic was real. Was it so far-fetched that other things, like werewolves, could exist as well?

"Wait, what?" Ellie's eyes went wide. "Your *mate*? What in the hell does that even mean?"

Colin leveled his gaze on her. "I think you know what that means, Ellie."

"Well, yeah. I know what the word means." Wolves mated for life. Was it the same for werewolves? "But . . ."

"You're mine, Ellie. I knew it the second I laid eyes on you at the Sourdough. The wolf knew it. I know it's crazy and hard to believe, but it's the truth."

Um, ya think? Ellie stared, disbelieving, at Colin. "'Hard to believe' is an understatement. And I'm just supposed to believe you because you say it's the truth?"

"It's physically impossible for a werewolf to lie to his mate," Colin replied as though the explanation were simple.

"And I'm supposed to believe that because . . . ?"

Colin finished her thought. "Because if I lie to you, it will cause me intense pain."

Ellie pursed her lips as she studied him. "Prove it."

Colin let out a sigh as though he'd hoped she wouldn't ask him to do just that. Well, too damn bad. He might have moved unnaturally fast, but that wasn't enough to make her blindly believe everything he told her.

"Fine." The determination in Colin's hard gaze was enough to make Ellie wonder if she should have asked him to prove himself to her. He pushed himself up from the couch, slowly. "I am *not* a werewolf, and you are *not* my mate."

Colin's jaw clenched as he doubled over and then went down hard on one knee. Either he was an Academy Award–worthy actor or he truly was in pain. One arm wrapped around his torso as though to hold himself together. He let out several panting breaths before bringing his head up to look at her. "Anything else you want me to lie to you about?"

Ellie's lips parted and she sucked in a breath. She didn't know what to say, how to think or to feel. For the second time in her never-ending existence, Ellie's world had been turned upside down. The things Colin told her terrified her and, at the same time, filled her with hope. Maybe she wasn't as unique and alone in this world as she'd thought.

"Are you . . . immortal?"

Colin braced his palm on the coffee table and pushed

himself to stand. Ellie cringed; guilt stabbed at her chest. He'd already been through a lot and she'd caused him even more pain. Ellie might have been infallible, but she was no stranger to pain. Physical. Emotional. Mental.

"As immortal as any supernatural creature." Ellie's brow furrowed at his esoteric reply. "I don't get sick, I heal quickly, but I have weaknesses. Silver is one of them. But I can die. Nothing in this world is truly immortal."

Ellie looked away. Apparently, she knew something about the supernatural world that Colin didn't. "How old are you?"

Colin settled back down onto the couch. He gave her a wry grin that did traitorous things to Ellie's insides. It was totally unfair that he was so breathtakingly handsome. "A little over five hundred years." She didn't miss the hint of arrogance in his tone. "Give or take. After a while, you sort of lose count."

He was older than her. It had been centuries since Ellie had met anyone older than her. She couldn't help the smile that curved her lips. "That's pretty old."

"Yup."

Ellie found herself wanting to tease him. To get a rise out of him like she had that morning at the Sourdough. "You're sort of robbing the cradle, don't you think?"

Colin laughed. The deep rumble vibrated through her and settled in her lower abdomen, creating a warm glow that pulsed from her core outward. This was dangerous. The more they talked, the more comfortable she became. The more she wanted him. She felt an optimism she hadn't experienced in hundreds of years. She'd known disappointment for so long, she didn't think she could afford to hope for happiness. She definitely didn't know how to feel about Colin claiming her as his mate, but the prospect of having someone she could confide her own secrets to, someone she could perhaps be friends with throughout the long, endless years, was almost too good to be true.

Don't forget, Ellie. When something seems too good to be true, it's because it usually is.

"Obviously, age isn't an issue for my wolf. So . . . I've got a few hundred years on you." Colin hiked a casual shoulder. Ellie's eyes were drawn to the play of muscles from the simple act and her breath caught in her chest. "Age is just a number, right?"

His playful grin was as brilliant as the sun. It warmed Ellie from the inside out. Sweet Jesus, she was in over her head. Age might have just been a number to him, but for Ellie it had always been a reminder that she was doomed to an existence of loneliness, isolation, and unhappiness.

"I don't understand any of this." She wanted to. She wanted to be accepting and on board with everything Colin told her. "I don't even know you. How can I be your . . . mate?"

Colin's expression fell at her skeptical tone. "It's a lot to process. I get that."

He pushed himself up from the couch again. He rounded the coffee table and closed the space between them. Once again, Ellie was struck by the sheer size of him. She should have known he wasn't an ordinary man. Nothing about Colin conveyed ordinary. His gaze grew hungry and that strange golden spark lit behind his irises. His proximity sucked all of the breathable oxygen from the room until Ellie felt as though a weight pressed down on her chest.

"I see it," she whispered.

Colin's brow furrowed. "See what?"

"The wolf," Ellie said on a breath.

Colin reached out and smoothed her hair away from her face. Ellie stared in wonder and she couldn't believe she hadn't recognized that foreign presence behind his eyes the first time she'd noticed the beautiful gold glint. She was frozen in place by the intensity of his magnetic stare. Held captive by those beautiful, feral eyes. She waited for the tremor of fear that would no doubt pass through her, but instead Ellie was infused with a delicious warmth that only served to awaken her desire.

Colin took a deep breath and held it in his lungs. The simple act carried a sensuality that added gasoline to the building flames of Ellie's passion. She couldn't help but want him. He was the epitome of male perfection. And she'd been alone for so long. Too long. Loneliness had been her purgatory.

"You need to stop." Colin's husky tone sent a shiver over Ellie's skin.

She swallowed and took a breath to try to slow her racing heart. "Why?"

"Because the scent of your desire is driving me out of my fucking mind."

Whoa. Ellie was definitely in over her head.

CHAPTER 7

Colin balanced on the edge of his control. The need to put his mouth to Ellie's, to taste the sweetness of her lips, was almost more than he could resist. The mate bond formed an immediate physical attraction. But that was animal nature. Instinct told him Ellie possessed qualities that would make her his ideal mate. Instinct didn't have a fuck to give about emotions, decorum, or anything else. Instinct was logical. Biological. A force that couldn't be ignored or denied. Colin was helpless not to answer its call. Ellie was his. And only death could sever that bond.

Her scent drove him wild. Rich. Sweet. Heady. Her chest moved with her breath and her heart raced in her chest. His heightened senses allowed Colin insight as to how Ellie felt without having to ask her. Without having to guess.

The strands of her hair slipped through his fingers like silk. Colin's awareness of her vibrated through every cell that constructed him. How could he possibly resist her when everything about her beckoned him closer?

"Ellie, I'm going to kiss you now." He figured she deserved a little warning. An opportunity to tell him no if she didn't want this. Didn't want him. He'd hit her with one hell of a life-changing surprise today. They still had a lot to discuss—

her knowledge of witches for starters—but right now he *needed* to kiss her.

Her lips parted and her lids drifted shut. If that wasn't a sign, he didn't know what was. Colin's head bent to hers. Their lips met and a contented growl echoed in the back of his mind. He shut the wolf out, unwilling to let the animal intrude on this moment. Ellie tasted just as sweet as he knew she would. Dewy and fresh, like a spring morning. His arms went around her as he pulled her against him. She rose up to her tiptoes and threw her arms around his neck as the kiss graduated from shy and tentative to urgent and passionate. The floodgates opened and there was nothing either of them could do to stop it. They kissed as though they were starved for each other. As though they'd waited centuries for this moment. Colin supposed that in some strange way, they had. And neither of them was willing to waste another second.

Colin's hand crept up her back and his palm came to rest at the nape of her neck. His mouth slanted over hers as he deepened the kiss, thrusting his tongue between her lips. Ellie responded with equal fervor as their tongues wound in a sensual dance. He took her bottom lip between his teeth and sucked, which caused the scent of her arousal to intensify and bloom around him. Dear gods, Colin didn't know it was possible to want someone with such intensity and raw passion.

Ellie's arms left his body. She reached for her own shirt, quickly unbuttoning it and peeling it down from her shoulders. Colin hadn't expected such an enthusiastic response, but the fact that she wanted him with the same burning intensity was a boost to his ego that made his chest puff with pride. He didn't dare move his hands from where they were anchored to her body. She was in charge. However far this went was up to her. He wouldn't make a single move until she gave him the green light.

His lips abandoned her mouth, greedy to taste the rest of her. Colin kissed along her jaw, beneath her ear, down the slim column of her throat, to her bare shoulder, and across her collarbone. Ellie's head fell back on her shoulders as she let out a contented sigh. He kissed from the swell of one round breast to the other. Her opposite shoulder. The other side of her throat and beneath that ear. Back to her jaw, and to the opposite corner of her mouth.

Ellie reached behind her and unfastened her bra. "Colin," she murmured against his mouth. "Take your shirt off."

She didn't have to ask him twice. He was still a little sore, but a few bumps and bruises weren't going to stand between him and his mate. He was desperate for the skin-on-skin contact and unbuttoned his thick flannel shirt before shrugging out of it and letting it drop to the floor. Ellie pressed her chest against his. The cushion of her lush breasts seared his skin. The tight points of her nipples teased him as they brushed against the crisp hair of his chest. She reached for the waistband of his jeans and tugged the button loose.

All bets were off. Heat swamped Colin's gut. Desire flooded every nook and cranny of his mind. He kissed Ellie with every ounce of passion he felt while he reached for her pants, jerking the button free and pulling the zipper down. He couldn't get her naked fast enough. They devolved into creatures ruled by instinct and base desire. Their mouths met and parted. Hands groped and fumbled. Boots were kicked off and flung to various corners of the house as socks were toed off and tight denim pulled down the length of each other's thighs. The only sounds in the room were those of their panting breaths. When finally not a scrap of clothing stood between them, Colin reached for Ellie and pulled her along with him down on the couch.

He settled her on top of his lap, once again putting her in the position of control. He needed her to understand that her needs, her safety, her wants came before his own. As her mate, Colin would protect Ellie from any and all threats. Even if one of those threats was himself. "Ellie." He laid his palm to the side of her cheek as he looked into her eyes. "This can stop. Anytime you want it to. I know we're moving fast and I need you to know that—"

Ellie put her finger to Colin's lips. "Shhh." She smiled and the expression was so gods-damned seductive that it sent a rush of heat through his veins. "I want this, Colin. I want you. Stop trying to talk me out of it."

She put her mouth to his and once again logical thought took a backseat to desire. Ellie came up on her knees and positioned herself over the head of Colin's cock. She dipped and rolled her hips, brushing his sensitive flesh along her slick, wet folds. He sucked in a sharp breath at the delicious shock of heat and swallowed down a groan as she repeated the motion. The way she artfully teased him, touching without penetration, was hands down the most erotic thing any female had ever done to him. He didn't want her to stop, and at the same time Colin wasn't sure how much more of this amazing torture he could take.

Ellie gripped his shoulders and her head rolled back as she continued to pleasure herself. The sway of her hips adopted a gentle rhythm and Colin gritted his teeth at the soft, wet caress that ended with the stiff bead of her clit brushing over his crown. He was certain she could make him come this way. Without an inch of penetration. Gods, how he wanted—*needed*—to bury himself deep inside of her. But that wasn't going to happen until she decided it should.

"Colin." She said his name with such heartfelt relief that it stabbed through his chest. "I feel so good. You have no idea how much I need this."

He would give her everything she needed and more. *Anything.* As she was his mate, Ellie's needs were his to satisfy. Colin kissed her bare shoulder. Her chest. Over the swell of her breast as he worked his way to the center. He took her nipple into his mouth and sucked gently before dragging his teeth along that very sensitive part of her. Ellie shivered and her nipple hardened even more against his tongue. She let out a low moan as she slid down the length of his shaft and settled fully on top of him.

Gods. Utter fucking bliss.

The years of loneliness and isolation had eaten away at Ellie until she'd felt like a hollowed-out shell. A dried-up husk of what was once human. Empty. In a few short moments, Colin had managed to reawaken all of those emotions and sensations she'd thought long gone. Had Ellie realized she could feel this way, she would've gone off in search of a werewolf a long damned time ago. Well, she would've at least searched as far as the curse that bound her to this land would have allowed her.

Goose bumps rose on her skin and she shivered as Colin's tongue circled the tight point of her nipple. He used his teeth to heighten her pleasure and a moan gathered in her throat. She couldn't wait another second to have him inside of her, and so she settled down over the head of his cock and her eyes drifted shut as his rigid shaft slid along the sensitive inner walls of her pussy.

He continued to kiss, lick, suck, and bite. He paid such lavish attention to her breasts that Ellie thought she'd passed out from the intensity of pleasure. His arms wound around her waist and his hands settled at the small of her back. The tips of his fingers kneaded her ass, urging her into an easy rhythm as she rode him.

Ellie wasn't a stranger to the one-night stand. Because of her unique existence, it was a necessity. She couldn't have entanglements of any kind. No relationships. No intimacy. Already it felt different with Colin. And that instant connection worried her more than it probably should have. She refused to let her worries ruin this. Over the past few centuries, her moments of happiness had been few and far between. When one presented itself to her, she was damn well going to take it.

Colin's left hand abandoned her back to cup her breast. He lifted his head, and when his eyes met hers Ellie's breath stalled in her chest. The naked, raw heat in his expression was unlike anything she'd ever seen. It set her on fire, drove her out of her mind with want, and stole every coherent thought from her head.

His mouth once again seized hers in a passionate, desperate kiss. Their mouths slanted, tongues lashed out, and teeth grazed. Ellie couldn't get enough of Colin. The way he smelled, the taste of his mouth, the fierce, wild glint in his eyes, his body packed with lean muscle, and the way he held her tight as he fucked her. He'd unleashed something in her. Unlocked some hidden part of her that she didn't know existed. Without common sense or reason. Abandon the likes of which Ellie had never experienced. And now that she'd gotten a taste of it, she never wanted to go back.

"That's it, Ellie," Colin said against her mouth. "Just like that. Take it deep. Don't stop."

Heat unfurled in Ellie's stomach, reaching outward through her limbs like seeking vines. Her muscles tightened, her heart raced, as anticipation built within her to the point that she didn't think she could take another second of the intense sensation. She shut her eyes to block out everything so all that was left was the sound of Colin's breath in her ear, the sensation of his touch, and her own body's response to him.

"Oh God!" Stars exploded in the dark universe of Ellie's mind as she came apart. The orgasm rolled over her like an ocean wave, powerful, aggressive, relentless. She cried out as intense pleasure pulsed throughout her body, leaving her weak and shaken, her muscles warm and tense.

Colin held her tighter. His thrusts became wild. Hard and disjointed. Almost desperate. Each ragged breath ended on a low growl that sent a thrill through Ellie's bloodstream. He fucked her like the animal he claimed to be and he let out a low growl as his muscles tensed, his hips drove deep, and his head jerked back to rest on the couch. His cock pulsed against her sensitive flesh and Ellie was flooded with heat as he came. His right hand came to rest at the back of her head and he pulled her to him for a slow, indulgent kiss that Ellie swore lasted a lifetime.

"Wow." She was rarely at a loss for words, but Colin had managed to render her speechless.

"Mmmmm." The low hum of Colin's voice sent a shiver over Ellie's skin. He kissed every inch of her that his mouth could reach. Arms, shoulders, neck, chest, and torso. He kissed the hollow of her throat, her jawline, under her ear. Her forehead, temple, cheek, and back to her mouth. He seemed to enjoy kissing her more than anything else. He took his time as he kissed her, and each time the heat of his mouth made contact with her skin it only made her greedy for more. "I think 'wow' might be a bit of an understatement."

Ellie laughed. In a few minutes, Colin had managed to accomplish something she couldn't in twenty-four solid hours. The stress and depressing thoughts that plagued her melted away in an instant. Her worries diminished. The future that stretched out infinitely before her didn't seem half as bleak. He was a one-man antianxiety antidepressant.

But he wasn't a man, was he?

"What's the matter?" Colin's tone turned to one of concern.

"What do you mean?"

Colin ran his nose along Ellie's throat and she shivered. "Your scent changed. I can smell your worry."

Not a man at all. No, Colin Courtney was *extraordinary*. His keen senses posed a problem, though. How was Ellie to have any privacy when little things like a change in scent could give away her mood and thereby her thoughts?

"Today's just been sort of intense. That's all. Like you said, it's a lot to process."

Colin held her against him, as though unwilling for their bodies to part. The tension in his arms kept Ellie in place, and rather than pull away, she allowed her head to come to rest on his strong shoulder. It seemed such a natural thing to do. Almost too easy. She had so many questions she wanted answered, but she knew if he opened up to her Colin would want a few answers of his own. Ellie didn't know if she was ready to open up to him. She barely knew him. Her secrets were buried deep in the darkest recesses of her heart. Unearthing them after so long might be more painful than Ellie could endure.

"Intense," Colin agreed. "And amazing."

His words warmed her heart. Her fingers moved as though of their own volition and threaded through the silky strands of his tawny hair. "I don't know if it's all been amazing," Ellie said with a laugh. "Rolling down an embankment couldn't have been any fun."

"Totally worth it." Colin placed a kiss on her shoulder. "I'd fall off that cliff again if it meant you'd be the one to find me."

His words affected her much more than they should have. She didn't want to feel anything for Colin. She couldn't. She steered the conversation away from pretty words. "Where were you when you fell?"

He let out a slow breath. "The top of the ridge. Near the trailhead."

Holy crap. If that was true, she'd found him a good three-quarters-of-a-mile drop from where he'd fallen. A fall like that would've killed anyone. If the fact that he was still alive didn't prove Colin was a supernatural creature, she didn't know what did.

"You're lucky you didn't die."

Colin gave a gentle laugh. "Luck had nothing to do with it. Werewolf."

Werewolf. Ellie still couldn't wrap her mind around it. In the blink of an eye her life, her entire existence, had changed. She didn't know if she was prepared to deal with the fallout.

CHAPTER 8

Despite his having fallen off a cliff yesterday, Colin's afternoon was certainly looking up. Ellie remained on his lap, their bodies still joined as they talked. It was an intimate moment, one he wouldn't have expected to happen so soon. Colin wasn't about to complain, however. Both he and the animal that inhabited his psyche hadn't felt so content in years. Hell, decades. The mate bond was truly an extraordinary thing.

"You're so hot."

Colin chuckled at Ellie's remark. "Thanks. It bodes well for me that you think I'm good-looking."

Ellie laughed, and he swore it was the most beautiful sound he'd ever heard. "No. I mean your body temperature. Your skin is on fire!"

Thanks to his werewolf metabolism, Colin's body temperature always ran warmer than the average human's by as much as twenty degrees. "Ah. So you don't think I'm good-looking?"

Ellie delivered a playful swat to his shoulder. "I have a feeling you know you're good-looking and don't need me to stroke your ego."

"Oh, honey, there's plenty that I need you to stroke."

Ellie's head dipped, and her forehead came to rest on his

shoulder. He loved how easy it was to get a rise out of her. To embarrass her. To stoke the flames of her desire. She might have behaved modestly at his little joke, but her scent told him she was more than willing to help out with whatever he needed stroked.

"Seriously." Her voice went low and quiet. "Are you always this warm?"

"Pretty much. Part of my biology, I guess."

"Wow. I bet you're nice to sleep next to in the middle of winter. Who needs a fire when there's a werewolf around?"

Emotion swelled in Colin's chest at the prospect of a winter when he wasn't sleeping alone in his bed. It was true that pack life meant he was never alone, but it was entirely possible to be surrounded by bodies and still feel the crushing weight of loneliness. He'd worried about Ellie's reaction to their bond. About her inability to believe in what he was and what had happened. That she already had knowledge of supernatural creatures was a bonus. However, Colin sensed that her previous experience with his world hadn't been a pleasant one.

As much as he wanted to hold her close to him and keep their bodies joined, Colin needed to have a serious conversation with her. That wasn't going to happen when he was still inside of her and ready to have her again. He gripped her by the waist and lifted her. He missed her soft heat and considered putting conversation on the back burner for a little while longer. But that wouldn't get them anywhere, and Colin wanted their bond to start on strong footing. He shifted so she rested on the couch and he tucked her body against his to keep her warm. He put his mouth close to her ear and breathed in her delicious scent.

"Ellie, how do you know about witches?"

She shivered. Her scent soured with fear and Colin's

wolf rose up in his psyche, ready to defend their mate against any perceived threat. She tucked her body even closer to his and guided his arm around her middle. He'd seen so many sides of her in the short time since he'd met her. This Ellie was vulnerable and frightened and it made him want to hunt down whoever had made her feel this way and make them pay. Silence stretched out between Ellie and him to the point that it sent a ripple of fear down Colin's spine. They'd barely met; she had no real reason to trust him. She wasn't a werewolf, no preternatural senses whatsoever, and yet he hoped she would somehow sense the power of their bond and trust him.

"Ellie?" He'd do whatever it took to coax her out of her shell. "You can talk to me. You can trust me."

She let out a slow, shaky breath. "I want to trust you. But . . . I don't even really know you. And I know, considering what we've just done, that's sort of a ridiculous statement. It's just that I've never told anyone."

No one? It made Colin's heart ache to know she had no one to confide in. No one to lean on. Secrets were terrible burdens and they only became heavier the longer you carried them. Colin vowed that she would never be alone again. That in him she would always have a confidant. A protector. A lover. And, in time, he hoped a friend. The bond created an attraction between them; it connected them on a spiritual level. But anything other than that, like, for instance, a relationship, whether romantic or not, was entirely up to them.

"I can understand why you've never told anyone." Really, who would believe a story about an honest-to-God witch? Humans had a tendency to be cynical and disbelieving of such things. The supernatural world existed all around them and they were blind to it. It was easy for creatures like Colin to hide in plain sight. Humans didn't want to believe. So many of them were reluctant to open their minds to new possibilities. "But maybe it would be easier to talk to me about it, since this is technically my world were talking about. You don't have to worry about me not believing you."

"That's true. . . ."

Colin didn't want to pressure her. He wanted her to open up to him on her own, because she wanted to. Not because that's what he wanted. She had to come to him willingly in all things. "We can just lay here if you want. Take a nap. Relax. Whatever you want."

Ellie's fingers twined with his and she squeezed. "I thought you were a jerk that morning at the Sourdough."

"Yeah, well, I thought you had an unhealthy attachment to cinnamon rolls," he teased.

Ellie let out a chuff of laughter. "I had a lot on my mind. You weren't the jerk; I was."

"I will say you were a little cranky, but hardly a jerk."

Ellie tilted her head up to look at him. Her lips quirked into a petulant pucker. "Oh, I was *absolutely* a jerk. The biggest jerk. Honestly, I'm lucky John only made me take two days off of work instead of firing me."

Anxiety tugged at Colin's thoughts. It was too soon to discuss the dynamics of their mate bond, but he would eventually want her to move to Stanley. He couldn't leave the pack without formally being considered a rogue. A rogue werewolf was never looked upon favorably. It could potentially affect his position as a sentry and he couldn't have that. But neither could he live away from his mate. The distance between them, no matter how short, would agitate his wolf and make him volatile. Ellie would have to move to Stanley. And likewise, she would have to become a werewolf. It was the only way. Colin only hoped that when it came time to broach the subject Ellie would continue to have an open mind.

"For the record, I'm glad you had a couple of days off. If you'd been at work this afternoon, I'd still be laying in a tangle of brush."

"True. Maybe it was fate that brought you into the Sourdough to steal Frank's cinnamon roll."

Colin laid his lips to her temple. Whatever the outcome, he was damn glad fate had decided to intervene.

Ellie worried her bottom lip between her teeth. She wanted to open up to Colin so badly that the words practically leaped out of her mouth. Who better to understand her plight than someone familiar with this life? Ellie had always thought things like witches and spells and curses belonged in fairy tales. Never in her quiet, sheltered life would she have ever thought those things could be real. That is, until she'd been on the receiving end of malicious magic.

Maybe Colin could help her? Maybe he could find a way to set her free.

"Colin, how old do you think I am?" Ellie was almost fearful of his response. Worried about his reaction when he found out the truth.

"I don't know," he mused. "Twenty-six? Twenty-seven?"

"I was born February 23, 1817."

She was answered with a pregnant pause that caused her stomach to tie into an anxious knot. Colin reached down and tilted her head so she was forced to look at him. He studied her face, his brow furrowed with confusion. He took a deep breath and held it before letting the air out of his lungs slowly. "I could have sworn you were human. There's a faint scent of magic around you, but not enough. You're not a shifter, or a vampire, or anything else."

"No." Ellie cleared her throat and willed her voice to be stronger. "I'm not any of those things."

"Then how is that possible?"

Ellie didn't have to have superior supernatural senses to know Colin was a little afraid. And for some reason, that scared her even more. She'd always known being cursed wasn't a picnic. But now she couldn't help but wonder if it was even worse than she'd always thought.

"A witch cast a spell on me." God, it sounded even more ridiculous saying it out loud than it had in her mind all of these years. "I'm human, I guess. Honestly, I don't really know what I am. All I know is that I can't die." She drew in a deep breath as she was about to speak the words that gutted her every time she thought about them. "And I can't ever leave this place. Never."

Saying it out loud lifted a weight from her shoulders that she'd never realized had been there to begin with. She'd been carrying this terrible secret for so long. Lived through lonely lifetimes without any true friends or anyone to confide in. It felt so good to tell Colin what had happened to her. It was almost as if the witch's curse had less power over her now that someone else knew about it.

Of course that wasn't true. It would never be true. But Ellie appreciated the momentary relief.

Colin held her gaze. His hand moved to cup the back of her head and for a long moment he simply stared into her eyes as though to gauge the truth of what she'd just told him. He hid his emotions well and kept his expression passive. But the eyes never lied, and when a golden light lit behind his Ellie knew her words had upset him.

"Ellie . . ."

She wouldn't give him the opportunity to downplay what had happened to her. "I tried. To die." Admitting that was almost harder than admitting she believed in witches to begin with. "Everyone I knew and loved grew old and died and I was stuck here, in this body, in this *age,* unchanging and trapped. I threw myself off a cliff into the river. I didn't break a single bone. I didn't drown. And I don't even know how to swim." Her rueful laughter burned with regret. "I tried to set myself on fire, but I didn't burn. I walked out into a blizzard and stayed outside in the wilderness for fourteen days, but I didn't freeze. I tended those with scarlet fever, and worse, and never got sick."

"Dear gods." Colin put his forehead to hers. Sorrow, commiseration, pity, and anger vibrated off of him, the emotions almost tangible as he drew in a breath through his nostrils and then let it out in a rush. "Who is this witch? Tell me and she's as good as dead."

Ellie brought his hand to her lips and placed a gentle kiss on his fingertips. "All I remember about her was that her name was Sarah. She was a sour, bitter, hateful woman and I was punished because a man I didn't love, loved me."

Colin swore under his breath. He kept his forehead braced against hers as he breathed through the apparent rage that caused his limbs to quake. "She condemned you to immortality?"

"She condemned me to an eternity of loneliness," Ellie whispered. "In a place she vowed civilization would never find. She bound me to the land and I can't ever leave here."

People always wondered why the tiny town of Lowman never grew into anything. It could've been a booming tourist hub. Instead, Sarah had used her magic to draw heat from the earth, which created hot springs all along the river. Because of the mineral deposits, fish didn't thrive in these waters. Devastating fires devoured the forests every several years, driving out the game. Businesses opened and failed and people continued to pass through Lowman on their way to somewhere else, barely pausing long enough to blink.

This place was as lonely and isolated as Ellie felt. She was tied to the land. They were one and the same. What would Colin think of her now that he knew the truth? He claimed she was something important to him. Something she still couldn't grasp the concept of. But he had a life beyond this place. He had a job and, she assumed, a family. No matter what he claimed Ellie was to him, she couldn't see him giving up his life to live in isolation with her. Who would want that? He'd shrivel up and die here just like she saw others shrivel up and die here before him. She couldn't condemn him to share in her fate no matter how desperate she was for companionship. If she asked him to stay with her, she'd be no better than the spiteful witch who had done this to Ellie in order to hurt her for something that wasn't her fault.

"Have you tried to leave?"

Ellie had just told Colin that she'd tried to set herself on fire in order to escape immortality. Did he seriously think she hadn't tried to walk beyond the borders the witch had set for her?

"Yep. You know that saying 'what doesn't kill you makes you stronger'? Well, what doesn't kill you nearly drives you crazy with unimaginable pain."

Colin pulled away to study her face. His brow furrowed with worry and gold blazed hot behind his irises. "Pain?"

Well, "pain" was sort of an understatement. But it was the easiest word to get her point across. "The border of the curse starts just past where the Sourdough is now," Ellie replied. "It runs within a perimeter that encompasses about thirty square miles. After Sarah had cursed me, I walked right up to that line and stepped over it. I wanted to prove to myself that I didn't believe her hateful words and that there was no such thing as magic. I believed in magic after that day. And curses. I can't even describe to you what it felt like, it was that horrible. Blinding. Excruciating. A torture that has no equal. I experienced that pain three more times as I tested every single border that boxed me in. I never crossed those lines again. I haven't come within ten feet of them in two hundred years."

"Ellie, I promise you we're going to figure this out. I'm going to help you."

The fierce resolve in Colin's voice made her heart ache. Because she knew no matter how much he wanted to, he couldn't help her. No one could. Her fate had been sealed a long time ago.

CHAPTER 9

Colin's wolf snarled in the back of his mind. The animal was enraged and thirsty for blood. He was ready to hunt, to track, to maim, and to kill. The animal needed to avenge their mate, to free her from this vile curse and protect her from the unimaginable pain reflected in her deep blue eyes.

Easier said than done. The animal, on the one hand, was driven by pure instinct. Colin, on the other hand, used logic. The odds of finding the witch who cursed Ellie were slim to none. If she still lived, she could be anywhere. No amount of skill, or instinct, could help them to track a ghost. That didn't mean he was giving up, though. He was incapable of lying to his mate. He'd meant every word. He was going to help her out of this situation no matter what.

He just needed to figure out how.

"You know," Ellie began, "you're not a jerk at all. You're actually a really nice guy. Werewolf. Whatever. But you can't help me, Colin. No one can."

Werewolves never backed down from a challenge, and one as insurmountable as this was the sort of bait Colin couldn't refuse. He'd prove his mate wrong and in the process earn her respect and gratitude. He'd free her from this gods-damned curse if it killed him. Luckily, he wasn't without resources of his own. The only problem was, he'd have to leave her to do a little research. And gods, tearing himself away from her was going to take more willpower than he thought he could muster.

"I'm glad we've established I'm not a jerk." Colin was determined to do what he could to add a little levity to the conversation. "But don't underestimate me, Ellie. When I put my mind to something, I see it through to the end. You are my mate. Mine to care for. Mine to protect. I *will* find a solution to this problem."

The look Ellie gave him was so close to pity, it set his wolf on edge. She doubted him. Doubted his ability to help her. It was true they didn't know each other well, but Colin was determined to prove himself to her.

"Colin." Her voice couldn't have echoed her expression better. "Sarah is long gone. And I don't know any other witches; do you?"

Not personally, but Colin was far more connected in the supernatural world than Ellie was. "Give me a couple of days."

Her lips curved into a sweet smile that banished her sadness. "I get the feeling you're sort of stubborn."

Owen had once told him that a brick wall was less stubborn. "You have no idea."

"I just don't want you to expend a bunch of energy on something that isn't going to pan out." Ellie looked away. "I'm not worth the trouble."

Dear gods. She truly didn't understand exactly how worth it she was. "You're my mate, Ellie." Colin commanded her gaze with his authoritative tone. "I know you don't understand the magnitude of that bond, but believe me when I tell you there is nothing in this world more important. You are *absolutely* worth the trouble and then some."

"You don't know that."

"Someday, Ellie, you'll realize why and how I know it. But until then, you're just going to have to trust me."

Ellie laid her palm to Colin's cheek. "Hope is a very dangerous thing for the hopeless to feel. Do you understand that, Colin?"

She'd lived such an isolated life for so long. Too many endless nights to contemplate her fate and wallow in despair. Colin had never tackled a problem and failed to beat it. Ellie's problem would be no different. He was going to help her. There was simply too much at stake to accept anything less than success.

"You've got me now," Colin said. "And I'm going to bend over backward to give you more hope than you know what to do with."

"No offense." Ellie's lips twitched. "But I don't need a knight in shining armor. I might've been born before feminism, but that doesn't mean I haven't changed with the times."

Never once had Colin considered Ellie anything other than strong, capable, and independent. His wolf wouldn't have chosen her for a mate if she'd been weak, helpless, or dependent. His wolf saw in her an equal partner. Someone who would not only make them better but whose traits would complement theirs also. The animal could sometimes be a raging pain in the ass. Pushy and overbearing. But in this the wolf made no mistakes. Ellie was perfect for Colin and he was going to do everything in his power to hold on to her.

"I need to get back to Stanley." He'd been gone for almost two days. It wasn't unusual for Colin to be out for a day or more when scouting for game, but he had a lot of loose ends to tie up with Liam before he could get to work finding a witch to break the curse put on Ellie. "I just need to check in with my alpha and do some research. I won't be gone long; I promise. Just overnight. I'll be back tomorrow."

Ellie put her mouth to his for a slow, gentle kiss that only served to stoke the flames of Colin's passion. Gods, he was tempted to spend the rest of the day and night with her. Naked, limbs tangled in her bedsheets until the sun rose again. But he was antsy to find a solution to Ellie's problem and needed all the help he could get.

"You don't have to make apologies or excuses." She kissed him again, just a quick peck. "I don't expect you to sit here with me. I don't need a babysitter. Besides, I'm going back to work in the morning. It's not like I'll be sitting here pining away."

Her grin widened and it made Colin's breath catch. Gods, he loved her snark. "Well, good to know you won't be *pining away.* I'd hate for you to despair of my ever returning."

She laughed. "Oh, you'll be back. For the cinnamon rolls if anything."

"They really are delicious." Colin brushed her dark mahogany hair behind her shoulder. "As much as I hate to see clothes covering your gorgeous body, I think we'd better get dressed. Can you give me a lift to my truck?"

"As much as I hate to see clothes covering your gorgeous body," Ellie countered, "I'd be happy to. But I should probably warn you, my truck is an antique. The suspension is pretty much shot."

"Bumps in the road don't bother me." Colin hoped she got the underlying meaning to his words.

"It's a good thing." Ellie's gaze warmed with soft emotion that stabbed pleasantly into Colin's chest. "Because it's probably going to be a rough ride."

"Bring it on." Colin wasn't afraid of a challenge.

He never lost and he wasn't about to start now that he was so close to getting everything he'd ever wanted.

Ellie walked through the front door, shocked she'd had the willpower necessary to let Colin go. She might not have possessed werewolf instincts, but she couldn't deny she'd formed a strange, almost instant, connection with him. Ellie rarely felt comfortable with people. Mostly because she couldn't stop thinking about the fact that she wasn't truly human anymore. She didn't have those crippling thoughts around Colin. He wasn't human either. They had that in common.

And the sex . . . *Wow.*

Ellie wasn't exactly worldly, but neither was she a shy virgin. She had a feeling the moments of intense pleasure she'd shared with Colin were only a precursor to what he could give her when he took his time. And she couldn't deny she was dying to find out.

Careful, Ellie. You're starting to hope again.

She couldn't afford optimism. And she'd meant it when she'd told Colin she wasn't looking for a knight in shining armor. She appreciated that he wanted to help her. That he wanted to find a solution to her problem. But she didn't want to suffer his disappointment when his efforts were unsuccessful. She didn't want to suffer her own renewed anguish at being reminded she was trapped with no way out.

She was being punished for eternity and she hadn't even liked Wendell Bates. The man had been insufferably arrogant, a bully, and a mediocre guide and tracker. He'd come to Lowman thinking he could strike it rich in the fur trade. Ellie snorted. Wendell could barely catch a cold, let alone the animals needed to net him a small fortune. He would have died that first winter, from either starvation or hypothermia, if Ellie hadn't given him a few pointers. Her fatal flaw was feeling sorry for even those who hadn't deserved her concern. She didn't think Wendell loved her so much as saw in her someone who could help him reach his goals. Ellie had been born in the Lowman area. Her father never had sons and so he'd taken Ellie along with him when he hunted, fished, trapped. She'd known the land and its secrets. Wendell wanted to capitalize on her knowledge, strength, and moxie. And all his unwanted attention had gotten her was the vengeance of a spiteful witch.

Sarah Allan had always kept to herself, which made the locals nervous around her. She was the sort of woman you gave a wide berth to when passing. A strange energy surrounded her like a dark, malicious cloud. Many suspected her of dark deeds. Witchcraft. Even the local tribes had been wary of her. To this day, Ellie had no idea what Sarah had seen in Wendell, but for some reason, she'd loved him. And instead of returning Sarah's affections, Wendell had pressed Ellie's father to let him marry her instead.

Lord, she wished she'd never set eyes on Wendell Bates.

Then again, if she hadn't she never would have met Colin. She would have been long since dead and she never would have had this wonderful day with him, entwined in his arms. She never would have seen his beautiful eyes, his charming smile, felt the heat of his mouth on her bare skin. Ellie stared at nothing as her mind took her back to those intimate moments. If it hadn't been for Wendell, and for Sarah, she would have missed out on more than simply centuries of life.

Ellie plopped down on the couch. The gravity of her situation crashed down on her. She liked Colin. Obviously. But her need for freedom, to leave this place and see the world, hadn't diminished with his crazy proclamation that she was his mate. She sensed that connection didn't mean to her what it did to him. That somehow a bond had been formed between them. She wouldn't deny there was something . . . a connection that went beyond the superficial. But was that apparent bond enough to derail what she'd wanted for so long? Was that bond more important than her own freedom and finally being able to leave this place and stretch her wings?

She knew so little about Colin. Maybe she was making assumptions. Maybe he had no intention of keeping her so close. Maybe the bond was something they could share without it becoming a shackle. Another prison.

Maybe you're just overthinking everything like always and just need to calm the hell down.

Ellie laughed. Her own brain tended to be her worst enemy. She overanalyzed everything. Psyched herself out before there was anything to get worked up over. Of course she'd received the biggest kick to the gut of them all. An actual magical curse. So could she really be blamed for always jumping to the worst possible scenario in any given situation?

Colin had promised to help her. And he'd demonstrated that it was impossible to lie to her. She had no doubt he was a man—male? . . . werewolf?—of his word. Maybe for the first time in a long time, it was okay to have faith in someone. In something.

Maybe it was okay to have faith in Colin and a bond she knew nothing about.

CHAPTER 10

"This is fantastic! Congrats, Brother!"

Colin rolled his eyes. Apparently, Owen hadn't been paying attention to a word he'd said. He let his gaze wander to his alpha, grateful that at least Liam was taking his words seriously. The three of them sat in Liam's office along with Mia, Owen's mate, and Devon, Liam's mate. Colin hoped that between the five of them they could put their heads together to find a solution to Ellie's—and now Colin's—problem. So far, Colin was seriously considering his brother as dead weight.

"Whereas congratulations are in order," Liam began, "this is definitely a problematic situation."

"Problematic" was an understatement. Colin's frustration mounted as he attempted to shake the feeling of helplessness that assaulted him. He'd be damned if he'd let Ellie down.

"You know . . ." Mia's brow furrowed with concentration. "There were rumors that circulated for years about a woman who'd been bound to the land by a witch's curse. I bet those stories were about Ellie."

Mia was a wood nymph whose family had lived for centuries in the national forest land that bordered the Bench Lakes. It seemed logical that word of Ellie's existence and circumstances would make its way throughout the local supernatural community over the years.

"I don't suppose those rumors covered how to break the curse?" It was a long shot, but Colin could hope.

"Not that I can remember," Mia replied. "But that doesn't mean no one ever talked about it. I can ask around, see what I can find out. It's worth a shot."

At this point, Colin would take all the help he could get. "Thanks."

"I had no idea. Wow." Devon spoke more to herself than the group at large. "I mean, I don't know Ellie personally, but I've chatted with her at the Sourdough. I feel awful for her. What a terrible burden to live with."

When Liam had found her, Devon had owned a bar on the outskirts of Lowman. She'd been human at the time, and after they'd faced a few trials of their own Liam had made Devon a werewolf. Colin would have loved to have Liam and Devon's problems. They'd been a bump in the road compared to what he was trying to fix.

"There's a possibility the curse can't be broken." Leave it to Liam to bring the pessimism. "She's human and hundreds of years old because of magical influence. What if you break the curse and it ages her? She'll die before you have a chance to save her by making her a werewolf."

Gods. Colin let out a forceful breath. He'd never considered that possibility. But Liam was right. He could bite Ellie to make her a werewolf, but the process was slow and the transition wouldn't be entirely complete until the full moon. "I could try to turn her now," he suggested. "Get ahead of the game."

"It might not work because of the curse," Liam said. "It would be like Owen trying to turn Mia."

He was right. Colin couldn't turn one supernatural creature into something else. But Ellie was human. The magic made her immortal, not her biology. He could give it a shot. But then again, what if it backfired? What if the curse had a fail-safe that would have adverse effects?

Fuck. Colin stood and raked his fingers through his hair. He'd never been so gods-damned frustrated.

"Don't feel disheartened yet, Colin." Mia stood and laid a comforting hand on his shoulder. "Let me make a couple of phone calls. I'll be right back."

Colin was down, but he wasn't out. As Mia left the room he watched, and turned to face Liam. "Can I have a second alone with Liam, everyone?"

Devon got up from her seat. "I'm going to go see if Mia needs any help." She placed a kiss on Liam's cheek and gave Colin a reassuring smile as she left the room.

Owen stayed right where he was. "What's going on, Colin?" It was obvious he wasn't going anywhere unless Liam gave the order. Fine. Whatever. It wasn't like the entire pack wouldn't find out soon enough.

"I've taken a position with the SMT as a sentry." There wasn't any point in sugarcoating it. "I met with Wade Robinson two days ago in Garden Valley to shore everything up. But he's not willing to follow through with any paperwork until my alpha gives the green light." Colin looked pointedly at Liam. "Considering his experience as a sentry."

Owen quickly covered his amused smirk with an impassive expression. Colin knew his brother wouldn't mind; it was Liam he had to convince.

"No one with the SMT is going to help you with Ellie," Liam replied.

Of course he would assume that somehow Wade had convinced Colin to join their ranks by promising their help in breaking the curse on Ellie.

"Liam, this has been in the works for a long time. I accepted the position from Wade before I even laid eyes on Ellie. If I hadn't been driving through Lowman on my way to Garden Valley, I never would have met her at all."

Liam's expression remained somber. "And if I don't give my blessing?"

Then it would make Colin's next decision a hell of a lot easier. "If you don't give your blessing, Wade won't hire me. And with Ellie's unique situation, it'll leave me with only one option: break from the pack and move to Lowman."

"Go rogue?" That got a rise out of Owen. He pushed up from the couch and rounded on Colin. "Sorry, but that's not happening."

Rogues weren't favorably looked upon by the supernatural community as a whole and even less tolerated among werewolves. They were considered volatile and disloyal. But what other option did Colin have if his alpha sought to derail his life, and his mate lived over fifty miles away? Those factors alone would make him volatile as fuck even if he chose to remain with the pack.

"This doesn't concern you, Owen." Colin respected his brother's opinion, but he wasn't about to let him butt in.

"The hell it doesn't." Owen turned to Liam. "You're not seriously going to let him leave, are you?"

If Colin decided to go rogue, not even his alpha could stop him. Owen knew that. Colin hated ultimatums, but he'd given one anyway. "I'll leave if I have to." He looked pointedly at Liam. "But *only* if I have to."

Liam's sour attitude in regard to sentries had nothing to do with Colin; rather, it was Liam's bad experience and his skepticism of the bureaucracy. Colin refused to let another male's prejudice shape his future. He turned to leave, more than ready to focus his attention on Ellie and how to break the curse that bound her when Mia came through the door like a warm summer wind. “I think I found something!” Her eyes lit with excitement. “I’m not sure about breaking the curse entirely, but I think I know how to thwart it in a way everyone can live with.”

It might not have been a permanent solution, but it was promising. If anything, it would buy him some time. Colin needed a win and he hoped to hell this was it.

Ellie sat on the couch, head tilted back as she stared at the ceiling. The silence she usually enjoyed nearly crushed her with its force, coaxing thoughts to her mind that she’d rather bury. It had been a full twenty-four hours since she’d dropped Colin off at his truck. And whereas she’d coached herself not to expect him to return, a small part of her hoped he’d come back.

She’d eaten every spoon-fed bite of his “you’re my one true mate” spiel and she had no one to blame for it but herself. She’d allowed herself to think, for just one ridiculous moment, that maybe he’d help her. That he believed her and wanted her to be free of this stupid curse as much as she wanted to be freed from it.

A knock at the back door gave Ellie a start. Adrenaline coursed through her bloodstream as her heart began to slow. She pushed up from the couch and walked from the living room to the kitchen. Through the cottage-style window of the back door her eyes met Colin’s, and her heart soared with elation. He’d followed through. Come back like he’d said he would. Ellie was ashamed she’d ever doubted him.

He was a man—er, werewolf—of his word. Truly one of a kind.

Ellie opened the door to let him in. “He—”

Before the greeting could leave her lips, Colin pressed her against the wall and put his mouth to hers. The passionate kiss was the sort of greeting between lovers who hadn't seen in each other in months . . . years . . . decades. It conveyed enough passion and heat to set a forest ablaze and it left Ellie weak and shaken. She didn't know it was possible to miss someone so much in such a short amount of time, but Colin's kiss made her realize the past twenty-four hours had been torture and she'd spent every single hour waiting for him to come back.

"I didn't think—"

Again, Colin didn't give her the opportunity to finish her thought as he kissed her again. Ellie's arms wound around his neck and she came up on her tiptoes as his mouth slanted across hers. Did words matter when their connection was so strong? Did anything matter other than this moment and the way his lips moved slowly over hers? Any insecurities she might've felt melted away. She didn't have to possess werewolf senses to know every word Colin had spoken to her had been the truth. She didn't have to have keen eyesight or a superior sense of smell to know he wanted her.

When Colin finally pulled away, Ellie wondered how her legs were still solid enough to hold her upright. Every inch of her felt like Jell-O. She smiled, a little embarrassed at her own giddiness. She couldn't remember the last time she'd been so happy—in fact, she didn't think she'd ever been this happy.

"Hi."

Colin brushed her hair from her face. "Gods, I missed you."

No one had ever uttered those words to her. She'd lived such an isolated life. She'd never gotten close enough to anyone to give them the chance to miss her. Her time with Colin had been short, but the fire that had ignited between them burned hot and bright. "I missed you too."

Colin's answering smile warmed her in a way the summer sun never could. "Good. Because I think I've found a solution to your problem."

"What?" Ellie's voice failed her. She cleared her throat, disbelieving what Colin had just told her and yet desperate for it to be true. "Are you sure?"

Colin's brow furrowed. "No." She appreciated his honesty, but her heart plummeted into her stomach anyway. "Not exactly. For the sake of argument, I'm about eighty percent sure. Either way, it's worth a shot. And if it doesn't work, then we'll just keep looking until we find a solution. I hope you're up for an adventure."

Ellie had quit trying to break the curse a long time ago. As a werewolf, Colin could bring something to the table she'd never considered. "I'm up for anything." It's not like any attempt to break the curse would kill her. Ellie was immortal. "When do you want to start?"

"Well . . ." Colin bent his head and kissed her throat, her jaw, and took her earlobe between his teeth and sucked. "As much as I'd like to stay right here and taste *every . . . single . . . inch* . . . of your body . . ." His tongue flicked out at the corner of her mouth. "I'd like to get started right away."

"Anxious to make me less of a freak of nature?"

Colin kissed below her ear and Ellie shivered. But she wasn't sure whether it was from his kiss or the tremor of fear that rippled through her. Ellie had never wanted anything other than to be human again. *Normal.* But since she'd met Colin, she realized that normal wasn't all it was cracked up to be. Would it be so bad to be bound to the land for eternity as long as he was here with her?

"You're not a freak of nature," Colin replied. "But I *am* anxious to take you home."

Ellie pulled back to look at him. "I thought I was home."

He smiled. "My home. And eventually, *our* home."

Ellie froze. How did this somehow become about dragging her out of Lowman? She wanted the curse broken more than anything, but not so she could be carted off to some other location and be just as bound and isolated as she already was.

"No." The word slipped from between Ellie's lips.

Colin frowned. Gold light shone behind his eyes, but Ellie wasn't about to demur. "No?"

"No." She needed him to understand how she felt. "I've never traveled more than the thirty square miles surrounding this cabin. I've never been *anywhere.* I've never seen anything but these hills, and this river, and the same stretch of damned highway for hundreds of years. You want to break this curse so you can take me *home*?" Ellie tried to control her temper, but she couldn't do anything to control the volume of her voice. "Colin. I want this curse broken so I can be *free*!"

Being Colin's "mate" didn't mean to Ellie what it obviously meant to him. It was like being in an arranged marriage without being let in on the plan. One day she was minding her own business and the next—*Hey! Here's the guy you're going to be spending the rest of your life with! Congrats!* She wanted it to have the same instant, resounding impact that it had on him, but she wasn't like him. She wasn't a werewolf. She couldn't see, smell, or sense the same things he could. She might have been immortal, but she was still mundane. That didn't mean she didn't recognize there was something between her and Colin. A future with him—maybe even love—wasn't at all far-fetched. But how would she know for certain if she didn't get out in the world and truly *live* first?

He stared at her, his jaw squared, a deep groove cutting through his forehead just above the bridge of his nose. His eyes sparked bright gold and she swore she heard a growl rumble deep in his chest. He was upset, and rightly so. But she owed him honesty.

"I'm so sorry, Colin. But I can't go home with you."

CHAPTER 11

Colin felt as though his heart had been scooped out of his chest with a rusty shovel. His chest cavity was empty. A hollowed-out cavern of hurt and rejection. His wolf let out a forlorn howl in the recesses of his mind that further gutted him. Ellie didn't want him. She wanted *out.*

Knock it off and stop being an asshole. The logical part of Colin's brain knew Ellie wasn't rejecting him or their bond. The part of his brain that understood how awful the years of loneliness and isolation must have been recognized why she wanted to leave this tiny corner of Idaho and get out into the real world. The part of his brain that knew Ellie not only needed her freedom but also *deserved* it didn't feel an ounce of hurt at her emphatic words. The part of his brain that trusted in the mate bond knew she'd come back to him because fate wouldn't have it otherwise.

He knew all that and more. And yet he couldn't help but yield to the crushing emotions that screamed past the voice of reason.

"Fine. Whatever." Colin put up a wall of apathy to protect his fucking fragile feelings and the wolf who whined and worried in the back of his mind.

"Colin, I—"

"Hey, it is what it is." The flimsy words didn't carry any

weight, but it was better than letting her see how much her rejection got under his skin. Whether Ellie wanted to be with him or not, it didn't change the fact that she was his mate. His to protect, to honor, and to support. He would never condemn her to an existence that might as well have been a life sentence. Colin had given his word that he'd help her out of this, and he never broke a promise. His spine lost a little of its starch as he looked into Ellie's sad blue eyes. This wasn't her fault. Hell, this wasn't her world. Had she not been cursed, Colin never would have met her and he would have gone his entire life never knowing his true mate. He was thankful that the spiteful witch had given Ellie enough time on this earth for Colin to have found her. But the workings of the supernatural world were as foreign to Ellie as the mate bond Colin insisted on pushing on her. His wolf could grouse all he wanted. It wouldn't change the fact that Colin was going to respect her wishes and give her a little gods-damned space.

No matter how much it might hurt him.

He brushed the hair away from her face and tucked it behind her ear. "Ellie, it's okay." He kissed her forehead and let his lips linger there for a bittersweet moment. "I get it. I can't even begin to imagine what it's been like for you. Living up here. Alone. Not being able to leave or to see the world beyond what you get from the internet or TV. I know we don't know each other. And I also know that a bomb like our mate bond is a lot to digest. We'll free you from this curse and then . . ." Colin refused to think about what "and then" would entail. "Just know that you have me and you have a family. When you're ready, *if* you're ready, you can always come to Stanley."

Ellie's expression softened. Gods, her beauty took his breath away. "Thank you for understanding."

Colin understood perfectly. His gut bottomed out as he took Ellie's hand in his. Was he really considering the possibility that he might have to sacrifice his own life in order for her to finally experience hers?

Ellie kept her hand in his and led him into the living room. She pulled him down beside her on the couch—the same couch they'd wound up naked on a couple days ago—and tucked her body against his. Her head came to rest on his chest and the simple contact made Colin ache with longing. He had to have faith in their bond and trust that everything would work out like it was supposed to. If he let his doubt overtake him, it would cripple him.

"So . . . tell me about this grand adventure," Ellie began. "Wait, first tell me how you figured all of this out. I mean—two days? I've been trying to think of a way to break this curse for two centuries!"

"Supernatural creature, supernatural connections," Colin said. He threaded his fingers through her hair, letting the silky strands slip through his grasp over and over again. "I have access to knowledge and resources that you don't."

Ellie let out a sigh. "Why couldn't I have met you a couple hundred years ago?"

Gods, Colin wondered the same thing. So much time wasted, and now . . . he had no idea how much time they'd have once the curse was broken. These next few days with Ellie might be all he ever got with her. He vowed to make the most of whatever time they had together, though.

"My brother's mate, Mia, should really get the credit. She's a wood nymph and her family has lived in the Sawtooths for centuries. Apparently, you're sort of a legend among the grassroots supernaturals in the area. The mysterious woman, bound to the land by a vindictive witch."

"Seriously?" Ellie brought her head up to look at him. Her brow pinched with honest curiosity. "I can't believe anyone would've ever heard anything about me." Her mouth puckered. "Would've been nice if one of those wood nymphs had come to visit once or twice."

Colin couldn't agree more. If the supernatural community had tried to integrate her a long time ago, maybe the idea of a mate bond with him wouldn't have been so disconcerting to her now. But Ellie wasn't a supernatural creature, not really, and his world was an esoteric one. So far, her indoctrination had been anything but smooth. And it wasn't about to get any less bumpy anytime soon.

"Sorry. I got a little off topic there. Back to Mia?"

"Right." Colin continued to play with Ellie's hair. His wolf was content to have their mate by their side and Colin was right there with the animal. Peace settled over him like a warm blanket. As though this was where he'd always been meant to be. With her. "I don't know a lot about witchcraft, but Mia does. Apparently, curses take a lot more effort than simply saying a few words and infusing them with magic. In order to bind you to the land, Sarah would have to have had a physical object to create the boundaries. Something personal. Mia thinks there are four items at the four corners placed along ley lines. She said if we find the items and destroy them, it should free you."

"Ley lines?"

Colin smiled. Gods, how he wanted endless days to teach her all about his world. Days he might never get. "They're like tiny highways that crisscross the earth and hold magical energy. The latitudes and longitudes of the supernatural world. Witches use ley lines to draw power, map spells, and even travel. In order to keep you within the confines of the boundaries she set, it's almost guaranteed she had to use ley lines. We just have to find them—along with the physical markers she enchanted."

Ellie's gentle laughter reached out like a caress. "It almost seems too easy."

Colin held her closer. That's because it was.

Something didn't add up. Ellie didn't know much about the supernatural world, but it seemed ridiculous that releasing her from the curse that bound her would be so easy. Likewise, she might not have had Colin's keen senses, but she knew he wasn't telling her the whole story. And whatever he was omitting had him on edge.

"Oh, don't worry," Colin replied. "It won't be as easy as you think. We've got to go old-school on this. No motorized vehicles, no electronics. Magic is tricky. We can't have anything with us that might disrupt it. And then we have to actually find the items Sarah enchanted and destroy them."

"How do we do it?" Despite the anxiety that ate away at her stomach lining, Ellie couldn't help but be a little excited. After so many years, day in and day out, of simply existing, she was about to have an honest-to-God adventure. True, it was within the parameters of her own prison, but still . . . And she was about to experience it all with a man—did werewolves still consider themselves men?—she couldn't seem to get enough of. "Destroy the items? Do we need some sort of special weapon? A sword or some sort of magical dagger?"

Colin laughed. Ellie didn't think she'd ever get tired of that sound. "Nothing quite so elaborate. According to Mia, in theory we should be able to simply smash the item with a rock, which will release the magical energy and nullify the spell."

"In theory?" There was always a catch, wasn't there?

"Don't forget, Ellie. You're bringing a werewolf along. I'm not exactly useless if we get into a pinch."

Thank God for that. "Does that mean I get to see some Superman-style feats of strength and speed?"

"Could be." Colin put his lips to her forehead. "But let's hope not."

Ellie could get behind that sentiment. The fewer roadblocks, the better. "How do we find the ley lines? And when do you want to head out?"

Colin laid a finger to his nose. "Leave finding the ley lines to me. And I think we should leave as soon as possible; don't you?"

"Like, now?"

He let out a slow breath. "Sure."

Ellie couldn't help but feel a twinge of disappointment that Colin was so ready to get going. She knew her earlier words had hurt him. But why couldn't he understand that wanting her freedom had nothing to do with *not* wanting him? Ellie wanted Colin more than she'd ever wanted anyone or anything. She'd simply needed to convey to him that if she managed to be free of this horrible curse she wanted the opportunity to spread her wings and truly experience her freedom. And why did he think that meant leaving him in Stanley? Why couldn't they have dozens—hundreds—of adventures together?

"Do you have a backpack? Sleeping bag? We're going to be gone for at least a couple of days. I brought my own gear, a tent, and some food. Thirty square miles isn't much to cover, but I think we need to be prepared for setbacks."

A lump formed in Ellie's throat. "Setbacks?" Sounded like another word for "trouble."

"It'll be okay, Ellie." Colin gave her a reassuring squeeze. "I won't let anything happen to you. I promise."

He barely knew her, and yet Colin was doing everything in his power to help her. To protect her. "Who's going to make sure nothing happens to you?"

"Werewolf." He always used the word like it was the explanation for everything. "I'll be fine."

Ellie certainly hoped so. Because if anything happened to Colin in the course of helping her, she'd never forgive herself.

"I've got a pack and a sleeping bag." If there was one thing Ellie was thankful for in the modern world, it was Amazon. "But that's about it."

"No worries. I've got the rest covered." Colin let out another slow sigh, as though reluctant to follow through with their plans. "Better go get ready. I want to get ahead of the sunset."

Thirty minutes later, Ellie was ready to roll. It wasn't tough to get ready when she had nothing more than a sleeping bag and a change of clothes to throw into her pack.

Colin was outside, unloading his gear from the back of his pickup. Ellie took a quiet moment to simply watch and admire him in all of his magnificent strength and glory. It was almost inconceivable that someone like him could actually exist. He was the perfect representation of masculine perfection. Tall. Strong. Gorgeous. And according to Colin, Ellie was his.

His.

She still didn't understand the significance of their supposed bond. All she knew was that it meant something to him. Was important. Sacred. And she needed to remind herself of that moving forward. He deserved her respect.

He turned toward the window as though he sensed her watching him. Ellie considered dropping to the floor, but instead she froze in place. *Crap.* Caught in the act of peeping. He flashed a cocky smile that damn near set her on fire. Colin knew the effect he had on her. Thanks to his superior senses, Ellie couldn't keep her own damned body's reaction to him a secret. She should have been embarrassed by her brazen wantonness, but she couldn't manage to muster even an ounce of shame.

She wanted Colin, plain and simple.

He strode through the door, the epitome of smug confidence. Ellie's breath caught. His slow, purposeful stride was 100 percent predator and it sent a thrill through her bloodstream. "If you don't stop looking at me like that," his voice dropped to a husky murmur, "we definitely aren't going to get out of here before sundown."

"Is that such a bad thing?" As much as Ellie wanted to break the curse that bound her, she could sacrifice a few minutes to reacquaint herself with the magnificence of Colin's naked body.

The light in Colin's eyes dimmed and his smile no longer beamed with arrogance. Ellie wished she had the superhuman perception necessary to read him.

"It wouldn't be if you could see in the dark." He tried to tease, but his voice lacked the conviction. "I need your eyes, Ellie. I don't know this land like you do. You're our guide."

"Me?" It was true, she'd walked every square inch of her landlocked prison again and again over the years. "Are you sure you want to trust me? I know the land, but I was obviously too stupid to figure out the terms of my own curse."

"You're not stupid," Colin replied. "Don't ever say that. You just didn't know what to look for. We'll figure it out. Together."

Ellie smiled. “Teamwork?”

“Exactly.”

“Okay, then.” If they didn’t leave now, Ellie would be hard-pressed to leave at all. “Let’s get going before I change my mind.” She went up on her tiptoes and kissed Colin once.

He let out a contented groan that helped to boost Ellie’s own ego. “Honey, you sure are a beautiful distraction.”

Would it really be so bad to go to Stanley with Colin? Ellie was beginning to wonder if her wanderlust would cause her to overlook what could be the greatest adventure of her life.

CHAPTER 12

Colin needed to stay focused on the problem he had a chance of controlling and not the one he was helpless to effect. Mia's help, though invaluable, had been superficial at best. They were operating on assumptions. What-ifs. Without knowing where to find the witch who had cursed Ellie to begin with, they were flying blind. Hoping the legends were accurate and they would in fact find four seemingly mundane objects that had been enchanted to create a sort of invisible fence to keep Ellie trapped within its confines. The only certainty in this scenario was that a witch would definitely need ley lines for her spell to work. Colin could sniff out the invisible trails of magic with ease. It was what happened after he did that worried him.

They started at the easternmost boundary of Ellie's territory. The spot just past the Sourdough that she'd first tried to pass. Colin parked his truck in the graveled lot and began to unload. Supernatural strength came in pretty handy on treks like these. Colin could shoulder the bulk of the weight, enabling Ellie to hike longer before she felt fatigued.

"Okay, you're in charge of this excursion." He handed Ellie her pack and she slung it on her back. "You know the general location of the boundaries. Know the land. I'm just here to be your bloodhound. You lead; I'll follow. If I catch the scent of magic, we'll follow it. Deal?"

Ellie studied him. He'd never get tired of the rush he got from her intense scrutiny. He welcomed it. Wanted to lay himself bare to her. Anything to keep her attention. "You can smell magic?"

Gods, he loved her curiosity. Colin put his worry to the back of his mind and simply reveled in the pleasure of her company. "Not exactly. But I can sense it. Magic tingles along my skin and sort of burns my nose."

Ellie grinned. "So I don't *smell* like magic?"

Aside from the faint trace of residual magic that lingered on her as a result of the curse, Ellie's particular magic was unique in that she was Colin's mate. It tingled along his soul. "No. You smell like the river in spring and wild lavender."

Color stained Ellie's cheeks. She looked up at Colin from lowered lashes and her mouth curved into a sweet smile that tugged at his chest. "Well, you don't smell too bad either."

Colin snorted. "Thanks." He hoisted his own pack on his back and secured the strap across his chest. They had rations and water to get last them for a couple of days. With any luck, they'd find the ley lines and break the curse before their provisions ran out. If not, they'd be back at square one, filling their packs at Ellie's house. "Ready to get this show on the road?"

"Yep. Let's do this."

Colin made sure to adopt a pace Ellie could keep up with, but he was pleasantly surprised that he didn't need to slow too much. Ellie was fit and agile, able to negotiate the trails and steep inclines that led to the high ridges with ease. Thanks to last winter's snow and a fairly rainy spring, there was still plenty of late-fall foliage that proved to be both an annoyance and a challenge. Whereas Colin wanted to stomp straight through the brush and leap over the taller bushes, it wasn't quite so easy for Ellie and she opted to circumvent those obstacles.

"Sorry. It's just too hard to navigate the brambles."

Colin didn't want her to apologize for a damn thing. He'd walk whatever crazy, winding route she wanted as long as it meant one more minute of time with her. An hour passed. And another. Time seemed to slip through his fingers, faster than it ever had as they climbed higher to the top of the first ridge. Ellie stopped to stretch and drink some water. "I love the view from here. You can see so much of the river canyon below."

There wasn't anything nature could conjure up that could compare to Ellie's beauty. Colin's wolf let out a low whimper and he cocked his head, focused his senses. Faint, but enough magic to stir the fine hairs on his arms. According to Mia, the items imbued with magic to create the invisible fence corralling Ellie in would likely be located at the four corners. Which meant the ley line he was tracking would have to run due east.

"Colin? Everything okay?"

He looked over at Ellie. "Magic. It's pretty faint, but it's there." He brought up his hand and pointed. "This way. Check your compass."

Ellie dug a compass out of her pocket. Since electronics interfered with magic and vice versa, they were going old-school on this one. No GPS, no Siri to lead the way. She held the tiny compass up and turned toward Colin with a wide, excited smile. "East," she replied. "Dead on."

Colin stepped up beside her. "Stay close to me from here on out." Not only were they close to Ellie's boundary, but also he had no idea what to anticipate moving forward. He didn't expect the witch to have gone through so much trouble to curse Ellie and not protect her magic. Colin was an expect-the-best-but-plan-for-the-worst sort of male. He'd come well armed, and he didn't count on running this gauntlet without getting into a fight or two.

Ellie didn't question or argue with him. She stepped up beside him, her expression wary. The sound of her racing heart distracted Colin from the magic he was trying to track. If he'd had it his way, Ellie would still be at home where he knew she'd be safe.

Ellie watched the compass as they walked east. With every step taken, the tingle of magic intensified on Colin's skin. They were definitely headed in the right direction. His wolf let out a warning growl in his mind as adrenaline dumped into his bloodstream. Something watched them from a distance. Not an animal—well, not exactly—and definitely not friendly.

"Get behind me, Ellie." Colin's right arm jutted out as he swept Ellie behind him. He brought his nose up and sniffed the air and then cleared his nostrils with a snort. The magic burned and put his wolf on edge. From the cover of trees fifty paces ahead, glowing red eyes zeroed in on them. *Shit.* To his left was a tall Douglas fir. Colin turned and lifted Ellie in his arms. He hoisted her up to the nearest branch and she let out a surprised squeal. "Stay up here. Don't come down for any reason. Do you understand me?"

Ellie stared at him, wide-eyed. "Are you freaking kidding me?" Her tone was half incredulity, half indignant anger. "I couldn't get down if I tried!"

Good. Then there'd be no chance of her trying to help him. Colin dragged his gaze from his mate and forced his attention to the threat directly in front of him. The creature that emerged from the cover of trees snarled, ready for a fight. Colin had never seen a hellhound, though he'd heard stories. The witch who'd cursed Ellie had certainly dabbled in some serious black magic. Only the darkest witches could create such a creature.

In this case, the witch had used a coyote. Much like she'd cursed Ellie, she'd changed the animal by infusing him with magic. Colin could at least be happy she hadn't chosen a timber wolf or bear. The coyote was relatively small, though now he had the benefit of supernatural speed, strength, and stamina. The damned thing had been roaming these woods for two centuries. It was a wonder Ellie had never come across him. Colin said a silent prayer of thanks that she'd avoided the borders of her landlocked prison. He'd be doing the animal a favor today by killing him. He deserved to be freed from the magic that bound him as much as Ellie did.

Colin hadn't been challenged in a good long while. And he was more than ready to prove himself to his mate.

Ellie's heart leaped up into her throat. She'd never seen anything like the animal stalking toward Colin with slow, precise steps. He was a creature that didn't exist in nature. Something out of a nightmare. Dark fur, red glowing eyes, teeth bared in a snarl. Colin shrugged out of his pack and drew a long knife from a scabbard at his back. Ellie didn't know which one of them looked more menacing as they squared off, circling each other warily. God, if he got hurt . . . She never should have let him help her.

She opened her mouth to shout out a warning and promptly snapped it shut. Her words would only serve to distract him, and Colin needed every ounce of concentration he could get. The animal, which looked remarkably like a coyote, growled and Colin responded with a growl of his own.

Bright gold swallowed the blue of his eyes and once again Ellie was given a glimpse of that wild part of him that lived just beneath the surface of his skin.

The coyote was the first to attack. He was unnaturally fast, but then again, so was Colin. Ellie had never seen anything like it. The fight was too quick for her simple human eyes to track. Smears of color. Blurs of movement. The glint of light off the blade of Colin's knife. A loud whimper rent the air and Ellie started. It echoed around her, off the surrounding hillsides, and faded into silence. Her heart beat against her rib cage as though it wanted out, and her hands shook. She craned her neck to see past a large granite boulder that blocked her view, desperate to know who had been hurt. Her breath raced in her chest and she let out a cry of relief as Colin rounded the boulder toward her.

"Oh my God!" Ellie squirmed on the tree branch, ready to launch herself to the ground below. "Colin, are you okay?"

He cleaned the blade on his pants and slid the knife back into the sheath before positioning himself below the branch. "I'm okay. Hop down. I've got you."

Ellie didn't have to be told twice. She pushed off from the branch and Colin caught her by the waist to set her feet gently on the ground. She threw her arms around him and swallowed down a sob. "Did you kill him?" She could barely hold back the tears. "Are you hurt?"

He kissed the top of her head. "Shhh. I'm okay. He's dead." Ellie's shoulders shook as she tried to quell the fearful tears that didn't want to stop. "Try to calm down." Colin's hand stroked reassuringly down her back again and again. "It's over. You're okay. It's going to get worse before it gets better, so you need to prepare yourself. Just breathe."

She took several moments to compose herself and let Colin's arms around her be her anchor. Ellie hadn't known fear like this in a long time. The thought of losing Colin had her more shaken than that of him simply being hurt. The intensity of emotions confused her. They barely knew each other and yet she knew not having him in her life would be a million times more crippling than the lonely isolation she'd experienced over the past two centuries.

"Ellie?" His soft voice in her ear coaxed a shiver to the surface of her skin. "You okay, honey?"

She let out a shuddering breath. "I'm okay." She eased away from Colin and dusted herself off. "You're sure he's dead?"

He responded without elaborating, "You have nothing to worry about."

"Okay. Good." If she never saw anything like that creature again it would be too soon. But Colin was right. It was likely to get worse before it got better. She had no doubt there were similar, nastier creatures in her future and she counted her blessings that she'd never encountered any of them while out here hiking on her own.

"Do you still have your compass?"

Ellie couldn't believe how quickly Colin was able to shift gears. One second he'd been in a dangerous fight with the supernatural animal; the next he was calm, cool, and back to business. "I do." She retrieved the compass from her pocket and held it up in front of her. She shifted until the needle swung due east to get them back on track and pointed. "That way."

They walked in a straight line until a large pine tree blocked their path. The tree was the largest in the stand of surrounding pines and Douglas firs. A large natural bole hollowed out its center and Colin turned to Ellie, his expression a strange mix of excitement and worry. "My teeth are practically chattering from the magical energy here."

He reached into the bole and felt around for several tense moments. Ellie held her breath and her muscles tensed. Colin's hand emerged and in his grasp was a delicate teacup.

"That teacup belonged to my mother," Ellie said with wonder as she let out a breath. "It was part of a set."

Sarah had stolen that teacup from her. Ellie's anger crested, as fresh and hot as it had been when she first realized what had happened to her. She took the cup from Colin's hand and without even thinking about the repercussions for her actions smashed it against a nearby chunk of granite. The delicate cup shattered and a palpable wave of energy crested over Ellie. She drew in a gasp of breath as her knees buckled. Colin reached out to support her and she gripped his arm.

"Did you feel that?"

His brow furrowed and he did nothing to hide the worry in his expression. "I did. And I think you just broke through the eastern wall of your boundary."

Her anger drained and was replaced with excited elation. Ellie stared at Colin for a quiet moment. She let go of his arm and rounded the pine tree to continue on the eastern ley line. She knew how far she could and couldn't go on every inch of this land. When she reached what she knew was the border, Ellie closed her eyes. Lifted one foot. And slowly took a step.

Her eyes flew open and she turned toward Colin. Joy bloomed in her chest and she smiled wide. "No pain! Not even a tickle! We did it!" She rushed back and flung herself at Colin, wrapping her arms around his neck. She pulled back and placed a long, fervent kiss on his mouth.

"One boundary down, three more to go!"

CHAPTER 13

One boundary down. Three more to go.

Ellie's elation settled like a stone in the pit of Colin's stomach. The hellhound the witch had created to guard the first boundary had been easy enough to kill. He could only hope any other guards set to watch the remaining boundaries would have been created with a human foe in mind rather than a more powerful supernatural. However, Colin wasn't about to underestimate a witch with enough dark magic at her disposal to conjure the sort of curse that had made Ellie indestructible. Mia's words came back to haunt him and Colin's wolf let out a forlorn howl in the back of his mind. *If the curse has kept her alive all this time, breaking it could kill her in an instant.*

She'd given his own fears a voice and solidified them. Nothing was certain except Ellie's desire to be rid of this burden that had kept her alone and isolated for so long. Colin would have to broach the subject with her eventually, but until then he'd keep a close eye on her and look for any signs that she might be weakening or changing.

"Is it weird that now I know I can walk as far east as I want, I sort of feel the urge to take off and walk until my legs give out?" Ellie turned to Colin and graced him with a brilliant smile.

She deserved every ounce of happiness she felt. Colin wasn't about to squash that with his own worries. They'd face any obstacles in their way when they got to them. He refused to worry until there was something to worry about.

"You can walk as far as you want, honey." Ellie's joy buffeted Colin's senses in gentle waves that calmed the animal inside of him like nothing else could.

She reached back and grabbed his hand. "Watching you fight that thing . . . wow. I didn't know anything could move that fast or be that strong. You're amazing."

Again, that she was pleased with him infused Colin with warmth that pulsed pleasantly through his body. He wanted to impress her. To prove himself to her. To show her he was worthy of her. The mate bond demanded it of him and he was helpless to fight it.

"We can keep walking east if you want," Colin said as he tried to brush aside her compliment. "Or we can head north and find the next boundary."

He knew Ellie's answer before she gave it to him. "North. But now that I know what we're up against, let's be more careful, okay?"

Totally fine by Colin. The hellhound had been an easy opponent, but there was no guarantee the remaining boundaries would be guarded by creatures as easy to defeat.

Ellie held her compass aloft until the needle pointed to true magnetic north. They set off through the brush, careful not to veer off course until Colin's senses could once again identify the next ley line. With any luck, they'd reach the second boundary before sunset and they'd camp for the night. So far, they'd been walking for just under four hours, with another four or so more to go.

"You said you were in law enforcement," Ellie remarked

as they walked. "But you never told me what agency you worked for."

Colin was grateful to have some conversation to distract him from his nagging thoughts. "It's a new appointment," he said. "With the Sawtooth Mountains Territory's sentry. Sort of a supernatural equivalent of the state police."

"Wow." Ellie shook her head. "I mean, I knew magic was real . . . but I still can't believe there's this whole other world that exists and no one really knows about it. So you're a supernatural cop?"

Colin laughed. "More or less. But like I said, the appointment is recent. I haven't had a single day on the job yet."

"Oh." He wondered at Ellie's sudden sullen tone. "So, you're pretty excited about it, then?"

"Yeah." He could talk about the sentry position all day if she'd let him. "I'm excited to have something that's mine and not a part of pack life or structure. My alpha, Liam, is less excited."

"Alpha?" Ellie asked. "Is he like the boss of your pack?"

Colin was sure Liam would love Ellie's interpretation of his role. "Pretty much. Liam worked as a sentry before he moved the pack to Idaho. He didn't have a very good experience with them, so he's a little biased. I was trying to convince him to put his prejudice aside when Mia told me her theory about your curse."

"Oh." Again, he sensed so many unspoken things hidden in the one word. "Does Liam not want you away from Stanley?"

"Not at all. The alpha oversees the protection of the entire pack. Liam worries that the sentry's leadership is too . . . cavalier in the treatments of its members. To put it in perspective, he's like an overprotective dad who doesn't want his kid to join the military."

"I can see why he'd be concerned." Ellie eased a bush out of the way and continued to walk in the direction the compass pointed. "But at the same time, he needs to trust that you're capable of making smart decisions and taking care of yourself."

"Exactly." Every minute spent with Ellie further proved to Colin that they complemented each other. That they were meant to be together. Gods, he wished Ellie could see it, feel it, sense it, in the same way he could. "Wade Robinson, the territory director, told me he wouldn't hire me without Liam's consent. I threatened to go rogue when Liam told me he wouldn't sign off on the appointment and my brother Owen went damn near nuclear."

"Rogue?" Ellie's step faltered. "What's that?"

"Werewolves live in packs just like our animal counterparts." Maybe if he could get Ellie to understand pack structure, she'd also understand why he wanted to keep her close. "That group structure is incredibly important. If you leave the pack or are excommunicated for some reason, you're considered a rogue. Generally, rogues are treated as outcasts. They're not trusted by the supernatural community."

"Wow." Ellie picked up her pace so she could stay alongside Colin. "I had no idea. That's awful."

"I'm not interested in leaving my pack. But I'm also not interested in letting Liam's fears dictate my life. I'm hoping that when I get back home he'll have had some time to think about it and realize he's being unreasonable."

"I've been alone for so long, I don't even remember what it's like to have a family, let alone have someone around to look out for me."

Colin's heart dropped into his gut. He couldn't imagine what Ellie's life had been like up until now. Keeping this secret about herself that she couldn't tell to anyone. Watching as the few people who lived in the area grew old and died while she remained unchanging and forced to do it all over again with the next generation and then the next.

"How did no one realize you were . . ."

"A freak of nature?" Ellie asked with a laugh. Colin hopped over a fallen tree and reached for Ellie's waist to hoist her over it. "I was an only child and both of my parents fell sick and passed shortly after it happened. At first I didn't believe Sarah when she told me what she'd done, but then she ran a knife through my chest to prove it." Her sad chuff of laughter stabbed through Colin and he swore he felt the same pain she had. "I hid myself away. I didn't want anyone to know. My family's cabin was tucked far enough away in the woods that no one bothered with me. It's easy to live off the land when you know how. Every few years, I'd wander into town. Work. Earn money. Make an excuse as to why I had to leave and hide for a while. No one wants to live here. It's too barren. Too far from civilization. People come and go. No one usually stays long enough to notice anything about me."

"Including your fan club at the Sourdough?"

Ellie's laughter was more genuine this time. "I've only been working there for a couple of years. That's as long as I've known Frank and his crew." Her voice went low. "They're old. They don't have much time left on this earth. Living so long made me realize how quickly a human life can pass. How fragile they all are."

"Ellie." Colin wished he had the words to comfort her. "You're human too."

"No." She graced him with a sad smile. "Not anymore."

Colin's gut tied into a knot. All too soon, Ellie might become more fragile than she thought.

Ellie never considered that pack life could be so structured. The thought of Colin being considered an outcast squeezed her heart. If she asked him to leave Lowman with her, to travel the world and leave his pack behind, she'd essentially be condemning him to an existence as a pariah. She didn't want that for him, which made their situation even stickier. If she chose to stay here for him—to be with him—she'd be cheating herself of a lifetime of experiences. If she left . . . Ellie worried she might actually leave a piece of her heart behind.

They continued to talk as they hiked. Ellie discovered that Colin's favorite food was pizza, he was a sucker for cheesecake, and his favorite sport was hockey. She shared that her favorite food was biscuits with butter and honey like her mama used to make, she was a sucker for *The Bachelor,* and she thought the e-reader was the most ingenious invention of the modern world. Their conversation flowed from one topic to the next without either of them having to search for something to say. Every minute spent with Colin became something Ellie held close to her heart and cherished. Even their quiet moments were spent in companionable silence.

Did adventures really matter if Ellie had to experience all of it alone? Without Colin?

"I found the ley line."

Colin shifted their course to the left and then readjusted back to magnetic north. Ellie followed. Tiny butterflies took flight in her stomach as they neared the second boundary. She checked her watch, another four hours eaten by the soles of their feet. The sun set low on the horizon. It wouldn't be long before twilight settled over the hillside. In the distance, Ellie spotted a set of glowing red eyes. Was it too much to hope that a supernaturally enhanced bunny guarded this part of the boundary?

"Ellie . . ." She recognized the warning before he finished saying her name.

"I see it." Ellie wished she were as preternaturally strong and fast as Colin. At least then she'd be able to help him. "I know the drill."

She headed for the nearest tree and Colin lifted her as though she weighed nothing at all. His gaze, already feral gold, met hers, and he smiled. "Two boundaries down."

He turned without a word and headed toward the animal whose low growl disrupted the quiet evening. Funny, the thrill of freedom didn't hold the same allure as it had a few hours ago. Ellie didn't have quite the vantage point as Colin fought whatever the hell evil creature Sarah had assigned to watch over the boundaries of Ellie's prison. Snarls were met with grunts and growls. The sound of brush rustling and the thump of a body hitting the ground were the only indicators anything was happening. The sun set behind the western mountains, casting a gray mantle over the sky. Tension pulled Ellie's muscles taut as once again Colin put his own safety—his life—on the line. *For her.* Worry pressed the air from her lungs and Ellie couldn't help but wonder why, after all the times she'd walked this same path, she'd never seen these creatures that so fiercely guarded the items Sarah had enchanted.

Why now? Was it because of Colin? Did Sarah's magic somehow know that he'd be capable of accomplishing something Ellie could never do on her own? The notion of her helplessness rankled almost as much as her worry for Colin's safety.

God, Ellie. You never should have brought him into this.

She counted off the seconds in her head. The minutes. Twilight gave way to full dark and the sounds of the fight grew faint, as though they'd moved uphill. Ellie clung to the branch that supported her. Her muscles cramped from trying not to move. Soon, even the sound of a scuffle settled into eerie silence. A lump formed in Ellie's throat as she waited. Waited. Waited.

"Ellie. Hop down. I've got you."

She let out a surprised squeal. She wobbled on the branch, so startled she nearly fell out of the tree. Colin hadn't so much as stirred a blade of grass as he approached. He moved with eerie silence, once again astounding her.

"Colin! Oh my God, you scared the crap out of me!"

He gave a low chuckle that didn't sound as humorous as Ellie expected he wanted it to. "Sorry. That took a little longer than I'd hoped."

Colin grunted and Ellie's heart rate cranked into high gear. "Are you hurt?"

"Damn timber wolf," Colin complained. "Looks like we're graduating to bigger guards. Got his teeth in my torso, but nothing serious. Now get down here and let's find a magical item to smash."

"Nothing serious?" Ellie pushed herself from the branch, and once again Colin caught her with ease. The fact that he treated a wolf bite like *no big deal* made her want to shake some sense into him. "I have a flashlight in my bag. Let me look."

"Not yet." Colin brushed her concern aside as though he'd only sustained a scratch. "It's getting dark. Let's find what we need to break and take care of it so we can set up camp."

Ellie's frustration left her lips on a sigh. "Fine."

She knew there was no arguing with him. It was best to

just do what he wanted so she could do what she wanted when they were done. She pulled her flashlight from her pack as they searched the ley line for anywhere Sarah might have hidden her enchanted boundary marker. Colin came to a stop at a large granite boulder that had a wide crack down the center and reached into the dark cavern. After a few seconds, he pulled out what appeared to be a weathered scrap of fabric. Ellie brought up the flashlight and his brow furrowed with curiosity as he unwrapped the fabric to reveal a delicate bone hair comb.

"That's mine too!"

Indignant anger choked the air from Ellie's lungs. Even after hundreds of years, it chapped her ass to know that Sarah had been in her home. Had stolen her possessions! She took the comb from the nest of fabric and threw it on the ground. She brought up her boot and smashed it into bits. Her knees buckled as the wave of magic once again stole over her, and like clockwork Colin was there to steady her. She brought her eyes up to meet his worried expression. God, she wished she knew what was eating at him.

His face was as grim as she'd ever seen it. "Two down. Two more to go."

CHAPTER 14

Colin couldn't shake his foul mood as he set up camp. His torso where the second hellhound had bitten him ached like a motherfucker and the punctures from the animal's powerful jaw had yet to heal. Luckily, they were close enough to the full moon that he would heal a little faster than usual. He wished it were as easy to repair his cranky attitude that showed no signs of letting up.

Ellie had remained quiet since destroying the second boundary marker and Colin didn't like it one bit. If anything, it contributed to his temper. He wanted to crawl right into her head and see what she was thinking. The silence between them slowly unraveled Colin. His own guilt at not telling her everything she needed to know before they started this quest gnawed at him. Had he perhaps let his own wants get in the way of Ellie's needs? Had he perhaps used his own knowledge of the situation to manipulate it to his advantage?

Of course he fucking had. Gods, he was an asshole.

He pushed the last tent stake into the ground and Ellie got busy putting the sleeping bags inside. It was bound to be a chilly fall night, but Colin's body heat would keep Ellie protected from the harsh elements. That is, if she let him. He'd hoped that this little adventure would bring them closer together. But he worried that every passing moment only helped to build a wall between them.

"Are you hungry?"

Ellie poked her head out from the tent. "I know I should eat, but I sort of just want to crash. I'm sure you're starving, though. Go ahead and eat without me. I'm just going to lie down for a while."

Colin scowled as Ellie ducked her head back into the tent. He swore under his breath as his frustration mounted. The wolf grew restless in the recesses of his psyche, wound up and just as agitated as he was. Colin stood and shot a glare at his backpack as though it had somehow offended him. He pulled back his leg to boot the damn thing down the hill and instead kicked out at a nearby rock, sending it flying downhill.

"I'm going for firewood. *Don't* leave the campsite." Colin didn't give Ellie a chance to respond as he marched uphill. He needed to move. To walk off his temper and calm the hell down.

Colin walked for a good mile. A half mile uphill before turning and backtracking so as not to put too much distance between him and Ellie. He carried an armload of firewood, scraps of branches and broken logs that he'd found along the way. He thought about Ellie. About the fact that she had never walked farther than what he just had. He thought about the land that bound her, the loneliness she'd been forced to endure. The way she'd tried to escape immortality time and again before giving up. All of it weighed on Colin's mind as he headed back to camp. But most of all, he worried that the road ahead would be much harder. And he worried that Ellie would hate him once she realized he'd backed her into a corner.

"Colin? Is that you?" Ellie's voice called out from the tent as he dropped the load of firewood on the ground.

He gathered a few rocks and fashioned them into a fire ring before stacking the wood inside and retrieving a box of matches from his pack. "Yeah. I'm building a fire."

Colin wasn't mad at Ellie. He didn't think he could ever be mad at her. He was mad at himself and taking it out on her and she absolutely didn't deserve it.

"It's getting pretty cold."

"Yeah, well, I'm sorry I took so long. Like I said, I'm building a fire." Gods, what was wrong with him? Colin knew he was acting like a first-class asshole and yet there was nothing he could do to stop it. The sound of the zipper shredded the quiet and Ellie poked her head out of the tent, her expression fierce.

"Are you seriously that thickheaded?" Her temper shone through in every word. "I don't give a damn about a fire. I want *you* to come in here and keep me warm. But never mind, I guess. Build your stupid fire!"

Her head disappeared back into the tent and the zipper squealed shut. Colin's shoulders slumped and he rested his head in his palm. Yep, he'd really fucked up this time. He finished building the fire, and as the flames began to lick at the dried wood he bolstered his courage and prepared to face the storm inside the tent. It might have been presumptuous, but he shucked his clothes outside the tent and climbed inside. She might have been mad at him, but that wasn't going to stop him from making amends. What Colin needed right now, the only thing that would calm him, was his mate's bare skin against his.

She'd zipped the two sleeping bags together to make one big bag. Apparently, Colin wasn't the only one who'd been presumptuous. He crawled farther into the tent and zipped it closed before climbing into the sleeping bag and tucking his body against hers. Gods, her soft skin was heaven as it caressed his.

"I'm sorry, Ellie." He didn't know what else to say.

"I wanted to look at your torso. Make sure you're okay. Couldn't even let me do that. I mean, did I do something wrong? I've been trying to figure out what I could have done to upset you for the past two hours."

She had every right to be angry. To complain. To feel hurt. Ellie had done nothing wrong. She didn't deserve to be on the receiving end of a shitty mood he'd created himself. "You didn't do anything wrong. I'm just a little wound up and on edge. We're getting closer to the full moon and it makes my wolf a little volatile. I know that's no excuse, and you have every right to be upset. I just got too deep into my own head. I really am sorry, Ellie."

She turned in the sleeping bag and regarded him. Colin doubted she could see much in the dark. The fire burning outside barely illuminated the inside of the tent. But Colin could see her perfectly. Every beautiful detail. Ellie was remarkable. Strong. Fierce. Stubborn and willful. And the thought of losing her crippled him.

"I never carry a first-aid kit." She spoke the words as though it were something she should be ashamed of. "I don't get hurt. I can't. So there's no reason for me to carry one. And now, you're the one who's hurt and there's nothing I can do about it."

Colin's lips curved into a smile. She really didn't have any idea how resilient he truly was. "I don't pack a first-aid kit either," he said. "When I told you I heal fast, I meant it. The punctures are almost completely closed up. You're not allowed to feel bad, do you understand me?"

Without a word, Ellie reached out and stroked her

fingertips along Colin's torso. His muscles tensed as pleasure radiated through him. His cock stirred between his legs and he swallowed a groan. Her simplest touch drove him out of his mind with want. Did she have any idea the effect she had on him?

"You're right," she said with wonder. "I don't even feel anything."

"Ellie." Colin's voice was rough with passion. "If you don't stop touching me like that, I'm going to be tempted to prove to you just how *un*injured I am."

Her fingers skirted lower, past his hips, and she took the length of his cock in her palm. Colin sucked in a sharp breath as she stroked him from base to tip. Her voice went low and husky as the words vibrated through him. "Good. I was hoping you'd say that."

Ellie's mood had tripped from annoyed to wanton in a split second. She'd wanted to hold on to her anger, but Colin made it damn near impossible. The second he crawled into the sleeping bag beside her, rubbed his naked body against hers, and spoke in her ear with that deep, rumbling voice, she'd been lost. In truth, Ellie had been lost to Colin from the moment she laid eyes on him. His silent stoicism had bothered her more than she wanted to admit. Something was on Colin's mind, had been since they'd set out on this adventure, and she was tired of him keeping secrets. If something was wrong, she deserved to know. And damn it, they were going to get everything out in the open. Just as soon as she answered the call of her own raging desires.

Her want of Colin was like a force of nature. She had no choice but to ride out the storm.

His reaction when she touched him was an aphrodisiac

in itself. To know he wanted her, craved her as much as she craved him, drove her mad with longing. She continued to stroke the length of his shaft, silk encased in steel, as she listened to the sounds of his breath. Colin was one of a kind, and Ellie still couldn't believe he was hers.

The quarters were close in the tiny two-person tent, and they were about to get a lot closer. She was still a little shaken up over Colin's injuries, supernatural healing or not. She'd lived with the constant reminder that life was such a fragile, invaluable thing. Loved ones could be lost in the blink of an eye. She didn't have to know Colin well to realize losing him would lay her low. The next day, the next minute, hell, the next second was always uncertain and Ellie didn't want to waste another iota of time spent with Colin.

Ellie rolled and flung one leg over Colin's torso. He adjusted with her, rolling to his back as she straddled his waist. She bent low so her head wouldn't brush the top of the tent as she brought her hips up. His mouth found hers in the dark as his hands came to rest at her waist. A shock of heat glided over her sensitive flesh as the head of his cock thrust against her pussy. He pulled her down on top of him and Ellie let out a cry of relief as his length impaled her. Emotion swelled in her chest at the sensation of rightness, of completion, that overtook her when she was with Colin.

"Ellie, you feel so good." Colin murmured the words against her mouth before he claimed it in another ravenous kiss. "I can't get enough. I need to be buried inside of you until the sun rises."

Ellie's brain nearly short-circuited from Colin's heated words. No man had ever spoken to her in such a way. But Colin wasn't a man, was he? He stood head and shoulders above them all. His fingers dug into her waist as he guided the motion of her hips. Ellie matched the easy rhythm and her head fell back on her shoulders, pushing her breasts toward Colin's mouth. He took one nipple between his lips. Licked, sucked, and nibbled until Ellie was breathless, writhing, and sobbing with pleasure as she rode him. He paid the same lavish attention to her other breast, building the sweet anticipation to the point that she knew she wouldn't withstand another second of the delicious torture.

Her hands dove into his hair as she held his mouth against her. Her hips ground against his, each seductive roll urging him to take her deeper and harder. Ellie's hand came down beside Colin as though to anchor her. Every nerve ending in her body fired, heat swamped her, and a rush of warmth spread between her thighs. The sensation of Colin's mouth on her breast, the strength of his hands as he held her, the thrust of his hips and the intense pleasure he evoked as he fucked her, drove Ellie past the border of her restraint. Desperate sobs wracked her as the orgasm burst through her. Each deep pulsation was more intense than the one before it, a never-ending, churning sea of sensation that tossed Ellie with each dip and crest.

Colin fell back onto the sleeping bag as his muscles tensed. "Ellie!" Her name burst from his lips as he came and she was once again flooded with warmth.

They came down from the intense high together. Bodies joined, breaths synced up as one, gentle caresses, easy thrusts of hips, and openmouthed kisses that not only sated Ellie but also made her hungry for more. Would it always be this way with him? Moments of insatiable passion that satisfied momentarily, tiding them over until their hungers for each other needed to be sated once again?

You'll only know if you choose to stay.

Ellie had never been so torn. She'd always been a decisive woman. Knew her mind and her path and stuck to it.

Colin took everything she knew about herself and turned it on its head. He made unpredictability seem commonplace and she wondered if she opted to go out in search of adventures she might just be passing up the greatest adventure of all.

Colin shifted, rolling so Ellie rested half on his chest. She let out a sigh as their bodies parted, already missing his heat and the way he filled her so completely.

"I'm sorry I was a cranky asshole tonight."

Ellie smiled as she tucked her head against his shoulder. "I have a feeling you weren't half as much of a cranky asshole as you're capable of being." His attitude hadn't bothered her. She could be pretty cranky and obnoxious too when she wanted to be. She'd been petulant because she wanted him close. Wanted his arms around her and his mouth on hers. Maybe that's what they'd both needed. A calm to follow the storm.

Colin laughed. "True. But I'm still sorry. You didn't deserve my shitty attitude."

"Hey, you're doing all of the heavy lifting here. I owe you. Big-time. If you want to have a hissy fit along the way, go right ahead."

He stroked her hair and Ellie swore it was the most comforting thing she'd ever experienced. "Only if you promise to temper my mood the way you just did."

He didn't even have to ask. "Deal."

A space of quiet passed and Ellie shifted to rest her head against Colin's chest. The sound of his heartbeat lulled her, relaxed her from head to toe.

"Are you asleep?"

"Mmmm." She placed a kiss on his chest. "No. Just content. Thinking."

"About what?"

"You."

His heartbeat sped up a little and it sent a riot of butterflies swirling in Ellie's stomach. "What about me?"

"Just that you're amazing. And that I like you. A lot."

"I like you too." His teasing tone made her heart race alongside his. "A lot."

They could be so much more if Ellie just let herself fall. They could be amazing if she simply trusted in the bond Colin had so much faith in. Why was she letting her screwed-up notion of freedom ruin what could possibly be the best thing to ever happen to her? Why did she have to overthink something that Colin made seem like it required no thought at all?

"Ellie." His tone became serious and her nerves ratcheted tight. "I need to tell you something."

"Tomorrow." She didn't want anything to ruin this perfect moment. Ellie had no idea what Colin wanted to say to her, but she was certain it wasn't good. "Tell me in the morning, Colin. I'm going to go to sleep."

"All right." His tone dropped an octave and she swore she felt it in the pit of her gut. "Tomorrow. Good night, Ellie. Sleep well."

She turned her head to kiss his chest again as she settled in against him. "Good night, Colin."

Emotion welled in Ellie's chest and she swallowed it down. She knew, without a doubt, that tomorrow everything would change.

CHAPTER 15

Colin woke to the smell of breakfast. Well, as close to breakfast as you could get with the backpacking rations he'd brought. He climbed out of the tent to find a fire burning and Ellie cooking. She flashed a brilliant smile that made his heart stutter in his chest.

"Good morning!" Her gaze raked his naked body and Colin damn near grabbed her and dragged her back inside the tent. "I know you're a werewolf and have crazy supernatural body heat, but for the record it's freezing out here! Get some clothes on!"

She scooped some eggs onto the plate along with some cured Canadian bacon and a dollop of oatmeal. She gave him a look that indicated he wouldn't get a bite to eat until he put his clothes on and so Colin quickly dressed and settled down by the fire.

"It's sort of a mixed bag this morning," she remarked as she handed him the plate and a fork. "The oatmeal's thick enough to mortar bricks. It's definitely going to stick with you today."

Colin chuckled. "Nah. We've got sixty miles to hike today. We'll burn it off in no time."

Ellie smiled. She plated her own food and settled down

beside him. "You're probably right about that. At least it's all downhill from here."

At least something today would be easy. Colin suspected the downhill trek would be the only break they got. He'd hardly slept the night before. Instead, his mind raced as he held Ellie close and pondered not only the possibilities of his future but also Ellie's reaction when he finally told her what he'd been withholding from her since yesterday.

They ate in companionable silence. Ellie seemed anxious to get going and began to break down camp as soon as she had the last bite of once-dehydrated eggs in her mouth. It definitely wasn't a gourmet meal, and Colin was worried about her energy levels since she hadn't eaten dinner the night before. But one thing he'd learned about Ellie was that she was a woman who knew her mind. He wouldn't dare point out to her that she needed a few more calories for today's hike. If she wanted to eat, she'd eat.

"So, about last night."

Ellie turned to look at him and smiled. "Last night was amazing. I'll take that over a sixty-mile hike any day." She turned away and focused her attention on rolling up the sleeping bags and tent. Once again, she was using avoidance to keep him from telling her what he needed to say.

"Last night was amazing. But—"

"Oh, no butts about it," Ellie teased. She set the tent and Colin's sleeping bag by his pack and took his empty plate from him. "Better finish packing up so we can go." Her tone was much too cheery. "We've got a lot of ground to cover and we're burning daylight."

Damn it. She was going to have to listen to him sooner or later. Putting it off wouldn't make it any less unpleasant for either of them.

Colin packed up his gear and hoisted his backpack onto

his shoulders. Ellie was a captive audience; she couldn't thwart him for long. They were going to have this conversation whether she liked it or not.

"Time to head west." She pulled the compass from her pocket and turned until they were headed in the right direction. She took point despite knowing Colin wanted her to stay back from here on out. Just another avoidance tactic. "Let me know when you feel the ley line and we'll adjust course."

Her pace was fast as she hiked and Colin figured it would only be a matter of time before she tired herself out. When that happened, they were having a conversation whether she liked it or not.

It only took a half hour for Colin to find the ley line. He picked up his pace and walked beside Ellie as they continued west to the end of her boundary. Colin suspected whatever guarded the western boundary would be a little tougher opponent than the last. Part of him admired the witch's tactics. He assumed the magic self-adjusted. Starting off easy depending on which boundary Ellie tackled first. It was curious she'd never run into these guardians before. But he had to assume that once she'd realized she was trapped and figured her curse was inescapable, Ellie never again came close to where the witch had hidden the boundary markers.

Minutes turned into hours. Colin tried again and again to broach the subject of her curse and Ellie artfully deflected each and every attempt. By the time they reached the third boundary, Colin felt a resurgence in his cranky asshole attitude from the previous night. Especially since this section of land had no cover, no trees, no brush, nowhere for him to tuck Ellie away and keep her safe. *Son of a bitch.*

His attention would be divided, which would make for a sloppy fight. Colin had no choice but to suck it up and face whatever challenge the now absentee witch decided to throw his way. What he really wanted was to meet the witch face-to-face and have the chance to avenge his mate.

"Do you see anything?"

Colin didn't miss the worry in Ellie's tone. He shrugged out of his pack and dug in the front pocket. "Here." He pulled back the slide before handing her the GLOCK. "There's no safety, so it's ready to go. Don't hesitate to shoot, understand?"

Ellie nodded. Her scent soured but not enough for Colin to worry that she was too frightened to shoot if she had to. Ellie was brave. The bravest woman he'd ever met. She'd had to have been to endure what she had. She could handle herself.

"Watch out for sharp teeth this time, okay?" Ellie dropped the gun to her side and pointed it toward the ground.

Magic danced along Colin's skin and he looked up to see an enormous bull elk cresting the hillside toward them. His eyes glowed red and Colin took a breath as he readied himself for yet another challenge. "I don't think his teeth are what I'm going to have to look out for," he remarked. "Okay, Ellie. Stay back and remember, don't hesitate to shoot."

Her eyes went wide as she spotted the elk. Definitely bigger than the timber wolf and an animal that could be just as deadly. His enormous six-point rack of antlers could impale Colin any number of ways. His hooves could easily stomp him into the ground. The animal was a formidable opponent, which only confirmed Colin's assumption that each boundary would be harder to claim. He could only imagine what he'd encounter at the end of the line. That is, if he and Ellie chose to finish what they'd started.

He circled the massive bull, careful to keep a safe distance from the antlers. The animal threw his head back and let out a blood-curdling squeal that echoed off the surrounding hillside. A prize like this would feed the pack for months. Too bad the sadistic witch had thought it better to enchant the animal and let him go to waste. Colin hated to kill needlessly, and so far the past twenty-four hours had been filled with needless killing. All because the witch was too much of a coward to come out of hiding and face them herself.

The elk bucked his head and Colin jumped back to narrowly avoid the wicked point of its antlers. He pulled the long knife from the scabbard at his back. If anything, this would be an interesting fight. . . .

Ellie's jaw dropped. So far, she'd been a peripheral witness to Colin's fights, watching from high up on a tree branch, with her view obstructed by pine needles and tall brush. The hand that held the GLOCK shook as she brought it up, prepared to do what he asked and shoot the second it looked like she needed to protect herself.

Or him.

She'd be damned if she stood by and watched him risk his life for her again and did not do something to help. The quarters were close and there was a chance a wild shot might hit Colin, so when it was time to fire the gun Ellie needed to be sure that he was clear and her aim was true.

The bull was *huge*. Elk like that only got to be that size by being the toughest, smartest, most aggressive bastards in the herd. It didn't hurt that the animal had magic on his side, making him faster, tougher, and smarter still. Colin fought with equal ferocity. Equal strength and speed. He tossed the enormous animal like he weighed nothing, sending him sprawling thirty yards downhill, legs pointed to the sky. It didn't take long for the elk to right himself. He pushed to his feet and charged, head down, the tips of his antlers pointed directly at Colin.

Ellie aimed the gun and gently squeezed the trigger. The bullet struck the elk at his shoulder and his step faltered as his back legs kicked up into the air. He tossed his head wildly before changing course and charging straight at Ellie. *Crap!* The bullet had only managed to piss the animal off and now he was coming straight for her, prepared to impale her with his antlers.

"Ellie! Gods-damn it, get out of the way!"

She cringed at Colin's angry shout as she threw herself out of the path of the charging animal. The air rushed from her lungs as she struck the hard earth and the thundering of hooves echoed in her ears. Ellie covered her head with her arms in an effort to protect herself as a second set of footsteps surrounded her and then immediately cut off.

Her head came up in time to see Colin launch himself at the elk. They went down in a tangle of limbs and hooves and came to a skidding stop not ten feet from where she'd landed. Colin's arm came up in a blur and stabbed down. Once. Twice. Three times. The elk let out a thundering squeal and Ellie covered her ears as the ominous sound faded into eerie silence.

The poor animal ceased his flailing kicks and died in the tall grass.

Colin pushed away and rushed toward Ellie. He dropped the knife from his grasp and scooped her up in his arms, flinging her upright so fast, she worried she'd get whiplash. He inspected every inch of her from the top of her head to her boots. Lifted the hem of her shirt, checked her jeans for any rips.

"Are you okay, Ellie? Are you hurt?"

"I'm okay." Filling her lungs with air seemed almost too

great a feat to accomplish. She let Colin support her as she worked to still her trembling limbs. "Are you?"

"A couple of scratches, but nothing bad."

Thank God.

Knowing he was okay allowed her to finally take a deep breath. She took a few more seconds to calm down and simply enjoy the strength of Colin's arms around her. When she knew her legs would support her, she eased away.

"Okay, let's find that marker and smash it into bits."

Storm clouds gathered in Colin's eyes, the gold light of his animal nature flashing like lightning against the deeper blue of his irises. "All right. But afterward, Ellie, we *need* to talk."

A dark sense of foreboding settled in Ellie's stomach. She'd been trying to avoid this conversation and Colin wasn't going to let it happen. Whatever he had to say, Ellie knew without a doubt she wouldn't like it.

It didn't take long to find the teapot that rested under the crumpled remains of an old rail fence. Ellie took a rock and smashed the delicate porcelain. As before, magic wafted over her. And also as she expected, the magic seemed more powerful this time, its force bringing her to her knees. Colin waited patiently for her to gain her composure and helped her to stand. She'd hoped that maybe her apparent weakened state would prompt him to have mercy and avoid the conversation he wanted to have, but she knew better. She wasn't a delicate flower by any stretch of the imagination. Time to pull up her big-girl pants and face the music.

"The magic is getting stronger the farther we go," she remarked. It was as good a line as any to get the ball rolling. Colin scowled. He knew it as well. "Are you worried about what we'll encounter at the southern border?"

"No." Colin grabbed a rag from his pack and cleaned the

blood from his knife and his hands before sliding the weapon back into his scabbard. "I'm worried about what will happen to you once you break the final marker."

He turned and started walking. Ellie hurried to catch up, digging the compass from her pocket. She changed course slightly to get them on the right track and Colin shifted without even looking at her, as though he instinctually knew which direction her body had shifted.

"Me? Why?" Worry ate at Ellie's stomach lining. "I mean, I'll be free. That's a good thing, right?"

"Of course it will be." Colin spoke so low, she had to strain to hear him. "But Ellie, there's a chance . . ." He stopped dead in his tracks and turned to face her. "There's a chance you might die when the curse is broken." She opened her mouth to speak, but Colin didn't give her the chance. "That's why I think we should leave the spell at the southern border intact, just to be safe."

If Colin's assumption was correct, it would mean Ellie would never be truly free. Some part of her would always belong to Sarah and her malicious spell. A part of the world would always be blocked from her due to the magic that traveled the southern ley line. Her brow furrowed as she studied Colin and a wave of anger crashed over her.

"That's why you wanted to start at the eastern border, isn't it? Because it opened up the way to Stanley. You figured I'd go with you if I didn't have any other choice in the matter. You *tricked* me!"

The words left her mouth before she could think better of it. She hadn't meant to accuse Colin. She wasn't mad at him or suspicious of him or anything else. She was simply mad at the world. At her lot in life and her own misfortune. And Colin was on the receiving end because he was standing before her, the only other person on the planet—besides a witch who might well be dead—who knew the truth about her life.

"Never mind. Forget I said anything." She didn't want to fight. She didn't want to do anything right now but sit on the ground and cry. But crying never helped anyone do anything, so she kept walking, probably toward her own damned doom.

CHAPTER 16

Forget she said anything? That would be damn near impossible considering she acted as though she'd rather take a chance with death than be confined to the eastern part of the county with him. A butter knife to the gut wouldn't have hurt as much as her words. Ellie certainly knew how to cut deep, and unlike most of the wounds Colin sustained, supernatural healing wouldn't help with this one.

"So I should forget that you'd rather be anywhere on the planet than close to me, is that what you're saying?"

Ellie continued downhill without turning back to acknowledge him. Colin fought the urge to reach out and snatch her by the arm to pull her behind him. Whether she liked it or not, she was his mate. Her cavalier attitude in regards to her own safety after they'd established things would be more dangerous from here on out drove him insane.

"That's not what I'm saying." Her arms swung with purpose as she walked. "I told you to forget it."

"Yeah, well, that's not going to happen. Especially since you accused me of manipulating you and backing you into a corner."

Ellie stopped dead in her tracks and turned to face him. The accusation in her gaze was as good as a slap to the face.

"Are you going to stand there and tell me that's not what you did?"

Colin's jaw welded shut. She made it sound so much worse than it actually was. But he couldn't deny that he'd planned all of this in a way that he hoped would give him an advantage. "I was trying to protect you."

"You were trying to control me."

Colin's temper spiked. "Don't forget, I tried to talk to you about this. *Several times.* And you blew me off. You didn't want to hear what I had to say. That's not my fault."

It was Ellie's turn to stand in stunned silence. She couldn't deny she'd put him off. "It still doesn't change the fact that you knew I'd essentially be trapped."

Colin raked his fingers through his hair. She absolutely infuriated him. He wished she'd at least try to understand his position. Then again, he hadn't exactly done a bang-up job of explaining himself, his nature, and their bond to her. "Ellie. I didn't ask for this any more than you did. But that doesn't change the fact that there is a bond between us. You don't understand because you're not a werewolf. You don't feel it in the same way I do. The connection isn't superficial. It's soul deep. If anything should happen to you, I wouldn't recover from the blow. The wolf would slowly drive me mad and I'd have to be put down. Once we find our mates, the bond is eternal. Only death can break it."

Ellie's brow furrowed. "What do you mean, put down?"

"A werewolf who's gone mad is a dangerous thing. A werewolf who's lost his mate is even more dangerous. My alpha would have no choice but to kill me, and believe me, Ellie, it would be a mercy."

Ellie stared at him for a quiet moment as she digested everything he'd said. "Why didn't you tell me this before?"

"I didn't want to burden you with that. Not when you're already dealing with so much. I knew you wanted your freedom, and I knew if I told you everything about our bond you would feel obligated to stay. And as much as I want you to stay, I would never want you by my side out of obligation." It was a tough admission for him to make. "If you were a werewolf, you'd understand. But I know I can't make you feel what isn't there. I should have told you sooner. I should have let you know my fears about breaking the curse before we even left your house. The mistakes are mine and I own them. I tried to control a situation that was out of my control and I'm sorry."

Ellie reached out and cupped his cheek in the palm of her hand. "Of course I feel something for you. We wouldn't be here right now if I didn't. Everything is happening so fast after centuries of slow motion. I shouldn't have said the things I said. I know you're just trying to protect me."

Colin let out a slow breath. Their disagreement might have been smoothed over, but the underlying problems were far from resolved. They needed time to find equal footing. Problem was, time was currently in short supply.

"This is your life, Ellie. And these are your decisions to make. Where do we go from here?"

She worried her bottom lip between her teeth. "I think we should see it through to the end. Find the marker and I'll decide then what chances I want to take. But these aren't my decisions alone, Colin. We're in this together, and so, the decisions have to be made together."

Together. Colin liked that. "I think we should see it through to the end. But whatever's guarding the final marker is going to be tough to take down. I think I should shift. The wolf is stronger. Faster. His instincts are better. We're going to need every advantage we can get."

"You can do that?" Ellie's eyes went wide. "I sort of thought it had to be nighttime and the moon had to be full."

"The transition is more painful outside of the full moon and takes a physical toll," Colin explained. "But it can be done. I just need a few minutes."

"You want to do it now?" Ellie's tone hitched with alarm.

"Yeah. If something jumps us, I won't have time to shift. It's better to do it now."

"Can I still talk to you?"

Colin laughed. "You can talk to me all you want. I just won't be able to talk back."

"Oh." Ellie looked away as though embarrassed. "Right. Of course."

"My senses will be keener," Colin said. "It won't be as hard to locate and follow the ley line, and I'll likely recognize a potential threat before it manages to show itself."

"Okay," Ellie said slowly. "Those all seem like pluses. What about afterward? After we've dealt with those potential threats?"

"I'll shift back. The process will be a little slower, that's all."

"You're sure it'll be okay?" Ellie fixed him with a narrowed gaze. "You won't get hurt?"

"It's better this way," Colin assured her. "Promise."

"Okay." Ellie let out a slow breath. "I guess it's time I saw this other side of you."

Colin gave her a reassuring smile. "Everything's going to be fine, Ellie." He shucked his backpack and began to undress. "The transition isn't exactly pretty and is definitely not something I want you to see right now. I'll be right back."

Ellie waited patiently, despite her curiosity. Her appreciative gaze followed Colin's naked body as he trotted through the dry grass and disappeared into a tiny dip in the hillside. She'd never considered the logistics of transitioning between human and animal form. Colin wasn't exactly modest, which led Ellie to believe werewolves often trotted into the woods buck naked. Not that she was complaining. She definitely enjoyed the view.

Minutes passed and Ellie became more anxious. Colin had prepared her for this, told her it would take some time, but it didn't keep her from worrying. She looped her fingers into the straps of her backpack and had prepared to check on Colin when an enormous dark gray wolf crested the hilltop and came toward her.

Her jaw dropped. No wolf found in nature could compare to the size of the animal that trotted in her direction. He was huge. Bigger than any timber wolf Ellie had ever seen. "Colin?"

The wolf came toward her and Ellie froze in place. Their eyes met, and she knew without a doubt it was him. Those same golden-brown eyes had stared at her before, only now Ellie was face-to-face with the animal that hid beneath Colin's skin. He sniffed the air around her before extending his neck and running his nose along her torso, across her chest, and into the crook of her neck. Ellie giggled and her hand extended, hovering just above the wolf's head. Would Colin be insulted if she ran her fingers through the length of his fur?

He answered the question for her as he bucked his head under her palm, urging her to touch him. Ellie went to her knees and combed her fingers through the soft fur, her eyes wide as she took in every breathtaking detail. "Colin," she said on a breath. "You're beautiful."

The wolf let out a chuff of breath as a pleasant rumble echoed in his chest. Apparently, he liked the compliment, and Ellie smiled. "Are you ready to finish what we started?"

The wolf bucked his head once again. Ellie stood and gathered up his clothes, stuffing them into her pack. There was no way she could carry his pack and hers, so she left his propped against the rail fence, knowing no one would mess with it here. She and Colin would come back for it later, after they found the final boundary marker. At least that's what Ellie hoped.

The wolf was careful to keep a pace Ellie could manage. Downhill wasn't always easier, especially in areas with this steep a grade and chunks of decomposed granite that rolled out from under her feet as she negotiated the path. The wolf stood at shoulder height to her and offered support when she needed it. He stayed close to her, close enough to touch at all times. Ellie couldn't help but be amused. She had a feeling the animal had a wicked overprotective streak. Ellie warmed at the thought. She liked that he cared enough to make her safety his priority. Ellie had never really been anyone's priority before.

The sun moved across the sky, marking the miles that disappeared beneath their feet. Ellie didn't need a compass or ley lines to lead her to the final boundary. She knew it like the back of her hand. Had spent countless hours there. It was her favorite place in her landlocked prison, and she let out a derisive snort as she thought about all the hours spent there and all the while one of the keys to her prison had been right under her nose.

"We need to cross the highway and hike down to the river."

The wolf let out a low warning growl. Obviously, he sensed the magic and knew they were close as well. Ellie took a deep breath and held it in her lungs. Colin wasn't certain breaking the final boundary marker would kill her, but Ellie wasn't sure if she was prepared to take the chance. Before she'd met Colin, there were days Ellie had yearned for death. For release from the loneliness and isolation that crippled her on a daily basis. But since she had met Colin, a world she didn't know existed had been opened up to her. Did it really matter that she could never travel farther south than Lowman? And what would a lifetime's worth of adventures matter if she couldn't experience them with the one person she wanted by her side?

Without even realizing it, they'd crossed the highway and made it to the river. The South Fork of the Payette might have been cold and barren, but it was the most beautiful stretch of water Ellie had ever seen. Crystal clear, and the most amazing shade of light green. She loved the sound of the water rushing over the rocks. She loved the grace of the swift current. Most of all, she loved the way being close to the water made her feel at peace.

The wolf let out a low, menacing growl, and beneath her palm the fur rose on the back of his neck. Ellie brought her head up whip quick as a flash of tawny fur caught her attention. The cougar stalked them with silent grace, and as she got closer to them Ellie realized she wasn't a run-of-the-mill mountain cat. Like the other boundary guardians, the cougar had been enhanced by magic. Her eyes glowed red as she bared her teeth and hissed. Much bigger than an average cougar, she nearly matched Colin in size and, Ellie assumed, in strength. The cougar's razor-sharp claws scraped along the rocks as she approached them and Ellie came to a decision in an instant.

"Let's go, Colin. I don't care about the last marker. Leave it."

Nothing was worth risking his life. Not even Ellie's own freedom.

The wolf turned to look at her, his eyes narrowed. His low whine couldn't have conveyed to Ellie what he was thinking any better than if he'd spoken the words aloud.

"I'm positive, Colin. It's not worth the risk, to either of us." Ellie meant every word. She knew he could smell the truth of it. She wouldn't sacrifice either of their lives for something as stupid as a few extra miles. Besides, there were ways to circumvent boundaries. She'd been boxed in before, but no longer. And the world was round, wasn't it? Maybe Ellie could push Sarah's final boundary to its limits. But she'd never find out what those limits were if she risked losing her life and Colin's by smashing the final marker to bits.

Ellie had made her decision, but apparently the cougar hadn't gotten the memo. The animal continued toward them, hell-bent on protecting the marker. *Dammit.* Had they come too far? Was there no way out of this? The wolf laid his massive head into her and nudged Ellie out of the way. His low growl sent a shiver of fear down Ellie's spine. Colin was going to fight, and there wasn't anything she could do about it.

CHAPTER 17

The wolf was in charge and he wanted to fight. Colin had known this would be a possibility when he'd given his body over to the transition. Whichever of them possessed the physical body controlled the mind and will. Colin could of course make suggestions, as the wolf often did with him, but the animal was under no obligation to listen. The wolf wouldn't suffer any threat to his mate to live. It didn't matter what Ellie wanted. It didn't matter what Colin wanted. The wolf wanted to fight and the animal would have his way.

The cougar wasn't simply another enchanted animal. Neither did Colin suspect she was a shifter. She was something else entirely, a creature born of magic. And she wouldn't be easy to kill. His wolf had no such qualms. The animal was an overconfident fool.

The rocky, uneven riverbed made for unstable fighting grounds. The cat was agile and her balance was impeccable. The wolf was fast but not as graceful. The river itself posed another threat. Deep and swift, if he fell in he would have to fight against the current, which would likely exhaust him. The shift had already taken a lot out of him. He couldn't afford any more disadvantages.

The wolf was careful to retain his footing as the cat circled them. A strategic move and smart, as it kept them from being maneuvered into a less than advantageous position. The cat lunged and let out a menacing scream. She tried to goad them into an attack, but both Colin and his wolf were smarter than that. They could wait all day and into the night if they had to. They weren't budging.

The cat lunged again, this time toward Ellie. A threat to Colin and his wolf's mate wouldn't be tolerated and the wolf quickly adjusted to throw his body between her and the enormous cougar. A battle of wills no longer, this would be a fight to the death.

The wolf and the cougar went down in a knot of limbs, claws, and snapping jaws. Colin gave himself over to the pull of instinct and let the wolf do what he did best. Adrenaline coursed through their veins and pain no longer registered. The cougar was faster than they'd expected. Stronger than they'd anticipated. Smart and calculating. She showed intelligence beyond base instinct, which bothered Colin more than anything. The fight became less of a one-on-one contest and more about running interference. The cat went after Ellie time and time again and the wolf had no choice but to focus his and Colin's attention on keeping her safe.

This wasn't about protecting the marker at all. This was about Ellie.

The cat latched on to his and the wolf's throat and yanked. Her massive jaws were like a vise as she tossed them in the air to clear the way. They landed at the edge of the cold water, stunned. Colin pushed his awareness to the forefront of the wolf's mind, urging the animal to get the hell up and get to Ellie before the cat did.

A shot rang out, echoing like thunder off the surrounding mountains. Ellie's aim was true, and though it stunned the cougar, it wasn't enough to put the animal down. Enraged, she opened her jaws wide and let out a scream that chilled Colin's blood. The wolf felt no such fear and didn't waste a second pushing up from the rocks and charging toward their mate.

Ellie brought the gun up and fired another shot. It was the perfect distraction to keep the cougar occupied so he could attack. The animal might have been preternaturally strong, fast, and cunning, but it was apparent from the blood spilling from the gunshot wounds that she didn't heal like a werewolf. The wolf's massive jaws locked on to the cougar's neck as they leaped onto her back. Using their body weight as leverage, they rolled, careful to keep their jaws locked. The coppery taste of blood flowed over their tongue as they tore the vein open and the cat went down as she bled out on the bleached river rocks.

Ellie brought her hand to her mouth as her eyes went wide. As the life drained out of the cougar, her form began to shift and change. Four legs became two arms and two legs. The tawny fur transformed to a head of golden hair. The sleek animal became a woman and Ellie let out a choking sob as she watched in horror.

"Oh my God!" She brought her gaze up to meet his. "It's Sarah."

The witch. The wolf cocked his head to one side, curious. The witch had used her own dark magic to transform herself into an animal, guarding the boundaries of Ellie's invisible prison. Sarah's jealousy and hatred had spanned centuries and all it had gotten her in the end was her own death. A new sense of worry overtook Colin as he fought his way once again to the forefront of the animal's mind. He didn't know much about dark magic, but what if it died with the witch? What if it didn't matter whether he and Ellie broke the marker or not? As he watched the naked woman bleed out on the rocks, Colin's own fear choked the air from his lungs.

Every rattling breath in her chest might well bring Ellie closer to her own end. He'd never felt so gods-damned helpless. He'd torn open the witch's throat. He knew of no way to save her.

"Colin?"

Ellie's wide, fearful gaze told him she'd contemplated the exact same possibilities. She went to her knees beside him. Silent tears streamed down her face as she stared into his eyes. If Ellie died, he'd pitch himself into the gods-damned river. There was no way he could live without her. None. The wolf let out a long forlorn howl. Colin's own heart felt as though it would be ripped in two.

"If this is the end," Ellie said through her tears, "I want you to know that you were the greatest adventure of my life."

Ellie was more than likely about to die and she'd never get to hear the deep rumble of Colin's voice again. The wolf was the most beautiful creature she'd ever laid eyes on. She knew that Colin was in there. Could see him in the animal's forlorn gaze. But she wanted to see Colin's face. His expressive blue eyes. His full lips that spread into the most dazzling smile she'd ever beheld. If she was leaving this world once and for all, she wanted to look at him one last time. That wasn't going to happen, though. Once again, her fate seemed to be sealed and there wasn't a damn thing she could do about it.

She dragged her gaze from the wolf to the woman who lay dying not two feet away. Sarah looked the same now as she had two centuries ago when she'd cursed Ellie. Funny, that revenge could feel so bittersweet. For so long Ellie had wanted nothing more than to be rid of the curse that bound her. Now she'd do anything in her power to get it back.

Angry words sat at the tip of Ellie's tongue. So many things she'd wanted to say to Sarah. So many questions she'd wanted answered. But what good would speaking her mind do now? Sarah was dying. The wolf had gone for her throat and the spiteful witch wouldn't have been able to answer Ellie even if she'd wanted to. No, it was best to stay silent. Sarah was paying the price for what she'd done and soon enough Ellie would follow the same path. Funny, she wasn't so much afraid of dying as she was sad.

Colin deserved her words right now. Colin deserved her attention. And that's who Ellie planned to spend her final minutes with.

She turned her back on Sarah and turned to face the wolf. The animal bucked his head and Ellie cupped either side of his face in her hands. "I know you understand me, Colin, and I want you to listen. No matter what happens to me, you have to fight, okay? I know what you said about the wolf and what would happen to you without a mate, but you can't let that madness take you." The wolf's low whine tore at Ellie's heart. "You're strong enough to survive. You both are." The wolf pressed his body against her and she bit back a sob as she threw her arms around his wide neck. "Every single endless day of the past two centuries was worth it. I'd do it all over again for the opportunity to be with you. Even for a couple of days."

Behind her, Sarah coughed. Ellie turned around. Her tears started once again as she watched the witch slowly fade away. *Damn it.* Wasn't it just her luck that she'd spend her entire life wishing she was dead and then, when she finally got her wish, she wanted to live forever?

"I think I could have loved you, Colin." She couldn't bear to face him as she said the words. "In fact, I'm sure I could have."

Sarah let out one last, shuddering breath. Her eyes stared sightless at the sky and an eerie silence settled over them, drowning out the sound of the rushing river not five feet away. Ellie's heart leaped into her throat. Her eyes closed as fresh tears spilled down her cheeks. She waited for death. For the endless dark that would assuredly swallow her or the bright light of the afterlife to welcome her. She didn't care much which. Neither place would have Colin. Heaven, hell, or in between, it didn't matter.

Ellie waited. And waited. And waited. For something, anything, to happen. No pain . . . no rapture . . . *nothing. Good lord.* If Sarah's spell was supposed to be broken, she wished whatever the hell was supposed to come next would happen already. The suspense might kill her before anything else did.

"Ellie."

Maybe she was already dead. If so, heaven's angels spoke with Colin Courtney's voice. If she kept her eyes closed, she could pretend they were still together. If she kept her eyes closed—

"Ellie."

"Don't stop talking." Whatever angelic force drew her toward the afterlife could ask for her soul and whatever else it wanted as long as she could hear Colin's deep, rich baritone speak the words.

"Ellie, look at me."

"If it's okay, I think I'll keep my eyes closed. No offense, but I don't want to ruin the illusion."

She was answered with an amused snort. Whoever this angel was, he had Colin down to a T. "And what illusion is that?"

Warm hands rested on her shoulders and Ellie responded with an indulgent sigh. "The illusion that you're a gorgeous werewolf who, for some reason, seems to like me."

His warm laughter rippled over her skin like summer rain. “Ellie, open your eyes. You’re not dead, and if you want to know the truth, I like you for *so* many reasons.”

Ellie didn’t know if she could trust her ears. She didn’t want to open her eyes and be disappointed. “So many reasons? Like what?”

He leaned down beside her and Ellie melted into the contact. If this was heaven, it might not be too bad to spend an eternity here. “Your spirit, for starters. Your strength. Your kindness and big heart.”

She pursed her lips. Apparently, angels could see the good in anyone. “I’m not so kind or bighearted.”

“Oh no? I bet Frank would disagree. I’ve never seen anyone guard a cinnamon roll with such ferocity. I also happen to like your feisty personality, your fiery passion, and sweet tenderness. I especially like your lips. The way you kiss, the soft caress of your fingers, the way the light plays off your hair and sets it on fire. I like the deep ocean blue of your eyes and the almost microscopic freckles that dot your cheeks. But most of all, I love the way you look at this land with such affection even though it’s been your prison for centuries.”

“You love the way I look at the land?” No one had ever said anything like that to her before. But there was only one word in the sentence Ellie had actually paid attention to.

“I do.” Fingers threaded through Ellie’s hair and her bones turned to Jell-O. “And you said you thought you could love me.”

Ellie’s eyes opened. The river rushed beside her. The sun shone down on her and a light breeze kissed her cheeks. She turned to face the source of the rich, warm voice that never ceased to give her chills. “I’m not dead?”

Colin smiled. “You’re not dead.”

“And you’re not a wolf anymore.”

"You catch on quick." It was definitely him. She didn't think an angel would tease her during such a serious moment. "While you were in your, uh, meditative state, I figured it was safe enough to allow the transition. I'm a little wiped out, though, so if we could wrap this up and crawl into bed, that would be great."

Ellie searched his face, committing every detail to memory. She didn't know why she wasn't dead, but she wasn't about to take it for granted. "Bed would be amazing." Unfortunately, it wasn't going to be so easy. "But I don't think we're done here."

"No." Colin's expression became serious. "We're not. First things first, we need to find the boundary marker. And then, I need to make a phone call."

Ellie swiped at her cheeks and took a deep breath. She'd been on an emotional roller coaster that didn't show any signs of stopping. There was no time to take a break. No time to gather her composure. She had no choice but to put her feelings on the back burner and get to work. She dug through her pack and retrieved Colin's clothes. He took them with a smile and began to get dressed.

"Thanks. I definitely wasn't looking forward to crossing the highway naked."

Ellie's lips curved into a soft smile. "I'm pretty sure the sight of your naked body would cause a few accidents."

Colin's gaze warmed and Ellie wondered if there would ever be a time when she wouldn't want him with such immediate intensity. It was just another aspect of this crazy emotional ride she needed to adjust to.

"Will you be okay here while I hike back up the hill and grab my pack? I need my cell so I can call Wade Robinson and get him down here."

Ellie nodded slowly. "Of course, I'll be fine. I'll look for the marker while you're gone." Sarah's body lay on the rocks, nearly forgotten in the trauma of Ellie's near-death experience. It served to reason that Colin would call in a supernatural authority to handle this, rather than involve the local sheriff's department. Ellie wanted to laugh and cry at the same time. She'd love to see the deputy sheriff's face when she told what had happened here.

Colin finished dressing and gave her a quick peck to the cheek. "I'll be right back. It'll be a quick trip."

Ellie watched as he hiked up the hill and disappeared across the highway. She had no doubt it would be a quick trip. She'd seen how fast Colin could move and it still astounded her. She began to wander the riverbed in search of the final marker. Now that she knew she wouldn't break it, Ellie decided her best bet was to take it with her and keep it safe. The last thing she needed was for it to get accidentally broken out here. She wouldn't run the risk that anything would take her away from Colin again.

She walked in the direction the cougar had approached from. Ellie might not have had supernatural senses to sniff out magic, but she knew how to look for a hiding place. She found a section of river that narrowed and dropped into a deep falls. The smooth river rocks gave way to larger chunks of granite. Ellie started nearest the river and searched backward toward the steep embankment that bordered the highway above. A dark shadow caught her attention and she walked thirty yards toward where she knew the southern boundary began. She'd never ventured this far. The tiny cave was a perfect hiding spot.

It was barely big enough for a small animal to fit inside. Ellie took a deep breath as she went to her knees and crawled as far as she could inside. She reached into the darkness and felt around. Her hands made contact with a small wooden box and she pulled it out to inspect it. Inside was a delicate gold locket. Ellie let out a slow breath. The necklace had been a gift from Wendell. When Sarah had confronted Ellie all those years ago, in a jealous rage, she'd given the locket willingly to the witch, telling her she wanted nothing to do with Wendell or his gifts. Apparently, her verbal rejection and willingly relinquishing his gift hadn't been enough to satisfy Sarah. Ellie had no doubt the necklace had been the first item Sarah had enchanted. Now it looked like the gift Ellie had once given away would be with her for eternity. She looped the delicate gold chain around her neck and fastened it. It seemed heavier than it should, a reminder of everything she'd endured.

It was a burden she would gladly carry, however. Ellie saw her long life in a different light now. It was no longer bleak and endless but exciting with the promise of adventures to come. A tingle raced down her spine and she looked up to see Colin striding toward her. He brought up his hand in a wave and flashed a broad smile. Ellie's heart soared in her chest as she smiled back and walked toward him. In the end, Sarah had given her a rare gift. And Ellie wasn't about to let that gift go to waste.

CHAPTER 18

The knock at Colin's cabin door might as well have been delivered with the force of a jackhammer. The last thing he needed was for Owen's nosy ass to barge in and want an update when Colin and Ellie had some much-needed sleep to catch up on. It had been a full forty-eight hours since their little adventure, most of which had been occupied by meetings with Wade and sentry officials who needed to document everything pertaining to the witch's death.

"Fuck off, Owen!" Colin shouted from the bed. "Come back in a week!"

"It's Liam."

Well, shit. He could blow off his brother, but he certainly couldn't disregard his alpha. Ellie lay on her side, watching him, and her lips twitched with amusement. Gods, she was the most beautiful thing he'd ever seen and he still couldn't believe he'd been lucky enough to find her.

"He didn't sound amused," she remarked.

Colin leaned down to kiss her forehead. "No, he didn't." He climbed out of bed and reached for a pair of sweatpants. "Hang on!" he called down the stairs. "I'll be down in a sec!"

Ellie moved to get up as well. She'd been through so much in such a short amount of time and Colin knew her emotions were still a little raw and on edge. He didn't want her to be anything other than comfortable and relaxed.

"Stay in bed," he gently urged. "There's no need for you to come down. I'm sure Liam just wants to make sure I'm okay. Well, that and he's going to want a detailed rundown of everything that happened. Just rest. I'll give him the CliffsNotes version and be back up before you know it."

Ellie responded with a sleepy smile. "Are you sure? It's sort of rude, considering I'm a guest here."

Ellie was going to have to get used to the fact that she wasn't a guest. She was pack. Family. "You're absolutely not a guest," Colin replied. "Stay here and relax; I'll be back in a few minutes."

Colin threw on his T-shirt as he trotted down the stairs to the front door. There were still a lot of unresolved issues between him and Liam, mainly Colin's status as a potential sentry, but he could wait to tackle that particular issue once Ellie was more settled. She was his priority now. And he knew that was one thing he and Liam would agree on.

Colin opened the door to let his alpha inside. Liam's expression was pleasant, though no less authoritative, as he walked past the threshold and into the modest living room.

"Sounds like you've had an interesting past couple of days."

That was an understatement. Colin followed Liam into the living room and sat down on the couch, making sure to position himself lower than the alpha. After a moment, Liam settled down in the chair beside him.

"You know," Colin began, "when we first moved here, I thought it was a mistake."

"Believe me," Liam said. "You weren't the only one."

Colin laughed. "But so far, it's proven to be the right decision for the pack."

"I agree." Liam sat back in the chair and crossed one leg over the other as he regarded Colin. "Which is why I've decided it would be unfortunate to make decisions for members of this pack based on my own bias and experiences. I'm not a dictator, and if this move is going to work for every member of this pack I have to allow for certain leniencies. I have to be flexible. And I have to let each and every member of this pack live their best life."

Colin nodded. He wasn't about to open his mouth and insert his foot when it seemed as though he might be getting close to some sort of compromise in regards to his career choice. He hadn't planned to discuss the issue of the sentry position with Liam today, but apparently his alpha was ready to come to a resolution.

"I'm wary of the sentry and you know this. But I also know that Wade Robinson is an honorable male who came to my aid when Devon and I needed it, and I also know he recently helped you as well. I contacted Wade this morning and let him know that you had my blessing to join the organization. I think you'll do well within their ranks, Colin."

He'd been prepared for a long, hard fight. Instead, Liam was handing Colin what he wanted on a silver platter. Everything in his life was falling into place and he couldn't be happier.

"Thank you, Liam. You have no idea how much this means to me."

Liam pushed himself up from the chair, and after a moment Colin followed suit. He followed Liam to the door and pulled it open for him. His alpha paused as his gaze ventured to the staircase. Colin's attention followed, to find Ellie standing at the top of the stairs.

"After you've rested, bring Ellie over to the main house for dinner. I'm dying to hear the story."

Colin found it hard to tear his gaze away from his mate. She commanded his attention as surely as the moon. "We will," he assured his alpha. "Soon."

"Good. Oh, and just so you know, I sent Owen out with a hunting party this morning. He won't be around to bug you two for a while."

Colin smiled. He and Owen would definitely have a lot to talk about when the hunting party returned. "Thanks."

"No," Liam said with a grin. "Thank you. From what I've heard, the area you scouted near the Kirkham trail has plenty of game. It was lucky you came across it."

With that, Liam took his leave. Colin closed the door behind his alpha and turned to face his mate. He certainly had been lucky, but a bountiful hunting ground for the pack was the least valuable thing Colin had found there. He looked up at his mate, who smiled brightly. Finally, Colin had everything he'd ever wanted. And he couldn't wait to start this new chapter of his life with Ellie at his side.

Ellie's heart nearly burst with happiness for Colin. She wasn't usually much of an eavesdropper, but she couldn't help herself. When he'd left the bedroom, she'd thrown on some clothes and crept to the top of the stairs. It showed how engrossed the two of them had been in their conversation that neither of them had noticed her. Ellie had learned pretty quickly over the past several days that a werewolf could hear a pin drop in the next room. Pretty tough to be stealthy up against keen senses like that.

"Looks like I've got a new job," Colin said with a wide grin.

Ellie walked down the stairs as though she couldn't help herself. Since the moment she'd laid eyes on him, she'd felt a magnetic draw to Colin. She might not have possessed a werewolf's instincts, but when it came to matters of the heart a human's natural instincts could be just as powerful.

"Congratulations." Ellie hit the bottom stair and Colin was there waiting for her, arms outstretched. She leaned into his embrace as though she'd always been meant to be there. His arms went around her and she let out a slow, contented breath. The thought of eternity used to frighten Ellie, but now she welcomed it in the same way Colin had welcomed her. With open arms.

"I'm sure Wade will be in touch, but I'm going to tell him I need a couple of weeks before I can start."

"Why?" Ellie asked.

"I just think we need time to settle, don't you? Everything's still so up in the air."

True, but Ellie was starting to realize that a little uncertainty made life more exciting. "Colin, we don't have to have everything figured out right now. It could take two days, two months, or two years. And that's okay. No one should ever have to put their life or their dreams on hold for anyone else. If Wade wants you to start tomorrow, I think you should."

He searched her expression for a few quiet moments before leaning in to give her a gentle kiss. "Has anyone ever told you you're amazing?"

Ellie returned his kiss, lingering a bit longer this time. Her hand came up to stroke the weathered oval of the gold locket around her neck. For two centuries she'd shunned any notion of love. She'd formed her relationships keeping a wary distance in order to guard her own heart. Colin had opened up a whole new world for her. He'd given her hope, affection, passion, and adventure. "You're the one who's amazing," she said against his mouth.

"I'm okay," he teased. "But my mate is extraordinary. Immortal. Invincible. Resilient. Strong. Beautiful. And hands down, the *best* kisser."

Ellie laughed. She couldn't get enough of Colin and couldn't wait to spend eternity learning everything about him. They had all the time in the world and Ellie vowed never to waste a single second. "I don't know if I'm the *best* kisser," she teased back. "But I give my best effort."

"Oh, believe me." Colin's voice went low and husky, sending a thrill through Ellie's bloodstream. "You're the best." He put his lips to hers in a slow, openmouthed kiss that nearly made her knees buckle. If anyone was the best, it was Colin Courtney. One of a kind.

When he finally pulled away, Ellie could hardly quell the intense want that overtook her. "You should call Wade now and get all the details worked out." As much as she wanted to go back upstairs and spend the day in bed with Colin, she knew he was anxious to solidify his position as a sentry.

Colin put his arms around her and lifted Ellie off her feet. She let out a surprised squeal as he carried her up the stairs to the bedroom. "Not a chance, love. We're spending the rest of the day in bed and I don't want to hear another word about it."

So bossy, her werewolf. Ellie wrapped her arms around his neck as a contented smile curved her lips. *Love.* The word sounded so right when he said it. As though he'd always been meant to say it to her. She wrapped her legs around his waist as he climbed the last several stairs and headed for the bedroom. She'd always thought she needed to be free of the boundaries that boxed her in in order to live her life. But she was beginning to realize that a million adventures alone would never compare to a single adventure with Colin.

"An entire day in bed," she mused. "How will I ever endure it?"

"Don't worry," Colin murmured as he deposited her on the mattress. "It'll be tough, but we'll get through it together."

Together Damn, Ellie liked the sound of that.